Heaven And Hail

K.R. Brendlinger

This book is a contemporary romance intended for mature audiences of legal adult age. It contains strong language, explicit, graphic sexual scenes, dark and raunchy humor, violence, heavy sarcasm, social anxiety, mentions of miscarriage, gun violence, impaired driving, mentions of abuse, trauma, and mental health. This book is not intended to be a guide, a reference, glamorize any specific act or trait, or idealize relationships. <u>This book is a work of fiction.</u>

Your mental and physical health matters.

<u>National Mental Health Hotline (USA)</u> 866-903-3787

<u>Crisis Text Line (USA)</u> Text HOME to 741741

<u>National Domestic Violence Hotline (USA)</u> 1-800-799-SAFE (7233)

FOR ALL MY SARCASTIC WEIRDOS.

Contents

Pronunciation

Raine – *Ray-n*	***Calle*** – *Cal-ee*
Nollan Broack – *No-lan Broh-aa-kk*	***Casey*** – *Kay-see*
Nash – *N-ash*	***Ivy*** – *Eye-vee*
Declan – *Deck-lan*	***Sebastian*** – *Si-bast-ee-uhn*
Estella – *Eh-stell-ah*	***Elias*** – *Ee-ly-uhs*
Karson – *Cars-en*	***Bailey*** – *Bay-lee*

Dictionary

Envenom – make poisonous

Resentment – bitter indignation at having been treated unfairly

Vitiate – destroy or impair the quality

Immerse – dip or submerge in liquid

Epinephrine – synthetic adrenaline

Divinity – like a god

Cessation – being brought to an end

Vehement – intensity of emotion

Dopamine – neurotransmitter playing a role in how pleasure is felt

Affliction – cause pain or suffering

Legacy – a gift left behind

Sempiternal – everlasting

Landslide – slope downwards

Opacity – lacking transparency

Teleport – transport across space instantly

Ammunition – material used for attacking or defending

Valiancy – worthy, courageous

Fortitude – courage in pain or adversity

Manifest – clear of obvious to the eye or mind

Prologue

Nollan Broack

"Nollan! Get off of him!" Raine screams, fisting my navy short-sleeve Henley.

I managed to get banned from two bars in one night on my twenty-third birthday. Being the first birthday in a decade that I didn't spend with Raine, I found it justifiable. That was two weeks ago. Sparrow—the third and shittiest bar in this town—was the only one left. If I knew she would be at this hole-in-the-wall, I would've convinced Declan to hit Smit's outside town.

"Nollan!" She grows louder.

You want my attention, Raine? It's yours.

"Whore!" I swing a pointed finger, pulling my knee from the hard floor.

Lights shower the walls of the fifteen-square-foot bar-room, courtesy of Larry—the town's discount DJ Pauly D. Matching spiked hair glued to perfection, he fist pumps a little differently than I do. "Six months ago, you loved me!" The sweat transfers from my skin to hers as I press my nose to her cheek. She turns away, and my lips meet her ear. "Now you're getting dry-humped by this douchebag." My eyes fall to the hunched-over, plaid-sporting pussy spitting blood onto the floor.

I *tried* to let it go. I fucking tried, and I couldn't. His hands were on her hips, taunting me while I slammed back shots of Wild Turkey. Dropping one after the next till she would become a blur…It didn't work. I should have known better. At best, she was a drowsy nightmare. His greedy fingers slid over her beautiful curves in that sleazy little tank top, and he brushed those tiny heat-induced curls from her face. It lit a fuse I couldn't diminish. I couldn't allow his hands to hit her low-rise jeans one more fucking time. She didn't get to have a good time while I was liver-deep in misery.

Raine pulls away the minute my skin is absent from hers. Her heated green eyes reach mine, narrowed and murder- ous. Her lips are right there. Soft and probably salty. If I could unclench my jaw, I could kiss her. I'd take her face into my hands and remind her of what she lost. I'd make her regret the day she left me vacant. I hate her and the pain she's put me through after I gave her *everything*. I wanted to break his jaw like she broke my heart.

Hurt him.

Hurt her.

I'd do it again and again to every temporary replacement that we both know will never last. Fuck, everyone knows. I can guarantee someone is calling her a bitch, and someone is replying with worse. And while I agree, I'd knock their teeth down their throat if I heard a whisper.

"We were just dancing," she yells over the thumping bass. She looks around me at the sad excuse for a man on the floor, cupping a hand over his nose. He's not even her type. "I'm not your property, you fuck-face!"

I reach for her as she tries to walk through me, but Declan grabs my shoulders, pouncing from behind. I barely flinch in his attempt to pull my attention from Raine. "Cops!

Nollan." He shakes me. "Man, the cops are on the way," he calls once more, knowing I'm not listening. "Raine, he's got to go. He's already been arrested twice for fighting."

"Are you serious?" She cries in shock. Her eyes shift around as if she's arguing with her emotions.

Do you still care, rainbow? Admit it. You can't be angry with the monster you created. I will never be happy without you. Every asshole who dares to mutter your name will leave bloody-mouthed. It's you and me. We're supposed to be together.

I stare intensely at her, my jaw tightly locked, while Declan keeps pulling at my shoulder.

"He needs to go!" Declan yells, shoving his hands to the back of my shoulders till I budge and pass Raine, walking toward the exit. Fights break out in all corners of the bar amid our shuffle through the crowd of riff-raff. One spark, and the place goes up in flames, courtesy of yours truly.

I look back, meeting Raine's glare. Never letting anyone tell her what to do, Raine pushes people out of her way like the world's smallest linebacker, following close behind. She hates me. *I hate her more.*

"Declan!" Candice yells out of the crowd. I look back, catching a glimpse of the little bleach blonde with a busted lip. The blood trailing from her mouth matches the bandana she calls a shirt that's wrapped around her tiny frame.

"Shit," he murmurs and turns back to me.

I know that look. That's the look I give him, not usually the other way around. He's begging to go find the idiot responsible for inadvertently clocking the only woman he would throw a fist for...his eighteen-year-old baby sis.

"I'll get him out of here," Raine calls. "Go get her."

As I walk out the door, I nod to him, stiffly parting ways.

Cars are parked in makeshift rows, marked by whoever showed up first, and stretch across the right side of the building.

I don't want Raine's help, but I'm out of options. My dad and, truthfully, his entire firm will kill me if I get in any more trouble. *Broack's kid is in the slammer again.* It probably wouldn't matter if *our* last name wasn't one of the three along the side of that building.

"Declan drove. How am I getting home?" I pace backward through the parking lot and swing my hands out.

Raine walks silently around me. Fifty percent anger and fifty percent fear—she always tries to hide the second part. I missed her so much. Fighting with her is better than not hearing her voice at all.

Following, I wait for a brilliant plan to unravel. She stops at the driver's side door of her rusting ninety-seven, turning back to me. I told her not to buy a used car that spent years in upstate New York.

"Here's my key. Take it and get out of here. I'll deal with the cops."

"Why are you helping me, Raine?" Because you still love me. Say it's because you still love me.

The sirens ring in the near distance, and she grabs my hand, forcing me to take her keys. It's the first time her skin has met mine in weeks. Her sweaty palms, her soft fingers, and her Emerald nails scratch my swollen knuckles as she closes my hand around her green Ungrateful Dead bear keychain.

"Nollan, just fucking go!"

I cross my arms above my head and turn away. Looking up at the dark, clouded sky, I'm fucked. It's my only option. *Damn it!*

Letting my arms fall, I pinch the key between my fingers. The bear dangles, tapping the side of my hand. I turn back to her and take her face in one more time. Her green eyes are dilated in the dark tension.

I love her.

I hate her.

I wish she stayed the hell at home. Then again, I didn't need her here tonight to pick a fight with someone. I'm pretty good at doing that on my own.

She steps back, waiting for me to open the door. I slide into her beat-up sedan, sticking the key in the ignition. Before I can think about it twice, the tires chirp as I peel out of the parking lot. Tears fill my eyes, and I wipe them away.

"Fuck!" I yell, slamming my hands into the steering wheel. I smack them into Raine's fuzzy cover again and again before clenching my hands tight. Why wouldn't she come with me *or drive*? Drop me off at my place? Why would she stay? Was it him? That piece of trash who doesn't deserve her? Was it because she couldn't stand to be trapped in a vehicle next to me for eight minutes? What's she going to tell the cops?

I reach over to the water bottle, sliding across the passenger seat, swerving. The plastic slides from my fingers.

"Fuck it." I have to get off the road before they come looking for me. Pressing the toe of my all-black Vans closer to the floor, I speed into the empty night. The streetlights blur, and I blink several times, following the yellow line. Two more blocks.

"Raine left today," Declan announces the moment I turn my back.

I wanted him to choose my side, but Dec is Switzerland. I walk across the garage to the mini fridge, grabbing a glass bottle from the door.

"I know," I admit. "Guess she finally gets what she wanted...out of this town."

"Man, I think it'll be good for you." He sits on the old, musky green floral couch, adjusting the truck nuts on his skateboard. His tangled, blond waves fall over the front of his red spiral tie-dyed t-shirt.

I sink into the cushion, resting my elbow on the ugly upholstery. "Two years ago, I thought I'd be married by now," I reply, tilting my beer back. Instead, I'm back at my teenage hangout, debating if I should get high or drunk. I shouldn't be doing either in navy dress pants and a pale blue button-down.

His dark blue eyes blankly steady on my face. "She's not the one. Move on." Declan immediately goes back to spinning a wheel.

"You're right." A smile grows on my lips. "I have bigger plans...Broack Automotive Rentals. Wanna borrow a Ferrari this time next year?"

"Hell yeah!" He picks up his half-empty bottle from the floor, holding it to mine. "Here's to the journey." We crack glasses, and I take a sip before looking around the concrete box.

The memories of Raine still live in between these walls from the last eight years. Her name is still spray-painted in hot pink on the wall next to the rest of the crew, even though she never liked the color. The dusty white walls are covered in her pieces. The hole in the drywall next to the fridge from sword fighting with pool sticks never got repaired. I see her in every night after school spent on this cement floor. Our weekend Pong tournaments. Christmas break from university, when we'd avoid our moms. Passing out on the pool table... making love against it... and getting caught.

Broack's will have no trace of her. It will be the fresh start I've been desperate to find.

My heavy gaze drifts over my friend's long face. Not only did he lose Raine—a woman who was like a sister—Candice moved out two weeks ago. His nights are spent alone and here I am, crying like a bitch about my ex.

I raise my beer again, catching his eye. "If you need anything, let me know."

"I'm good. No worries." A toothy grin takes away any doubt. "I'm a mountain goat, bruh. I adapt."

"Yeah." I nod. "I wouldn't repeat that."

Chapter One | Envenom

Raine

Somewhere along the lines growing up, I was convinced every happily ever after started the same way. A distressed princess needs rescuing by a knight in Kevlar armor.

As the story goes on, the knight—who turns out to be a prince—uses his savvy tactics to overcome the barriers, and the beautiful damsel is wooed by his spellbinding charm.

I've never been *her* and I can't remember the last time I believed in fairy tales.

My destination is determined by how badly I want it.

Firmly grasp that shit. Grasp it in your hands, babe. Similarly said in a more PG manner by the best square sponge in the deepest blue sea. I'm holding on for dear life every time I fly back to this town.

Easton, Florida. The place where I grew up chasing boys on skateboards and showing them up when I finally caught them. It was my distraction from misery. After all, suburban emo kids are drowning in generational expectations that feel like the end of the world. I wish it were a phase, Mom.

Is that overly dramatic? *Misery.* I can't stop asking myself this ugly little question. I had a picture-perfect suburbia life. I should be happily married, with a cute little house in a cute little neighborhood, and my cute little car, which nestles a cute little car seat in the rear. *Vomit.*

There are always whispers. Starting with how I turned down Nollan's proposal. *Who would say no to that beautiful man*, especially knowing his family's esteemed reputation? His dad is a partner at Broack, Baker, & Franklin Law Firm—one of the most successful businesses to come from this bland little town. Not that it's an exciting job. *Personal opinion.* Sure, it's important, but I'd rather get paid to be an influencer. Being shipped around to all the coolest locations and the most exciting events for simply filming myself in exchange—hell yeah.

I turned Nollan down, and then *I* put six states in between us. It's been seven years, and I still can't live the notoriety down. Despite the rumors, I didn't leave this town because of him. I left it *for me,* like I always said I would. Tell me how terrible I am once more. To my face this time. Pretty please with sugar tits and cherries. I'm dying to fulfill their pitiful lives with something worth gossiping about.

Ya know what? ...I'm built to be Pele. A goddess of fire and volcanoes...the fun in that. The only power I have, though, is more of a curse. If I believed in monsters, I'd say one cursed me with curves. Curves that wrap an invisible hand around the throats of men, choking them till their existence no longer matters, before I move on to the next poor bastard. They should just enjoy the wild ride. Most would, but every now and then—stage four clinger. I'm not the girl you take home to Mom.

Ivy's twins have my head stuck in Wonderland, or whatever fictional planet that has my brain speaking in a mythological tongue. Thanks to those two, I know far more than I've ever been inclined to about princesses and the evil witches that cross them. The witches are truly more interesting. It's how quickly they are judged and how it's never asked, *who hurt you?* What damaged you to the point of disaster, batshit witch bitch? They all have some type of trauma.

I wish I could blame who I am on a horrible event in my life, but *nope!*

I've been blessed with normalcy. Yay me. My parents have been happily married for thirty-one years. I grew up in a community where high school football was the highlight of a Friday night. And local events were never short of volunteers. Struggling to pay for college was never a thought in my head. Mom and Dad had that fund set up when I was in diapers.

I would have settled down with Nollan and been raising two or three crotch goblins by now if Mom had it the way she planned. New York is home, not this...litter box.

If I had stayed in Easton, I'd be miserable. I wouldn't have met Ivy when she was hired at *Eleanor* a year after she had the twins, and I was assigned to be her trainer. I should have listened to my best friend's advice months ago, but I played with fire for shits and giggles, and now I'm...I don't know, anxious? *Blame Nollan.* He answered my drunk-as-a-lovestruck skunk text. He agreed that our heated conversations would be on a limited-time basis. I ended it. *Not as quickly as Ivy suggested.* Now that I'm back in this little toxic wasteland and on edge. I *really* did it this time. *Blame Nollan.*

Only if I could go back to last weekend, far away from here. Oh gosh, Lily. That little shit. She had me rolling with her impression of her "grumpy daddy" at the princess festival. I can't help smiling. Ivy's sassy six-year-old's hands ball on her hips. Using her *monster* voice—which she insisted was what her father used—she yelled, *no princes, no princes!* The sight of her running down the hall, chasing Lia with a butterfly net, replays in my head. They're cute and all, but college was the first and last place I plan to live with someone who expects me to pay for everything and tuck them in at night.

I used to be labeled as rebellious for my choices. Seventeen never seemed so far away and still so close at the same time. It was more acceptable to be this way back then...determined to live a life I don't want to take a vacation from. With one year left of my twenties, I'm tired of hearing how I'll regret not having kids or whatever else society—AKA mommy dearest—thinks I should be doing at this point. *Go to college, Raine. Get a job with stability, Raine. That skateboard won't pay adult bills. Marry Nollan.* I won't waste time with someone who thinks they can change my mind. *Not again.*

Besides, do the princesses of fairy tales set out for a prince? Is it ever really the goal? Cindy just wanted a day off from her hellish life, and, well, Belle surrenders her freedom for her father's exemption. It wasn't to live in a palace with a dark prince. Although that's a little intriguing. I bet he had a trick or two up his sleeve. Serve me a bowl full of bad boy with a cherry on top. Van cherries, preferably. *Mm.* The point was that neither of their goals was to land a prince. Yet I still have to hear about being the singleton cat lady. I don't even have a cat.

Subconsciously pondering what arguments I'll hear this week from my conventional mother, I've overdone the lateral raises. My arms shudder as I lower the dumbbells to the floor, exhaling warm air from my mouth.

Great, spaghetti arms. Limp wet noodles, over-boiled and heavy.

My brain filled with more thoughts than I could properly sort out, and I found the first available gym to escape into—the hotel's ghostly-white box of assorted iron and equipment. Returning to my hometown entails another day of sitting through a lecture, another weekend filled with fake smiles covering drawn eyebrows and loose lips, and yet another opportunity to indirectly be compared to Calle, the perfect daughter. The negativity this town holds is more than enough to remind me why I left in the first place. Missing my family is one thing. Missing what each visit entails is another. Man, why won't it let up? I'm sick of the past dragging me into the landfill. Is chilling next to the dirty diapers or the used condoms worse? Putrid shit or sticky jizz? *Double vomit.*

I tuck my ankles beneath my butt, reaching for my phone at the edge of my yoga mat. When I scroll through my playlist and click on a song, I stretch my arms to the right and repeat to the left.

Ooh yeah. That feels amazing.

Exhaling the tension and built-up angst, the music sweeps me away as my thoughts had, finding peace in my lonesome once again. This feeling of being weightless in every aspect surges over me. The gravity that had been ripping in my chest since I walked into Valley Airport last evening is finally beginning to evaporate.

The smooth guitar riffs pick up, and I let my heavy eyelids close. Sliding my hands down my thighs along the buttery fabric of my slate leggings, I sway side to side with every note.

There are very few things that feel better than getting lost in rhythm and beats. I lift my hips, orbiting them slowly, my body and soul engulfed in the heavy instrumental, taking me farther into serenity.

I love this song.

"I didn't think you could dance like that to a Bring Me The Horizon song," a smooth voice startles me.

The door latches behind what I'm certain is a Greek god just shy of gold luster. Holy fried meatballs, Batboy. What the hell is that? Am I that tired that I'm hallucinating?

The waft of unsavory gym odor strikes before I can make a fool of myself by staring drunkenly. Heat pours into my cheeks as I look up from his wide chest to meet his dark brown, hooded eyes. His nefarious grin is full of amusement.

This is my luck. He's real...and he's entered my bubble of chill with cynicism.

What are the odds of someone showing up at the hotel's gym at this time?

I run my eyes over his sinewy body. Colorless ink covers the man, extending from under his chin to his knuckles, as if he were merely a walking canvas. A black sleeveless shirt masks his chest. I imagine the hidden skin matches. It must. He definitely sat through days of six-hour sessions to perfect his highly cared-about physique.

While his body is impressive, it's his baby face that I've been stuck on for a minute too long. A strong chin, framed with a soft yet strapping jawline, lures me to his rosy lips that release his smile as his tongue skims over the bottom. Below his manicured brows, virtuous eyes wait for my response.

A face sculpted by angels and a body handcrafted by the devil. If beauty is in the eye of the beholder, my eyes are deceiving me because I've never seen a man more obscure and instantly attracted to his enigmatic appearance. He's what? Twenty-two? And on 'roids. I've heard they shrink the goodies. *Itty bitty teenie weenie, couldn't get in my bikini.*

I hope he's not one of those oversharing types who think they need to help every solo woman at the gym. I don't care how appetizing he may be. I'm doing just fine, even if I'm not sculpted in muscles. Exercise does wonders for the mind, and I certainly need that clarity right about now.

"I'm sorry. I didn't mean to startle you," he continues, his dulcet tone filling the room as I turn the sound down on my phone, not moving from my mat.

"You didn't." I pretend like his presence doesn't bother me, refusing to make eye contact. It's not a total sense of dislike. I don't even know the guy. It's the bubbling in my gut and racing in my chest that has suddenly reappeared. Fucking anxiety. Once I'm on that edge, it takes a while to fully come back down. Being alone with a stranger—a very large stranger—at this time of day is somewhat nerve-wracking. Despite this place being full of security cameras, he could easily slice my throat before surveillance would even walky for help. And the crazy in me wants to stick around and see how this turns out. See if the nightwalker is bloodthirsty. It's the most alarming thing...hating the uneasiness I get from this town while loving that exact same rush when it comes to everything and anything else. There is a fine line between adrenaline and anxiety.

"You a fan?" I ask casually, stretching my arm across my chest and leveling it with the opposite. I can sympathize with anyone who connects with the same music as I do. I've seen them twice.

"Well, we just met." A smirk drags from his lips, and I'm hesitant to hide the curl casting mine.

Smart ass.

He walks around a stationary bike toward the weight rack, setting his water bottle on a floating shelf inside the *rectangular sweatbox* we now share.

"Of the band." I scowl, following him with my eyes.

I switch to the opposite arm, stretching deeply with a slow exhale.

Analysis:

Threat? Unknown.

Weapons? Sarcasm and double-barreled triceps.

Flirtatious meter points to exceptionally goofy.

"No. Not really," he replies.

Docked points.

He's knowledgeable enough to know the sound of the band, yet he lacks the taste to appreciate powerful lyrics and catchy beats. Scrunching up my face in disgust, I continue pushing my body to its limit of flexibility.

This is why I have a makeshift home gym. No bros, weirdos, or pervy gym addicts. This one is probably all of the above.

"I hope you don't mind sharing the equipment." His voice carries.

Not that it matters. He's already pulled weights from the rack. The three hundred and fifty square feet is adequate for both of us. All bronze and no brain.

"It's a public gym."

Am I being a bitch? I'm not trying to, but, okay, maybe I am. It comes naturally. Even if I could keep eye contact with him, I'm not in the mood to entertain his mildly terrible flirting. And I'm hungry. This place should offer a twenty-four-hour breakfast for hangry women who can't sleep. Today's plan didn't involve waking this early to hit the gym, but here I am.

"Technically, it's private. The gym is for hotel guests only." He talks with his hands, swinging them in front of his chest, and my gaze gravitates to the ink on them again. It's hard to avoid. Graffiti is everywhere. If he didn't want people to look at the mural he put on his body, he shouldn't display it. Too bad if my staring makes him uncomfortable. He's...beautiful...*anyway, um...*

I narrow my eyes at his retort, hiding any indication of my attraction to him. A mutually agreed-upon monogamous commitment is far more ideal than a rando tryst. Why is the thought of a one-night stand marginally imploding everything else in my brain right now? *He's not that good-looking.*

Hell, I'm lying to myself. The man is an inferno. Spicy. Scolding. Somebody call the fire department before this bitch goes up in flames.

Still, I'll never see him again. He probably lives in Texas. For some reason, I feel he would live in Texas, far away from New York. Either way, I won't *ever see him again.* So what's the point of becoming infatuated?

Hi. You're hot as fuck. Thanks for letting me scowl at you for twenty minutes. So-long. Poof. Gone with the wind. Ejec-to-seato. *Strangers.*

"Do you always hit the gym this early and blare metal music?" He asks, picking up the set of dumbbells and alternating his arms up and down. His veins convex outward with every lift.

A flush of warmth heats my skin, and I look away, avoiding becoming a drooling animal. *I'm exaggerating.* My poker face is prime.

The scant flames of desire diminish, only to be replaced with sarcasm and satire, my natural rude state. My resting bitch face and all, in tow. "I like to work out without an audience," I sneer. "Peeping Timmy can get his jimmies off to something on the boob tube instead of my assets."

He chuckles before pushing through another rep. "I would too if I had a habit of breaking out in dance. Do you sing too? A full concert."

Maybe he gets by with his looks, and women don't pay attention to what's coming out of his mouth. Shit, I bet the insults work. Sometimes red flags look deep pink and pretty. As I wrinkle my nose, my brows contract. The fifteen-pound dumbbells I used still lie to the left of my mat. Standing, I grab them and return them to the rack, ignoring his existence.

"Are you always this aloof?" He asks, still alternating arms. He'd rather annoy me than count reps.

Only mockery comes from his mouth, yet I'm stuffy for not giggling like a childish schoolgirl at his snide remarks. I'm caustic and too blunt when I stop holding my tongue and speak my mind, but he's more venomous behind his sneers. He wants to get a reaction from me. He can keep his beautifully packaged poison. A few words from his mouth were all it took to reassure me that I will definitely not be going to his room, not give him my number, and am not interested. I'm one-hundo percent judging the fuck out of him right now. Nonetheless, I have the urge to word vomit all over his adorable black Converse.

It's like sitting at the bar with just enough alcohol in your system to tell the guy next to you about your shitty day, knowing he couldn't care less. It's cheaper than paying a therapist to listen to your first-world problems.

"I was woken up at four in the morning by my drunken ex," I casually word, spilling the beans before I can fully think all the consequences through.

There are none, though...right? What consequences would there be for venting to a total stranger? I suck my lip inward and roll my yoga mat up, suddenly needing something more to do with my hands.

Stop. Don't puss out. Yeah, I didn't need to validate myself or let my personal information slip, but...Gross, I don't like this feeling of...*vulnerability?* Yeah. I'm naked without my bulletproof vest, so *fuck around and find out*. Blurt it out, Betty needs to pack it in and zip her lips before I'm actually naked. The *pretty boy* here could smooth-talk his dick into me when I let my guard down. Fatigue and emotional distress will be the whore of me.

"So you don't always work out at four-thirty in the morning then."

He didn't ask about *the ex* or give me some kind of *his loss* bull. Not even a *oh, you're a single lady?*

"If four-thirty is so early, why are you here?"

His smile grows up his face, highlighted by a set of beckoning dimples. He probably got into a fight with his girlfriend, and she kicked him out. I could see that. Him having a girlfriend and her kicking him out with the scoffing words that seamlessly flit off his tongue. Most women would be appalled, or at least not understand his...*sense of humor*. As much as I'm sure he's a sarcastic asshole already, so am I.

"I just got in around four. Couldn't sleep," he returns, switching stance and dropping one dumbbell. His thick fingers skim over his dark hair, brushing it to the side.

"You haven't slept yet?" I ask in astonishment. I wouldn't be functioning. My lack of sleep is already taking its toll.

Let me get this straight for my clouded brain. He's made of muscle, has an entrapping voice, and doesn't sleep. He's a fucking siren. *Puh-lease, don't start singing.* Wait, there are male sirens, right? Okay, I have let my overly active imagination take control at this point, and I clearly should be hibernating in bed.

"A buddy of mine likes to close the bar. I took a nap earlier," he says through breaths.

"You're telling me, you went out drinking, then came back to the hotel to work out before calling it a night? And I'm the one on trial." I let out a breathy laugh.

"Hey now, I'm sober. I had one Scotch, that's it," he tries to justify, stopping his row to make the point. He is completely colorless, from his head to his black Chucks. Diddle my skiddle, and I'll lend you some of my rainbow.

I walk to the nearest open wall with my mat and water, setting them on the floor beside me and pressing my back against the wall while I line up to squat.

"So you're in town visiting a friend?" I look straight ahead, focusing on my movement as much as I can, as if the serial gym killer has wandering eyes.

"That's more of a perk. I'm in the area for business." He walks to the weight rack and exchanges his dumbbells.

"Oh, that's why you're Sober Sally," I mock, watching him reposition.

"You're almost as brazen as me," he exhales through the lift. "Not quite, but I admire how candid you are." If I were as candid as he believes, I would tell him exactly what I think of him. His pompous, flirty ass can...slide right over here and let me touch those enormous pecks. *Shit, did I just jerk my head? Did he notice?*

He has this charm. I don't want it.

I do.

Do not.

Do.

Enjoyable bickering back and forth? I want that too. This confliction! *What is wrong with me?* I need help. *Siren.*

"I wish I could be that arrogant." The scorn spews out of my mouth. Maybe I'm being much more brash than I typically am with men who show interest in me, but it's easy, and he feeds it.

He lowers his hands to his sides, both gripping a dumbbell. "You're better at dancing than I am." A smile drifts upward from his lips. "I'm not arrogant. I give credit where due." He winks, rolling the weight in the palm of his hand.

"Cute." I roll my eyes. He is...something else. What's the word? He's turning my intellect into ignorance.

"So, you think I'm cute?" *Seriously?* "That's flattering. Really, I appreciate it," he grunts as he pulls a dumbbell toward his face.

"You have an air-filled head, don't you?"

"I thought it was average-sized, or are we talking about a different head?"

The heat rushes to my face, and my legs shake unrelatedly. I break my wall squat, slipping as I scramble to stand and reposition myself. I can't believe he just said that to me. I also can't believe I just told this *stranger* he's an airhead. I'd reserve such comments for my friends.

"Those are some bold words to say to a stranger, yet a lady."

"Madam, forgive me," he bows with his arm across his abdomen, the dumbbell still in hand. "You can handle it, though. The words, not the questionable big head."

The smirk drags across his face, locking his eyes on mine. He glides his tongue across the bottom of his upper teeth, and I stare as he pulls his lip into his mouth.

Stop flirting with me, you seductive, foul-mouthed beast. How do I even respond to that? Is it an apology, a compliment, or an insult? I'm never short on snappy comebacks, and I won't start now.

After staring at him for a week and two days, which translates to ten seconds, the words finally make it to my mouth. "I love how men lie. If they have a big dick, they say it's small and when it's small...well, keep that confidence, babe."

A deep laugh rolls through his throat. His Adam's apple bobs, and I'm stuck scanning his art again. He tips his head back, allowing me to catch a glimpse of the sea turtle under his chin.

"Please, though, tell me how you know what I can handle?" I egg him on once more.

"Observation." He drops the dumbbells and sits on a bench. The look he gives me—it's how I imagine getting struck by lightning feels. A shiver travels along my spine; my body tingles throughout, and the hair on my arms stands tall. I ignore it, refusing to disconnect, not letting my body and mind break the hold his eyes have on mine. "You're here alone. You listen to *metal.* You're sarcastic and witty. And you haven't tried flirting with me yet, at least on purpose anyway." I stare blankly at him, his alluring voice filling my thoughts. "It's in the details, doll. You're clearly an independent, intelligent woman, even if your taste in music is subpar, but I get it. It intimidates anyone thinking of approaching you. You can handle your own. As for big head...I'm sure you can take whatever you set your mind on."

This dumbass just insulted my musical brilliance and me, and I'm still trying to talk myself out of making a decision I know I'll regret because being derided by a psychopath is something I'm into today. I love being a woman. *Do the minimum, babe. Watch me fall for the peen.* At least there was one compliment in there this time.

"You're a bit piquant," I reply, blatantly.

"Piquant?" He laughs, enthralled.

"Yes. Piquant. Google it." I bob my head to one side, widening my eyes.

"Did you read the dictionary this morning, too?" He jests, lifting his brows.

"Last night, actually. It's my nightly ritual. I write down three words per week that I can use to badger random men. My goal is to make a grown man cry in less than sixty seconds. It's a work in progress." I slide my back against the wall until I'm sitting on the floor.

"See, I'm right about you. You can handle it."

Oh, wouldn't he just love to know how I would handle *it*?

He stands back up and begins lifting again. I grab my phone, disconnect it from the Bluetooth speaker, and gather the rest of my things. I almost want to stay longer. Hell,

I do want to stay longer. If anything, the entertainment has eased my overactive brain. If it were a different time and place...

"This has been fun and all, but I'm heading out. Going to brush up on pages fifty-five through sixty of Webster's before sunrise. The gym is all yours."

He lowers his weighted hands. "Sounds *riveting*. It was nice to meet you. I'm Casey, by the way."

I hold my yoga mat under my arm while my hand rests on the doorknob. I rock back on my heels, debating if I should give him my name. It's just a name...but why does it matter? A name to go along with the memory of the woman who insulted your pretty ego?

"Raine," I respond, pulling my lips awkwardly tight together.

I can't understand the calculus that's going on in my head, trying to convince me to stay a little longer. This is my weakness, men—men with a red flag waiting to shoot up in the air like fireworks into the night sky, squealing before it pops. *Nollan had one. Leo had many.* I'm sure under that hubristic exterior, he's full of them.

I should go. Shower. No, I'll probably take a bird bath for now and catch a few z's before breakfast with Calle because I'm dragging, and I didn't work up much of a sweat anyway, thanks to being interrupted.

A moment of awkward silence prompts me to move, or at least say something. He's merely standing there, staring at me, and I'm idiotically doing the same while my brain talks densely between my ears.

"Don't forget to get some sleep, Mr. *Businessman*," I reply, straight-faced. I'll never see him again.

His smile widens, amusement falling across his face. "Sleep is for weaklings, Raine, but you already know that."

I squint, staring at him for a moment before turning the doorknob.

Chapter Two | Resentment

Raine

Looking down at my phone, my hair cascades over my eyes, hiding my face. It's just after nine, and I've been sitting in the lobby for about *ten*? Yeah, it's been about ten minutes now. Where is Calle?

I'm not surprised she's late. That's Calle. She'll show up to her own funeral late. *Fashionably.* Calle's last testament probably requires several outfits and a panel of judges to choose the cutest, pinkest pantsuit. I hope I die first.

I missed her so much. A week turned into six months quickly.

In the few visits I've managed to make every year, it's been pretty easy to avoid Nollan. Last night was the first time he's called me in six months, and it's been years since I've seen him face-to-face.

He's still here in this town, except now he's the owner of Broack's Automotive Rentals. Very luxurious vehicles, from what I've heard, and of course from the mouth of my mother. Anything she can do to hype Nollan. She would give any amount of money for me to return home and *settle down* with him. After the phone call this morning, I'm just waiting for him to appear. *Conspiracy theory awakened.*

Five years have changed a lot, but it hasn't changed the people in this town. When my deranged ass disappeared, our families and friends all supported him. My move wasn't that crazy. I'd never been quiet about getting out of this town. The women around here should have a reality TV show: The Real Gossiping Grannies. Hah. I crack myself up. You're either bred with the talks-a-lot gene, or it skips you, and you become the subject.

Irradiant sunshine pours through the stretch of windows. Heat warms my face as I pull my hair back, tucking my phone into my eight-year-old Kate Spade crossbody. Why did I put a hoodie on? How could I forget how warm it gets here, even in late October?

A slight breeze accompanies the lobby door closing. "Raine?" A familiar voice utters my name, pulling my sight to deep blue eyes and a half-baked smile.

Oh. Fuck. Me.

His fingers run through his slicked-back, messy blonde fringe. *I jinxed myself. I called it.*

Nollan Broack, what do I owe the pleasure of this visit? Seemingly not hungover either. It makes me wonder how drunk he was when he made that call.

I stand to greet him, tucking my phone into my pocket.

"Rainbow!" he yells passionately. *Ugh, that detestable nickname.* He wraps his arms around me, lifting my feet off the floor. I try to ignore his sedative scent, pulling back from his constraint.

"Nollan," I greet him calmly.

Adjusting my hoodie, I look down at my black Capri leggings and cross my arms over my chest. A part of me—a very microscopic part—covets his thirst. Like the Cheap Trick song, *I Want You To Want Me*. If it were any other man, it would be fine, but for me to want Nollan to pine over me...it's terrible, and I can admit it. At least I'm not in denial, but I am humming Cheap Trick in my head now. It'll be stuck on replay for a week.

"I didn't think I would run into you today." His lips curl into a playful smirk.

"Kinda seemed like you did from the voicemail I got this morning."

"Guess I can't handle my liquor like I thought." He throws his hands in the air, shrugging. The light scattering of freckles that travel up his arm reminds me of all the times I teased him for being an overripe banana. I could have died from laughter when he showed up at my door one Halloween in a banana onesie. The dick jokes rolled in all night, but that's Nollan. Always was the life of the party.

"Honestly, I'm not here to *accidentally* run into you." He air quotes. "I'm picking up a friend for breakfast." An upward nod toward the front desk temporarily removes his flirty eyes. He doesn't skip a beat, shooting his shot with typical Nollan flair. "I'm not sorry, though." Ensnaring me in his mesmerizing blue eyes, I could easily get lost in them and make him wish he had never run into me today. That's the difference between Nollan and the random men I meet. Even though we rarely speak, no time passes when our eyes meet. That connection will always exist. I haven't been this close to him—this physically close—in five years. It feels like I never missed a heartbeat...Nothing changed, and we're teens searching for a good time. He's just as handsome as he was the last time I saw him.

I love it when my mind tosses me a flashback of swooned distraction. The reality is that *attraction* was never our problem. I miss that skater boy, but he's more mature now with this *three-day beard* stubble look happening. The lean muscles I once rested my face on are a little more pronounced, and a tan t-shirt covers his chest, meeting his black slim-fit jeans. Calle would approve of his stylish upgrade. Especially those pointed-tip boots.

The warmth of someone approaching captures my attention. At first glance, it doesn't quite register. *Then it does.* When I snap back to his face for the second time, confusion fights with my resting bitch expression. *Casey.* The *I'll never ride his—uh, never see him again*—businessman from the gym.

He smells really good...like...sandalwood and birch? Sweet. Smooth. Smoky. Strong. Stronger than Nollan's cologne. Thank the graces, Nollan stopped dousing himself in Phoenix body spray. I don't need those warm memories of inhaling against his chest to drop another nostalgia bomb on my morning.

Casey's hands snugly fit into the pockets of his navy dress pants, encircling his thick, muscular thighs. Big hands in tight pockets. *Tense from pocket to pocket.*

What I don't get is why this man is ignoring my existence. He *thought* he'd come to my rescue. Save the damsel being harassed. By all means, save me. *I'm simply incapable.* Clear your throat and ask, *"Is this man bothering you, miss?"*

As the saying goes, *assuming makes an ass out of you and me.* It makes an ass out of me, now staring at a man who is hooked on my ex-boyfriend as if he's the one who needs saving. *He's right.*

"Corner Café?" Casey's lips move, and for the second time, I'm stuck in a delayed mode, struggling to process the words...the question. *Corner Café?*

I shift between the two men, searching Casey's face. I blame him for the rapid beating in my chest. My flushed cheeks. The creeping...anger?

He tricked me. He. Tricked. Me. *He's Nollan's friend.*

It's not anger. It's astonishment. How did I miss the signs of a fake hand of cards?

He's Nollan's friend!

The friend that he was out with last night until the bar closed.

And did Nollan call me *while* he was with Casey?

It's step one in his plan to get me back. Why can't the man move on already?

This bullshit reminds me of the time he repaired my favorite skate deck after he whipped it at Luker. There was a reason the two kept their distance. They always got into it. And I fucked with Nollan, telling him how a new board wouldn't have the *memories* this deck had. They had two more like it at Dudley's. Exactly the same. Yet, I gave him the impression that my heart was set on repairing my fucked deck.

You can epoxy it, sand it, and apply new grip tape, but it's only a matter of time before that baby will break again. Two weeks, or two years. It'll break again. Nollan can't repair us, and I'm not giving him any hope.

Casey's eyes navigate my expression, and his lips curl upward.

"The usual," Nollan replies, optimism in his voice.

I blink rapidly, probably looking like I'm having a seizure or stroke *or something*.

I don't think Nollan has a clue that we've already met. He certainly doesn't know the details of our semi-flirty conversation. Unless he's grown from the insecure, possessive man I once broke the heart of. Let's test the theory.

Today on Obsession Busters, we meet Nollan. He's a two-time Obsession Offender. Has he changed, or will he bite off his friend's face in the name of love?

Crossing my arms over my chest, I look at Casey. "Did you get any sleep?" I ask impassively and await his response.

Scrunched eyebrows cross my blond, blue-eyed ex's face. He looks back and forth between Casey and me.

"I got an hour or two." Dark eyes fixate on mine momentarily before he smiles at the other man in this triangle. "Friend of yours, Nollan?" He asks, unbothered. A calm and collected demeanor emanates from him. The arrogant fuck never eases up.

"Something like that," Nol mumbles. "How do you know each other?" He could never hide his emotions. I shouldn't be surprised by his lack of change. He wears his heart on his sleeve.

"I met Raine in the gym this morning." Casey shifts, looking in my direction.

Dimples. He's stupidly cute.

"I had to spot him." I roll my eyes. "He got it up pretty easily, though." His amused simper tugs upward.

"Oh, really?" Nollan's heart-shaped face is deadpan. Whoop, there it is. The snap. The crackle. The popped brain cell lit a fuse. "Maybe Raine would like to join us tonight," he adds. *What?* Do not invite me anywhere. "We're going to Sparrow."

My second double-take of the day, and it's not even ten AM.

Sparrow. He said...Sparrow! What!

Of all places...he said, Sparrow.

I need to wipe the gawking look from my face and return to Earth. That was a long time ago. I've moved past it. He's fucking with me...and if he's not, well, I'm not in the mood to repeat mistakes. Going with Nollan to *Sparrow* tonight is equivalent to pouring gasoline over a wildfire. He knows better. I know better.

This ends right here. *No* to Nollan. *No,* to his friend, Casey. *No* to all of it. I'm not doing this. Breakfast with Calle and a quiet, drama-free—or as free as possible—weekend. Then it's back to New York for another month until I have to return and risk my sanity again.

"I'm going to my parents today. Probably won't be back till late. Thanks for the invite. Another time." Partial truth.

We may have been apart for years, but that hasn't stopped the force that pulls me to him. When I moved away, I was certain I left him—I left us behind. Then I got fucking drunk. Oh, those blurred lines.

It was late fall. Ivy and Audrey convinced me that wine tasting would be fun. *Soo* fun. It was a bad idea. Being single for a while, and eh, a little tipsy—well, a lot tipsy—combined with a lot horny, I was convinced one little texting session wouldn't hurt. I pulled him back into my sticky little spider web. He's not completely innocent, either. We both needed that outlet. His dirty demands suited my bratty tendencies, and we got each other. It was fun and hot, and *over.*

Nope. Don't go back there.

As cliché as it is, Nollan is like gravity. Everyone is pulled to him, and I'm no exception. It could be his smile, his confidence, and his humor, or it could be nothing but familiarity. Whatever it is, I ended it for a reason.

I've always been straightforward. He agreed. Either of us could have called it quits at any time. It was pure, dirty fun until I did what I do best and cut him loose. It should have been longer than six months ago, but I did it. Guilt-free, the bird is released back into the wild. Fly, little pigeon. Fly into a four-door fucking Ranger.

"Raine." Nollan nearly growls as his tone deepens.

"Nollan," I retaliate.

"Sparrow," he orders.

The memories drown out our surroundings. Everything else quickly becomes unapparent...or irrelevant.

"Your parents never stay up late."

"Do I have to state the obvious?" I reply impudently and drop my hands to my sides as I take a step toward him.

He leans his head to the side, taunting shamelessly. His brows flex as if this is comical. "Oh, you don't want to see me in handcuffs?"

The distance between our bodies feels more narrow than it is, and his astringent squint trials me to say something. He's begging me to unload everything right now. Make a scene. Make sure his friend knows exactly how bat-shit crazy I am. No matter how frustrated he makes me, in the presence of others, I won't rudely disagree.

Calle's boisterous voice unlocks my eyes from Nollan's. With a quick exhale, I step back and turn to my chair. Plucking my purse from the cushion and pulling the strap over my shoulder, I'm finally saved by a face I can appreciate.

There's nothing to worry about, Nollan. I don't want either of you. The jealousy is flattering enough to fulfill one of my dark desires for the next decade. Try not to subtract from the population on account of me.

"Oh *boooys*," Calle sing-songs. "She's mine!" Strutting over in oversized neutral tie-dye, her hair swings in a high pony. Her high-waisted shorts are made of a flowy, pleated material that looks comfy, but I'll pass.

My darling, attention-grabbing kid sister takes the spotlight with every entrance. I'm just background noise when Calle is in the room. The older I get, the less I give a shit. It used to bother me until I realized I could use it to my advantage. When Mom was focused on Calle, she wasn't nagging me. I wish I had taken the opportunity to experiment into a goth era. Dressing head-to-toe in black and chains would have heavily freaked her out. *Satan worshipper*.

A recent salon trip has lightened the ends of her strawberry blonde tresses, no longer matching mine. She stops when she reaches us, putting her hands on her hips. Denying we're related would be wild, though. We share the same diamond-shaped faces and matching eyes that we inherited from Mom.

"No Nash?" Nollan asks as if a switch had flicked, and he's no longer ready to hate-fuck me on the floor of this lobby.

I guess it's fitting that one of us ends up with a Broack. Calle has been dating Nollan's younger brother for a few years now. I can understand her infatuation with him. He's just as fine as Nollan. *Gross.* He's going to be my brother-in-law one day. Nah, fuck it. I'm gonna ask her to be my sister-wife.

"He's with Declan. We're not always together." She shoots him a disapproving look. I wonder how much time she spends around the Broack family these days. They're like bickering siblings. How cute.

"I'm hungry," I say, blankly looking at Calle.

"Okay, let's go," she agrees with a little bounce, her hands still on her hips.

I scan over Nollan's familiar face once more. That's the end of that.

"It was good seeing you, Nollan," I lie. Shifting to Casey, I'm met by his daring eyes. "Nice meeting you." I clear my throat. "Ehm, Casey."

He nods, suddenly a man of few words, maybe wishing the circumstances were different. *I don't.* Not anymore.

"I'm sure we'll run into each other again." Nollan's shifty grin is draining. *We won't.* I'll try my best to avoid the Nollan plague for the duration of my stay in Hell.

Can it be Tuesday, like, *right meow*?

Chapter Three | Vitiate

Raine

"Did you see Dad's last YouTube video?" Calle asks. Her tight grin says it all.

Swirling my straw, I push and poke the lemon around in my glass of water. Mrs. Kay's Place looks the same. I could close my eyes and visualize it in detail hundreds of miles away. Ceiling-to-floor red and white, it's hard to mistake for any other diner on Earth. Leather—or look-alike leather—booths and chairs in perfect condition give the *retro feel* that I love from my favorite diner. I'm partial, on account of the fact that I've been coming here for breakfast since I was a kid. It was a childhood staple that I always walked away from with a warm, understood feeling. Who doesn't love a stack of melt-in-your-mouth, fluffy, fresh pancakes? *Oh shit.* People who are allergic. That would be as bad as peanuts. Peanut butter *and pancakes*? My condolences.

"How cringe is it?"

Our waitress arrives with Calle's sugar-filled coffee—one of those frappuccinos or lattes, I don't know—and my OJ. I push the short marbled vase filled with yellow carnations from the center of the table to the side. I would have opted for a booth if there were any available. A waiter joins the woman, holding a circular tray with our food. You don't get service like this in the city...or a meal that doesn't run you thirty bucks for appetizers alone. Okay, it's not oysters, either. Strawberries are said to be just as powerful an aphrodisiac, not that I'm getting laid.

The server unloads it, and I thank her before taking a bite of my toast, shutting down the gurgling in my stomach.

"His camera angles are pretty good now. Nash has been helping him."

"It's been what...a year since he started his channel?" I try not to inhale my food, talking with soggy bread pushed to one cheek.

"Yeah. Sounds right."

"What's his following?"

She holds her tall mug to her face, inhaling the rich darkness hidden under caramel accents. "Three thousand."

"Three thousand people watch our dad talk about boats and fish?"

"Mhm," she hums.

Impressive. Three thousand people decided they liked his content enough to hit that subscribe button. A marine mechanic upgraded to service manager turned into a YouTube sensation. I'd fail miserably at that three-second hook. All the props to him for recruiting his customers at the service center and learning something new in his late fifties. I'm a little more cemented in my routine.

Calle gets her likability from the old man and her outgoing nature from Mom.

"Do you still go out?" I pause to chew. "On the boat."

She picks at her colorful omelet with hesitation. "When I have time. I've had a lot going on lately," she trails off, staring into the distance with each chew. After a moment, she jumps back into the conversation without giving me time to question it.

"We have to spend Christmas at your place in New York this year!"

No.

What?

Why?

Vomit.

I take another bite of my toast, looking away so she doesn't see my eyes bugging out.

"Please." Her whine is accompanied by a pout. "I'm desperate for a snowy Christmas," she continues when I don't immediately answer.

She's not going to stop till she gets her way. I can't remember a time when my little sister heard the word no and accepted it.

"Do you really think Mom would allow that to happen?" I fork more food into my mouth.

My eyes roll as my shoulders melt forward.

My damn. These are the most perfect pancakes, powdered sugar and all. Orgasmic to the taste buds. Who said I wasn't getting laid? *Nom.*

"Hello," she sings. "Have you met me? I can talk her into it."

My eyes take a second spin. Picking up my glass, I take a drink and swallow before finally answering.

"Can I watch?"

Her laugh is as bubbly as the core memories held in a jar in the museum, locked away in my head. "The secret ingredient is inviting a boy over. She wouldn't want to cause a scene in front of her future son-in-law."

"All I'm saying is, I'm not sure of your plans when you die, but if they don't play My Humps by The Black Eyed Peas at the service, I'm not coming." As if Calle would die from the scorn of our mother before I do.

"Spiteful." She hums the tune. "How do you plan on keeping that promise?"

"Uh nu." I shrug.

"That's going to be stuck in my head all night."

"So would I'm N Luv, but can't have a song about stripper lovers without at least one pole, and I'm sure that's too tacky for you."

"At least my ex wouldn't be grinding a skateboard on those poles."

"Grind poles. Lay pipe. Deface my corpse."

Her upper lip wrinkles in a disgusted pause. "You are so twisted and disturbed. I'm making a memo tonight for all musical choices to be picked by Nash in the unfortunate event I die before my kook sister."

The waitress places our bill on the table and rushes to the next with a tray full of drinks. As I wait for her to drop the tray, I watch her make her way to the table and glance back at Calle, who is too preoccupied with her phone to notice. I would have spilled that entire tray, tripping over thin air. I remember the summer after high school, when I worked as a server in this place. Atrocious.

"Mom still thinks I'm destined to marry Nollan."

"I could find a reason for him to visit." She shimmies her shoulders.

"I'll slip Exlax in your drink." I bob my head at her. "And I'll put plastic wrap on every toilet in the house." Calle nearly chokes on her coffee. "I can't seem to convince Mom that a seven-year break is not a thing, but if you want to fuel the fire...Let the games begin, little sister."

"It was a joke! I swear, I won't. But how about Mr. Casey Pierce?" She tucks her chin and bats her lashes. "You met him this morning, didn't you? He's a cutie."

Incredibly cute. I've never seen a man so cute that I also wanted to see naked, at least not since high school. A rugged, bearded man would be better. Casey's clean-shaven face and perfectly tapered, slicked-back fringe with that clean undercut...it's maintained better than my wild locks most days. He's *too* pretty. He is everything.

"He's...something," I say with tight lips as I try not to smile.

"Grits?" She points, trying to convince me to clean her plate.

One foot out of Calle's little red car, and Mom starts hollering. "Come here and give me a hug!" She waves.

Her dark blonde hair blows in the breeze as she wraps her pink cardigan around her slender frame. This is the beginning of the cold season for her, as usual. I wrap my arms around her shoulders, and Calle joins. I tower over the two of them in silence. It reminds me of being a little girl. She would hug me multiple times a day, and it made everything better. My teenage self protested everything.

"Both my girls are home!" She exhales.

"Easy, woman. I don't want *death by hug* on my obituary."

She shakes her head. "Oh, Raine. It's good to have you home."

"What's this box?" I lightly kick the cardboard on the edge of the porch, and it rattles with noise. I hope it's there because it's junk.

"I was cleaning out the garage and found all these old CDs."

Is retirement that boring?

I bend down and peel open the box, immediately transported to my teenage years. "Holy shit, *We The Kings*." I smile, staring at the pop-punk album in my hands.

"Raine!"

"Sorry, Mom." I shrug.

"Didn't you go to see them live?" Calle asks, kneeling beside me to peep the albums.

"Yeah. I did."

I had the stupidest ear-to-ear grin, yelling lyrics over singing them in a crowd full of jumping strangers. I don't even know how I liked those massive crowds back then, but I did. I lived for the thrill. Still do. It's just different. A lot quieter.

Nollan watched me like I was the main attraction, star-struck. His smile was fueled by mine, and I was so in love with it. When everyone loved Nollan, he loved me. He saw me.

It was fun, but what sticks in my head the most from that night...the drive home. The five of us eighteen-year-olds that went—the four guys and my craziness—all hyped off of the concert and hungry, decided to stop at this coffee shop two blocks from the venue, ten minutes before closing. They ended up giving us two dozen donuts for free, since they were just going to be tossed. Free donuts — score.

Minutes down the highway, I pulled a mystery donut out and took one bite. It had some weird coconut filling, and my foolish teenage self decided to throw the nasty thing out the car's open passenger window. It flew back inside the rear window, smacking Declan right in the face. He got coconut creamed. I took his cream-pied virginity. It started a whole-out donut war, with donuts flying everywhere. We were so stupid and reckless. Nollan was swerving, dipping in his seat to avoid the food fight. How we're still alive after the stunts we pulled amazes me.

Every time I hear "Stay Young," that's what I picture. Back when we thought we were invincible and our love would never die.

"I'm taking this one."

Spending the day hanging out at the house wasn't half bad. Dad showed me some of his videos, walking me through his boating trips, and Mom gave me a tour of all the DIY projects she had been working on. It's been a pleasant day. What a shocker. Mom hasn't even mentioned moving back home once.

"Who took you shopping?" I lift my elbow from the table. Dad sporting the *in*-fits? I'm not convinced it was all they had in his size. Calle swapped his cargo shorts for something else when he was out fishing. She smirks, chewing her mouthful.

"How was it?" Mom asks, pointing to my empty plate.

"Bussin." Sitting at the kitchen table, it's like no time has passed. All my childhood memories remain freshly intact every time I pull a chair out and run a finger across the grain. Planning the bi-annual cruises we took from the time

I was twelve to seventeen. The worst *two-minute talk* about maturing bodies. Having college laid out in front of me like a four-course meal. Telling them I was moving to New York.

I psych myself out, expecting the worst every damn time...and I call Calle dramatic. I'll protest that Cree women trait till my voice becomes as hoarse and I unsteadily whack youngsters with a golden dragon-head cane. I'm cautious, not dramatic.

"I made your favorite dessert too, key lime pie! Imagine if you lived closer. I could make it for you every week!" *Whomp, there it is*. The casual *you should move back to Florida* footnote.

"It wouldn't be as special then, and I'd have a double chin and half an extra ass cheek," I respond, and Calle snickers, like I knew she would.

"Speaking of *special*." Calle uses the opportunity. "Wouldn't Christmas be extra special if we spent it in New York this year?" Her grin is huge. She looks directly at Mom, waiting for her reply, while we both know any argument she could come up with already has a counter-argument awaiting it. Calle fucked up, though. Her lover boy isn't here to be a distraction. Something about helping Nollan—*vomit*—with a software issue at the dealership.

"Well." Dad wipes his mustache clean. "How do you feel about that, Raine?"

"Calle talked me into it. I'm fine with hosting this year." I glance at Mom, and she looks back at Dad — one of those glances that translates something like *you better agree with me or no poon for you*. Oh God. Why brain! Why did you do me dirty like that? I'm having disturbing visions. No, nooo.

"Kimberly?" he asks.

She looks pissy and bent out of shape. How dare we challenge traditions?

"Joshua." She glares over at him for putting her on the spot. He knows damn well that she's not interested, and yet he can poke the bear without getting bitten. "I like our traditions. What's wrong with having our normal Christmas celebration?"

I fight my rolling eyes, stopping them before they reach my lashes. I'll get the attitude speech like I'm seventeen. I don't know why she has to be defensive. She takes everything so personally.

"Mom." Calle opens her mouth of persuasion. "How amazing would it be to have a snow-covered winter in the beautiful mountains?"

"What about Nash?" Mom argues, scrapping for any excuse.

All of our local relatives gather for a party the week after Christmas. It's always the four of us on Christmas Day...and the past few years, Nash. She's shoveling down instead of out. Every year, Mom asks where Nollan is and encourages Nash to invite him over. It's freaking weird. I should hire someone to be my date.

"He would come with." Calle's eyes spring wide. "In fact, it would be a spectacular time to finally propose. Maybe on a ski lift?" She has the biggest, shittiest grin on her face, and I finally understand her motivation behind this winter wonderland Christmas. The beach is nice, but a proposal in December on a snow-covered mountain is swoon-worthy. It's every one of the fifty-three-holiday movies where Prince Charming kneels in the snow. How he avoids the wet spot on his pants, I'd be inclined to know.

"Do you think Nash can pull off something that romantic?" I taunt and lick my fork clean, picturing that pie on my empty plate.

"A girl can dream, can't she?" Calle admits with a shrug.

"Don't worry, the Broack boys always have something up their sleeve," I sneer.

"I think it's a nice idea. Kim, what do you say?" Dad sets his bifocals on his gray, bushy, hair-covered head, oblivious to my derisive remark. "We could make a trip to Outworld Pioneer, too." Slick Dad-e-o. Casually slip that in there.

"Who's going to do all the cooking?"

I've been taking care of myself for a good while now. I'm pretty positive I can manage to make dinner. We'll have my specialty, blueberry waffles fresh from the toaster, and microwavable breakfast sausage. For dessert, surprise lemon-lime gelatin shots. Spoiler: The surprise is finding a tequila shot mixed in with the vodka.

"Mom, I can cook," I answer flatly.

"Fine. We'll have Christmas in New York if that's what everyone wants."

Calle looks at me with another big grin, squeezing her eyes shut. She *always* gets her way. The little shit.

Now that it's settled, I can make my way to that pie. Clearing dishes from the table, I round the island to the dishwasher, opening it, and laying plates into the rack.

"You know what would be nice?" I hear Mom's higher-pitched tone from the table. *Ah hell.* This isn't going to end well.

An hour later, I'm about to rip my hair out. Very fucking follicle. And I swear, if one person makes a Britney comment after my mother-driven makeover, I'll oops their hair off in a pile next to mine. This wacky woman thinks I should invite the entire Broack family to celebrate Christmas in my one-bedroom apartment in New York.

It's ridiculous. She's going senile. I'm packing her shit and putting her in a home.

I made my way out the backdoor to the Florida room a while ago, getting comfortable in one of the wooden rocking chairs and casually paging through my socials while I tried to tune her out. The same boring posts brighten my screen until I open up my favorite app — Knack. I swipe past the first short film, stopping on a new book trailer. *Eventide Kooks.* The group of friends reminds me of the idiots I grew up with, only richer. What's romance without a millionaire trope every other month?

Won't she shut it? My patience and tolerance are wearing thin, but I continue to bite my tongue for the most part and quickly add the book to my TBR saves.

"Just because you're friends with the Broack family," I mutter. "Doesn't mean I should invite them to come to New York for Christmas. If you want to celebrate with them, then make arrangements when you get back home." My monotone is certain to annoy her.

Pushing my toes against the cool ground, I rock the chair and continue to stare at an article about director Bennett Larson and a new *Hollywood darling* he's dating. I can't make it past the first paragraph with Mom's voice drowning the words to mush.

"You've known them since you were in grade school with Nollan!" She barks and paces.

"Mom, today is the first time I've seen Nollan in *five* years."

She stops, placing her hands on her hips. "I know you talk to him. He told me that you texted him before."

Oh God. If only she knew what words we exchanged in those texts. It wasn't about getting back together.

I slide my phone into my pocket, taking in the pink sky as it begins to set.

"Raine, you will invite them, or I am not coming," she exclaims.

"Bullshit," I fire back, snapping a look at her. My brows wrinkle as my parted lips hang. She's lost her fucking marbles. Nursing home! Make her somebody else's nightmare.

"Don't speak to me that way." She blinks. "I am your mother, and you will respect me."

"I'm sorry I cursed, but I'm not being disrespectful. What you're saying is ridiculous."

"Excuse me!" Another outburst, claiming I'm a degenerate. I'm an adolescent. If I made the remark out loud, she would carry on for ten minutes about how I don't act my age, and mother knows best, and yadda yadda, fucking beat me like a piñata.

Standing from the wooden rocking chair, I make my way to the back door. "I'm done with this conversation."

Calle and Dad are in the living room, openly avoiding getting pulled into the shitshow. I partially blame Calle for this. I told her Mom wouldn't *just* agree.

"Can you take me back to the hotel? I'm tired. Didn't sleep well last night."

She nods and grabs her purse in the same breath it takes me to find Mom hovering behind me with her arms crossed. *Oh, here we go again.* Why won't she just drop it? The Broacks are not invited. Nollan has no business at *our* Christmas party. She's acting insane. And does she realize that she's trying to get me together with my sister's future brother-in-law? If I don't already get looked at as the weird one in the family, can we add hooking up with my sister's husband's brother? Someone call *Jerry*. I can hear the chants now. *Jerry, it's true love. So what if their babies are double cousins?* That's reaching. My bad.

"Raine Violet Cree! You will not walk out while we are having a conversation."

Conversation? Conversation!

I've reached my threshold. I can't hold it back anymore. I've been down this road over and again with her. Nollan and I will never get back together!

"This is not a conversation. This is you once again trying to tell me how to live my life!"

"I am not telling you how to live your life! Josh, does it sound like I'm telling her how to live her life?" Dad's slippers shuffle across the floor till he's between us with his hands raised. A subtle head shake is all that needs to be said. "I'll tell you what, that man won't wait for you forever, and you'll end up single for the rest of your life! Is that what you want?" She cries out.

"Absolutely!" I yell, throwing my arms in the air. "Do you have a problem with that?"

I love how she assumes I'll be single forever without Nollan, like nobody else would want me.

"As a matter of fact, I do! I won't have my daughter sleep her life away."

Dad shuffles in between us in his awkward attempt to diffuse the scene. "Come on now. Let's all have a seat."

"I don't care." I point. "It's not your choice."

"I can't believe I've raised someone this selfish!" She cries out and pulls at Dad's arm, trying to remove the human shield from her vision.

I step back and pace twice. I never speak to either of my parents this way. Years of bottling it up, holding back from telling Mom off when she always tells me what I should and shouldn't be doing...it was a matter of time before I exploded. Especially when it comes to Nollan...like I'm still the worst person after all these years for breaking his heart. For Christ's sake, I can't do it anymore. I can't be the calm rain...I'm a thunderous storm.

"I want to be selfish! Why else would I break up with a man who wanted to marry me? I don't want to live your life, Mom. I don't want to be Nollan's wife or the mother of his children. I want to be free to do whatever I want, whenever I want, and this is exactly why I moved away." The heat is pouring into my face as I finally explode. "Sorry, I'm not living up to your expectations, but this is my life. I'll never be good enough for you, will I?"

Nothing.

A thick silence consumes the room.

Not one word?

I'm over this.

I walk to the front door and stop.

Damn it.

I take a deep breath and slowly release it, trying to calm myself down. I look at Calle, who has been invisible for the first time in her life. She forces a half smile and says her goodbyes. I take another deep breath and look at my parents. Everything inside me screams not to leave this way.

"I love you," I mumble, dryly. *I want to light your Azalea's on fire.* "I'll call you tomorrow."

My face hasn't changed, and my shoulders remain stiff. If I've learned anything since leaving Easton, it's that everything can change in a moment.

Calle pretended nothing happened the entire drive back. We both know it will blow over. Her attention is now on finding ski gear that fits her curves perfectly. No gaps. No basic colors or generic patterns. I don't know what else she said because I was too busy talking myself off the ledge. I agree to make the trip to Blake Boards in Orlando tomorrow, so she'll let me out of the car.

I stand on the sidewalk, hanging onto the door frame. I want to walk away and be alone, yet…I don't want to. "Text me tomorrow."

"Oh, wait," she stops me before I close it. "If you want to go out tonight, a few of us are getting together. Just let me know, and I'll pick you up."

I nod. "Okay, thanks."

Do I go out with Calle or sit alone in the dark with my earbuds in, drowning out any thought of the last few hours? I'll reevaluate my locational depression in an hour.

Chapter Four | Immerse

FRIDAY, 7:30 PM

I flop backward, disturbing the crisp white linens. Wouldn't it be nice to have someone make my bed for me every day...without paying them. I could lie here for the next two hours, zoning out and listening to Sum 41's Underclass Hero on repeat.

Popping my earbuds in, I pull my phone out of my pocket and tuck my fingers along both sides of the Galaxy Pop Socket. Out of six playlists, I'm not in the mood for any of them. Not even Shred Sauce.

I key "pessimistic" into the search bar. It greets me with several playlists. Both "Sorry Mom" and "Sad Bitch Vibes" are tempting. Meh, I'll go with the first one. It's fitting.

I stare out the window that stretches across my third-floor suite. A full moon reaches over the clouds, separating a spiral of pink and blue that seems to deepen by the minute. The beauty creeps into the darkness of the night, and I give it my best to escape reality once more.

It's tiresome — not being able to evade the memories of an ex-boyfriend. It's a scar that everyone wants to know about. The only celebrity downfall I relate to.

What can I say? I met Nollan in the first grade when I dropped my carrot sticks on the floor in the lunchroom.

43

The long rows of tables. The ugly off-white floors had matching walls filled with giant laminated fruit and vegetable art. And the stretch of stainless steel where I slid my tray till I got to the end and tripped over air. Messy hair swept over both shoulders, and a pair of baggy bibs—I think they had embroidered flowers on the leg—I dusted myself off and looked up to find a smiling blond boy in front of me.

I've always been clumsy. One of my awesome attributes. Today, it's an inside joke—*falling with flair, tripping with talent, so gifted I can feed my boobs and my face at the same time.*

That day, this thoughtful yet goofy six-year-old offered to share his veggies. What kid wouldn't want to give theirs away?

A fohawk, a washable Ninja Turtle tattoo on his freckled forearm—he probably did on the bus without his mom knowing—and two carrots tucked under the sides of his top lip like a walrus. Luckily for me, he didn't plan on sharing those. He slipped them into his pocket for safekeeping. Our friendship only grew from that day. *Clumsy* and *goofy* stuck together.

The time Tessa Laurence tripped me on the basketball court during gym class and busted my knee open, he sat with me on the ground, holding a paper towel on it until the nurse arrived. Some of the other boys were even grossed out by that one, but there he was — telling me jokes that were only funny out of his mouth.

It turned out that we only lived a block apart. Most days after school, we would hang out at the park on the corner, and, as much of a control freak as Mom is, she would let me go for an hour every night without hovering. If I wasn't home by seven, she would be outside with her hands on her hips, calling all the parents in the neighborhood to see who has eyes on the park.

By the time we hit high school, most nights were spent in Declan's garage. I love Dec, but I secretly loved the nights I hung out at Nollan's more. Every time his mom would get the photo albums out and share his elementary pictures with his little round metal-framed glasses that he hated. It made me smile. A time with less pressure and expectations, I guess...and he was so cute. It's funny that already, by fourteen and fifteen, I felt the heaviness of not being what adults wanted me to be.

By tapping the skip button on my lock screen, I replace the ugly tugging inside my gut. That's the funny thing about memories. One minute you're smiling and the next...you're not. And I'm outtie five-thousand.

Maybe I should go out with Calle tonight. It would keep my head quiet. The trade — entertained via creepy men who confess their undying love for *blondes* on the dance floor. And when I'm a cold bitch, it's time for the classic one-liner — *can't a guy be friendly?* No, *bro*. I suck at friendships. I don't want it anymore. I suck at relationships, too.

Nollan was the only guy I gave a chance to in high school. I'll chalk it up to high standards or because of Mom and Dad. Mostly Mom. Them being uncool with their teenager dating? Accurate. But I think it had more to do with my intimidating most boys. I was born with a resting bitch face and a dry attitude — a rub some salt on your wounds kinda girl.

One of the boys — a saying I didn't mind till I hit puberty. Was I a prehistoric woman with a thick piece of wood in my hand, a unibrow, and crazy *pit hair,* embodying my underarms like *Armpit* from *Aaahh! Real Monsters*? Nineties cartoons were on another level.

Thanks, guys. The confidence boost was higher than Declan on a Friday night behind the away team's bleachers, hitting on some rando from the opposing district. If it wasn't for Nollan flirting with me, I'd have assumed I was destined to be a virgin until college. That might have been the reasoning behind my decision to give him a chance. Do Broack or do college with an unplucked cherry waiting for a miserable one-night stand with a frat boy who couldn't point out the clitoris on a labeled diagram?

Our first date...Man, I couldn't forget it if I wanted to. It was an eye-opener.

The battery-operated candles. *Oh my God, stop smiling.* It was so long ago.

The grape juice mimicked wine. The sunflowers. Yes. Those sunflowers. The dinner for two was on his parents' patio, waited on by Nash. He was only, um...thirteen at the time. Oh, seventeen and smitten.

He was my first everything. My first kiss. It was a few years before he asked me out while playing cards in Declan's garage. I snapped at him. "This isn't spin the bottle!" It's what he deserves for catching me by surprise. That big anime smile took half his face, and part of my icy heart melted. The cherry-popping heartthrob...heartache...*heart-fucking attack.*

Five years. Five years, neck deep. Through college, too. Then he ruined it.

And I broke it.

I stop fisting the comforter and check my phone screen for the time. It's not as late as I thought it was.

It took me two years till I finally left Florida. I could have stayed. I could have made it work. My job's flexible.

Instead, I put three thousand miles between us. I closed the door...But I didn't lock it.

My dating life has been less successful since I jumped a plane and high-tailed it out of there. Well, I can't say *less* since my comparison is dating only one man. New York had a few new candidates for me.

Austin was fun for a while. It's not uncommon for me to take a guy's number if they look good on a snowboard. He was cute underneath the helmet. It reminded me of Nollan with his blond, sandy hair and lively blue eyes. That's as far as their similarities went.

My first *scarecrow*. A complete mama's boy and far too sweet for me. It takes someone with tougher skin to deal with my rude ass commentary. Lacked brains...at least the humorous part.

And then I met Leo. Accurately, he was a *lion*. Leo's outlook on life...He was bold and confident, with a hunger for adventure. The risks that man could get me to take. Oh gosh, that time he talked me into skyscraper climbing. Well, he asked once, and to this day, I'm convinced asking once is the same thing as talking me into something. I wish he had...He deserved better. Always settling for less, never seeing his worth. His pride interfered with his...no. I don't want to think about him. I can't go there tonight. Pack it back into my suitcase and save it for a rainy day when it doesn't matter, where the tears blend in.

Am I the *Tin Man*? Heartless?

Impossible standards or unwilling to meet someone halfway? Sounds like my M.O.

You're either the wife or the whore. If you dare to be any-thing else, they'll find a label for you like "refusing to grow up." "Mid-life crisis." Oh, my personal favorite... "the mis-erable cat lady" because you can't be happy without being in a relationship, nor could you be a dog or iguana person. I'm gonna need at least two years to get the baby-talk down. *Come here, my little bootsy-wootsy, pumpkin-pie, cutie-patootie.* Needs work...just like my complaining. How many times can I bitch about *labels* before I fully convince myself that I don't care?

A *long*, hot shower will cure my problems.

I've been seeing rave reviews about Carrington Suites' recent remodel. The bathrooms are three times the size of mine at home, and the shower...*oof*. Admit it. As stupid as it sounds, I wouldn't lie about booking solely for the shower that's straight out of Home TV. I need to brag about it to someone. I texted Ivy a picture later. It's the tits, and if it makes me a grownup for being excited about it, call me Ella and slip on the glass pump. I'd hand out death stares like I'm a pissed-off customer with an inverted bob on a mission to demand a refund for *my* fuck-up if anyone actually called me a princess.

It looks like the pictures. A smoked glass sliding door opens to emerald-tiled walls. The rainfall-style shower head is suspended in the center with two traditional heads that line the sides. It's a fucking oasis, and I'm on the verge of switching songs again. It's a Rich Girl moment. Thank you, Gwen Stefani, for that catchy hook.

I regret noooothing! After the last few hours, I wouldn't mind living that pampered princess life for a minute. The *warrior princess* life. Hell yeah. I slay dragons, not play hide-and-seek with them. *Soldiers guard my quarters whilst I soak my overworked muscles in the raining heat of repair. You shall not peep a glance, except you, guard number three. Siiike. Got your hopes up? We all know I'm secretly meeting my enemy's brother to service those needs.*

I force myself to get up and turn the lights on before pulling the curtains over the window. Making my way towards the bathroom, I'm caught up a few feet from my *spa* when someone raps on the door.

Noooo. *"What now?"* I whisper to myself, letting my head drop as if it's too heavy to hold high any longer. It is. My head is overflowing. It might very well tell me to pop whoever is at the door in the pie hole if I don't get some *woosah* ASAP.

"Raine...it's Nollan," he announces.

Nollan? What is he doing here?

Cracking the door, I answer flatly, "What's up?"

"Can I come in?" He walks into my room before I can reply. His body is so close to mine, I feel like he's going to hug me, and yet I'm shocked by his warm hands suddenly hoisting me up. His palms clench my ass, and a gasp escapes my throat like a bleating goat. The fear of falling pressures me to hold him tight. I wrap my legs around his waist and lock my ankles.

The psycho casually kicks his foot back, closing the door. He pushes his back against it, jerking my chest to his. His hands clench tighter, certain the door is secured. Jolting and twisting, I smack him in the chest. "Nollan! Put me down," I yelp, ready to go thumbs to the eyeballs if necessary.

With a sinister grin, he agrees. "Okay."

As he runs toward the bed, I hang on to his shoulders, digging my fingers into his skin and baring my teeth.

This fucker!

I fall to the mattress, immediately putting weight on my elbows to get up. Trapped beneath his hovering body, his hands push against the linens, and I fall to my back. An authentic laugh leads me away from reality. Our eyes meet...His slowly wanders to my lips and back up.

No. This isn't happening.

Yes. Let it.

No. We can't do this again.

Ugh.

The static between our untouching bodies shallows my breathing. His defined arms on both sides of my head taunt me. I crave to feel the ridges of his biceps. To pull his overpriced cotton t-shirt right off. To feel his beautiful body against mine.

No! For the last time, no! Shit. I *can't* do *this* with *him.*

"Damn it, Nollan! What are—"

"I love hearing my name from those pouty lips." He cuts me off, swiping his thumb across the flesh of my lower lip.

"Noll-*hey!* Stop it. How did you get my room number?" I bet it was Mom. He could have talked his way around the front desk, too. I should start using an alias. *Freda Winkle or...Anita Dick.*

Staring into the distance, my eyes trail the texture of the curtains. He drops his chest into mine, reeling me back.

"Don't worry about it." His familiar fingers trail my jaw, and his voice lowers. "Say my name again."

I tuck my chin, sending daggers through my eyes straight to his.

"Fine," he grumbles. "Tell me, what's going on with you and Casey?"

"Jealousy doesn't look good on you, Nollan. It clashes with your eyes." It's also none of his business who I *talk* to. I wiggle my shoulders, hoping he'll move. He doesn't budge. *Fine.* "Nothing, okay? Absolutely nothing. Why does it matter?" I scoff.

"Do you like him?" So serious, Nollan.

Instead of relieving his grave mind, my savage thought is to fuck with him. He doesn't need to know that Casey and I have nothing besides a few words between strangers.

"I'm going to his room in an hour. What's it to you?"

"Funny and a failed lie. I don't want you to see him again."

"Well, don't you sound like my mother. Here's a lesson that neither one of you has learned yet. You don't have any control over who I'm friends with," I assert.

His hands stress my wrists as he pins my arms above my head to the mattress. His eyes darken, and he pushes my arms wider. His lips veer over mine...yearning for a taste. Averting, he grazes my ear with his teeth.

"Friends or *friends*?" He whispers. Stuck in place, he awaits my reply.

"I don't kiss and tell."

"Oh, come on, rainbow. Do you have a roster?" His mouth never leaves my ear. "I doubt it," he whispers. Every word is another sultry breath against my neck. He shouldn't have come here. Mutually, we want each other, and mutually, we have the power to destroy each other. "*Oh, baby girl*, he croons. "Do you text all your *friends* things like mm, I don't know...*I wish you were here right now...I wish your hands were on my body...I need to hear you moan.*" A shaky sigh vibrates down my spine. "Are you getting wet for me now, baby?"

My stomach flips and knots. Twice over.

I...I can't.

My words become a whisper. "That was months ago. We ended whatever that was." My brain says it's over. My heart has healed that wreckage. Yet, my dumb bitch vagina keeps pulsing every time his breath hits my skin, and his fingers trace a vein.

"Did we really, Raine? Are you sure you're tired of me telling you all the dirty things I know you love to hear? I can give you what you want. I could rip these leggings right off of you." He pinches the fabric along my thigh between his thumb and finger. "And bury my face, pushing you to the edge over and over till you're *begging* for me to stop." His voice thins out, airy over that single word. "And I won't stop until you're *screaming* for me to let you cum."

I hate that he's the best fuck I've ever had. It's his extensive knowledge. Everything that easily makes me squeeze my thighs together is locked in his thick-ass skull. It's past tempting. I could ride the high...It's the letdown that weighs on me. It keeps me grounded every time I want to give in.

When he brings his mouth back to mine, his tongue laces between my lips. My supple skin clutched between his teeth, he drags my lower lip as he pulls away. The anger in my stomach is overpowered by the heat rising through my body—the want—because I want him *so bad*. If I do this—have sex with Nollan—he could get attached. He could think I want to be something more. I could break his heart and mine all over again. The past is supposed to stay there. I'm not reopening a healed wound.

"You taste like Christmas—"

"Cookies." I crack a smile. He told me that the first time we explored the sacred number sixty-nine. Fucking idiot. I told him he tasted like water. Much less charming.

Breathing him in, my head fills with countless memories like this, like every taboo place we stripped down to when we were stupid kids. I only ever wanted to taste him once more. To feel every smooth ripple, vein, and contour of his body. Not now. "*Fuck*," I breathe out. "All I have for you is lust."

With shivering hunger, a familiarity overwhelms me. His blue eyes refuse to release me. The silence is exasperating.

"I don't want to hurt you again," I plead, pulling my arms from his grip. He doesn't budge as I push into his chest. "Don't make me." I push into him again.

He won't move and just keeps staring at me. What the hell is his problem?

"Noll-damn it!" *Why do I keep saying his name?* Kinky bastard. It's not helping my case at all if he's getting excited every time I say it. Knowing I'm turning him on only makes me want his touch more...and I can't. "I bet you're going to jizz in your pants if I say your name again!" I drop my head back and roll my eyes.

He dives into my neck's crook, laughing. Warm air catches my shoulder, and he lifts his face, unburying the smirk that draws wide. I crack a smile when I see his, unwillingly. That magnetic effect that pulls positive energy out of my soul, forcing a prodigious grin.

"How am I supposed to not love you when ridiculous shit like that comes out of your mouth?"

Love you. I wish he hadn't said those words.

"You have been teasing me too long, rainbow. Every dirty little text you sent me at one in the morning, I'm holding you to them. I'm not here to complicate anything." He pauses, smoothing loose, dark blond strands out of his face. "I've kept every filthy word in my head for months, hoping you would get hungry enough for me. I know what I am to you. Maybe I'm still fantasizing about a dream with you...that's my problem." He bows his head. "Give me one night, Raine." Don't do this. Please. "I'll give you everything you missed. Nothing else, I promise. When opportunity arises, take it."

This became *complicated* the moment Nollan called me. Phone sex with my ex, who lives thousands of miles away, when we're both single and horny, was one thing. It was fulfilling, yet not emotionally attached. This is that simple. We have too much history. I wish I didn't care. I wish I could keep him when it's convenient and tell him to leave when I'm tired of it...like Austin. I didn't care about hurting his feelings. He was fun to have around, until he wasn't. I'm sure he and his mommy talked shit on me, and he got over it. Nollan won't. How can I...sleep with him...and go back to our separate lives?

"I need you. I know you want me, too." His hands continue to bracelet my wrists as he flicks one thumb up and down my palm. "I can feel your pulse racing."

"It's not racing," I deny.

"Are you sure?" His lips take to my neck, and his teeth rake my skin. "Still not racing?" He stretches my arms wider, and his mouth drifts to my shoulder. His warm breath nibbles against me, and he kisses tenderly. "How about now?" The pressure from his hands on my wrists deepens. The warmth of his tongue swirls across my clavicle, reaching the neckline of my tank top. It cascades over my spilling breasts. "I can feel it. You want me as much as I want you. ..You can't lie to me. Tell me you want me."

"Nollan..." His hand weaves into my hair, wrapping a section around his fist. He leans in to press his lips, full of peppermint, against mine. Giving me the advantage, I roll my body on top of his, pinning his arms to the bed. All I see are blue eyes...eating me alive. He stares into my mind with the intent to attack and strangle my doubts.

He's offering...and I'm taking.

I glide my hands into his gentle palms, sliding my fingers in between his. His excitement rises against me. I lean into him, my breasts tight against his chest, stopping within inches of his lips.

"Safeword is Worcestershire," I murmur through a smile.

His brows draw tight, and he cocks his head, quickly shaking it out to reply. "Safeword means game over." He smiles back, trying to catch my lips again.

"I need a shower," I whisper, pushing myself up. He looks over my body while I still straddle him on my knees. It's going to be a long trip back to memory lane. Here's to a sensual start and an explosive night. One more time.

"I'll join you."

"I don't know," I joke. "Sharing is caring, and just because I'm getting naked with you doesn't mean I care."

His brows near again, wrinkles crossing his forehead. "It's part of the package deal. You gotta share."

"It's mine. I paid good money for this fancy-pants suite and its luxurious shower from the almighty Heavens."

He narrows his eyes. "Really?" An amused smile crosses his lips. "I don't care if it's made of gold and lined with diamonds. You are not getting in without me. I know how that brain of yours works. Let me see this *amazing* shower."

I slide off the bed and onto my feet. Grabbing one of his hands in my two, I pull him up, shuffling backward with him in tow. If he didn't protest, by the time I got out of the shower, I would have talked myself down...or gotten off in the shower with the idea of him walking in on me, two fingers deep, on my knees, moaning.

He glances inside. "It's nice."

"Nice? Just nice?" I scrunch up my nose, likely for the millionth time, and walk over to the shower. With a nudge, I slide the glass door to the side. "It's better than nice, and if your dirty mouth doesn't admit it, you leave me with no choice. I'll have to wash your mouth out with soap till you come to your senses."

"Fine." He twists his neck from side to side. "It's more lux than the bathrooms in my house, but my master shower is just as big," he gloats. "You would like it. My house."

Nollan, don't ruin this high. Don't tell me that you painted the bedroom my favorite color next.

"Let me guess. You want to give me the full Cribs tour, too? Garage packed with shiny cars and all?" I nearly snort, pushing my hands outward. "Do you have a home the-ater? Oh, oh, wait! You know what I *really* love...a good, screened-in patio. Keep the crawlers out. Well, you know what? We don't have that problem up North." I can't help myself; I'm bobbing my head to the side and biting the tip of my tongue between my front teeth.

"Why are you so fucking sardonic, Raine?" He asks, walking over to the sink. I follow him, unable to reply. His hands take my waist, lifting me onto the vanity. They glide from my hips to my side booty and pull me closer. His lips press deep into mine, matching his body between my legs. I can feel his excitement rising in his jeans. My lips brush his shadowed jaw, calling me one step closer to stripping naked. I weave my fingers through his sandy hair, pushing back the strands hanging in his face.

It was too sweet. Too gentle and...romantic. I don't want any of that with him. I want to stay present while detached. It's the perfect recipe. Letting my guard down isn't an option.

He grasps my neck, lacing his fingers around each side. It's as if he's thinking the same thing. His lips connect along my decolletage. A soft moan escapes my lips.

Leaning my head back in a euphoric rush, I drop my hands to the counter, suddenly needing the support to hold my body in place. His lips sweep across my jaw to my ear, and his teeth scuff my earlobe, gently tugging. A growing fire aches in my core, stiffening my breathing.

Stop teasing. Undress me.

"Still don't want to share?" He whispers.

"No," I argue anyway. Even when the depths of me are screaming to drop my panties to the floor, I fight, waving the white flag.

"You know you want to. You share, then I'll share." His lips brush my jaw. "The water running down your naked body, down my naked body...down my abs. You want to touch them, babe?" He glides my hand underneath his shirt. "Water running down my legs." He smooths my hand over his thigh. "Over my cock." His length twitches against my fingers. "I know you want to get it wet for me. Be my girl tonight."

"I'm wet enough for both of us. You want me, you got me." I wrap my hand around his, holding it to my neck, and pull his lips from my jaw to my mouth. Devouring him, I suck his mouth into mine.

We're not teenagers sneaking around, nor are we college kids annoying our roommates. Yet, this feels scandalous, sneaky, and wrong in every right way…and it's incredibly fucking hot.

He releases my neck, stepping back to pull his shirt off. Nollan walks to the shower, leaning against the mirror in awe.

This is happening. God, he's sexy.

He turns the knob to let the waterfall, then stares at it for a moment. His wrinkled brows alarm me.

"What's wrong?"

"The water's not flowing," he answers, turning knobs.

I slide off the counter, joining him in certainty that he's incompetent. "What do you mean?" My voice is stilted.

You have got to be shitting me. Who knows how long it will take to fix this. Cock blocked by the shower.

Talk about flicking a switch. I'm already crashing.

No, we can savor it. We…can…we can still do this. Maybe skip oral…Oh, fuck it. It's one thing after the next, and I'm tired. If he didn't show up, I would have already found this out and called the front desk. I could be lying in bed reading a book, escaping all else. Nope, now I'm just frustrated with a half-naked Nollan Broack in my broken hotel bathroom.

"Babe, relax." He caresses my forearm with two fingers. "I'll figure it out."

Maybe this is a sign to put an end to this—whatever *this* is—right now.

Nollan wraps his hands around me, resting them on my lower back. He's mind-reading again.

"Seriously, go relax. I'll call the front desk to get someone to take a look at it."

"I can handle it, Nollan." I pull his hands from my body.

"I'm not leaving, Raine. This is on pause." Grabbing my wrist, he tugs me to his chest. "Don't even think you're getting away from me. I'm still getting that pussy tonight." His firm grip squeezes around my less-than-bubbly butt. "Let me deal with this." He lets go, walking out of the bathroom. I follow, watching him pick up the phone to dial the front desk.

I'm cock clouded.

I let him walk in here after six months of not speaking and seven years without so much as a face-to-face conversation, only to take control like I forgot how to function. And they say pussy is power? She who coined that phrase must've had a low libido or damn good *mind over matter* muscles.

"Hello. Yes, this is room 128. I have no running water. It needs to be inspected immediately." Look at him, all grown up. Such a serious tone, Mr. Broack. *No!* This is not attractive. This is the bare minimum. Red flags, dumbass! Red! Red, you're dead. *Reeed.* He is not strong and demanding, and sexy, and déjà vu...déjà vu, déjà vu. I wonder if that's like Beetlejuice. Say it three times and watch your world unwind.

"Thank you." He hangs up the phone. "They're sending maintenance now."

"I'm not a ceramic doll," I scold him. "I could have called."

"I told you, I got it. Don't be mean to me," he pouts, walking back to me. I look from his eyes to his bare chest. Light freckles compass his shoulders. The two-inch scar across his left bicep from the night skateboarding at two AM on Main hasn't changed. He has a small tattoo along his side that I've never seen. What is it? "Raine?"

I quickly pull my sight to the floor, but hesitate. "I don't know if this..." He rolls his tongue and chirps at me. The awkward skater kid that I loved to tease...I don't know him anymore. I will always see that part of him in his time capsule eyes. "Noll…" A dramatic exhale calms my tired mind. "I had a huge fight with my mom. All I want to do is forget this day."

His mouth pulls long, breaking my straight-lipped glare.

"What's that shitty grin for?"

Walking back into the bathroom, he grabs his shirt, pulling it back over his head. Propping a pillow up on the bed, he lies down, adjusting the still-hardened length in his jeans.

"Go get dressed."

Is he on a power trip from assessing my water situation?

"Do I look naked? Cock-blocking shower ring a bell?" I thumb over my shoulder.

"You know what I mean. Go change," he insists. "For the bar. You're coming with me to Sparrow." His eyes leisurely travel up and down my body. Is he checking me out or judging my outfit?

"Why would I go to Sparrow? The last time I was there, I was escorted into the back of a cop car. Or did you forget, Nollan?"

He laughs, somehow finding it humorous. "Can you hand me my hat?" In a seamless transition, he points to a distressed black baseball cap lying on the floor inside the door. I missed him dropping it. It's taken me this long to notice the color of the cotton cloaking his thighs. I'm *so* detail-oriented. It's the same black jeans and tan short-sleeved shirt he had on when I ran into him this morning.

"I have to change, but you're wearing that?" I argue.

"What's wrong with it?"

I hand him the hat again, my face full of bunny lines, as I shake my head mockingly. Simon Says doesn't get to boss me around without backtalk. Ignoring his question, I lean against the bed and cross my arms over my chest. "Who's going?"

Sparrow seems to be the place to go around here now. It wasn't that popular when we were eighteen, trying to sneak drinks at the bar with our green bracelets hidden. Nine times out of ten, we got away with it. The scene was far more enticing when it was illegal. These days, getting my kicks on snow-covered mountains is more my speed. Hangovers and flashing lights can shove it.

"Nash and Calle. It's rare that I don't see them together. Glued at the fucking hip. Declan. Probably whatever girls he's hanging with. A couple of guys from work might show, but we usually barbecue or take the boat out. They have wives and kids." A low sigh susurrates between his teeth. He adjusts his hat and continues. "I don't go to Sparrow much, believe it or not. Only when they have good bands booked and when Casey's in town." *Show pony.* He makes a good wingman, doesn't he? "Yes, Casey is going too. Don't even think about it, Raine." Nollan's threat is parched, and in the same, it doesn't mean he's joking. That's where I come in.

I stand up. "Oh, come on, Nollan. Never wanted a threesome?"

He sits upright, running his hands through his hair before putting his hat on backward.

"You don't need to talk to him at all if that's what you're working on."

"Afraid of a little competition, huh?" I sneer, stepping between his legs. With a hand on each of his thighs, I taught with unyielding fingertips. I can't resist. He's easy to rile.

His hands slap on top of mine, holding them down. Fervid eyes captivate me instantly.

Oh rawr. I missed this possessive problem. A smirk pulls at my lips, and I play into his grip. That's the thing about Nol. Most of the time, he's submissive and sweet, which always worked out well when we were together. It's his other side...the one that comes out when I push him to the edge, that most people don't see. The one that snapped when I broke his...I broke his heart and transformed him into a heavy-fisted monster.

"Do you want to take a ride in the back of a cop car again?" He pokes a soft spot under my ribs, making another joke. It's not funny, and coming from me—the least serious girl on the planet—it means something. Sympathy floods and drains from my heart in the same breath. The air thickens between us, and as much as I want to scream at him, I can't. "Don't fuck around, Raine."

I pull my hands from his abruptly, walking away. "Like you would pick a fight with that man."

"So you were checking him out?"

"A straight man wouldn't have been able to look away. He's nearly six feet tall, with enormous arms and a freaking neck tattoo. And to put your mind at ease, I'm not interested. I'm going back to New York in five days. You get one night, remember? Don't do anything stupid."

Reaching the foot of the bed, I kneel to unzip my suitcase that's lying on the floor. I pull out an oversized, burgundy V-neck tee with distressed letters on the back. It's barely legible anymore, but the vintage tee is cute with my gray high-waisted jeans. I toss the outfit onto the bed and stand to pull my charcoal tank top off. Sliding my leggings to the floor, Nollan leers over my half-naked body, partially cloaked in a black wireless bra and white cotton undies. Without needing a suggestive movement or dirty words,

I tease him, slowly grabbing my t-shirt and pulling it on. Then I tie a knot along the side. His focus never wavers, stony, as he silently watches me step into my jeans. I pull them up to meet my knotted tee.

He looks down at his feet, and his voice softens. "Raine, I'm serious about Casey. You know I want you, but with me or not, tonight or never, stay away from him."

"What's that supposed to mean?" I ask, vexed. "Me no share friends," I proudly vaunt as a pissed-off prehistoric man would.

His eyes return to me, unamused. "It has nothing to do with that. He has something going on...I don't know what it is. Don't get involved, please."

"What does that even mean?" I ask, grimacing. *"Don't get involved,"* I mimic his low octave. It's not like I plan to see the gym rat again. Nollan's appetite to control me is pushing me to be petty, though. Yeah right. It would take a lot more for me to use his friend in my plot of vengeance. And vengeance requires more effort than I care to contribute.

"I like Casey, but can you trust me on this? I've known him for a while...Wolves in sheep's clothing exist everywhere, not just in fairy tales. Just...don't go pissing him off, at the very least. *Don't do something stupid,"* he teases.

"Ha!" I laugh. "I only do stupid things when I'm with you."

"I'm a bad influence. What can I say?" He smiles, tight-lipped, throwing his arm up in the air before returning to the mattress.

Wolf in sheep's clothing? Casey already looks like a wolf. Is he the sheep or a true big bad man killer? My smile lengthens. I turn to the full-length mirror. All the times shit went spiraling with Nollan...In different ways, neither one of us has an off switch, especially when liquor is involved.

It's probably one of the defining reasons I hardly drink any-more. We arrived with inevitable eradication everywhere we would go together. Wanting to go two different paths in life wasn't the only reason for our demise. I spin around, checking out my butt in the mirror, and swiftly switch the conversation's direction.

"So, what time do you want to leave?" I ask, glancing over at him. I'm kinda...excited...for a night out with some old friends. *Not with Nollan.*

Oh, the times we would hang out, drinking in Declan's garage. I wonder if his dad still works the graveyard shift. His mom took off years before they moved here. I doubt he thinks much about her these days. If I had a dime for every time we drew dicks on Nollan's face because he was always the first to pass out, I'd have a hefty piggy bank now. I could buy new bindings for my snowboard like those four-hundred-dollar Atlas' I've been eyeballing. Those are the days I miss...before everything got...serious.

Nollan's locked on his phone when I bend back down to my suitcase, grabbing a small cosmetics bag along the side. I wish I had that shower now. I'll probably smell like sweat, booze, and smoke by the time I get back to the hotel tonight, anyway. Fuck it. Roll on a bar of lavender, or did I bring the vanilla? Whatever.

I don't miss that part of the bar scene. Waking up with smoke-drenched hair. I have to change my pillowcase. And heaven forbid if I passed out before taking off my make-up. I caked that shit on wavy, heavier back then, too. It looked like I got socked in both eyes following a night out. Damn, did I clog up the pores.

A knock at the door supervenes. "Maintenance," a deep voice yells. By the depth of his voice, I imagine he's a lumberjack of a man.

"I got it," Nollan says, walking towards the door. "Raine, it's only eight. You have plenty of time." Bingo. He's a minimum of six feet. Nollan chats away, attempting to establish a solution to my shower problem. Meanwhile, I tune them out, dragging the bench from the foot of the bed to the full-length mirror to spread my small collection of cosmetics out on it.

Nollan's phone rings twice before he murmurs, "Nice timing." Then answers. "Hello…Yeah. I'll meet you in the lobby at nine. I'll drive tonight."

He must be talking to Casey. Who else would meet him in the lobby?

Over the next half hour, I pull myself together, trying to stay out of my head. The simple, smoky gray eye with a nude glossed lip will surely be wiped off before we even get to Sparrow. Beachy waves were created with my flat iron to complement the crease from my hair tie. And to think, I almost didn't bring it with me.

Nollan is paging through his phone when I plop down next to him. His wide smile warmly greets me. I pull my old black and white Converse low tops on.

"You could have used the bathroom." He slides his phone into his pocket. "For your hair and stuff. It didn't take long to figure out the problem. Your magical shower awaits you tonight," he assures, waving his hand in the direction of the door.

"*Hilarious.* What was wrong with it?"

"Water supply valve got flipped off. Someone's stupid mistake on maintenance. The boss man didn't sound happy about it." He sucks in his lips, widening his eyes. "I told Casey I would meet him in the lobby at nine. Whenever you're ready."

"Let's go." I grab my keycard and license from my purse, tucking them in my back pocket.

My head is heavily in the clouds, floating away while my past self takes over my present body. It's going to be a shit show. A complete fucking train wreck. And who cares? I want to dance, laugh, and pretend I'm not going to have a one-night stand with my college boyfriend. Is it a one-night stand if you have history? Old dick, new night. I shrug it off and wait for Nollan at the door.

Casey walks off the elevator into the lobby in slow-mo like a thirst trap reel. Oh, like, um, like that one with the naughty dancer. Hell, what was his name? He's in a Vegas show with a couple of other celebrity lookalikes.

A black button-down shirt with the sleeves rolled off may cover most of his ink-covered arms, although it won't do him any favors when he's in a crowd of warm bodies. God, look how those dark wash jeans are fitted to his thick, muscular legs. And his lips—I don't even know what he just said, but the way his mouth moved when he said it…Bacon and mozzarella! He looks good enough to eat.

No. Shit no. Shut the fuck up, brain. Bad brain, bad! I'm a horny little toad. And men like him are so full of themselves, anyway. They only date size two models with flawless skin. Perky, sweet, intelligent girls with a plan. Unlike this flawed size eight, future crazy cat lady with an attitude problem. Meh. Why not embrace the label? Plus, he's like an evil spy, as Nollan warned. *Don't go near him, Raine. He's the devil in disguise. His dick isn't as big as mine.*

"Casey, you know Raine already." I hear my name and return to reality. "She's going to be tagging along tonight," Nollan says, winking at me. Casey smiles, pushing his sleeve up farther. If he pushes the seam any higher, it is likely to creak. The imaginative sound glues me to his jutting veins.

I follow both men from the near-empty lobby to the parking lot on the left side of the building. The overhead lights are lit, and a few empty spots space some of the parked vehicles. My feet cement to the asphalt. "This is your car?" I yell in shock.

A striking night blue paint wraps the sports sedan, glistening in the moonlight. Its sleek, fastback-styled body and profile full of contours erupt with luxury. "This is at least a hundred-thousand-dollar car."

Nollan chuckles. "It's baseline, under a hundred."

I stare at him with my mouth ajar before doing a half-lap around it and opening the back door. It's covered in rich tan leather with black accents throughout. *He has a Porsche Panamera.* I have a Honda. At least it's not the old clunker I had years ago, but nonetheless, it's a thirty-thousand-dollar Honda. It's a reliable car. I like it, *but but but!* It's not a race car. It's a reliable, smart choice. Sure, I could afford one of these if I wanted to. That is more than I'd spend on a vehicle, especially when I don't drive a lot. Working at Zimmer's dealership those few years before I moved, I learned a thing or two. I'm not clueless when it comes to price tags. Touching anything mechanical is a different story.

"I rent expensive cars out for a living. Half-million-dollar vehicles. Job perk, I get to drive them." He leans in and rests his hand on the door frame. "Want to take a Lamborghini next time?" He pinches the brim of his hat, adjusting it, and smiles at me as I climb in the backseat.

Mom wasn't underselling him. He's doing well for himself.

"And what are you renting?" I ask Casey.

"McLaren," he replies as if it's no big deal that he's been driving around a couple hundred thousand dollars in automotive machinery. I bet everyone's used to seeing these cars around here now. It wasn't this way when we were growing up. We had to drive to the next town over to catch a glimpse at anything fast.

"Explains why we took the Porsche." Four seats versus two.

Nollan starts the car and pulls his door closed. "Welcome to my world, rainbow."

Oh, shit on my birthday cake. It's going to be an *interesting* night.

Chapter Five | Epinephrine

Casey

FRIDAY, 9:00 PM

I knew Nollan would find a way to get her out here tonight. I should have known who she was this morning. It didn't click till it was too late...because of her commotion, her unpredictability—it was exactly what I was looking for to replace the thoughts drowning me.

Her full peachy lips wrap around the mouth of a Blue Moon, and she turns away, strawberry blonde waves skating down her back. She's incredibly sexy in those jeans. Tauntingly tight, they cling to her heart-shaped ass. As she talks to the redhead behind the bar, she teeters back and forth. Occasionally, I glance around the noisy bar, but to anyone paying attention, it's obvious I'm staring at her. Stuck on her.

She reaches for Nollan's arm, turning to face my direction again. What's she whispering in his ear? I bet she said something sassy with a grin that big. She's...pleasantly *alarming,* and...here she comes.

The girl next door walks towards our booth—the same booth Nollan always picks—and she looks right through my glass shell. Every curve of her body persuades me to make bad decisions. I didn't get this far in life without taking calculated risks. Hooking up with one of your friend's

69

women is a sure-fire way of burning down bridges and getting punched in the nose...despite their size.

Beautiful women are a dime a dozen. They usually come with false pretenses and hidden agendas. I've met plenty of them—everything I could desire physically, but emotionally, they're like white rice. Bland. It's my fault for thinking I should date someone who lives in the same wealth bracket as me. The gold diggers are just as predictable. The first question on every date is always "What do you do for a living?" *I smuggle drugs up my asshole. Last week, the guy on transport security recommended his favorite enema kit.* If I had the balls to be that dickhead, that would end a date quickly. I wouldn't treat a woman poorly, despite her deserving it.

Raine smiles softly, sitting down on the opposite end of the curved, vinyl-covered bench.

"How's that Blue Moon?"

"Hmm?" She asks as if she didn't hear me. Then she looks at the glass bottle like she can't remember what it was called. "Oh, it's good. Have you tried this harvest pumpkin before?" She seems more chipper. A little less bite than this morning. Sleep must've done her well...or something—someone else.

"I haven't. The occasional scotch will do it for me. Honestly, I don't drink much," I tell her, raising my glass.

"Ah, I see. Here, I just thought the businessman couldn't work and play at the same time," she mocks. "Turns out, you just can't handle the booze at all." Her lips wrap around the bottle again.

There she is. I actually like her more when she's popping back those Sour Patch Kids, throwing her sardonic bullshit at my every wisecrack. She doesn't fall to her knees for me or pretend she understands my dark humor. She actually gets it. She doesn't ask me stupid questions, like Am I single? Do I like cute brunettes? What's my sign? Because if I weren't a Scorpio, what would they say? Oh darn, we're not compatible? No, they just switch to my favorite—*I love your tattoos; what does this one mean?*

"My body is my temple." I raise my glass again, simultaneously with my brows. Her illuminated green eyes even.

It's been blatantly obvious since the moment I met her that she's different from the women I'm used to. Not one in a million. That's bullshit. *She's not like other girls?* I'd be as bad as the women trying to win me over if I pretended that was something legitimate. She's refreshing.

This pretty wildcat is straight and solitary by nature. She's unlikely to be swayed easily, and the challenge intrigues me. I can already imagine her arguing about everything. She would be a complete pain in the ass. A girl like that is the type to get away with murder, bury a poor bastard in her backyard, plant a bed of flowers over him, and cry seamlessly at his memorial. If she decided to fill me with lead, I'd laugh a ghostly howl watching her try to move my robust body. I'd take my chances if it wasn't for Nollan.

As I watched her in the lobby this morning, sitting there looking at her phone, she was pretending or praying she wasn't going to run into me again. She waited for her *evidently late* sister with her nose to the floor.

The way she looked up at me when Nollan introduced his *friend,* well, it's nice to know she's not completely unruffled in my presence. She hides it well. I wonder what else she's hiding behind those vivid green eyes and why she's here with Nollan when she was...*less than willing* to have a conversation with him earlier.

She keeps watching Nollan at the bar the same way I've been studying her. What is she thinking about? The thought of her tongue circling the head of his cock in the parking lot sprawled over those leather seats? *Nah*. That's probably my wishful thinking. I want her to be as animalistic as a deprived man. It's been far too long since I've been laid.

I have an aching feeling she's pure vanilla, generic, and unmemorable. This amazingly interesting exterior is a set-up. You lose the mind games and either become Nollan—unable to get past his high school sweetheart—or you get a mediocre lay and move on to the next. Even when Nollan has Bailey—the good-looking brunette who runs his front office—practically on her knees, he still craves the taste of his college days. I've seen Bailey around more times than I've heard a word about Raine since I've known him. Regardless, if he hadn't dragged her here tonight, I don't know if I would have seen her again...and I'd be lying if I said I didn't want to.

She rubs her arm anxiously.

"Do I make you nervous?" My sight settles on her fingers.

"No," she fires back. Her hand moves more quickly over her skin. "I knew you were arrogant, but fuck. Not every woman is interested in you." Her eyes fall to my mouth and back up.

"Why are you rubbing your arm so much if you're not nervous?"

"I didn't say I wasn't nervous. I said *you're* not making me nervous." Her hand falls. "Are you some kind of creepy therapist?"

She earns my low chuckles. "Are we going to keep doing the back and forth, or are you going to tell me what has you on edge, love?"

Her mouth draws wide with a fabricated smirk. "Is that any of your business?"

I look back at the bar and see a short brunette making her way toward Nollan. *Bailey* showed up. Her shoulder-length, rich chocolate hair bounces, and she wraps her arms around Nollan's neck. His height makes her push to her tiptoes. I try not to chuckle as he pushes her arms down quickly, flashing a look at our booth. He's checking to see if the ex he brought with him tonight saw it.

I study Raine's diamond-shaped face. The tiny beauty mark above her mouth, uncovered from her ivory makeup, her concave nose, and her modest, low-arched brows that match her hair. She sucks her bottom lip inward, letting it slip from her teeth, wet. If I'm not the cause of her nerves, it must be something logical. Nollan.

"Raine, that is your name, right?"

"I think we established that already, Casey. My mom would have never named me *love*, although my accomplishments may as well be in line with dropping my panties on a Tuesday night at The Prickly Pickle." She steals my laughter again. Taking a short sip from her bottle, she peers toward the stage to the right of the bartenders.

"Where's the Prickly Pickle? It sounds *earthy*." I play along.

"Take a left from here, drive two blocks, loop around at the gas station, and drive straight for about four and a half miles. You can't miss it." Her arms raise into parallel lines, stretching straight out as she continues. "Big ole prickly pickle. Tons of prickles."

"You should join me."

"Not my scene, but I'll write back if you send me a postcard. For reference, I'm a titties girl." She tucks her hair behind her ear. Five black studs line the cartilage o her lobe.

"I'm more of an ass man."

She shrugs and wets her lips. "Guess I have nothing to worry about then."

My eyes descend to hers, smirking. She's ambiguously serious. She's wrong about her ass. Right about having nothing to worry about. "Piquant—pleasantly stimulating or exciting to the mind."

"What?" She tries to hide a smile, failing.

"You told me to Google it." I rest my arm on the back of the booth, looking at her.

"Well, damn. You listened. Good boy," she says, carelessly. "Glad I could be of assistance in extending your glossary."

"You're wrong."

"Huh? How so?"

"We can agree to disagree on many, many things, but I'm not a good boy. Exciting and stimulating, easily." I noisily inhale a sharp breath. "A good man. A *bad* boy." Slowly tilting my glass back, I take a drink without releasing her from my gaze. She stares at me until she hears Declan yelling through the crowd. He raises his glass bottle in the air, avoiding collisions. Two women follow in his footsteps.

Oh, I recognize them. Both are friends of Bailey. They were with her two months ago when I was in town. I couldn't recall their names if I wanted to. Neither of them could be over five and a half feet, and...purple hair tonight? That woman had blue hair the last time I saw her. Creative hair and dark make-up match her deep chocolate eyes. She fills out her short, black, scalloped dress well. Bold with the softest voice I've ever heard.

Declan must have the others' attention. She hangs off his arm, looking up at him with love-sick admiration. When I met her a few months ago, she was so shit-faced I was surprised she was still alive. Serve three shots of tequila to a pint-sized woman and watch the havoc unfold.

Her caramel hands glide up and down over Declan's sun-kissed arm, brushing his bleach-blond hair around. She's just over a hundred pounds soaking wet and has to arch her neck to see his face. Gently peeling her manicured nails off, he takes in her emerald slip-like dress, vastly.

His relaxed smile grows the closer he gets. "Raine, girl, it's good to see you!"

"Come here, fucker. I missed your bum ass." She stands to give him a hug with the biggest grin I've seen yet. Then she smacks him in the back of the head. "Pick up the phone and call me once in a while." He's unfazed, expecting worse. Must be old friends. "Don't tell me you still live in your dad's garage?" She laughs gingerly.

"Whole house is mine now. Dad moved in with his girlfriend a few years ago. Anytime you want to come down, I have a couch."

"If it's the same couch from ten years ago, I'll stick with the hotel."

"Suit yourself." He winks.

"Pierce! Hey man, how's it going?" He greets me by my last name, like many others do, with the notion that Casey is too feminine. I'm not bothered by it. If anything, it would be my last name that bothers me. A dark halo hangs over it, courtesy of the man who gave it to me.

The past is the past. Most days, I don't even think about him or my mother. Recent events have served up a plate of old memories on a rightfully silver platter. It doesn't matter. It can't be changed. Why live in agony over it? Take it and move forward.

"Good. Great. You want to sit?" I slide towards Raine. My knee brushes hers, and our eyes meet for a brief moment.

Stay.

She looks away, moving over just enough until our knees no longer touch. I can't take my eyes off of her, only catching pieces of the conversation.

I gather the will and manage to pull myself away, glancing towards the bar to find Nollan and Bailey again. Nollan's brother weaves around the congestion, interrupting him with a pat on his shoulder. His girlfriend—Raine's sister—wraps her arms around Bailey's shoulders, giving her a hug.

"Nash said you're going to teach Calle to snowboard?" Declan's words draw my attention back to the table, finding Raine's face. She snowboards?

"Yeah. She's making me go to Blake Boards with her tomorrow for gear. I guarantee she's going to lose her mind when she sees the butt pads."

"She's going to need all the pads! Just buy the whole store." He laughs, and Raine joins in. Her lively amusement vibrates past my sternum, directly to my heart, where it settles and warms me to the core.

"Where do you go snowboarding?" I interrupt.

"New York, where I live," she answers. Her eyes leave me, and she looks at Declan like I'm the weird kid that nobody knows who invited into the group. You'll have to try harder to depress me. Being the odd one out is kind of my specialty.

"Oh, really. What part?"

"Cattaraugus County."

"I live in Essex." I've been to that resort. It's a six-and-a-half-hour drive. Three or four by air.

"Have you been to Whiteface?"

"I've been going there for years." It's been more like a decade. Aspen, Vail, Snowbird, Zermatt, Whistler. The list goes on. If you name it, I've been there. One of the only perks of growing up a Pierce.

I look to the left of Raine. Nollan and the crew at the bar are making their way in our direction. How's he going to play this? Two women who both think they're going home with him tonight.

"Bailey!" Raine jumps up, sliding out of the booth. Her arms fly around Bailey's shoulders. Apparently, they know each other. Most nights out with Nollan aren't this compelling. Entertain women and talk cars. That's what brought me to him. Specifically, a Nissan GT-R in Super Silver Quadcoat.

Sure, the cars brought me to Nollan. I'm not sure what's kept me in his circle. The backyard barbeques and the family atmosphere? A sense of belonging.

"I didn't know you were going to be here tonight! I was going to call you tomorrow."

Everyone knows everyone. Small towns. I smile to myself and hide it with my glass. She's...cute.

It grows louder in the bar as the band takes the stage. The platform is surrounded by people drinking and dancing. A long-haired blonde man plays the guitar—a mild alternative rock song—next to a porcelain woman with a dark pixie cut who begins singing and tapping her foot.

Raine turns back to the booth, picking up her beer. Her eyes don't leave mine while she slams it back and sets the empty bottle back on the table. This time, I'm the one stuck on her mouth.

What was that about? Intimidation? A notice to fuck off? Flirtation? I can't settle on one reason or another, only spinning thoughts of another place, another lifetime. There is no hope of getting with that girl, and all I can do is watch her. Create a reflection of the person I think she is inside my head. Hold that thought hostage. The only power that matters—self-control—despite what mankind fights over.

She grabs Bailey's hand, yelling over the noise. "Let's go!" She steers her friend towards the crowded floor, pointing at the band.

Calle pulls Nash by his shirt's tail, disappearing into the crowd, and the other two women quickly slide out of the booth and follow, leaving Declan, Nollan, and me. Dec's women push to the front of the crowd, and I lose sight of them. I lean back, slouching against the vinyl, and scan the crowd. Beautiful young women everywhere, dancing seductively and with intent...And then there's Raine, jumping up and down like a fucking kangaroo.

She plants her feet on the floor, moving her body effortlessly to the music. Her fingertips kiss her swaying hair. They cascade down to the back of her neck and release back out into the air. Her full hips move side to side. Circling, shaking—I don't know what the fuck she's doing...but damn...she's sexy.

The rhythm gets heavier, and she jumps to her feet, hopping up and down a few times before returning to rolling her hips. One hand in the air and the other settling to her hipbone, she's tormenting the hell out of me and has no idea. She's not even trying—not even so much as a glance in my direction—to look for Nollan. She's just enjoying herself. She doesn't care what she looks like...who's watching...who's judging.

"Well, shit, man. I'm not letting the ladies have all the fun," Declan shouts over the music, pulling me out of my dazed coma. He slides out of the booth and takes off into the crowd.

Nollan stiffly tips back his beer, staring at me with dead eyes and a tense jaw.

Fuck.

The groan echoes in my head. That look—I've seen it from every jealous boyfriend who has tried to pick a fight with me every time I go to a bar. Casual people—pretty women—watching isn't a crime worth punishing.

"You good?"

"Good." His lips roll in.

He's not fucking *good*. I press my teeth into my tongue, wanting to bite it until it pours red. Instead, I bail on the fantasy of fucking the smart-mouth woman I met at the hotel gym. Before he gets bent anymore, I'm shutting this down.

I lean forward, pushing my sleeve up as high as the cotton will inch over my biceps. "It's hot in here. Let's go outside for a minute. Get some air."

He puts his empty bottle down and stands, following me to the exit through the crowd. We make our way through sweaty bodies and smoke-choking men, exiting the building. The parking lot is well-lit, with spotlights along the roof and poles throughout each section of cars. A group of people to the left is smoking something that earns a short exhale as I step to the right and turn to face my bitter friend. As he brings his face inches away from mine, the distance closes. I stay put, dauntless. It doesn't phase me. I've stood in this place many times and never swung a fist. Despite what people say, they still judge a book by its fucking cover. I'm a lover, not a fighter.

"Casey, I'm only going to say it once. When it comes to Raine..." He hesitates, pressing his lips together tightly. Then, he steps back. He can't intimidate me, and Nollan is far from ignorant. "We have history."I understand his plea. *Don't fuck my ex.*

"We're good. We are good," I reassure him, placing my hand on his shoulder. "You want a shot? Crown?" I squeeze the tense muscle and glide him around, back through the door, and into the crowd. The advantage of being height-endowed—I can easily search the room and spot the ocean-loving bleach blond.

"Declan!" I yell. "Shots?" Pointing to the bar in our shuffle through the maze of people.

"Hell yeah!" He calls back, following as we push to the bartender.

"Three shots Crown," I tell the redhead. If it will ease the rapacious look on Nollan's face, I'll hit on her. The chill guy I befriended in this town has a possessive and jealous side. Everyone has a downfall.

"Natural?" I ask her.

"Natural? I hope you're asking about my hair, hunny," she replies with a meager southern drawl. "My hair is natural, absolutely, but it's no secret the ladies ain't." She shimmies.

I pull my elbows from the counter, glancing at her ample cleavage. "I don't judge." With a wink, she dips forward. Intentionally or not, her breasts spill further from her tight black tank top. *Motorboatable.* She pulls shot glasses from below the counter and fills the row of three. Nollan drops it back quicker than she can tuck the bottle of liquor in its place.

"I saw you in here last night. Out of towner?" She asks.

"Yeaaa—" I string out, taken aback by Nollan's hand gesture. An indicator to *Red* that he wants another shot. She pours it before I can form a full sentence, and Nollan leans backward against the counter, throwing the second shot down his throat. His eyes search for Raine in the crowd before he slams his glass to the counter and stands up, walking off.

The bartender collects Nollan's empty glass, placing it below the counter. Then she reaches into the sable apron hanging from her hips, retrieving a long, claw-style hair clip. Separating a layer of her hair, she clips it back. "Your friend is on a mission tonight."

"Something like that," I reply.

Declan takes the seat next to me, quickly finding the shot with his name on it. Leaning on his forearms, he mumbles before gulping it down. "Bro, I love Raine, but Nol...Nollan gets pulled into the riptide every time he sees her." He picks up his hanging face to look at me, flicking his head to the side to shake his shaggy hair out of his eyes. His face is long and slightly annoyed.

I raise my glass to him and drop it back. That will be it for me tonight.

"The dance floor is calling your name." I look over my shoulder to find Raine's grin.

Nash walks around her and leans against the bar next to Declan, followed by Nollan. He squeezes his brother's shoulder as he rejoins us. The juice either kicked in or something else perked him up because he's in a better mood. His usual yellow aura recoils with a smile that can spark comfort in a stranger.

Declan is right. I've known Nollan for a few years, and I've only seen him get trashed once. Last night, when he found out she was in town. There's a lot of history here I'm missing, and from the sounds of it, this isn't his first offense going off the rails when it comes to her.

Lights spill across the walls of the dark bar, turning her light hair rainbow colors. She has a smile that would radiate energy at zero points. "I didn't peg you for a party girl."

"You're not very good at pegging women at all, are you?"

"Don't make yourself sound ignorant."

"Half the girls in here are drunk. They'll still think you're doing a good job." She taps my knee.

"How much have you had to drink, Raine?"

"Not enough to be one of those girls, businessman."

The smile on my face is impossible to avoid. She's a meteor, crashing into my atmosphere and burning my throat like cinnamon whiskey. Every word that escapes her mouth is unfiltered and somehow fulfilling. She reaches over to Nollan, pulling his hat off and putting it on her head. She's drunk, unquestionably more intoxicated than she wants me to believe, swaying side to side with the music.

Nollan takes his hat back and dips close to her before pointing to the end of the bar, where the pool tables are. He nods at me, then turns to follow Nash and Declan. Raine's fingers wrap around my wrist the second I stand up.

Oh, she's going to fall.

"Dance with me."

Oh. I'm confused. *She's confused.*

"Me?" My fingertip hits my chest.

"No, the Queen of Narnia," she sneers, straight-faced. "Let's see who the better dancer *really* is."

"Uh, I don't know if that's a good idea." I searched for the guys, but I am unable to see the pool tables from where we stand. Nollan is going to bitch out. I'm the not-dickhead that shits on his friends and takes their girls. No matter how tempting or unbinding their relationship may be.

"Ouch, rejected." Her head hangs.

God, she looks good. Ahh...fuck it. It's one dance. There are a few hundred people here tonight. If it's not with me, it'll be with someone else. "Alright." I cave. "Let's see what you got, Happy Feet."

She bounces on her toes and walks off. I follow her through the bar, toward the stage. She buries us in the middle of the crowd, cleverly hiding from Nollan's view. We're on the same page. Neither of us is interested in a psychotic meltdown courtesy of alcohol and hurt feelings. We all know he's showing off. Nollan doesn't go out like this often and doesn't drink the way he's been drinking tonight. We go to the race track and sometimes catch a band. He barbecues. The guy has a patio setup that a chef would adore. If this was who he was when they were together, it makes sense why it ended.

Her swaying hips swing, and she dances around me. "Is this what your idea of fun is? Drinking and dancing?" I yell over the music.

"No...and yes." She doesn't stop, closing her eyes briefly. She looks...at ease. Her problems have disintegrated and gone with the wind.

"What does that mean?"

She softly smiles. Her beautiful peachy lips curve with comfort. "I like dancing. At home, I take a fitness dance class."

"Oh, you jazzercise." I bite my lip, trying not to laugh at her dropping jaw.

"I do not jazzercise! It's not the eighties, Casey. Did you get that line from your grandma?"

"I'm hip. I know what the cool kids call it. Other than to jazzercise, why'd you come out tonight?"

Her eyes roll upward with the glare she gives me. "It wasn't to drink. I know I called you out…but I'm not much of a drinker either." Her lips pillow together. "You know exactly why I'm here," she adds, returning to dancing.

"For sex," I taunt. Her face is priceless, stoned over and gawking, although she gives me no leeway before snapping back.

"Absolutely. I decided I was going to walk into a bar that holds terrible memories with my dumbass ex-boyfriend along with his dumbass friends, just for some cock and canoodling." She gives me another hard look. I'm one of the dumbass friends.

"That's shitty. If you're going to pay for prime entertainment, it better be worth it." She bobs her head around, and I can't tell if she heard me or not. "I bought a ticket, and I'm a little lost. What am I missing?"

"Unfinished business," she answers between a twirl.

"Poltergeist of the past. What did he do? Throw too many tantrums? Refuse to grow up?" My brows furrow, followed by a sultry smile. It's as smooth and confident as I am.

"I'm the—Are you going to dance or just ask questions you know the answers to all night?" She shut me down.

"Love, the only reason I agreed to come out here is to annoy you with questions." Staring into her vixen green eyes, I need to know one more thing. "Last question. I promise."

"Promises are easily broken."

"The cons to this promise-breaking are relatively low."

She shakes her head with a slight curve to her lips. "What is it?"

"I saw you in the lobby around seven."

"Yeah?"

"Who pissed in your cereal?"

"That's your question?" I nod, and she rolls her eyes. "I got into an argument with my mom."

Mm. "Sorry to hear that."

She sighs. "She...my mom and I, we have different ways of thinking."

"Hmm." I raise my thumb and pointer finger to my chin, tracing the short length. "And how do you feel about that?"

"Well, Dr. Pierce, I have this horrible feeling your rates are out of my price range. I'm not paying for a therapy session," she sneers. "Shh. Dance."

I like her laugh. It's bold, yet delicate. She grabs my hand, spinning herself around.

Darling, you're not getting away that easily. Refusing to let her go, I spin her again until her back is tight against my chest. She smells so good. I brush her sweet coconut hair to the side and spin her out.

Abruptly pulling her into my chest, she gasps, and I gently squeeze her waist, swaying left to right. I run my hands up her sides, over her cotton t-shirt, along her ribs, to the warmth of her skin. She moves slowly beneath the presence of my fingertips, which glide toward her elbows. I lift her hands, placing them tactfully around my neck. I rest my palms over hers, and she stares up at me. As we drift to music, I lose myself in her eyes.

Beautiful.

Gliding my fingers down her forearms, I settle my hands on her hips.

"You're fucking breathtaking," I mutter, not positive she heard me. I glance down to her mouth, her lips parting before she looks away.

She gasps again as I spin her by the hips ninety degrees until her back is against my chest again. I imagine that same shock when I get her into bed with me. She'd rethink that pegging comment. As we drift to the beat, my hands rest lightly on her hips. She slides them onto my thighs, moving her hips faster.

Woman, please stop trying to give me a public erection.

Her soft hair brushing against my face, her curves moving against me...I want to...Damn. Everything she does evokes the side of me that I *desperately* want to show her. How I dangerously want to give her that.

The song comes to an end before I'm ready to return to an empty reality. The music cuts, but neither of us moves.

"Ten-minute break folks. Let's slow it down in the meantime with DJ Slater," the blonde man announces, tapping the microphone twice. The song immediately plays. Smooth saxophone and acoustic guitar strings followed my higher-range male vocals.

I gently grab her hands, pulling them away from my thighs. Taking one delicately in mine, I spin her around. "Stay with me," I persuade, draping her hand over my shoulder. She's caught up in me, too. Her adorable, dreamy-drunk expression mimics the internal twisting that pulls me closer. We waver like teenagers at a high school dance with my hands on her hips. "Maybe I am a better dancer than you." I smile devilishly. Every time I say something unimpressive, she gives me the stink face. I'm surprised, her face isn't stuck in that position. "What's with that face? You always make it."

I won't fight for her, ever. I won't beg for her to stay. I won't wallow in pity when it doesn't last. I'll move forward, like I always do, as I've always had to do. If she lets me in, I'm taking the offer. Nobody has to know.

"*That face?*"

"The nose wrinkling thing. You do it a lot," I point out. "You might want to stop."

"Stop being an arrogant prick, and maybe I would."

"Take a look around, sweetheart. I'm not out of place. Every girl in this crowd has glanced over at least once. The group of brunettes next to us is drooling. Do you even see how much they envy you?" She looks around, taking in the staring women around us. Some of them offer her similar glares, and others hide their faces in a rush. Don't bite your lip, love. "Hey. Look at me, please. Don't let anyone make you feel self-conscious."

She tries to hide it. Her eyes darken, and she purses her lips. "I don't need a lesson in self-esteem. I get it; you're confident. You're hot. Any woman would love to tear this stupid white shirt from your chest."

"Stupid?"

"This isn't Vegas. Wear a fucking t-shirt to the bar." Her eyes roll to the side.

"I'll wear what I want. Hey, look at me." Her chin tucks as her eyes grow wider. Yeah, I didn't ask this time. "I am confident, but here's a secret." I inch closer to her ear. "I hate crowds," I whisper. "Loathe them. It's overwhelming." Her lips tighten while she tries to fight a smile. "Oh, are you enjoying putting me through pain?" *That smile.*

A clash comes from the top of the room near the pool tables, erasing her joy. Instinctively, I bring my hands back to myself and search as far as I can see. Raine steps past me, pushing her way through the crowd towards the noise. I follow her, staying as close as I can.

A bar stool flies in the air, landing in front of her as she reaches the opening. She steps back, glancing up at me. "Are you okay?"

She doesn't answer, her mind lost in the madness. Declan's arms are tucked under Nollan's, crossing over his chest in restraint as he pulls him off a man that's double his size. He keeps swinging one arm and pointing with the other as he yells.

"Keep running your mouth, bitch! See what happens!"

Declan stands in front of him, barking. "Nollan shut the fuck up." He shoves his hands into Nol's chest. "Come on!"

Shit. I need to help him.

I unintentionally run my hand across Raine's back, trying to steer her out of the way.

"No." She wags a finger. A scowl from hell drives home, telling me to stay put.

I look back at Delcan, slapping Nollan's face between both hands. He holds him long enough to get his attention. "You need to chill!

It's pure chaos. One woman is in a man's face, screaming at the top of her lungs. Music and smoke suddenly lie heavy. The crowd grows, and all I can do is flex my shoulders, hoping people will keep their distance from the intimidating tattooed man.

I spot Nash sitting on the floor with his woman standing over him, giving him hell. She's fucking pissed. I want to get the fuck out of here. People are backing up, nearly tripping over each other, trying to get out of the way with the same train of thought. I'm done.

"Fuck. I'll get the car," I say, walking away.

Move. Move it. Fucking move.

Nollan's not entirely foolish. He gave me the keys earlier, as if he were foreshadowing this.

Freedom and fresher air. People are scattered all over the place, half of them unaware that it's going to be swarming with cops soon. I speed walk to the car, unlock it, and start it up. The engine roars as the lights brighten the parking lot.

Raine, Declan, and Bailey are standing outside the door when I pull up. My heart heavily races, ready to speed out of here at any moment. I don't have to be the one on the run to be injected with epinephrine. I eat up the untraditional high, feeling a thousand times better being outside. Waiting to drive off gives me a taste of the adrenaline I knew long ago.

"Are you sure you don't want me to come with?" Baily's concern hardly affects Nollan. Raine's eyes wander between the two. By now, she has to see that something is going on between them.

"No. I'll text you," he says, pulling away. Declan knocks the top of Nollan's fist with his, followed by the bottom, and without a second glance, walks back into Sparrow to look for his women. Bailey hesitates, glancing back at Nollan, but follows behind the girlfriend rescuer.

"Let's go," he says, sliding into the rear passenger seat. The moment Raine jumps in behind me, I don't waste any time, peeling out of the parking lot.

"What the fuck?" She yells, smacking his knee.

He flinches. "Sorry."

"Sorry?" She sneers, mocking his word in a nasally deepened voice. "Care to elaborate other than *sorry*?"

"The guy wouldn't leave Bailey alone. He didn't take it well when I told him to fuck off. He threw the first punch. When Nash tried to break it up, the guy's friend sucker punched him. So I hit the fucker with a stool and then...I might have thrown it across the room."

He looks like he did all the punching. His fist is bloody, but his face looks fine. Not a mark. I watch the road, occasionally looking in the rearview mirror at them.

"Yeah, I found that stool at my feet."

His chin knocks up, and their eyes meet for a heavy moment. "I didn't know you were there." Nollan's vacant gaze turns on me. "Where were you two, anyway?" He pulls his shirt off and wraps his hand several times.

"That's going to stain your shirt," Raine scolds him, ignoring the question.

"I'll buy a new one, Mom."

She's giving him that look now. Even if I can't see her expression, only getting a glimpse of her when the street lights shine over the car, I can hear it in the static between them. She leans over the center console, touching the side of his ribs, and he winces. That must be where he took punches from his opponent.

"I said, don't do anything stupid. If you're behind, I'll catch you up. This falls under the stupid category," she sasses. I chuckle, and she looks at me with an uninviting glare.

"House or hotel?" I ask, finding Nollan in the mirror facing Raine. He waits for her to answer.

"Hotel," she finally replies.

Pulling up to the hotel, I make the last-minute decision to pass it. Something is off.

"Um, hotel?" Raine leans forward, pointing. "The big grey building to your left."

"We're being followed," I reply, calmly.

"What? What do you mean by *followed*?" They both turn and look out the rear window. "Who would follow you, Nollan?" She smacks him in the back of the head.

"A dark SUV has been tailing us since we left. I didn't want to jump to conclusions."

"Never saw it before," he mumbles.

I don't know if it's someone looking for more trouble with Nollan or if it's someone looking for me. Either way, I don't plan on finding out. Just the possibility of it being someone Cameron sent to keep tabs on me is enough to ensure that fleeing is a better option.

"Hold on." I barely give them the warning before I push the gas pedal to the floor, pull the steering wheel hard, and turn the car in a one-eighty. Crashing fists smack against the leather, gripping and holding on for their lives. As I accelerate, I speed past the SUV.

"For Christ's sake. It's a cop," I murmur. "How fast can this thing go?" I impassively joke. Raine sits back and fastens her seatbelt. It's amusing watching this woman who appears impervious to me suddenly become vulnerable. Nollan leans forward, almost sitting on the backseat's center console. He presses his hands against the leather in front of him.

"Turbocharged V6. Don't fucking wreck it," he replies, suddenly sober. A sinister smile crosses my face as I look between him and the road.

"I swear I'll stab both of you fuckers if I end up in the back of a cop car again in this town!" Raine yells.

I laugh. "Again? Is this a normal occurrence around you?"

"Easy, Casey, she's said she's going to stab us," Nollan utters. "Go faster!"

I push the pedal further, allowing the needle to climb the speedometer.

"You're both *soo* hilarious," she exaggerates.

Nollan moves to his seat and looks behind us. "You got it. You got it."

I gap the cop several car lengths before forcing the brakes to the floor and whipping the wheel again. Slamming into reverse and abruptly backing into the dark alley, I park next to a two-car garage bordering the street before cutting the engine. The lights quickly go out, and the moment is silent...until it's not.

What's *that*...light panting?

I turn around to find Raine no longer belted in. Her right knee is pressed into the console's leather, her left knee on his seat, and her ass is pushed out with the arch of her back. She has his hands pinned to the headrest, entwined in hers. Her mouth levitates over his, teasing him.

Well, I'll be damned. The adrenaline turns her on. Explains why she likes to board, the little adrenaline junkie. Shaking my head, I look back to the street, eyeing her in the rearview mirror. She's not vanilla, is she? Not simple and innocent with a smart mouth. Nollan's warning wasn't for his sake. It was for mine. Once you're in her trap, you do what you can to stay. Maybe...who knows?

Letting my eyes wander, she digs into the depths of my brain, worming her way through me like a disease. Fuck, to be her toy right now. As much as I don't mind watching her, none of us are going to jail tonight.

The cop accelerates past the dim alley, lights flashing as he speeds away. I'm not waiting for him to figure it out and turn around. Twisting the key, the motor purrs, and I put the car in drive. Pushing the pedal to the floor, I speed back onto the main road. Whipping the wheel, my palms slide across the leather, and bodies collide in the backseat. Raine flies sideways into the rear passenger window, instantly calling out in pain.

"Fuck, Casey!" I glance back to see her rubbing her head. "A little warning next time? *Asshole*."

If it means you'll yell my name like that *next time*, no way. No warnings, because this is as close as I'll get to hearing you moan for me. I'm sorry. I'm sorry. I want you. I'm sorry, I want my friend's girl…or whoever she is to him. You don't get to choose who you're attracted to. Only your actions. I shouldn't have done that.

"Nollan only told me not to hurt the car. He said nothing about the passengers." I flash an obnoxious smile at her in the mirror, cloaking the self-disappointment. Nollan laughs, hugging the headrest in front of him. Then I find her again. As she settles in her seat, that look burns into the back of my head.

I'll find her missing smile. "What band sings this?" I ask, tapping the volume up on the steering wheel.

"Atreyu," their voices synchronize.

"Do you actually like this one?" She sneers. "Or are you going to add insult to injury?"

"I'm into it." My chin tips up as I catch a glimpse of her in the mirror. "Pop-punk isn't the same as your *screaming* music."

"Have you ever been to Sound Fest?" Nollan slaps his hand down on the console's leather, catching our attention.

"It's been a while since I've been to a concert."

"Sound Fest is more of an experience. Try ten bands, signings, food, and good vibes. Raine and I used to go every year." She nods, tight-lipped. "What was your favorite show, babe?"

Her smile stretches in the streetlights. "Cream pie donuts."

"You listen to a band called Cream Pie Donuts?" They both laugh. I must be missing something.

"No. She's talking about after, um, who was it?" He snaps.

"We The Kings. They're pop-punk."

"Yeah! On the way home, Raine threw a donut out the window, and it flew back in the rear window, pie-ing Declan in the face." He bows his head, laughing again. "You had to be there."

"I get it. I've had some crazy parties with my friends."

"*Mr. I don't drink* gets crazy?"

"Young, wild, and free doesn't mean you have to be drunk. I think you know that...and for some reason keep trying to get under my skin."

She has little to stay, all in good timing. Here's the hotel. I park at the farthest end of the lot. The car will be less likely to be spotted if the cop patrols the area looking for it. Nollan gets out, double-checking that I didn't get a scratch on it. I turn back to Raine, stalling her settled hand from pulling the door handle.

"Hey."

"What?" She's still pissed.

"How's your head?"

"Don't tell me you care." She wets her lips. "I'll be fine."

"I'm sure you will." I smile, glancing toward Nollan passing her door, and making his way to the front of the car.

"We both will," she answers sharply. "It was nice meeting you...again." She pulls the handle and steps out. Then she walks to the front of the car, meeting Nollan. This is it. A weird fucking night and a hello-goodbye to one of the most intriguing women I've met in a while...There are more fish in the sea.

I get out, joining them to hand Nollan the keys. "No scratches?" I chuckle, turning away.

"Looks good. Nice driving!" He yells.

Without another look in her direction, I briskly find the entrance and let them have their reunion, minus the third wheel.

It's two in the morning, and my flight leaves at ten.

I stretch my arms out, lie flat on my back, and reach for my phone. Six missed calls from a blocked number border the top of my illuminated screen. Two less than yesterday. My phone slips out of my hand and falls to my bare chest. The abrupt hit makes me cave inward.

"*Son of a...*" I mutter aloud.

Pulling the pillow from behind my head, I hold it over my face.

Go to sleep.

This has been a shitty trend for the past two weeks. The past haunts me at night. I was over it. I buried it six feet under. I moved on. Now it's back, draining my energy. And it's because *Cameron* wants something. At least tonight, something new, *someone new*, is distracting me. This unpredictable woman, whom I have no business entertaining myself with. To be a fly on her hotel room's wall. That's *not* creepy. I sound like a stalker.

...If the shoe fits.

I open Insta and search her name. *Raine Cree*. Thanks for telling me her full name unintentionally last night, Nol. I click on the first search result. *That's her.* She has a cute smile.

Are these reels? She has reels snowboarding?

Knows what she's doing...and there she goes, taking a spill. This is...it's a fucking compilation of falls. Is she making a snow angel?

For a few minutes, I indulge in her snowbound trips before I click back to her profile and scroll. I immediately stop on a picture of her in a skin-tight, full-length black dress and find the caption. *"Had to take a picture at my cousin's wedding or this dress never happened. If you leave a rude comment, I will print out your profile pic and add it to my dart board without a second thought. Kidding. No, I'm not. Congrats to the beautiful couple! #wedding #playingdressup."*

She looks phenomenal...The things I'd like to do to her. Morning wood should rise at seven AM, not two. What could go wrong? I ruin some hotel sheets? I have a fantasy, a hand, and a closet full of towels.

I reach toward the nightstand again, grabbing my glasses by the frame and putting them on. My cock is as hard and long as her black and purple snowboard. On the dance floor, her body grinding against mine and then that stunt she pulled with Nollan...I was expecting this. I hate being single.

Slipping my hand down the sparse, dark trail from my lower abs to my groin, I stroke the length of my stiff cock. If she were here with me...If she were here...She'd be touching me. She'd be moaning for me. She'd be in shock and awe, and fuck, she's good with her hands, wrapping them both around me because one isn't enough.

"That's it, love," I mutter. "Don't stop." The veins in my forearm cord, and I tap the screen with my thumb to keep it from dimming.

Nollan will get over it. Her history with him is still far less complicated than anything I would bring to the table. He wouldn't know. I can't get a grip on her...and I should do it. I should make a move. Send her a message. Tell her what's on my mind. Tell her what I'm doing right now.

Holding my hand up, I spit on it and roll my palm over my dick's head. Stroking down with the twist of my wrist, it's her ass grinding against me that's on replay. *Dance on me, darling.* I want to see that scrunched-up face, telling me to turn off the hip-hop and play some metal. She would drive me fucking insane with that shit.

She's funny. I could handle the ear-piercing music for one night with her. Digging my fingers into her thighs till they're bruised, so she'll remember me days after I'm gone. Lord knows I couldn't forget her. I wasn't designed that way.

Sebastian would tell me to go for it. For a man who locked a girl in when he was only twenty-two and she just turned eighteen, he still cheers me on with these no-direction relationships I get into. Always short-lived, but Raine...I could break my own rules. *No one-night stands.* It's not a rule, per se. It's who I am. She thinks I'm a fuckboy. It couldn't be farther from the truth.

Bash, being my only childhood friend that I'm still close with, besides Ky, I was surprised when he suddenly got married. At twenty-six, I still can't see it. Not when Cameron is breathing down my neck.

Fuck. I can't do this.

I drop my phone to the sheets, releasing my cock. It's not enough. I can't get this fucking shit off my mind, despite the fantasy of her.

I want a woman to occupy my time, like Bash's wife, Estella. She's the opposite of him. She's gentle and reserved, nothing like the big mouth.

I should be content, knowing Bash is going to be at the mediation tomorrow. He was born a lawyer. I wouldn't trust anyone else.

It's the biological residents I share blood with that fuck my lonesome nights over. Karson has the best lawyers daddy's money will pay for, not that I think any of this will make it to court. My sister is just like our father, Cameron. She stops at nothing to get what she wants. Between the two of them, I'm stuck here, beating off with no happy ending.

Neither of them bothered me till...Grandpa passed away two weeks ago.

A heavy sigh leaves my lungs empty.

Two weeks already since I heard his reassuring voice.

I adjust my sweats and punch in the sides of my pillow until I'm comfortable.

The four years I spent living with Gramps before graduating high school changed my life. I owed him my life. He was a stern man, but he was a better father to me than Cameron ever had been. I imagine our bond is the reason he willed the majority of his belongings to me. Karson, being the spoiled brat she is, can't handle that. She has yet to officially state what she wants, but my guess would be the villa.

The villa is as nice as Pierce Estate, Cameron's mansion. The house itself is over seven thousand square feet with five bedrooms. Each has its own bathroom and walk-in closet. Despite only being built twelve years ago, the detail is exquisite. He insisted he had to bring Tuscany home. Filling a small portion of the massive patio, an in-ground pool with a waterfall is the first thing to draw the eye, next to the covered outdoor bar, cast in stone. The property also has a five-car garage and a six-stall horse barn on its twenty acres.

She can have it. Whatever it takes to keep her out of my life. Leaving my family, aside from Grandpa, was the best decision I ever made.

Bash, Ky, Alistair, and Benji are more of a family to me than the people who created me have ever been. The only thing Cameron ever taught me was to protect the dynasty at all costs. Generations before him opened CP Banking, handing him the golden ticket. I don't fucking want it.

A quick internet search easily connects me to my wealthy family, but I've worked far harder than he ever has to create something that is mine. This is mine. Fuck Karson. Fuck Cameron. They won't get to me.

I *will* move forward from this and from them. Temporary pain grows strength, resilience, and courage.

Another sigh empties my lungs.

I'm not getting to sleep anytime soon. I might as well go for a walk. Tire the body, overpower the mind.

Chapter Six | Divinity

Raine

Friday, 2:15 AM

I slide my key card into the door, and Nollan follows me into my suite. Dropping my purse on the bench, I sit on the end of the bed, pull my shoes off, and let them fall to the floor.

Ugh, I drank way too much. The first rule of playing stupid games...always keep your feet on the ground, or you'll spin round and round.

He stands in front of me, taking my face in his hands. I look into his dopey eyes. He dropped his blood-covered shirt near the bathroom door, while I gave myself a pep-talk about the swirling world of intoxication. His knuckles are dry and swollen now that I see them in the light.

"You should put some ice on that."

"I'd rather put some of you on me."

"Nollan," I hesitate, knowing what I'm about to say is going to change the mood. He has *or had* something with Bailey. I'm not getting in the middle of that for a trip down memory lane. "Are you...interested in Bailey?"

"Why does that matter?" He takes a step back.

"It matters because it matters. It's a simple question."

"It has nothing to do with us."

"It kinda does." I ruin my face with lines. "She's still my friend, and if she cares for you in that way, she's going to be crushed if she finds out about...*us.*" *Us.* That's not a thing.

"She has no say in what I do," he fires back.

"I don't think you two are on the same page, then. She seemed..." I shake my head, smoothing my hands over my thighs.

"Seemed what? What are you talking about?" He pinches the bridge of his nose.

I scan his body, his naked chest, and his bruising ribs. "My eyes work pretty well. She kept touching you. Then you got into a fight because of her. And I was right there when she asked if you wanted her to come with us."

He rubs his hand over his closed eyes.

"Talk to me," I practically plead. "What's going on, Nol?"

He drops his hands in surrender. "We started hanging out a while ago, but in the past five months it's been a lot more." His legs cave as he plops down on the bed beside me. Taking off his hat and tossing it to the side, he falls backward onto the mattress. He pushes blonde strands of hair from his face, swiping them to the side and threading pieces back between his fingers. I scoot farther onto the bed and roll to my side, tucking my arm under my head. "She wants a title. Something official and...I haven't been able to give her that." Nollan reaches out, brushing my hair behind my ear. His thumb rests on my jaw, holding me gently. "It's you, Raine." My eyes wander back and forth as I search for words. "You cut me open, ripped my beating heart from my chest, and sewed me back up. And I had this hope you would come back holding my heart in your hands." His warmth leaves me absent. "Instead, you moved away like...nothing," he sighs. "You run, Raine. Every time you see a fracture, you take off, not giving a damn about who falls in the process. You ruined me, and I still want you. I always want you. No matter who I date, I'm still thinking about you, comparing them to you." He rolls to his back, looking at the ceiling. "A good girl wants to give me the world and I'm waiting on your torturous hurricane to sweep in and fuck me over."

My heart beats in my stomach. It's louder than the grumbling of the after-bar munchies. I keep staring at his face, watching the agony in his blue eyes. I'm paralyzed. I didn't run away from anything. I ran towards myself. It's not my fault he can't let go.

He takes my chin in one hand and kisses me softly. It's confusing and conflicting, and I don't care because I want his heat.

"This is the last time I'm going to see you. I need to live my life without you because, Raine, I'm an addict. The pain you leave me with is the consequence of my high," he exhales. "It's time I finally stop relapsing."

"Asshole," I mutter, snapping out of dick-vision and seeing his true colors. It blinds me with disbelief, wrapped in anger and agony. He wants one last rail and bail to sew his wild oats before he settles down with the prom queen. Like what the Friday fuck?

In my emotional distress, my words slowly make sense, coming out more calmly than either of us anticipated. "You knew this since you called me this morning, didn't you?" Pausing for a moment, I shuffle through my thoughts. They become increasingly violent, shaking me awake. "You knew I would hook up with you, and *what?* You would then tell me, *by the way, I don't want to see you again. Raine's* in town. Here's my chance to get it in. Get the hall pass. The bachelor night cum slut. One final hoorah. What the hell, Nollan!"

I sit up, heat rushing to my face. "You couldn't just be honest?" I've never lied about my intentions. He agreed to them. We...*we agreed*. Is this his petty revenge? It's pissing me off the longer I look at him.

"And say what? I want to tap that one more time before I never talk to you again? I'm sure you would have agreed to that, Raine."

"You malicious asshole. Asshole. Asshole!" Hell, I drank too much for this. "I never once lied to you! Not when we were dating and not when we were doing...whatever the hell we were doing." I throw my hands up. "If you wanted one last ride before you moved on to your happily ever after, you could have just said that. Like, do you even know me?" I stand from the bed, and Nollan finally sits up.

"Would you have said yes?"

"I don't know." I cross my arms over my chest, avoiding his eyes. Maybe. If it was my last chance to fuck him... It would sink in eventually. If he had given me a heads-up, I would have overthought it and said yes. His not being there when I'm desperate for a man on the other end of the phone...Our absolute ending.

"See, you wouldn't have. You purposely torment me, staying just at arm's length but never fully out of the fucking picture. You've done this since the day you broke up with me. I go out, and there you are, at the same bar as me, flirting with every Tom, Dick, and Harry in the place." His hands fly in the air as he talks, mimicking the commotion I made ninety seconds ago. "I thought I could finally move on when you moved away. Then you had to text me, holding on with an inch." He pinches his fingers together. "You're selfish. I was always a second thought. Now you want to make me out as the bad guy," he exclaims.

"Selfish!" I yell.

This is the second time in twenty-four hours someone has used that word on me, and I'm tired of it. I'm tired of letting people talk *to* me and not hear, *really hear*, what I have to say. "You're right. I'm a selfish bitch. Let's talk about why we don't. Back to that night in Sparrow. I wasn't dating you that night. I was single, and at the bar with my friends, and *still*, I went to jail to cover for your ass! I didn't even know you would be at Sparrow. You always went to The Rebel! Apparently, starting fights and getting kicked out. I didn't even know who that person was. It wasn't the Nollan I remembered. If I were so selfish, why did I take that bullet? Why did I cover for you? That was one of the most *terrifying moments in my life!*" I yell. "And not because I might have damaged my future plans. No. Because I didn't know what happened to you. I spent hours wondering if you made it home in one piece. If you hurt yourself or anyone else. I let you leave. I told you to go, watching you take off in my car with who knows how much alcohol coursing through your veins, so *you* wouldn't get arrested again." I point at him, close enough to touch him without making the connection. "What do you want from me, Nollan? You know exactly who I am. Yeah, we both changed since then, but you fucking know that I've always been honest with you. I know I'm not the same person I was all those years ago, but you...You can put a suit on and parade around, but underneath it all, you're the same punk, aren't you? Starting fights because you didn't get what you wanted. Me. Do you know how it felt to be back in that bar tonight, witnessing you throw punches and—Nollan, a fucking chair?"

He stands from the bed and wraps his arms around my shoulders, hugging me. I'm frozen again, my arms pinned to my sides, not knowing which emotion I should give in to.

"Fuck, Raine," he says, sympathetically. He holds me, and I inhale alcohol from his warm breath mixed with the spice in his deodorant. The silence between us is dulcifying.

He pulls away, holding onto my arms. His rugged hands slide to my shoulders, and he pushes me backward onto the bed. I inhale. Unstable emotional waves crash around me. The sullen turbulence of lust and desire buries my rage and agony. As Nollan wraps his hands around my thighs, the nightmares of memories fade. He pushes me onto the edge of the bed, my toes brushing the carpet. His stony scowl and cold blue eyes hold me, but I don't want to move. His hands slide from my thighs up to the button of my jeans, and he pulls at my zipper. Then, in a sudden prise, he yanks my jeans to my knees, pushing them off my ankles. Inching knee-by-knee, he straddles my thighs. The same way he hovered over me hours ago, winning my agreement.

"Nollan." I have more to say, but it's too late. We're past heartwrenching words.

"Shh," he whispers. His lips meet mine briefly before he pushes me off my elbows and onto my back. I don't want him to stop. I don't care what either of us said moments ago. I don't care about Bailey's feelings. I only care about the heated friction increasing between my legs the farther his lips drift down my body. His warm hands fold around my ribs, underneath my shirt. I close my eyes with his lips caressing my abdomen, down to my pelvic bone, making me squirm and my core muscles shutter in anticipation.

Nollan's soft hands massage over my skin, hooking his fingers around my panties. I'm so glad I shaved yesterday…Wait, it's like *something* o'clock in the morning, so two days ago? Two-day stubble. Whatever. He won't notice.

The light tug makes me reflexively bow upward. He unhooks and pushes my hips back to the bed. What's he…Why did he stop? I open my eyes and lower my chin to my chest to catch his abruptly haunting eyes just…watching me.

"I don't want you to stop."

"Oh, is that right?" His brows twitch upward and settle back in place. He slides his fingers over the gusset of my panties. With one finger looping and pulling to the side, he exposes my wet flesh. My entire body ignites, and I throw my head back with the slip of his finger rolling over my clit. "You want to melt beneath my hand?" Fingers lace into my hair, and he drags me back up on my elbows. His words come out as clear as the sun on a cloudless day, finding a way to boggle my intoxicated mind. "Too bad."

"What?" I exhale.

"I'm not going to give you what you want, Raine." His mouth says one thing, and his finger says another. They keep moving in slow strokes between my legs.

"You…" I begin to buckle, stopping myself. "You know what it is, too. What's the problem?"

"Eight months ago, you texted me around two in the morning. Do you remember what you said?" In a condescending taunt, his head tilts slightly to the side. I push his hand back and adjust my panties.

"Eight months ago? What, like March? What are you fucking talking about?"

"Yes, Raine. Think." A finger gun taps his temple. "It was Saint Patrick's Day weekend. Do you remember what you said?" He hovers over me.

I remember that weekend, unfortunately, and exactly why he's pissed now. He held a secret grudge this long? When did we become this? When did he start lying?

That weekend, I let the girls talk me into going to a winery. It was the first time I had a drink in, I don't know how long, much like tonight. I woke up with the worst hangover and a slew of text messages I regret.

"It's...a game," I murmur, biting my cheek. He grabs my chin. I sigh loudly, knowing exactly what I said that night. "I already apologized for that." I was an asshole. It was a turning point, which is why I told him I wanted to end our arrangement. I haven't had alcohol in six months. I shouldn't have had any tonight. Then...everything went wrong, and he showed up, and I make stupid decisions when I'm around Nollan. I hate this town. I partied. I stayed out all night and slept all day. I took every wild adventure that was placed in front of me. Recklessly endangering myself was how I escaped. Nothing changes when I come back here. I try to get away, yet somehow I end up begging for fuel to ignite my fire.

"What did you say, Raine?" He grinds his teeth, and I bat his hand away.

An increasingly annoyed sigh vibrates out of my lips. *"This is a game. I'll never stop fucking with your head."*

He stands up, looking at me from the bed's edge. His dark jeans clearly display a protrusion. He's tormenting both of us.

"Fuck!" He throws his hands to his head, fighting his demons as much as I've been fighting mine. "I wish I could just leave you here wanting more. Leave you like you left me..." His hands swing violently to his sides. "I can't. I don't want to walk away from you."

I stand up, grab my jeans, and pull them back on.

"What are you doing?" He asks.

The building rage hits me. Both of my arms fly up in a passionate vexation, striking his bare chest several times until he grabs my wrists, stopping me.

"This is what you wanted!" Nollan shouts.

"I never wanted any of this!" He holds my wrists as I struggle to hit him. "I wanted you, but you wanted more. You couldn't just be happy with me. No, if you didn't have the ring on my hand, I wasn't good enough!" He releases my wrist, and I step back from him. He's not the only one with pent-up animosity. I swear, I dealt with this before. I was past it.

"Any other woman would want that. Why am I wrong for wanting to marry a woman I love and raise a family with her?"

"Just because *you got me*—" I shut down, feeling the tears starting to well up in my eyes. Why did I fucking go out with him tonight? Why did I drink? Why? Fuck! Why?

"You can't even talk about it with me?" He asks. "You... it's like you decided to quit since we lost—"

"Don't," I cut him off. "I did not quit. I never wanted to be a wife or a mother, and if you had paid more attention, you would have known that. You should have known that. It wasn't a secret! We have been friends since we were six!" Pacing the length of the bed in a miff, I turn back to him. "You need to move on, Nollan. Like you said, it's been seven years. *Seven.* We can't keep doing this."

"How? Tell me how I get over you. I've been trying for each and every one of those seven fucking years!"

"We can't be friends." I close my eyes and rub my brow.

"We can't be friends?" He strokes his hair back.

"You said it first. We need to cut ties. We haven't been friends in a *long* time. We fuck around with each other. We play games. We're *toxic*, undoubtedly, but friends? Can't hold a friendship when you are still in love with me and I still want to fuck you."

"Just like that?" He drops his hands and stops.

My mouth hangs, silently stuttering. "Ah—I'm not saying I'll never see you again, but... like, you'll never be dead to me, Nollan. You said it first. Us being anything to each other is impossible."

"You're not as tough as you pretend, Raine." He steps closer to me.

"One of us has to be." Real or otherwise, why not me? I'll break what's left of us.

"This is how you want to end it?" He gently wraps his hands around my waist.

"Fuck," I call out, stepping back and pushing his hands off of me. "No. I don't want to end it, honestly. If you said nothing was going on between you and Bailey, I would have slept with you tonight." Hair sticks to my skin, and I brush it from my face. "I can't fight the devil on one shoulder and the angel on the other anymore. We can't be anything to each other."

Two strangers who had something once upon a time. That's it...like normal people. Morn it and move on.

He runs his hand through his slicked hair and grabs his hat from the bed, fitting it back on. Rubbing his face down, Nollan searches for the words before he looks at me, lull.

"Yeah, the devil and the angel on *your* shoulders. It's still about you. You're not ending this *for me*."

Quickly picking up my shoes and wiggling them on, I nearly fall on my face and hop to keep my balance. I can't handle any more of these bipolar games. I can't do this. I can't.

"What are you doing?" As he reaches for me, I avoid him.

"I'm...I need to get some air." My lip quivers, and I try to hold back my tears.

"Raine, wait." He grabs my hand. "Please. I'll do whatever you want. Whatever it takes to get you to stay."

I take a deep breath, slowly letting it out, trying to hold myself together. "You'll choose to never marry? To never have kids?"

"I'd do whatever you want me to do, Raine." I pull my hand away from him and hug my chest tightly.

"You'll regret it. You'll never forgive me for taking those things from you."

"I've been in love with you since the tenth grade. I'm never going to stop."

Why won't he accept it? We're not meant to be. "Could you pick up and leave Florida? Leave the business you built here? Leave your family and friends? Leave everything you have called home all of your life?"

"We can work something out."

"That's the problem. I don't want to compromise any-thing, and you shouldn't have to compromise on every-thing." I crush the hope in his eyes.

"Raine...don't do this." He reaches for my hand again.

"No." I push his hand away. "We're both drunk and...I just need to get some air. Crash on the pull-out sofa. You're not driving home. Hate me or not." I grab my key card and phone and walk out of the room. When the door latches, I fall to the floor, pulling my feet out from under me and leaning against the room door. As I melt into the empty hallway, tears stream from my eyes. Blocks weigh down my chest, and my limbs are tied tight. I sink lower into the dark abyss, capturing my sanity. My control. I want to lash out and break free, and all I can do is gasp for air. Then I hold it in, preventing my squeaky sobs from growing.

I ran towards me. I chose me. I didn't think, in the process, I would scar him. How could he think I wanted that? Am I truly a horrible person? Is it not an act? Is this who I am? The flood of tears coats my flushed cheeks, and I hide my face on my knees, letting drops of frustration and defeat darken my jeans.

"Raine?" A smooth voice calls. "Hey, I didn't know you were on my floor." *Casey.* Noo. Go away. I couldn't mistake that tone. It's him, and there's no way I'm going to let him see my bloodshot eyes and snotty nose. I'm a pathetic mess. "Are you okay?" I keep my head buried, ignoring his presence. Why did he have to be on my floor? I just want to be alone. His leg brushes against mine when he sits down beside me, just like it did in the bar. Only this time, I don't pull away from his warmth. "Where's Nollan?"

"Inside," I weep.

"Do you want to talk?"

"No." *Go away.*

"You sure? I don't have anywhere to be."

"I'm Pele," I mutter, wiping my soaked face with the sides of my hands.

"You are *what*?" The amusement in his voice dwindles.

I elaborate, as if he would understand my nonsense. "Fucking *Pele*. The goddess of fire and volcanoes, known as a villain that's ready to curse you and...I don't know, throw fireballs or something. I only ruin people's lives."

He laughs deeply. "Well, the goddess part, I can believe."

"You don't even know me." I stare at him. "Haven't you paid attention to the back and forth...between Nollan and me." *And between you and me.*

"It's none of my business, but yeah. I see you."

"What does that mean?" He sees me. Woo-hoo. I'm saved. Praise the highest power. "You see who I am. The fucked-up, the flaky, the drunk off-her-ass skank? And what? You're here to save me?"

"No, *skank*. I'm here to prove you wrong because if you're right, I'm a tall, handsome tool." With the slightest pressure, he leans into me. "We have something in common, besides both being wildly attractive." His sultry smile puts me at ease for a breath. "Raine." His tone becomes more serious, and he speaks slowly. "I know we just met, but I've spent enough time around you to see it. You and I, we do what we fucking want, despite what everyone tries to cultivate upon us. We lead like Gods, not follow like sheep." Corny. Fucking corny. What's his point? "People like us create the life we want despite what everyone conveys." His teeth drag across his lower lip. I can't take my eyes off him. "The community standard can't dictate our actions. They love to hate when we walk outside the border. Be weird and sarcastic and blunt and flirty. Don't let anyone make you doubt yourself. If you're a lava monster, burn every fucking bridge that doesn't accept you."

Burn bridges. Leave when I'm not accepted for who I am, with my middle fingers in the air. Give this man an Oscar. Elect him into the fucking presidential office. Someone I've known for twenty-four hours has understood me in a way that people I've known my entire life have yet to achieve. And it makes sense. Why am I fighting for acceptance here?

I narrow my eyes. My brick walls have magically become glass, waiting to be shattered. Shattered by confident, gentle chestnut eyes and simple words that piece together a collage of pain and beauty. It's what I needed. He's what I needed. He's what I need. He's so cute.

I lean toward him. Closer. Closer, till my lips meet his.

What am I doing?

I pull away and freeze in panic.

Oh, no...oh no, oh no.

He takes my jaw in his hands. Gentle. Firm. Comforting. Confusing.

What the shit is happening? Why's he looking at me like that? My mascara must be running.

I raise my hand to rub my eye, and Casey moves in, passionately diving forward. His lips press against mine, and his tongue parts my lips, sliding along the supple skin. As the tip of his tongue meets mine, mint caresses my taste buds. Ten seconds of his touch. Ten seconds...I can't erase. He pulls away and heat darts through my body, leaving me conflicted once more. What do I do? Should I slap him? God, no, *dumbass*. I started it.

Casey slips his hands behind my knees, pulling my back from the door. He wants me closer. His thick fingers curl around my leg, tugging in one swift motion until I'm facing him. His muscular thighs sandwich me, hugging my knees like bolster pillows. I glance over his body, unsure of what I'll find on his face.

What's he wearing? It masks how large he is. Charcoal sweats and a loose tee. I take the side of my thumb across my lash line again. My makeup must be sweating and smeared. It's not fair. Men don't try. They roll out of bed, and they're pretty. I wasted an hour, only to look like The Joker.

He scoots closer, and my knees touch the sides of his abdomen. I rest my hands on my shins, blinking away the heavy sleep in my eyes.

I'm...I'm okay with this. There aren't any nerves or what-ifs. Blame it on the sweet poison altering my brain chemistry, or...maybe it's the lack of consequences. Anything I tell him right now won't matter. It won't follow me. I...I don't care if I look like a gutter clown either. I've never been more content with the possibility of him being a serial killer, in fact. I want to see how that would play out. Don't run up the stairs and hide under the bed. He'd snatch me up by the ankles and drag me away as I clawed at the ugly shag rug. Be the kid from Home Alone, not the girl taunting the guy on the other end of the phone.

His hooded eyes capture me in silence. He presses a finger to the bottom of my chin, pulling me into another kiss. Soft...and gentle. He trails down my jaw to my neck with light suction.

I'm in lurve. La-la-la-loove. I'm in love with brown eyes and bazooka biceps and sensual lips, and *don't stop there. Please do* drag me to your lair of doom.

I'm an idiot. Be the Home Alone kid. Not the phone girl. *Oh, God.* Why does he do this to me? He makes me want to break fake rules and bend bullshit promises. I would live in this fantasy forever.

Whispers fill my ear. "I've been waiting all night to do that."

"To sweep in and steal me from your friend?" I whisper back.

He pulls away, and his tongue rolls across his teeth. "Guess we're both villains," he replies, leering.

The difference between me and him...nobody cares if he's a villain. It could be as big and bright as a full moon, and they would justify it. He's likable and hypnotically beautiful...at least his eyes are. That's more acceptable than a woman scorned. A bad boy is desirable. A bad girl is crazy and heartless.

"I knew that from the moment I met you, Mr. Pierce."

"Don't call me Mr. Pierce. It's Casey, love."

"Fine, Casey. Don't call me *love*," I reply. "You're not British." That sounded more intelligent in my head. Not my best quip.

"It's an endearing term. I don't have to be British to use it. Would you rather hear, *babe*? Or worse, *bae*," he mocks.

I roll my eyes to the right. "I've been told I rip beating hearts from the chests of men and make them crave more. Doesn't matter if you're the *babe type* or the *darling, sweetheart,* or *baby cake* type."

"If you rip my heart out, you're doing me a favor. I mean, I still get to crave more after you rip it out, right? I'm not dead? No zombie shit happening either?" He weaves his fingers in the air playfully. I resist smiling at his stupid joke for barely two seconds before I snort, tucking my chin.

"Long-term effects are yet to be determined. *Apocalypse delivered via Raine.* You're welcome." I twirl my wrist, taking a bow.

"I like a little danger. I'll take my chances."

I close my heavy lids, slowly exhaling. When I open my eyes, I blurt out the first thought to make it to my lips. "The way you drove tonight...what kind of business are you in?"

I call mafia. Is he allowed to tell me if he's in the mafia, or is there like a *we don't talk about our club* kinda code?

"Yeah, tonight...how's your head?" He brushes the hair along my forehead. "I'm sorry about that."

Avoiding the question...That's not concerning at all.

"No, you're not," I shake my head. "You wanted me for yourself. You threw me off of Nollan."

"That was brutal. I can admit it was an asshole move. I was an asshole. Please, forgive me." His eyes beg.

"Complete asshole," I agree and smirk, grabbing my phone from the carpet behind me. "Who did you think was following us, anyway? If you really thought it was the guy from Sparrow, what was he going to do? Pick another fight in the parking lot? Kinda suspish."

"You're right, smarty pants. I wasn't worried about that."

"You're a spy, aren't you?" Leaning in, I narrow my eyes. "Did you go rogue, and your boss has a hitman out looking for you?" My theories are endless.

He laughs. "Not exactly. It's a long story. Maybe I'll tell you someday."

I nod, sucking my lips in. Nope, not suspicious at all. Holding up my phone, I press the button on the side to wake the screen and glance at the time. "It's three. I should go."

If I spend any more time with him, I won't be getting into my bed tonight. With enough persuasion, I could easily find myself in his room. Okay, with little convincing on top of the liquid encouragement running its course. Why do I keep blaming the alcohol? Because it's definitely not on me when I make another poor decision. That's what I'm sticking with, and...*oh*, his lips are...inviting.

I wouldn't argue if he kissed me again. God, he's...mm, yummy. He's a *Knack* thirst trap artist, playing with cookie dough while making suggestive gestures without his shirt on. Bonus points for the sexual appeal of tattoos. It's kinda the whole reason I still have an account on that *social media app,* though. So if he is actually posting videos, I'm going to find them. That reason, and for Phoebe Films. I love her short stories.

"I came out here for ice. I didn't make it there," he smiles, dimples at the beginning and end of his lips.

"Sorry," I whisper, clenching my teeth together.

"No need to apologize, those lips were worth it," he whispers back. "That Blue Moon isn't too bad either. My buddy would probably enjoy it."

"Your buddy would enjoy what exactly?"

"Oh, you." He tsks. "Filthy, filthy—"

"You were thinking the same thing. If you don't live every day in childish jokes, sexual innuendos, and consume at least one meal's worth of calories in the form of a beverage, we are not compatible. Give up now. Give up yesterday." I thumb over my shoulder.

"He'd like *you.* Not as much as I do."

I smile coyly, and a weird, nervous sensation overwhelms me. It's not anxiety. *Oh God*, maybe it's not him either. Tell me it's not the alcohol coming...coming back up. I shouldn't have taken those shots of whiskey tonight. With a deep breath, I slowly let it out, as I talk myself off the puking train. Don't climb aboard. Stay at the train station. Your broke-ass can't afford a ticket. Do not vomit all over the pretty man who just kissed you.

"I should get a few hours of sleep. I have a flight at ten." The queasy feeling slightly subsides in my revelation. *Shock therapy.* Is he leaving already?

"You're flying out in the morning?" I ask abruptly. Disappointment overwhelms the nausea.

This trip home was supposed to be uneventful, like every other one, but then I met *him*. He's the common denominator in everything that's gone wrong. I met him first, before it all unfolded. Before Nollan ran into me. Before Calle convinced me to host Christmas in New York. Before the fight with Mom. Before Sparrow. Before I was called a heartless heathen.

It's easy to put the blame on him. He would let me, too, wouldn't he? Take my wrath and move on with his life, for I was a girl he kissed one night. If only it were that easy for me to not care. I play it well. Yet, the meltdown I just had—mascara tears in the hotel hallway—proves I care what some people think about me. I don't *want* the liability of others' opinions on my self-worth. When the fuck are these daily affirmations going to kick in?

"You want to come with me?"

What?

Yes. One hundred percent yes. Take me away strange, dangerous man I've already developed an entire backstory for. A dethroned mafia spy who was manipulated by the wrong woman and needs a down chick to have a little fun with while he stays emotionally unavailable, running from his boss.

I push my elbows to my knees and rest my chin on the palms of my hands. "Absolutely. Where are we going?" I glance up and smile at him.

"Bangkok." He smiles suggestively. I drop my hands and lift my head.

"Oh, yeah, I've been there a few times. Weather is pretty nice this time of the year," I burst into quiet laughter. His laugh follows mine, leaning his body into mine. "Shh, it's three AM, remember!" I scold in a whisper, laughing more. He leans back, and I catch a glimpse of his smile again. His teeth are perfectly straight, his heavy lower lip is protruding, and small indents are dimpling inches from his mouth once more.

"I have to handle some business in California, then I'm making a stop in Benderridge for a few days."

"Bender? You're paying for my plane ticket, right?"

"Do I need to buy you a new board and gear, too?" His brows raise, then fall.

"You can just rent it," I say, waving my hand in a gesture of *no big deal*. "Pimp yourself out on the corner. You'll make the money in a few hours. And remember not to undersell yourself. Your worth at least...a buck fifty an hour."

"A buck fifty!" He whisper-shouts. "I was underselling myself. My last mark only paid forty-five plus a vanilla milkshake."

"Did she at least spring for the whipped cream and cherry?"

"Nope, but it's all good because I have another hustle that brings in a little more money." He nods.

"Well, again, renting is a-oh-kay."

"You won't reach gold digger status like that." His upper teeth dig into his lower lip.

"I'm a diamond girl." No, I'm not. Why did I say that?

"I'll keep that in mind."

"No rings," I joke. "Actually, skip the diamonds altogether." Swallowing, I shake out my hand. "Buy me something from Nollan's Porsche collection, or better yet...steal it." I casually split my anger towards Nollan in the conversation. I wonder if he'd be my accomplice in hiding Nollan's car down Shandy Avenue.

"I got you. 911? 918 Spyder?" As he speaks, he rolls his tattooed fingers down my forearms. "No, you want a Carrera, don't you? No worries, I can afford it. I'll buy you your own. No hand-me-downs." He says smugly. *Oh, please.*

"What's your net worth, Richy Rich?" I badger.

"Um...Macaulay rich." His smile fades as his eyes leave me. He shakes his head, muttering. "It's nothing compared to what I could have...Not that he's not extremely well off." He returns to me. "But loyalty requires more than green paper, you know?"

"So you're like back row at the Oscars." I mean, if he's not the hottest popstar turned actor, he's in the back row tonight.

"Not even invited to the Oscars." He winks, chuckling.

"Don't do Macaulay dirty like that. He's an icon." I giggle. It's true. Who graces the screens of millions of TVs every December more?

"Hey, don't put words in my mouth. I said I was not invited. Not the icon."

"Yeah, well, I'm not in the market for sugar daddies."

"You're not? Damn, I was hoping you would want to go on an adventure with me. At the least, save my offer for a rainy day?" *Please tell me, no pun intended.* It's so cheesy, but he's so cute, and maybe that makes up for my cringe. Nollan's sweet charm used to make up for calling me a fucking rainbow.

"That's cute."

He glances at my phone on the floor. "Put it in your calendar. *Rain date with Casey. No expiration.*"

"Are you being serious right now?"

"I'm not fucking with you. Come with me."

"Is Bender open for the season already?"

He's a stranger. A fucking stranger. Alarm, alarm. Wee woo. Don't hit ignore!

"They open in two weeks, but I know some people." *Of course, you do.*

How did I get here? This has been the craziest day, and everything is spinning. Wait, is it *physically* spinning?

My body reminds me of the shots I slammed earlier, as well as how I quit the mood juice months ago. The uneasiness in my stomach creeps up, and I jump to my feet, pulling my key card out. Slamming it into the slot as fast as I can, I hear the click and throw the door open. Running towards the bathroom, I drop my card and phone, hunching over the toilet. The contents of my stomach spew out. Ugh, mom's dinner. This better not ruin key lime pie for me. Key lime pie! Please, sweet baby Lord, not the key lime pie.

"Raine, I woke up Nollan." Oh, *whyyy?* Couldn't you have closed the door and left, Casey? This is mortifying. I tell one guy I don't drink often, then get gut-spewing drunk. And the other guy knows me from a stage of my life where I could handle my alcohol at the same level as the boys. Back then, I was proud to be one of the guys. Poker, beer pong, and shot-for-shot—I wasn't the girl they called *tits*. My invisible sack was hefty. Both of them can leave, allowing me to wallow in my pity and puke. I don't need either of them holding my hand.

I glance up from the toilet to see Nollan walk into the bathroom in his boxer briefs, half asleep. "I grabbed a hair tie from your bag," he says groggily, handing it to me. "Do you need anything else?"

"No. Thanks," I mumble, avoiding connecting with him.

"If you do, just let me know." His jaw tenses as he looks at Casey. "I'll be on the couch. I can't stay in here, or I'll be puking too."

The bubbles in my stomach are too distracting to worry about his feelings right now. I arch forward and spill my cookies again. When I sit back up, I pull my hair into a messy ponytail with the band Nollan gave me. The sound of a cabinet closing behind me catches my frazzled attention. I find Casey at the sink, with the water running. He turns to meet my unsteady eyes. His smile greets me, and a different kind of flutter takes my stomach again. The good kind. He kneels in front of me, running the damp washcloth over my cheek.

"Is that a no?" His smile widens.

"I'm going to Orlando with my sister tomorrow," I mutter, taking the cloth from him.

"Oh yeah, the butt pad one. Rain check it is."

"Coffee!"

"Noo," I groan and pull my pillow tighter. Wait, is that Casey? His voice...It's the last sound I remember before passing out. That and the flushing of a toilet.

"Wake up, fucker!"

Peaking from my blanket, I blink. It's too bright. He throws a pillow at Nollan, pegging him in the face. Nol's arm springs up, no longer dangling off the couch.

"Dick," Nollan grumbles. "Where's the ibuprofen?"

"On the table with your crummy coffee. Be glad I got you anything. I'm not your momma." Nollan slowly rolls off the couch and staggers to the dinette. "Next time, let's stick to grilling, yeah?"

"Hey, you awake under there?" I pull the blanket back from my face and smile.

"What time is it?" If I don't look like hell, my body odor is a new signature fragrance sure to please. On top of sweaty BO and tobacco residue, add a mix of edged pussy and smoked rotten milk. I hope I took my pants off *after* he left.

I look up at this nearly six-foot man dressed in body-hugging dark gray slacks and a tucked white shirt, rolled to quarter sleeves. He's a majestic eagle, and I'm a dirty little hamster.

Owch ow. No sitting up. Hell, my head hurts. Even in the death wake, I'm pretty sure he asked me to run away with him in the hour before my gut erupted. That was real, right? That shit happened?

He stands above me while I stay curled up in the fetal position with the blanket up to my chin. "It's nine. I can't stay. I have to get to the airport."

"Oh..." I try to recall everything we spoke about. "You have a flight this morning?"

"Do you remember anything from last night?" He chuckles.

"Um...you said ten, right? Mostly remember. A little fuzzy around the time I started puking my guts out." I force a sleepy smile. "How did I get in bed?"

"You passed out in front of the toilet. I carried you to the bed."

Oh. My. God. He held me up against that Hercules-chiseled body, and I don't remember it...because I was blacked-out shitfaced! Why did he come back this morning? Couldn't have saved me the embarrassment? Oh, that's right. I'm a solid exterior of *I don't give a fuck.* An oozing internal wound from hell-*ooo-no way* am I going to dry heave the imaginary contents of my stomach out now. Swallow that bullshit down. Do not *air vomit* on his suit. I pull the blanket back over my face.

It doesn't matter. I won't ever see this man again. He's not asking me to run away with him. We drank. We kissed. We...*We kissed.*

He pulls the blanket back, kneeling beside the bed. "When you're finished with Nollan, give me a call." With a dimpled smile, he slides a business card under my pillow. "Take it easy on the whiskey next time." He rises, leaving me in a whole lot of *what the fuck just happened.*

Wait. *Wait!* Don't leave.

He's not leaving. I'm not letting it happen.

I do the most reasonable thing I can think of...I grab his leg, wrapping my arms around him as I hang off the bed.

Shit. Shit, shit. *What am I doing?* I've gone and lost my fucktard mind. I'm like a child hanging onto a parent. *Daddy?* Shut up, brain! I can't even blame this on alcohol impairment. It's post-drinking delulu. *That's it.* I'm delusional from the hangover.

He bends back down, and stupid, douchey dimples frame his smile. "I don't want to go either, but if you're not careful, you'll lose your *friend,*" he whispers and up-nods towards Nollan, whose head is lying on his hands on top of the table.

"I already lost him, but I could make you lose him, too."

"Hey, now. Villains can stick together just like heroes. Don't burn me and I won't burn you." He winks, then glances towards the dinette before lifting my chin with one finger. His thumb traces my lower lip. "I'm holding you to that rain check."

"Maybe it'll happen. Maybe not." I pull the blanket up to my eyes, covering my unfaithful mouth.

His eyes drift to the side, and I'm dying for him to say what he's thinking. He doesn't. He walks over to Nollan, says something I don't catch, and leaves. It's going to be a long day of shopping with Calle while I'm hungover and mentally warped. It can't get any worse.

Is this like a life crisis because I'm almost thirty? Is that how those things happen? Fully sudden, with no warning, you just start making obscure decisions? At least I know one thing: I'll finally get in that shower this morning...as soon as Nollan gets his ass out of here.

Chapter Seven | Cessation

Raine

"What do you think of this one? Raine? Raine!" Calle scolds me. She spins in front of the full-length mirror outside the dressing room.

"Sorry. It looks good, Cal. I like the color."

"Just text him." She swivels back and forth, checking all angles of herself out.

"He's Nollan's friend." I stare deeply at her. "*Someone*," I add, with a hard pause. "Will eventually get it back to him. I just want to go home and get back to my life. *Peace the furk out, Easton.*"

She waves me off. "*Oh, please*! I don't even talk to him about you." She tucks a pair of Merlot waterproof pants back onto a hanger and hooks them outside the dressing room. "And I'm going to go out of my way to avoid mentioning your *name* around him if that's what you want."

"Don't make it like a thing, but yeah...you're a single child from now on." Calle knows what she needs to know—Casey essentially taking care of my drunk ass and his *invitation*. That's it.

It's been on my mind all day, from the moment I stepped into the shower to drown my headache. I had to talk to someone. May her gossip gene be weak, and her attention fish-like.

"It's not like you had anything to do with that fight."

"Stupid boys being stupid."

"So you closed one door, why not open another?" She obnoxiously raises her brows up and down.

"He seems like a fuck boy," I sneer, swiping my hand through a spiral rack of jackets, and pretending to look through them.

"Isn't that like, what you're into?" Gawking with her hands on her hips, I look over and scrunch my face at her.

"Yes, Calle. I'm into stupid boys and fuck boys," I stare at her impassively. "What I'm into is the one-in-a-million find, apparently," I gripe. "Someone who wants to enjoy life with me. That's it. No strings or expectations other than *enjoying life*." I page through the rack again.

"What about when you're sick or old? Don't you want someone to be there for you? You know, in sickness and in health?" She smiles at her banal marriage reference. I walk closer to the fitting room, leaving the jackets behind.

"There are no guarantees in life, buttercup. I could marry a man, and the dude could get knocked off before our first anniversary." I draw a line across my throat with two fingers. "Then what? I just try again after doing a bunch of legal mumbo jumbo? I'm good."

"Well damn, Raine, *knocked off*? What have you been reading lately? That's so depressing!"

"I'm *sorry*!" I yowl, long and sarcastically. I wrap my arms around her shoulders, pinning her arms against her sides in an obnoxious hug.

Rocking her side-to-side, she calls out. "Find yourself a sugar daddy, Raine!"

Dropping my hold, I take a step back, clapping my hands together.

"Yes!" I drag out with a whisper of a yell and lean into a slight bow. "A cute little old man! He wouldn't be a long-term commitment." Calle's laughter grows obnoxiously. "Maybe one with false teeth and a walker." I smile widely, and my cheeks hurt. Casey couldn't convince me last night that I needed a candy man, but when Calle suggests it, and I'm sober, I see the appeal in daddy energy. I'll spend my time, he'll spend his money. Everyone has a damn good time.

She holds her hands over her heart, gasping. "Oh my God, stop! You're making my chest hurt."

"Bonus points if he has daughters my age. Just call me Step-Mommy. Momma Raine?" We laugh in unison, starting to draw attention to us from the other shoppers.

She stops deadpan with her mouth drawn. "Wouldn't you want to marry him, though, so his fortune would be willed to you?"

"Let's say I was for marriage. You know I'm not making it to the honeymoon. As soon as he wants the slob on his half-baked cob, I'm out of there like a cyclist being chased by an ostrich." Calle towers over in laughter, her brain about to shrivel up from loss of oxygen. "Sign me up for the prenup and a cruise, so I can fake motion sickness." I look over my shoulder to see two women with disgruntled, curled lips. Oops. The sniggering consumes me until my laughter is as strangling as Calle's. Deep belly laughs that kick the air right out of my lungs.

"Ostrich!" She yells, gasping for air. "You're nasty!"

"Shh," I hush her. I should know better than to get her fired up. Her deafening laugh is going to get us kicked out—not me. Ugh, I missed her face. "Are you getting all of this?" I ask, grabbing the hangers on the left side of the fitting room.

"Yes, and these pants." She points to the crystalline purple bottoms she's wearing.

"Do you really need to buy all this for one trip?" I ask her, closing the door to her fitting room while she changes.

"Well, I was *thinking*," she sings. "Actually, Nash and I have been thinking...about moving."

"What? Why?" I can't imagine Calle leaving Florida. She's moving away from our family, her friends, and everything she loves. She would be one of those people driving around the concrete jungle with a salt-and-sun bumper sticker. Heart at sea, head in the clouds, because the only salt around here is on the roads when it snows.

"Nash found a job. It's temporary, but it pays well. Like *really* well. We would be there max a year." She avoids looking at me, squeezing her lips together, relaxing, and doing it again.

"What's the problem?" I ask sternly. "There's something you're not telling me."

"I'll be alone." She hesitates. "Everyone is in Florida. I'll be planning a wedding all by myself from another state. It's not what I wanted." I knew it. It's funny that she's already sure she'll be wedding planning, too. Calle's a social butterfly with a ton of girlfriends. Of course, she's going to have withdraw from her people. I moved, and we still make time for each other.

"And what am I? Stale fries on the floor mat of your cute little car? How close are you going to be to me?"

"Five hours," Calle answers with a pout.

"Weekend trips. We can meet halfway," I suggest. "You'll get to see me more than you do now." She walks back into the fitting room. "Calle, it's not that bad. You meet new people and make new friends. I have an entire group of people who accept my weirdness, and nobody likes me in Easton."

She opens the door, holding her ski pants. "Raine, people like you here."

"No, people like Nollan. I was accepted because I was with him. Bailey and Declan were the only ones I could hang out after *us*. I get it. I'm a weird, sarcastic bitch. Not everyone is equipped to handle that, but I found my people. That's my point. You will easily make more friends. Everyone likes you, Calle," I comfort her.

"You're my favorite weird, sarcastic bitch, Raine," Calle says seriously, making both of us smile. My charismatic little sister, may you have skin as thick as mine, and one of these days, may I be half as graceful as you. "You want that hat? Add it to my bill."

"I surely thought you'd hate it." I hold up the purple knit beanie lined with a visor.

She nods. "I do."

Stopping by our parents' for an early dinner after shopping, it's as if yesterday never happened. Just wait until Mom finds out Calle is moving away for an entire year. When is she going to break that news? Mom didn't have much to say, but we made it through the entire visit without a disagreement. She even invited me to check out a new flower shop with her tomorrow. That's what we do. Apologies are unspoken. Instead, we make it up with invitations and compliments.

Black Bear Creamery has a long line of customers waiting for their famous sundaes. Famous to the townies and surrounding areas, anyway. At this point in the season, they're only open on weekends. The crowd isn't surprising.

Calle dropped me off on her way back to her apartment, and Bailey should be here any minute. Tomorrow was the plan, but after last night, well, why not just rip off the Band-Aid? I look up at the red-orange Royal Poinciana above me. Low-hanging branches shade part of the parking lot. I could get in line, but I'll wait. She has to be close.

How do I even begin to address her? *Oh, hey, I just found out you're into my ex, whom I've been secretly sexting and almost physically slept with last night, but it's totally fine, and we ended it.* Yep, that sounds amazing in my head. I'm sure it will sound just as comforting out loud.

I spot Bailey getting out of a metallic gray Corolla. This is going to be just splendid.

I walk down the asphalt to where I spotted her. "Hey!"

"Hi. How are you?" She smiles. Her shoulder-length, dark brown hair is in loose waves. Petal-colored lipstick and matching blush are spread across her cheekbones. Her brown eyes have a light bronze shadow above them, and those must be lash extensions. Her natural lashes can't be that long and fluffy. And here I am with a messy ponytail, loose strands flying across my face, nothing more than skincare and a little mascara. At least I curled my lashes before I left the hotel. We have always been quite different, but we got along so well. Some things never change.

"Been better." I nervously laugh.

"Yeah, I bet," she says, hitting a button on her key fob to lock the car doors. "Did Nollan get home fine?" She continues talking as we walk the last few car lengths toward the growing line.

Hasn't she spoken to him at all yet? He left the hotel not long after Casey. We didn't exchange many words. A short goodbye, and he was on his way. It was apparent that he was feeling the after-effects of the alcohol, as I had been, not to mention the hits he took to his rib cage. He left with a shirt on, appropriately. At some point, Casey must have given him one of his. I'm waiting for something, *the something* that is wrong with Casey. He's been far too gracious. Far too good-looking. And he claims to have a heavy bank account. If I could find a flaw, then I could stop thinking about that rain check he left me.

"Yep. Casey took care of everything." I press my lips together, avoiding giving too much detail. We stand in a winding line of people waiting for our turn, and I lace my fingers together in front of me.

"How's New York?"

"It's good, *still*. I love it. Anytime you want to visit, just let me know."

"I can't believe it's already been two years. How's everyone else? Elias?" Her soft voice sounds genuinely curious, and I'd gladly talk about my life and friends as opposed to the last forty-eight hours.

"Ivy's girls are six now! They grew so fast. She and Scott have their hands full. Audrey has a new boyfriend, Mikey. He's nice. Rosalin is doing well. Her son turned nine a few months ago. And Elias actually works full-time as an instructor now at the resort." It wasn't long ago that Bailey spent a week at my apartment visiting, a few years after I moved. My friends are open and accepting. It's different as an adult. Everyone has a different past and present, different ages, and different experiences compared to our friend group growing up. They invited Bailey right in, and Elias even spent a day teaching her to snowboard.

Traditionally, a ski girl, spending spring break at her parents' timeshare in the Poconos every year in our early teens, was something I always looked forward to. Subconsciously, it had to have been the freedom that came with those adventures. Smoking pot in the cabin's attic with those two local seventeen-year-old boys we met freshman year was one of my first rebel movements that sticks in my core memories. I can't believe we got away with it when her parents got in earlier than expected, and they had to climb out the window while we sprayed air freshener. Then, I told her dad I wasn't feeling great and blew the bathroom up. It was nice to have two parts of my life exist cohesively. That was...so long ago.

"Oh wow, I'm glad everyone is doing well. Elias was a great teacher. That's the perfect job for him. And are you seeing anyone?"

"Nope." I look at the ground, avoiding any suspicion of the love triangle I went home with last night.

"What happened to um...Lee?" She asks, brushing her hair behind her ear. I don't remember mentioning Leo to her. Calle probably mentioned him.

"Leo. Ended over a year ago," I answer, vaguely. "But enough about me. How's life working at Broack's?"

"Chocolate!" An excited little boy behind us yells. I smile at the family and look back at Bailey.

"It's nice." She nods softly.

"Nice? Ice cream is nice. You have to meet a lot of clients, right? You're the front of the business. The face everyone sees first. Anyone famous cross our little town for a Lambo?"

"You know what, it's great. I loaned a BMW out to Bethany Hollander, the beauty influencer." I return her nod as if I know exactly who she's talking about. "She was sweet. And a woman who claimed to work for a famous producer. I didn't get his name. He used an alias. And I'm seeing Nollan now," she says confidently.

"Oh, how long have you been dating?" I pretend to be surprised.

"Eight months." *Eight?* Not four or five, even six?

"Really? Well, I'm happy for you." Truthfully surprised, Nollan's lies are stacking up.

"Raine, I'm trying to be nice since you've been a good friend since middle school, but I know he went back to the hotel with you last night."

My face flushes. I look at the family behind us with the little boy, hoping they didn't hear her accusation. The woman's mouth lifts in half a smile as if she's acknowledging that she overheard her, but isn't judging me for it.

I quiet my voice. "Bailey, I had no idea till last night that you two had something going on."

"You let him in your hotel room last night, right?" Her hands go to her hips, in fists over her sage-wrapped dress. She's getting a little louder, making me anxiously rub my arm. Couldn't she wait till we got out of this line and into a more private setting before confronting me? I came here to have this discussion with her, over sugared-up moods, without performing for an audience.

"I let him in so we could talk. Nothing else happened." I take a step closer to her, keeping my voice down. Something else did happen, but I'm not giving her the extra details right here, especially when she's already clearly pissed. I'd lie about anything to stop this from becoming an explosion.

"Oh, talk, like you talk when you text and call in the middle of the night?" She raises her voice even louder. Okay, she knows way more than she has led on, and she's obviously not happy about any of it. I don't blame her. It's Nollan's fault.

"It's come to my understanding that Nollan likes to lie."

"He's not perfect, and neither are you." Her eyes descend down my body, shaming me. I'm going to be the bad guy here. I can already tell Nollan won't be held responsible. People in the line around us are definitely starting to stare as the animosity increases in her voice.

I cross my arms over my chest. "Nothing happened last night. We talked, and he told me he wanted to move forward with you."

"He told me everything, Raine. You can stop lying," she barks.

"I don't know what he told you, but I'm not lying." I turn to look at the line in front of us.

Hurry up. I want to get my ice cream and get out of here.

"I know you tried to seduce him, and when he turned you down, you went to his friend. I thought you were a good person, Raine, but you have lost your way. You need to take a serious look at your reflection. When you get past this phase, feel free to give me a call, but until then, I don't think we should talk, considering Nollan's my boyfriend."

She stomps off towards the parking lot, drawing everyone's attention.

I glance to see the family behind me. The woman is now scowling. I offer a mild smile and shrug, but she doesn't let up, pulling her child close to her side. Now I'm the town homewrecker and whore. Keep adding to my resume. Bailey walks away, nearly reaching her car, while I avoid connecting with all the eyes that are on me. She had to have spoken to Nollan this morning, or she would know nothing about Casey last night, even if she has no idea what the truth is. The little bitch baited me. She stops a few feet away and turns around. *No, don't do it*. In disbelief, I tilt my head slightly to the side and drop my jaw.

"And don't text Nollan again!" She yells.

"Love you too," I mumble.

What the hell did he tell her that for? My cheeks are beet red. The hell with it. I'm getting my rum raisin even if I have to stand in the line pretending that didn't just happen.

I sit down at an empty wooden octagon table, adjusting the umbrella for shade, and lay my phone on the table. Scrolling through the numbers in my contacts with one hand and spooning ice cream in my mouth with the other, I stop when I see "*Casey Pierce.*" Clicking on it, there's a note added to the contact. *Rain check.* He must have added his number to my phone when I passed out. Did I unlock it for him? I'm never drinking again.

I tap the back button and hit *Calle*, holding the phone to my ear.

"Hello?" She answers.

"Hey, change of plans. Could you pick me up at the creamery?"

"What happened to Bailey?" Her voice vibrates through the phone. "You're on speaker, by the way. I'm folding laundry."

"Did you know she was dating Nollan?"

"Kinda."

"Calle!"

"She always says he doesn't like labels, but none of us are blind."

"She just flipped out on me in front of a line of people. It would have been nice to know, *like yesterday*," I whisper loudly, trying to keep myself from any more unnecessary attention.

"I'm sorry, but you said you haven't seen Nollan in years, so I didn't think—"

"Calle." I cut her off. "I was texting him *six months ago,* and either way, you could have just mentioned it."

"They started dating after you ended that thing," she groans.

"According to her, they have been together for eight months."

"News to me!" She chirps. "Besides, you always tell me to *skip the details*."

"Yeah, *details*, like the normal daily things we all do. I don't need to know you have an upset stomach from eating at Taco Tuesdays, and you've been glued to the throne all morning. Letting me know the guy I'm sexting is dating one of my friends..." *Friends*. I don't think we've truly been friends in a while. If we were, wouldn't she have told me months ago that she was seeing him? "Anyway, can you pick me up?" I ask, spinning my spoon in circles around my dish of ice cream.

"I'll be there in twenty," she agrees.

"Thank you." I hang up, dropping my phone on the table and palming my forehead. I lean my face against my hand as if my head is too heavy to hold up and take another spoonful of my melting ice cream. *I hate Nollan.*

It's only seven-thirty, but here I am, already showered and changed into my pajamas. *Two days.* That's all it took for me to be ready to leave this town. That's a lie. I could have left after the first few hours.

I slide into bed, pulling the fresh scented blankets over me, kicking my legs to loosen the bottom where it's still tucked along the end of the mattress. Rolling to my side, I see Casey's business card lying on the nightstand. House-keeping must have found it under the pillow when they made the bed. That's where I left it.

Casey Pierce
Pierce Investments
Wilmington, New York.

A phone number sits below the bold font on a simple em-bossed black rectangle. I roll the card between my fingers. Ink of a white fine-point marker lines the back in messy handwriting. *Join me in Colorado for a piquant time.*

I fight a smile that rushes to my face. I taught him a new word, and like every ecstatic kid holding onto a significant memory, he has to tell me it over and over again.

Maybe I should go. Nollan is no longer a concern to me. I fucking hate him. The more I think about him, the more I want to go to his house and give him a piece of my mind.

It would be the childish thing to do and only make it ten times worse.

I smack the card onto the bedside table and wipe the pissy look off my face. Sitting up, I let the blanket fall from my tank top as I lean against the flat plank headboard. Gingerly unlocking my phone, I stare at Casey's number. I close it and open Knack, typing "Casey Pierce" into the search bar. Nothing comes up. Clicking on my Insta app, I search his name again. Nothing. I scroll down my feed, noticing Bailey posted recently. A basket of conch fritters sitting on the hood of a gray Challenger. It must be a picture for Nollan's business feed. I'm sure she casually posted it on her personal page to send the message further home. She is with Nollan Broack. Congrats. He's your problem now. I couldn't care less. I wish I didn't care about how much of a lying asshole he is, either.

The post is tagged. A few clicks and I find myself on Nollan's page. My investigation leads me to a photo of him with Casey, dated a few months ago, with a tag. *Casey Raiden Pierce*. I adjust my position in bed, straightening up more. A heaviness warms my chest. *I found you.*

He has maybe twenty posts. A few photos of him snowboarding, another of him sitting in a Ferrari, several with groups of people, and one other that particularly catches my attention. It's a selfie. He's wearing a black T-shirt and black square-framed glasses. He looks studious. None of the posts are new. The last one is dated three months ago.

I slide back down the bed, pulling the blanket halfway over my face to hide my blushing cheeks. Closing the app and opening my contacts again, I stare at his number. I shouldn't be nervous to call him. He's just a man. Men don't get under my skin, *ever*. There is nothing to lose. He literally watched me puke my guts out, straddle my ex in the middle of a car chase, and found me crying on the floor all in one night. There was also that episode where I got caught dancing in the gym.

I hit the call button and listen to it ring, sounding twice before he picks up.

"Hello, Casey Pierce," He answers.

The sound of his voice chills my arms. "How do I cash in that rain check?"

"Hold on a minute." My phone dings, and I look at the screen. He wants to video chat. I'm in pajamas. *Pajamas.*

I can't ignore it. What do I do? *What do I do?* I'm gonna accept it. The hell with it. Tapping the button, my screen lights up, then darkens. A deep leather-wrapped interior surrounds the beautiful, muscular man. He's driving another luxury car. No surprise. His eyes skip between me and the front window. He's polished, and I'm in *freaking pajamas*!

"I'm on my way to a meeting, and you are...Are you still in bed?" He squints.

"Never left, best day ever."

"It's what, eight there? Has it been that great of a day?" He reaches along the headliner and pulls a pair of aviator sunglasses down, sliding them on his face.

"You have no idea," I grumble.

"I don't, but I am about to go into a meeting I'm dreading. I'll be in the same mood as you by the time I get out of there."

"That's supposed to make me feel better? *Oh, my life sucks too. Waaa.*" I stare, impassively. "You suck at pep talks."

"I know. I'm amazing at everything. Thanks for the confidence booster." *Like he needed it.* I sit up against the headboard, smacking my head. I wince and let my blanket fall to my waist. "You really are in bed. Pajamas and all. What is that yellow...ducks?"

"Only the most mature adults wear yellow duckies. I'd rather be in my bed than in a suit going to work." I rub the back of my head.

"I'd rather be in your bed, too." A slow, sinister smile drags from his lips.

"Does that line usually work for you?" I ask, tightening my lips to avoid a smile, although the side of my mouth curls slightly.

"I don't need lines. Walking into a room works for me."

A stiff laugh takes me over, and I throw my head back, smacking it for the second time. Damn it! I hide the pain, snapping a witty comment back at him. "The whole hoes in different area codes just don't work for me."

"Damn. I really thought I could be one of your hoes. That's a bummer."

"My fourth hoe in all my years. Not a very good player, huh?" I shift my eyes from side to side and shrug.

"What?" Casey replies, shocked. "*Fourth.* You never stop surprising me."

"Well, hell, is *hoe life* my whole aura?" I blurt out.

He laughs. "Noo. No, no." His laugh continues. "I didn't mean it like that."

"It was Nollan, wasn't it? That's how you got the impression I'm a loose girl?"

"Not directly," he admits. "You have history. I get it."

"Then why would you think...That kiss in the hallway?" I ask, wrinkling my face.

"Do you really want to know?"

"Abso-fucking-lutley. Tell me why you think I'm a hoe!" I bob my head.

He smiles. "Let's say *promiscuous*, not a *hoe*. And first, tell me why you didn't want to marry Nollan?" He lowers his sunglasses an inch, pressing his index finger between the lenses, along the center of the frame.

"How do you know about that?"

"Little towns like to talk." His tongue rolls over his lower lip.

"I asked you a question first."

He smiles and pushes his sunglasses back in place. "I'll give you an answer after you give me one."

"You're annoying." I sigh. "You wouldn't get it." I look away from the phone, staring out the window at the faint moon. "You won't understand."

"Try me."

Fine. I'm not ashamed. "I don't want to marry *anyone*. It's not just Nollan." His eyes stay focused in front of him. He doesn't respond immediately, but then finally looks back at the screen.

"You don't want marriage. You don't want to hoe around. So let me get this right, you want monogamy without the expectation of a lifelong commitment?"

"Um, yeah." Does he actually get it? My family still, after all these years, can't understand what I want, or at least doesn't understand why. "To be without someone for the pure enjoyment of being with them instead of the goal of building a future with legal paperwork and spawn."

"See, I understand you. It's not that difficult."

"Now tell me why I'm a hoe," I prompt.

Casey laughs. "You're relentless. Hold on, I'm at the parking garage." He removes his sunglasses and clips them to the visor. The screen dims as he drives through the levels.

Shadows and streams of light casually peak across his face. Is that a smile?

"What are you thinking about?"

He smiles bigger, ignoring the question as he keeps scaling the floors, his focus staying on the windshield. Light returns to the screen as he puts the vehicle in park. He releases his seatbelt and leans closer to the camera. A close-up of his face covers my screen, cut off just below his ink-covered neck, and a shadow outlines his lower lip.

"I don't think it was the whisky that had you grinding your body against mine and ten minutes later straddling Nollan in the back of the car. I almost want to know, was he a pawn or was I? Or do you just like the attention? I couldn't care what the reasoning was, honestly. That's what I was thinking about. You, in the back of my car, on the roof of this parking garage. You with the steering wheel in your back. You bent over the hood. You pressed against the fender with your legs wrapped around me. You're yelling my name just like when you yelled it in the back of Nollan's car. I wouldn't be able to return this rental by the time I'm done with you."

"The hoes are way more skilled in California."

What the fuck! I should just smack myself in the head again. I opened my mouth...I opened my sardonic, freaking mouth. He tells me he wants to do dirty, *oh unholy* dirty, *dirty things* to me, and I told him to go find a hooker! *Pick me.* I'll be her. God, that's desperate.

He laughs, leaning back, and his chin points to the ceiling. Would this be the angle I see when I look up at him? I make a weird face, puffing my cheeks out full of air. "You suck at flirting," he states.

"Who said I was trying to flirt with you?"

"You called me, remember?"

"Yeah, I guess I did."

"Cash the rain check in, love. Come play with me." I rub my neck, unresponsive. It's what I want. Why am I scared now? "How about I buy a ticket, and if you decide you want to have some fun, be at the airport tomorrow?" He moves his phone, shifting my view of him as he leaves the car.

"You're going to buy a ticket and hope I show up?" He either doesn't care about his money, or he's that confident I'll show, he's willing to gamble.

"No. I know you'll show up." Choice number two.

"Why?" Is he a freaking lunatic, and I'm marching myself right into my own death? I watch murder mysteries, man. Curiosity killed the cat, now watch me meow myself right into him? I won't be your next victim. I'll drug you first. I mean...yeah, I'll get on that plane, anyway, knowing it's a poor decision, but I swear, if push comes to shove, *you will* die first.

"I know you're feeling the same thing I am." He leans against the black vehicle, bringing the camera back to his face.

"And what's that?" I brush the hair from my eyes before reaching for my blanket.

"I want to see you again, and you want to see me again, or you wouldn't have called. You've been quite brutally honest with me this far, and I appreciate it. Please don't deny it now." He glances around, then back to me. "I have to go, you already made me late."

"*I made you late?*" I argue obstinately.

"I'll text you the information for your ticket in a few hours." His eyes draw up and down. "It was nice seeing you, Raine."

"Bye."

I slide down the bed, pulling my pillow around my head, squishing my cheeks, and silently squealing. He's right. The butterfly feeling is welling in the pit of my stomach, and I can't wipe this stupid grin off my face. I have three more days off work, and I really don't want to hang around here any longer. I'm back to tip-toeing around Mom, Nollan is a liar, and I hardly trust that he'll keep his distance, and Bailey's accusations will surely get around. I'm sure her display earlier is already being talked about. I'm going. I'm going to run away with the pretty-faced gorilla I just met yesterday like a grown-ass woman who isn't embarrassed to have a fling.

Ping!

A notification alert plays on my phone, and I pick it back up. It's a text message from Casey.

> I know I said in a few hours, but I had a minute. Here's your confirmation code. You can get your ticket at a kiosk or at the check-in desk. Your flight is at 11 a.m. and I'll pick you up at 3 p.m. It's a non-stop flight.

> Cya at 3.

> I knew you wouldn't say no.

I call my parents and Calle right away, making arrangements for breakfast in the morning. I can say goodbye to everyone and then get the hell out of here. I'll make up something about work and needing to head home early. I'll see them in a few weeks for Thanksgiving, anyway. It's the perfect escape plan.

This is going to be good. It'll be fun. Slopes, sexual tension, and a pre-paid adventure to end my mini vacation. What more could I ask for? I'd be crazy to pass this up. Eh, in case anything gets weird, I'd better make a backup plan.

Chapter Eight | Vehement

Raine

"Well, Raine, I heard that you had a little tiff with Bailey yesterday. Angie Kline also said there was a fight you may have been involved in at one of the bars Friday night?"

Ugh, Angie Kline, the biggest gossip queen of them all. I'm pretty sure it's her full-time job. It didn't take long for Mom to start with the questions, either. Calle and I literally just met her and Dad on the sidewalk in front of Mrs. Kay's.

"Raine, I'm concerned for you. I hear you're getting all wicked up at the bar and fighting with Bailey. That sweeth eart..." As we walk, she pulls me close to her with a side hug and rubs my shoulder. "If you need help, I am here. We can go talk to Bailey today, together."

"Mom. That is all out of context," I reply to her, grumpily.

"Maybe it was just a crazy night between old friends," Dad chimes in. I bet he has his own experience in mind.

I glance at Calle, and she gives me the look. One of please don't mention I was at Sparrow too, or I'll die of parental disappointment. I won't, and in return, she'd better keep her mouth shut about dropping me off at the airport where I'm flying out to see Casey and not home to New York like I'm about to tell our parents.

"I promise you, I am fine, and nothing happened that you need to worry about. I am, however, going to be heading home early. I have a flight out today." Mom gasps, and I cringe, baring my teeth. "I'm sorry my stay is shorter than I planned, but some work stuff came up." Does this prove I'm a responsible, nearly thirty-year-old adult? Nope. Because now she has something else to gripe about.

"They can't manage without you for two more days?" Mom complains as we seat ourselves in a booth along the window front. Before I answer her, I slide in. "I'd be speaking with management," she adds.

"It's fine. I'll get extra days off over Christmas." She's still sore over that topic, not saying another word as she sits down beside me. In my head, a reel plays—the mental image of tapping my fingers together and laughing evilly plays.

We eat breakfast and chat. Calle talks about her latest project she's designing for work, and Dad tells everyone about the boating trips he has planned for the month for the second time.

"It's ten," I announce. My packed bags are in Calle's car. We can go straight to the airport from here. She came up with a system last night while we went over the plan. That way, my impulsiveness won't get me on a missing persons list.

"Alright, let's head out," Dad says. He had generously paid the bill ten minutes ago. We say our goodbyes in the parking lot, and I give Mom and Dad hugs before heading off to the airport with Calle.

I set my carry-on behind me on the sidewalk and close the rear passenger door. "Oh, wait, give me your phone. I wanna make sure that app thing is connected." I take Calle's phone and hold it up to mine. "Now you can track me," I say, handing it back to her.

"Stop freaking out. If he were a bad guy, do you really think Nollan would keep his company?"

"Nollan isn't the most reputable when it comes to character lately. I'll text you when I land. Love ya."

Denver International is bigger than I imagined. Colder than Florida's seventy degrees, too. My phone reads a high of fifty-three for the day. The weather is similar in New York lately, and I packed a few warmer outfits for travel, but I need more layers now.

I make my way through the concourse to the Jeppesen terminal, level five, for my suitcase. Looking side to side, I take in the pieces of art. I quickly spot my suitcase, running over to grab it just as my phone pings with a notification. I shuffle my belongings around and move out of the way to check them. A text from Casey.

Casey Pierce: Level four, west, J-M.

Shoving my phone back into my pocket, I quickly find my way. Once I reach J-M, I walk out the exit to find Casey's intense brown eyes waiting for me. He's not the businessman version I saw last, nor the gym rat I met Friday. He's not even wearing the fancy button-down shirt that he wore to Sparrow, either. This is the guy I kissed in the hallway. His heather gray hooded sweatshirt disguises his muscular upper body, along with his dark blue jeans, those same black Converse shoes he had on at the gym, and a dark gray Under Armour hat covering most of his hair. He looks normal, less godlike.

"You like to rent the most expensive car on the lot, don't you?" I met him at the trunk of his SUV. "I'll take the one with the most zeros, please."

"Only if it looks fun to drive." Before lifting my bag into the trunk, his lips turn into a smile. He shuts the hatch and walks to the passenger door, opening it.

"Are you hungry?"

"I can open my own door," I reply.

"Easy wildcat." He throws his hands in the air in surrender. "Please?" He asks, looking at me with a pout and leaning his hand against the roof of the dark blue car. I brush against his chest as I climb into the seat. The slight touch sends darts into my stomach. He leans into the car, grabbing my seatbelt and latching it in place. I want to scold him again, but his face is inches from mine, and I'm caught in his upturned eyes.

He shakes his head, smiling. "Nothing to say this time?"

"You're purposely trying to get under my skin."

"I open the door for you and make sure your sour ass is safely belted. That's what gets to you?"

"I'm a capable grown woman."

"And I'm a capable gentleman. If I want to cater to my woman, then I will." He steps back and shuts the door, walking around the front of the vehicle to the driver's side, where he opens the door, getting in. He fastens his seatbelt and pulls away from the curb, looking straight ahead.

My woman. I'm making it difficult for him to cater to me because I don't want him to get even the slightest shred of hope of us becoming more. I don't want another dead-end relationship. I thought that was clear.

"Are you cold?" He asks, weaving his fingers through mine. "Your hands are freezing."

"Cold and hungry."

"Food, yes," he chuckles. "A hangry woman is something to fear."

"I'm sorry, okay. Can I blame it on being tired this time?"

"You'll say anything to get me to buy you food, huh?" He rolls his thumb back and forth over my knuckles.

"You'll say anything to hold my hand, huh?" I reply. "Can I have it back yet?"

"Nope. You're mine now." His smile curves higher while his focus stays on the road. With one hand on the steering wheel, he looks back at me. I swallow the saliva pooling in my mouth, choking back my desire for him to say that again.

"Mr. Pierce, you can't rent me like one of your luxury cars."

"I think you already made it clear, you're not the rent-to-own type either. How about leasing? It's a little more permanent than renting in my mind, like a long-term contract, still without the pressure of buying."

"You want to lease me?" My lips remain parted while my teeth are aligned.

"I like you, and you like me. You don't have to get defensive or, I don't know, uncomfortable with me now. I get it. I don't have any expectations other than the pleasure of your company. Let's see where things go." He shrugs. "If I find you in my bed tonight, I'm not going to complain."

"Can we start with food first?" I pull my hand away from him, warming my fingers between my thighs.

"It's a good two hours till we get to the hotel. We have reservations at six thirty with some friends of mine. Will something quick be fine till then?" Friends? Do they know that I'm here? Do they know how we just met?

"That's not what I signed up for."

"They won't be a problem. Bash is the most open-minded person I know." That's code for he won't think you're a whore. "If you're uncomfortable, we'll ditch them."

"What do they have to eat around this area?"

"Are you allergic to anything?"

I hesitate, glaring side-eyed. "Noo." I swear, if he feeds me something weird with a bunch of eyeballs, I'm out. I'll be on the next flight home.

"I got you."

"This isn't Fear Factor. I'm not eating anything hairy."

He glances down for a moment, then looks back up to smirk at me.

"What?"

"Nothing."

"That was an intrusive thought."

"It wasn't intrusive. More like an innuendo."

"Share with the class. I won't judge you," I insist.

"Um." He chuckles. "I guess I should have shaved my balls."

"Oh." I nod. "I think it is customary to groom the garden before a new hook-up, but considering this was certainly the most unexpected connection, there should be an exception." Wait. Did I just admit I want to munch on his balls like they're dinner? Yep. That happened.

"I was going to say Ocean Prime, it is."

"Seafood? Yeah, that's more appealing. No offense."

"None taken. Two more questions. You ready?" Does he want my blood type now? I half-roll my eyes, catching myself and looking back at him. "Do you like sushi, and can you eat while I drive without making a mess?" He asks, flicking his pinky finger up for the first question, and his ring finger next.

I have to give him that lecture about being a grown-ass woman again. "Yes, and probably not, but I'll try." I lift my shoulders, shrugging, and throw my hands up. So maybe he was right to ask, even if he was joking. I'm twelve...twelve and a half. Clumsy, messy, and make sexual jokes as if I'm a comedic genius.

"But you're a grown woman?" Casey taunts.

"Don't use my words to fuck me over. Come up with your own. And it's not like I'm dirty. I lack a little coordination from time to time."

"Oh, love, you can be dirty all you want. It's the lack of coordination; we have to work on that one." With his knuckles, he nudges my thigh. "And you're a snowboarder?" He jests. "I was expecting someone who could keep up with advanced riders."

I'm not even sure what part of that I want to address. The part where he tried to allure me? "The best uncoordinated snowboarder around, thank you. Don't worry, your pretty head. I'll keep up."

"If you make a mess in this car, you are going to be cleaning it up."

"It's leather. Wouldn't be hard." I run my hand over the console.

"You'd better hope so. I like to keep an upstanding reputation with my business transactions. And don't roll those eyes at me. I hate cleaning."

I purse my lips. "Soo sorry to be such an inconvenience. Don't worry, I'll be careful, Daddy," I play, leaning toward him. Oh, shit. I said that out loud this time. I look up at him to see him studying me for what seems like dangerously too long. He makes me so nervous that I sit up straight and softly clear my throat. "Watch the road."

"Why? Am I scaring you?" He simpers. "The tough chick."

"Stop staring at me and watch the road." I point.

"Tell me, do I scare you?" He refuses to look at the road and is intently glued to me.

"You're making me nervous. You make me nervous, okay?" I nearly yell. He smiles, and his eyes go back to the road in front of him. "Asshole!" I cross my arms over my chest. "You could have gotten us killed."

"I like daddy better than asshole." He leers at me, then reaches for his phone that's attached to a mount suctioned to the window. I palm my forehead, and he chuckles, hitting a button to unlock the screen. He taps on his phone again. "Haven't you learned by now, I'm a pretty good driver." You're such a good driver; you threw me into a window. "Call Ocean Prime," he commands the system.

The restaurant answers. "Ocean Prime, how can I help you?" I lose the woman's voice, only hearing his.

"I would like to place an order for pick up. An order of Ocean Roll and an order of Dynamite Roll. Yes. Casey Pierce. Thank you." He hits another button on the screen, ending the call. I don't want to stop staring at him, at his mouth. His tongue runs over his protruding lower lip. Every word he spoke, I couldn't take my eyes off him. That kiss from the other night...to feel them once more. He looks over at me, and I waver between his lips and his eyes. He's simply...beautiful...or um, handsome?

"Why are you staring at me?" He softly asks.

"Why do you always ask me questions you know the answers to?"

"I want to hear your voice." He shrugs.

"You're gorgeous, and I know you know it," I scoff.

"I'm just a normal guy, Raine."

"You are not normal. Things like this...meeting a guy, immediately being annoyed by him, thinking I'll never see him again, and then bam, I'm in his expensive car being catered to like a princess. I don't want that. I don't want to like you, and I don't want to..." My eyes widen as they fall to his crotch.

"You don't want to what?"

"I would be lying if I finished that sentence, so I'm not gonna do it."

"Mhm," he nods. "I'm not the special one here."

"Please," I sass. "I know I'm fucking awesome, but I also know I'm not a supermodel." He pulls the vehicle to a stop at the traffic light, and I follow his hand as he reaches for my thigh, squeezing it. "Stupid boys are attracted to wildfires."

"You're right. You have me doing things..." His hands fly up in the air, leaving me, and become tucked behind his head. "Stupid things." He exhales. "That I don't ever waste time doing. I haven't wasted time doing in...a long time." He drops his hands, one returning to the wheel and the other on the center console. "Dancing at a packed bar. The fucking crowds. Being late to a meeting, so I could schedule your flight before you changed your mind. I'm never late, love. I haven't been able to get you out of my head since I met your smartass, and I knew it, I, oh, I knew you would make my life miserable and complicated, and two minutes in, you're already poking the bear." His bottom lip protrudes out, and he shakes his head to the sides slowly, chewing on the soft skin. "You let it out. Set everything on the table and say it like it is. Well, so do I. We're both adults, and we don't want to stay away from each other. Stop fighting it. Stop fighting me." The light changes, taking the moment with it. "We're almost there." He runs his hand along the back of his neck.

Fine. I'll play nice. "Good. I am starving." I look away when his eyes meet mine, cracking my fingers against my palm. "And Casey."

"Yeah?"

"I'm in."

"You're in? Completely? Fully?"

"One hundo. You got me." I hold out my hand. "You're right."

He weaves his fingers between mine, pulling me closer. "Give me a chance to prove myself."

Yes, it's that easy, that simple to give him access to my heart that's incapable of everlasting love. It's not what he's after, is it? I'm the temporary love. Nobody has been able to handle that yet. Neither beauty nor money makes you less insusceptible. "As long as we're on the same page."

"No strings." He draws my hand to his mouth, kissing it gently.

We pull up to a two-story brick building. Broad windows cover the exterior. An outdoor patio with tables is surrounded by bushes and floral arrangements along the side. It's more elegant than I imagined. What dinner reservations has he made tonight if this is just a quick...um, brunch stop? What's the equivalent of brunch in the PM? A snack, maybe linner, or dunch? I don't even know what I'll wear.

"I'll get your order and extra napkins." He gets out of the car and closes the door, leaving me with a hanging jaw.

Every step he takes to the building, I'm invested. How many days a week does he work on those glutes? I inadvertently squeeze my knees together, watching him. The smile he flashes me as he looks back pulses waves into my core. The door closes behind him, and the waves simmer. The tension is going to build up so high by the time I decide to sleep with this man, it's going to be a letdown. If it's not...I'd be totally fine if he was a crazy kidnapper and wanted to keep me. Dick, snacks, and snowboarding sound way better than work, family drama, and snowboarding.

I pull out my phone and text Calle.

> Hey. I'm still alive.

> Yay! Did you get it in yet?

> Slut buttered his big ole dick all up.

> OMG! You nasty!

> I'm fucking with you. We didn't get to the resort yet. Just stopped for sushi.

> Have fun. Update me later.

Placing my phone on the seat along my thigh, I turn the volume up on the radio. The wide touchscreen lights up. "What the hell?" I think aloud. He said he didn't like this band. Did he turn the Octane station on for me? The driver's door opens, and he hands me a large white paper bag before getting in.

"You said you didn't like this band," I reprimand, pulling the bag onto my lap.

"I don't. Still trying to understand why you do." He reaches for the bag, pulls out a container of sushi, and sets it on the center console.

"Turn something on that you like to listen to."

"You don't want to listen to this?" He looks at me with raised brows, holding the second container in his hand.

"Oh, I do, but show me what's so much better," I say, reaching for the sushi container in his hand and stacking it on top of the other. His face lights up with the challenge as he sets the empty paper bag behind my seat, handing me an envelope with chopsticks and forks in it. I place one container on the floor between my feet, and then the other on a napkin on top of my lap. He switches stations and carefully pulls the car out onto the road. The music bounces through the speakers, and I immediately know what song it is. A classic nineties hip-hop song. With chopsticks in hand, I shimmy my shoulders back and forth, dancing in my seat. I start rapping the lyrics, and he does a double-take with scopic eyes. The priceless shock that spilled across his face is hilarious.

"Whaaat?" I laugh. "Is this your genre of choice?"

"I like a little of everything."

"Except metal?"

"I mean, I can handle some of it for you, but the straight screamo shit...Love, don't torture me, please," he says, drawing out his words.

"How about a compromise? I won't overdo it on the heavy music, and you won't...play jazz in the car, ever."

"Jazz? You want to hate on jazz? Come on, not even a little Miles?" Dropping his jaw in disbelief.

"If you want me to take a nap, sure," I say, before shoving a sushi roll in my mouth.

He looks back and forth between me and the road, dramatically. "We're good?"

"I didn't make a mess," I reply. He shakes his head at me again. I seem to be making him do that a lot today. This is me; take it or leave it. You wanted Raine; you get the whole storm system, too.

"I want one." He eyes the container. "I need help. Pop on in my mouth." His brows rise. "Don't want to drive recklessly, right?" He grins obnoxiously. "Please."

"Oh, now our safety matters!" I pinch a roll between my sticks and hold my hands underneath it as I lean over the center to meet his mouth.

He rolls his tongue over his lip, a dangerous smile appearing. "Mm, daddy likes."

"Never say that again." I look at him deadpan.

"Tell me the truth, you're into it."

I open a container of sauce, dip my pointer finger in it, and smear it down the side of his face. "How about I'm into that."

He slowly turns to me. "Look who's playing dangerous games now."

"But you're an amazing driver." I tilt my head back and forth as I taunt him. "So when are you going to tell me about it?" I grab a napkin and hand it to him, but he stares at me blankly. "What?"

"You put it there."

I draw my lip out, scrunching up my face. Pressing the napkin to his skin, I drag it down his cheek. His hand glides over my wrist, and his lips gently cloak the back of my hand. The flat of his tongue runs along my thumb and pointer. Time stands still for a brief second as our eyes meet. Then he looks back to the road like a responsible driver, leaving my ovaries on fucking fire. My God, man.

Get it together. I pull my hand away. "Stop avoiding my question."

He sighs. "My life is...complicated."

"Complicated. Like fucking your ex's friend complicated, or more along the lines of being involved in the criminal business complicated? A getaway driver, too."

"I only did that once." His tone is serious and believable.

I slowly look away. Truth or bullshit? Closing the container tightly, I set it on the floor to avoid making a mess.

"I haven't always been a stand-up citizen." He glances between me and the road. "My teenage years were especially rough."

"Were you actually a getaway driver? Rob a bank or something?"

"No...it was a gas station," he admits.

Um, what? Am I okay with this? Did he go to jail? How much did he get away with?

"Raine," he laughs. Oh shit, my mouth is open, and I'm staring idiotically at him. "I'm fucking with you. I didn't rob anyone...yet." I run my hand through my hair, brushing it to the side. "My grandfather got me started in junior drag racing after I got busted for street racing at fifteen."

"You had a car at fifteen?"

"More like had easy access. My..." His jaw becomes tight. "My parents would travel often."

"They would leave a fifteen-year-old home alone?"

"Not just a fifteen-year-old, but my twelve-year-old sister, too."

"I'm sorry." I look to the floor.

His hand takes the cotton blend along my leg, rubbing my thigh. "Don't be. We had plenty of maids and house staff." I see the anger in his eyes. He's trying to mask it with humor.

"Money can't compete with time."

"You're a smart woman." He points at me, smiling. I watch his hands slide back over the steering wheel, and the brightness returns to his face. Maybe I shouldn't have pushed it. I understand having parts of your life—dark memories—you don't like talking about.

"Duh." I return my gaze to him before glancing out the window. Casey rubs my thigh again, looping his fingers under the tear in my jeans, his skin meeting mine. His beautiful eyes scare me. He has the potential to ruin my life. The way he talks to me...touches me...looks at me. I haven't felt this...smitten in a long time. Returning to the scenery from my window, a wash of overwhelming serenity sets in, and I close my eyes, able to let myself relax. I'm safe here.

"Raine, not falling asleep, are you?"

"No, just resting my eyes."

"Raine, we're here." Casey's voice wakes me, and I open my eyes. I must have fallen asleep. "Welcome to the Alpine Cabin."

My ears pop as he opens my door. It's been less than three hours since I got off my flight, and I thought I was doing fine with the altitude. I'm not so much now. I'm tired, and a wave of nausea is beginning to hit me slowly and surely, just like the other night. I step out of the vehicle, losing my balance. Lightheaded, I hang on to the door to save face. My nipples could cut a diamond. It's freezing.

"Whoa there. Let me help you." He wraps his sizable arm around my waist. "Come on. I'll take you in first and then come back out for your bag."

I look up at the beautiful, rich red log cabin. The deck wraps around it, as far as I can tell.

"I'll be fine." I try to pull away from him. "Just give me a minute," I say, sitting down on the steps. "I thought we were going to a hotel?"

"We're adjacent to The Lodge Hotel." He replies while sitting beside me. "Let me help you, please?" He holds out his hand.

I feel like yesterday's hangover has crept back up on me with some kind of new-dimension hangover relapse. I just want to pull a blanket over my head.

"Please? You need water and rest if you want to make it to the mountains tomorrow."

Fine. I grab his hand, and he pulls me to my feet, wrapping his other arm around my waist again before leading me into the cabin.

"Hey there, how was your flight?" From the couch, a voice asks. A man about the same size as Casey stands. He's a little taller but muscular, with colorful tattoos lining his arms. His light brown hair is short, and his eyes are sky blue. As terrible as I feel, it's hard to miss another handsome man. Another one I'm making a poor first impression on, but I guess these guys are into hot messes. I sleepily smile.

"Hey, Bash. She got hit with altitude sickness. You want to grab her bag out of the trunk?" Casey asks.

"Yeah. Pills in the kitchen," he replies, walking past us, out the door.

"This way," Casey guides me to a room on the first floor. I sit down on the bed, and he lets go of my waist, making sure I'm steady. "Sebastian and his wife, Estella, claimed the second-floor bedroom. It's a good thing right now," he chuckles. "I'll get you a glass of water. Do you want ibuprofen or anything?"

I shake my head and reach down to pull my shoes off. As soon as Casey walks out of the room, I stand up to pull the blanket off the bed. Sebastian walks in behind me and sets my bag down on the end of the blanket. I'm just going to have to move it now, but I smile politely to the best of my knowledge.

"You'll be fine by tomorrow. Happens to all of us," he says and walks out the door.

Tomorrow? What about the dinner reservations? We should be leaving in the next hour. I grab my suitcase and move it to the floor, climbing under the blanket and curling up on my side. The moment I close my eyes, Casey's voice returns.

"Here you go, princess." Sitting the glass on a rustic bed-stand, next to a short bronze lamp, he leers.

"I'm not a princess," I murmur, closing my eyes again. "I'm ruining your dinner plans." He sits on the edge of the bed against me and pushes the hair out of my face, smoothing it back several times. Why is he taking care of me? It's giving me the ick. Is that what I am to him? A stray kitten he pities. I feel like that right now. I'm the ick, not him. Vomit. Twice have I put myself in these situations, and twice Casey has been trying to rescue me...and succeeding. It has to be an ego trip.

"It's not a big deal. I'll hang out with you here."

"I don't need you to take care of me," I grumble.

"I know you don't." He rests his thumb along my jaw. Smoothing my hand over his, I slowly lift and hold it in front of me as I scan his colorless art.

"How often do you have to redo these?"

"Redo them?" He chuckles, amused. "You sure you don't want anything?"

"Pain is my bread and butter. I'm fine," I insist. "A tattoo artist told me that hand and finger tattoos fade easily."

"It's been a few years since I've had them done, and I don't see a need to get them touched up yet. I think maintenance is required at some point with any tattoo. Why? Are you thinking about a hand tattoo?" With my pointer, I trace up each of his inked fingers.

"Just curious. I do have a tattoo, one."

"Oh yeah? Where at?"

"I got it when I was twenty. My mom still doesn't know about it." I let go of his hand and tug at the blanket. He slides to the floor and kneels beside me.

"Is your mom anti-tattoo?"

"She is...traditional, let's say." That's literally the best word to describe her in all aspects. Plus, it's better than nar-row-minded...if the shoe fits. I lean back and pull my hood-ed sweatshirt up, getting it stuck on my shoulders, while I'm flat on my back, and smack my hands off the headboard. He chuckles, then pulls it up over my head.

"Woman, you are zany." I ignore him and pull my tank top up to my ribs. "Where exactly is this tattoo?" He asks, raising his brows.

"Right here." I roll to my right towards him and push the band to my bra up along the side. The tattoo along my ribs is only visible when I'm braless unless I push the band of my bra up. I didn't get it to show other people. It was for me.

He trails his thumb along the black ink near my breast. I never got it colored in like I wanted. His eyes return to mine, and I'm quickly consumed with euphoria. This lightness of nothing can hurt me, and I'm not sick from the aptitude anymore. It's a false reality I don't want to leave.

"Very nautical," he nods, looking back at the anchor wrapped in a chain rode.

"It's basic. I know, but I got it..." I hesitate, closing my eyes. "I got it after a traumatic experience." I push his hand down and adjust my bra before pulling my tank top back down. "It helped me move forward."

"I get it. It's like therapy. Obviously, I've needed a lot more of that than you." He nudges my arm, standing up. I pull the blanket back over my body and curl my legs up to my chest. "Let me show you something." He pulls his hoodie over his head and then his t-shirt, laying it on the bottom of the bed. His beautiful bare body sits in front of my face as he kneels along the side of the bed. He takes my hand in his. "Do you see this one?" Guiding my fingers to it, he continues. "It's a Kraken. It doesn't mean shit. It just makes a beautiful piece of art." The octopus-like creature covers one side of his chest. "And this one." He presses my fingers to the back of his bicep. "My mermaid." I run my fingers over his smooth skin, looking at each individual design that combines into the masterpiece that covers his chest, arms, and neck. Most of it is nautical. A seahorse, a crab that is scary realistic, and a treasure chest. "We both have water tattoos."

"I don't know if it's really that special. A lot of people get nautical tattoos," I say, half smiling, looking up at him. "This had to take hundreds of hours," I whisper.

"The one on my back was the longest I sat for," he replies, turning around. His back is covered in the same achromatic art that the rest of his body possesses. A compass wrapped around the skeleton of a sailor or pirate. It looks like the compass is floating away, but still attached as the bone bag tries to keep it. I touch his defined shoulders and solid arms, drawing my hand back to myself.

Oh God. Pulling the blanket tighter, I close my eyes. My sickly body craves more than it can handle, reminding me that this high is in my head.

"Raine?" I let my eyelids open to see his saintly face. "Can I lie next to you?" The sincerity in his voice is comforting.

"Lie down, Casey," I whisper, letting the heaviness weigh my eyelids shut again. As he sits on the other side of the bed and lies down, the mattress sinks slightly. I roll to face him, weakly opening my eyes. His hands are behind his head as he stares at the ceiling. His still, shirtless body is next to mine, and I'm wide awake in my head, seeing every detail and movement I make in slow motion. Calculating, over-thinking, everything that I wouldn't normally overestimate. I feel powerless next to him. Starstruck and stupid. A sick, weak shell of a strong woman. I don't like it. It's terrifying. As if when the plug is pulled, I'll spin around and around, drifting down the drain with the dirty water.

"Casey?" I hum.

"Raine?" He turns his face to mine.

"What are you thinking about?" I ask hesitantly.

"Thinking I'm glad I ate sushi with you or I'd be pretty hungry right now," he says, impassive. Leave it to a man to daydream about food.

"Dunch."

"What?" He laughs.

"We had dunch. I'm trademarking it. It's like brunch but between dinner and lunch." People try to trademark everything now. Why wouldn't I join in?

He grins, rolling his head back to look up at the ceiling once more. "Fuck," he exhales. "I need you to marry me."

"No," I immediately respond, stony and frozen in my position, my eyes suddenly no longer heavy. Starstruck and stupid, sick or not, nothing could convince me to smile and nod.

"No?" He looks back at me, concerned.

"You can't ever want to marry me. Ever," I repeat.

"I just meant...I need to keep you." He rolls to his side and puts his arm around me, pulling me close, my face resting along his chest. "You're sexy and quirky and have this dark sense of humor...We're on the same page. Don't think twice about it." Casey's hand slides to my shoulders, and I look up at his five o'clock shadow and parted lips, becoming submerged in his eyes. His hand slides to my jaw, his thumb gliding back and forth along my chin. He rests his head on his other arm.

"I don't want history to repeat." The raw vulnerability I have around him is lucid. I want to keep him, too. It's insane. It's lust. Attraction and excitement...and a weird desire to let a man take care of me. I'm not completely convinced he's not a secret sociopath or the title of a new unsolved murder episode; The Snowboarding Murderer. Subtitle:

Where have all the snow bunnies gone? Although he's very convincing that he's not. Maybe a siren? The art lines up.

"I'm not afraid of your scars...everyone has their demons. You can't be suicidal over them. The past is the past, and today is right now. Stay." His thumb runs over my lips.

"Don't ask me to marry you, and I'll stay."

"Deal." He smiles, letting a deep chuckle out.

"I'm serious. None of that A Walk To Remember business." I squint, and he listlessly nods.

"I'm pretty sure she told him not to fall in love, nothing about marriage," he whispers. "Can I fall in love with you, Raine?" His warm breath creates a breeze across my forehead, and strands of my hair float over my face.

"As long as you'll be okay when it doesn't last," I murmur, burying my face into him. His silence reassures me. He doesn't believe my words...or doesn't think he'll fall in love with me anyway.

"Casey, what are your demons?" I ask, beginning to doze off.

"There is not enough time in two days to share them all with you," he answers, pulling me to his chest as he rolls to his back and drapes his arm around me.

Chapter Nine | Dopamine

Casey

Monday, 6:15 AM

It was...peaceful. I laid in bed with Raine for nearly an hour after she fell asleep, running my fingers through her hair, that addicting coconut scent surrounding me. It couldn't keep me from overanalyzing my legal dilemmas.

"She has no case. A judge will look at her like she has six heads! Crazy bitch." Sebastian's boisterous voice carries through the living room, trying to reassure me that Karson is making my life hell for no reason and will eventually drop the game she's playing over Grandpa's will.

"I thought she would want the Villa." I walk from the open kitchen to the living area and settle onto the couch catty-corner to Bash, rubbing my eyes.

"She has no case. She is a case. A nutcase," he says, then mumbles something I don't catch, but I'm sure it's an insult towards Karson.

"I'll worry about it when I have to," I reply, tired of talking about her.

"How's your girl feeling?" He asks, piquing Estella's interest. She glances towards me, lying on the couch next to Sebastian with her head on his lap and covered in a huge fuzzy opal blanket. It looks expensive and lucullan. He rubs her exposed shoulder, then pulls the blanket over it.

169

"I haven't woken her yet."

"Well, what are you waiting for? Get her ass up," he complains. Estella smacks him in the chest, glaring. Before muttering an apology, he gives her the same look back.

"It's not even six-thirty. I'm in no rush," I say, kicking my feet up on the solid oak coffee table.

"Why don't you take her some coffee?" Estella suggests.

"Yeah! Do that one. That's a sweet gesture," Bash agrees, pointing excitedly toward me, then looking down at his wife. He agrees with everything she says, even if it's preposterous. She's the only one that I've seen in my twenty-something years of knowing him that could turn him into putty. I would think it's her sexy accent or her beauty, but it's not, and he's been madly in love with her since the day he met her.

"You sap," I taunt him, standing up and walking to the kitchen to do exactly as she suggested.

Setting the coffee on the nightstand, I draw the curtains in the bedroom to let the rising sun in. She's lying dead center in the bed; her hair is everywhere, half covering her face, and she's drooling on her pillow. That is a deep fucking sleep. I exhale a chuckled breath. Never in my life have I spent a night in bed with a woman I just started seeing and only slept. I slip under the blankets beside her and take her in, trying to remember everything about her in case I never see her again after today, drool included. The woman has no idea how gorgeous she is. She rolls into me, and I caress her lower back beneath her tank top.

When she looks up at me, I greet her. "Good morning, wildcat. Feeling better?" Those green eyes of hers could take my life away. They're an anchor dragging me to the depths.

"Yep," she answers coyly.

"I brought you coffee." I pull her body tight against mine, which is petite in comparison to all the right curves. She stares at me. Then her eyes drift down my body, where she locked on with this blank look on her face. I could almost laugh, until I feel the wet warmth of her tongue along my clavicle, gliding up my neck till her lips meet mine, where she stops.

Fuck this. Without hesitation, I press my lips deeply into her velvety mouth. Slow, wet kisses that make me forget everything stressful. There's nothing more I want to do today than her.

"Does that mean you're happy about the coffee?" I ask, against her lips.

"No, I hate coffee." I feel her smile curl upward against my mouth. "You make me happy." As I pull her into my lips, our tongues intertwine. With each deeper flick and swirl, she sends heat to my groin, sending my heart racing. She abruptly withdraws, and I will her back. "Feels like you're happy to see me too," she whispers, against my skin. I thrust upward against her, my hard cock pressing to her hip.

"Keep kissing me like that, and you'll find out just how happy, I reply, pushing my teeth into my lip. Her hand slides down past my navel to my silk gray shorts, stroking downward, the fabric smoothing over every inch. She stops and looks me dead in the eyes. I chuckle at the shock on her face and run my tongue across my teeth. Her enlarged eyes drift away while her hand is frozen in place.

"You're—"

"Well endowed."

"Not wearing boxers," she replies, her eyes moving across my chest as she covers up her astonishment.

"He likes the breeze," I whisper, searching for her laugh. I feel her cheekbones rise against me.

"*He?*" She asks. "Does *he* also have a name?"

"Not yet. Any suggestions?"

"Sounds like a personal problem, but I have a few suggestions," she says, pushing away from me. "Pete The Dragon...Johnny Long Bean...Big Bernard...Harry Unstyled...Ro berto." I palm my face and reel her right back.

"The only problem I'm going to have is blue balls if you think you're just going to cut me off like that."

"Still, that sounds like a personal problem. And the whole *naming your party zone* gives me the vomit emoji. My face is going to turn green if you refer to your penis as *he* again."

"You're so lucky." I shake my head.

"What is this luck you speak of?"

"You're lucky I'm a gentleman and treat women with respect, but I do *so badly* want to disrespect you."

She laughs, pushing her hands into my chest. Is that...she's blushing. "Come back here." I grab her hand, pulling her on top of me. When her ass pushes against it, my cock twitches. "You like this cat and mouse game?" She pulls her tank top over her head, leaving a sporty black bra. I run my hands up her smooth thighs to the narrowing of her waist. "Do you know what you're getting yourself into?"

"I know exactly what I'm doing. I'm not the mouse."

Sliding her bra up, her breasts spill out of the bottom before she pulls it from her shoulders and throws it to the floor with her top. I keep my hands in place, catching her eyes, full of heat, and cutting into mine. *She's the cat.*

"Shouldn't we start with food first?" I smirk, mocking her from yesterday.

"This is why you invited me here, isn't it? Two consenting adults clearly attracted to one another."

"Shit, I thought it was to be your travel nurse since I'm taking care of you constantly."

"Aftercare is the only nursing I should need, but if you're too much of a gentleman—" She lifts her leg, trying to climb off of me.

"Tsk tsk." Grabbing her wrist, I pull her back, running my fingers over her inked skin before taking her breast in my hand. I roll my thumb in circles, tracing the outline of her hard pink nipple. They only get harder as she intently watches me. Her hums are full of pleasure, and my hands fit her hourglass body perfectly. Feeling down her back to her waist, I lift her up to her knees and push myself back, sitting up against the headboard. She scans my body as I pull my shirt off, handing it to her.

"If you want me to be your maid, at least supply a uniform and not one of those assless aprons. Something classy," she says, tossing it to the floor with her clothes. "Loose slacks and a turtle neck."

"Fuck, that's sexy. You'd have me wrapped around your finger. I knew you were after my money." I plant a tender kiss on her neck.

"A hoe got bills." She leans deeper against my mouth.

"Promiscuous girl, I already gave you an advance. A plane ticket to the all-inclusive Pierce Playland."

She slides to the side of the bed, standing to push her leggings off. My hands lace behind my head. I lean back and follow her palms, tracing down her legs. Panties left, her fingers straddling the top of the fabric, hesitant, almost as if second-guessing the decision. I reach for her hand.

"Am I still making you nervous?"

That got to her. She takes it as a dare, letting go of my hand to drop her black panties to the floor and step out of them. Every second I wait makes my dick harder. Her slender shoulders. Her heavy tits. B cup? Nipples slightly angling outward, her trim midriff, a horizontal navel below a crease that draws across her abdomen, those perfect, wide hips, and that ass that peers past them just enough. Her long, smooth legs and, mm, thighs...with just the modest gap before that pretty little pussy. It nearly disappears when she shifts her hips, until she does that thing again, where she pushes her butt out. I move closer to the edge of the bed, running my hand up her thigh to her ass. I clasp my hand around her plump cheek before smacking it.

"You're gorgeous. And these—" I squeeze. "I could leave them bright fucking red...if you're into that. You have to tell me what you like, beautiful. What do you want from me?" I find her eyes, gliding my hand over her thigh. She leans into me with a muffled moan. I want to hear it again and louder.

Slipping a finger between her legs, her wetness coats me, and I slide in slowly. She falls closer, pressing to her toes. Her knees push into the side of the bed, and her hands drop to my shoulders. She exhales a sweet noise. I release her, grabbing the back of her thighs and pulling her even closer. I circle her clit with my thumb, and she opens farther. "I like that, tell me you want more without telling me you want more." Her airy inhale softens as I lick her thigh with the flat of my tongue.

"Casey," she scolds. "Can you shut up?"

"No. You're going to hear my every thought until my voice remains inside your head when I'm not around. There are one-night stands, and then there's me. I'm going to take my time. I'm going to talk to you. And I'm going to learn what you like." She earns the look I give her, staring into her eyes before I go in for another taste of her. This time, it's exactly where she wants me. Fuck, she's canned peaches wet. She's sweet and musky and *so wet*. "Does that turn you on? When I'm straightforward and demanding?"

"No. Maybe. I don't know."

Won't she look at me? "Hey, look at me. Please." She finds me. "You haven't been talked to the right way in bed, have you?" I lap my tongue down and back to her clit. While I grip her thick thighs, her hands squeeze on top of mine. "How many men have you drowned to death and buried in your backyard?" I smile up deviously at her, licking my lips.

Her eyes burn me, not a smile in sight. "Take a guess?"

"Three?"

"Why three?"

"Because the fourth and fifth are still alive." *Nollan. Me.* "If the other three had survived, you would have more stalkers than I can handle."

"Hah, don't worry. The fifth will find his place beneath an avalanche in the near future."

I sink back. "Those are fighting words."

"And you're prepping to impale me with that thing—" She says, pointing at my standing tall erection. "Isn't a problem?" If there's been any indication to get my dick out, that would be it.

"This?" I point, pulling the elastic of my shorts outward. "That's what you want?"

"Actually, let's put this on pause. Sounds like fun.. making you wait all day." She bends over, gathering her clothes. "You did say you wanted to learn what I like." She gives me a once-over. "Hope you don't have *a bad day* on the slopes."

"If that's how you feel, I'll stay here and whack it." Pushing my shorts to my quads, I run my hand up and down my shaft. Her eyes hover hungrily over me, and her lips part, spilling her clothes onto the floor. "It doesn't look that intimidating, does it?" I slide to the edge of the bed, in between her spread legs, and drop my shorts to the floor. Grabbing her thighs, I look up at her. Her breathing is quietly labored, while mine is controlled.

"I'm letting you know now, I'll be immensely disappointed if this trip is nothing more than cervix stabbing."

"The free snowboarding doesn't make up for cervix stabbing? That's not a real thing, is it?"

"Pain, yeah. Pain from cock punching the cervix? Usually an indication of something else, but I'm not a doctor. Ask HelpMD," she sneers.

"I'll be a doctor. Wanna play?"

She has the cutest laugh, I swear. "You have an entire wardrobe for sexy time somewhere, don't you? A dungeon." She widens her hands, mimicking a big screen. "Casey & The Sex Chamber of Secrets."

Funny...sexy...authentic. To keep her would be too perfect. "You look so fucking beautiful," I murmur. Her long hair hangs down over her breasts, slightly covering her nipples, while I kiss her midriff, my gaze shifting back to her eyes. "Tell me this is what you want." I smirk, knowing that something sardonic will come out of her mouth. She tugs the flesh of her lip into her mouth and puts her hands on my broad shoulders.

"You'd better know what you're doing with that thing... *Daddy*," she says, rolling her eyes. I throw my head back in laughter. I knew she was into it and sure as fuck wouldn't ever admit it, but she wanted to say it again, even in the form of a joke.

"Do you have any doubts?"

"I know what I'm doing, Casey. Now cut the nice guy shit," she replies, glaring.

"I am a nice guy." I smile. "A good man...and yeah, love, I can be a bad boy. Don't say I didn't warn you."

"Wait." She stops me. "We don't need a safeword?"

"Woman, what kind of freaky shit are you into?" Her glare eats at me. "No. Not right now. If you want to stop at any time, tell me."

"I've never..." She sighs, letting her sentence hang.

I gently rub over her legs. "What is it?"

"I haven't talked about sex in this way with anyone. We talked, but...it was different. This is just...I just met you."

"Honestly, it's shocking that you're here. I can tell you don't put much faith in other people."

"I don't want to talk about that. Where's the bad boy?"

I wrap my hands around her leg, above her knees, and pull her thighs to the bed. She holds on to my shoulders till she's kneeling above my lap. She's not going to like it at first unless she is used to an above-average dildo. Her confidence is cute, though, as if I didn't have experience being a man with a dick with its own zip code. The first few girls I dated hated my size. I didn't know what I was doing either. Now I do.

I drag two fingers up her leg to the soft skin along her inner thigh, grabbing her ass in my free hand. The length of my finger slides between her legs, feeling her tender skin. I stare at her parting mouth, massaging her gradually up and down before slowly pumping in and out, separating and stretching them inside of her. Pulling my fingers out and dropping my wet hand to her round ass, I lift her. She pants softly. Anticipation? Or is she still pretending none of this makes her nervous? Suspended over my swollen tip, I rub it across her opening.

I need to feel her around me, squeezing me, trying to push me out, and then starving for my return. She's so fucking sexy.

"I should get a—God damn. You're so wet," I groan, lowering her. She lightly gasps and raises herself back up. Where's the fucking condoms?

Her hand fists my cock, rubbing the head along her slit, pushing at her opening again.

Fuck. Fuck! Where are they?

Fuck. She hasn't said anything about wearing one. Is this cool? Can I...Should I? Oh fuuck, stop sliding over me like that. Check the nightstand. Check it. Fuck. Fuck, fuck. I have to move her and...fuck it.

I slowly propel into her, lowering her down, and making her hand return to my shoulder.

"Fuck," she squeals. "Ouch." Something about the word coming out of her mouth—I want to hear it. It's a guilty pleasure.

"I'm sorry." My heart beats faster as she takes more of my length.

Her nose wrinkles and winces. "Slow, slow, slow," she exhales.

"Okay," I breathe out.

I've been imagining this moment for the last three days. Lying next to her last night was torture, wanting to touch her and knowing I couldn't. She pushes her ass out and arches her back, rocking in my lap. Then, she settles into a slow pattern, finding something that feels good to her. She jerks and adjusts, finding rhythm again. Her wetness runs down her legs and mine.

"You want more? You think you can take it?"

She hums and bobs her head. I thrust upward, nice and slow, driving my full length into her. Her loud moans boost my high. They're broken up by silent gasps. "It's okay, baby. Does that hurt? I fucking know. Fight it off. Find the pleasure. Use me till you get there. Dig your nails into my skin, grind and ride, shift and find it. Guide me to where it feels good. We're in this together." She rocks against me. Her nails dig into my shoulders.

I can't keep my eyes off her bouncing tits, but I draw myself to her face for a moment. Her closed eyes, riding me like she owns me...making me go where she wants. I'll be hers. Fuck, I always do this...fall deep for the pussy. "Was it worth it?" I whisper into her neck. "Was it worth cutting your family visit short to fly here to see me?" I'm a relationship person, and she's a situationship person. What am I doing?

"Yes," she moans, long and loud. Her breathing labored with her continuous grinding.

I hold in my laughter, but the louder she gets, the funnier it is that she has no idea Bash and Estella are lounging in the living room, feet away from us.

"My God," she yells.

"Casey, baby. Not God," I reply to her moan, biting at her neck.

"Shut...up," she exhales, pressing her fingers messily to my lips. I keep one hand on her hip and run the other over her breast, taking her nipple between my thumb and finger, tugging it till it can't possibly tighten further. She yells out, a yelp that turns into a moan, and her pussy clenches around my cock more and more with every circle of her hips. I push her down and hold her in place. She struggles to lift back up, but I don't let her. Her pants become a heavy panic, unable to breathe out more than a single word.

"Casey!"

"*Wildcat.*"

She moans, wrapping her fingers around my face and dragging me to her mouth, deeply kissing me through gasps for air. I pant against her neck, her hands falling to my arms as she tries rocking again, clenching around my dick.

"Casey," she moans, louder, trying to get me to release my grip. I don't loosen my hold on her, refusing to let her move, only pushing deeper into her. She never said *stop*.

Tap, tap, tap.

A light knock on the door quiets her, and her vivid green eyes claw into me like her nails. I'm betting she's going to sucker punch me when I tell her that we have an audience. I smile at her sinfully, almost laughing.

"Casey! These rooms aren't soundproof," Sebastian yells.

I pull Raine's ass up and slam it back down again. She heaves a sharp breath, followed by a moan, squeezing my biceps. I do it again, then throw my hands onto the bed behind me and lean back.

"Thanks, Bash. Now kindly fuck off," I yell.

Her face lights up, and she slams her hands into my chest, the same place I held her hands last night when I tried convincing her we had matching tattoos. She pushes her ass out again and rolls her hips. Watching her ride my cock, her soaking pussy dripping down me, sweat glistening across our bodies, and seeing her excitement over our audience is making it hard not blow my dick in her right now. Fuck, I want to do it and pound her till we're both left in a creamy mess.

I lean on one arm and circle her clit with my other hand. With each roll of her hips, I feel her clench around me tighter and tighter. Her breathy moans, her nails into my chest...I know those moans. They're shorter and uncontrolled in pitch. She's almost there, isn't she? God. Shit. Fuck. Fuck. I can't...I can't hold it back. My head falls, my eyes roll shut, and I erupt into ecstasy, pulsing deeper inside of her. Her breathless body falls to my chest, and I nearly drop to my back, using my strength to hold our bodies together as she bows in and out, and our hearts race against one another.

"You guys done now?" Sebastian yells from the other side of the door.

I take a breath and yell back. "Estella, put a leash on him!"

"This is a great way to be introduced to your friends," Raine says, trying not to laugh.

Exactly—blindly on opposite sides of a door, with my cock pulsing inside of her. I rub my hands up and down her arms and flex inside of her again. Her walls tighten in return. "Would you rather meet them when you're sick or getting dick?"

"*Ohh, okay, Dr. Suess,*" she mocks. "What time is it?"

"Around seven," I answer, tucking her legs to my sides and wrapping my hands around her hips. I roll her over, so I'm on top of her. "I never read a book where dick was a rhyming word."

"I have. You won't find it in the kids' section."

"That's a good thing." I softly kiss her jaw. "Why did you need the time? Hot date?"

"I need gear," she says, looking up at me.

"Estella has some stuff you should be able to fit." I place another kiss on her neck. "Whatever else you need, we can pick up or rent. Next time, I'll give you more than a few hours' notice." I nudge her chin with my knuckle. "Speaking of gear and kids, we probably should have talked about that before this happened." I nod downward, gesturing to my raw cock that's still soaking in her.

"Clean, covered. It's been a year since I've—" She wavers. "Well, almost wasn't—the whole Nollan thing. That doesn't bother you?"

"I don't care about what or who you do before me, nor do I care what you do after me as long as when you're with me, you're with only me."

"When is *after you*?" She asks, brushing her hair back from her face.

"Whenever you tell me you don't want to see me anymore."

"You just want me to fuck you and hang out with you and whatever, till I decide I don't want to anymore?"

"That's what you want, isn't it?"

"What if you don't want that?" She's afraid she's going to hurt me. I judged her right. She was never a villain.

"I can't make you stay, Raine. If you want me, you'll get me, and if you don't, I'm not going to chase you. I won't sit around in misery, pitying myself. I'm not Nollan. I won't start fights or create drama. I'm right here, you have me, literally," I chuckle, watching that beautiful smile reappear. Laughing with her is natural. I really hope she sticks around for a while. "And I'm clean, love. Actually...you're a first."

"A first?" Her head sinks back into the bed, and her eyes widen.

"Not *the first*, crazy. *A first*. First time I haven't used a condom."

"Why?" She scrunches her face up. "You should have said something."

"You make me stupid. I tried, but..." I flex inside of her.

"Oh gee, thanks. I'm a stupid inducer."

With laughter, my body shakes against hers. "Stupid inducer. Where the fuck do you come up with this shit?"

"My mom says I'm special." She shrugs.

"You are special...and maybe I trust you."

Her arms swing up and fall back to the bed with a thud. "I'm a stupid inducer," she mocks. "Who thinks, oh, *I trust this one, I'm not going to wrap it*?" She attempts to mimic my voice, but sounds more constipated than anything. "I bet they're in that drawer, too." Her eyes roll towards the nightstand.

"Hey, stupid inducer, you induce stupid, you're not stupid. Wouldn't you have stopped me if you didn't already have a backup plan?"

"Yep. Put all the trust in her; *she has a backup plan* because the woman you met *days ago* is shockingly honest? I wouldn't let the millionaire knock me up? I wouldn't give him an STD? Here's some shocking honesty...I thought you were a perv and a weirdo and a villain when I met you, so maybe, *just maybe* I wanted to be the hero to give you a venereal disease."

"Nah," I say, deadpan. "You're the same...a perverted weirdo."

She purses her lips, hollowing her cheeks. "I also thought you had to be some type of fucked up to look that good and be interested in me."

"Again...I thought the same about you. We were both right, huh? Two of the same fucked up that ran away to the mountains together."

"Here's some more honesty," she whispers. "Your giant dick is killing me. Can you pull it out already?" She's so straight-faced, it's borderline hilarious. "It's not funny!" She scolds, cracking a smile. "If I can't hang today, it's your fault."

"Easy, wildcat. We could just lie in bed all day."

"You sold me on Bender, not dick. That was just a bonus, like when you buy the sugary cereal for the taste, but it includes a mystery prize." She reaches out, tracing my lips with her finger. I flick my tongue out, grabbing her wrist and sucking her digit into my mouth. "I need a break...and ice." I flex inside of her again. She puffs out her cheeks, widening her eyes. "We're never going to get anywhere today if you don't stop that."

"I don't want to stop," I pout. "It's warm in here and cold out there."

"Then you're getting some cardio in because I'm not going to do all the work again," she argues. "I stand by my break."

I pull her with me to the edge of the bed, sliding my feet to the ground. Running my hands down her back, I pull her towards me, pushing myself deeper once more. As air escapes her lungs, her head falls into my chest.

"You fit me." With both hands, I grab her face and bend to her lips, kissing her softly. "I can be the perfect boyfriend you want once a month...or for two days. Let me know." Her lips call me in. I'm waiting for Sebastian to start yelling outside the door again—for him to ruin everything that is intoxicating bliss. It's only a matter of time. I drop my hands to her thighs and pull out slowly. Her back drops to the bed, and her chest rises and falls in waves. My cum slides down her ass out of her stretched hole. The sight just turns me on all over again. It's fucking hot.

I smooth my hand up her inner thigh, painting her tender, beaten skin with my cum. I spread it from her opening up and down her pussy lips. Fuck. I'm going to be erect all day. I stroke my cock, milking what's left down her leg, taking in the beautiful mess lying below me.

"I'm going to take a quick shower. Then I'll get clean blankets. I'll give you a minute. Looks like you need it," I simper.

"Arrogant!" She yells as I walk into the bathroom.

I return for a moment, dropping a washcloth on her. She sticks her tongue out at me when I smile at her.

"Hey!"

"What?"

"This isn't my mess to clean."

"As you wish, darling," I reply and mop up her thighs the best I can.

"Casey." She grabs my hand, stopping me from walking off. "What's your weirdest sex thing?"

"Thing?" I furrow my brows. "Define thing."

"A fact, a kink, a turn-on. You know."

"I don't think I have one that's very wild." She seems unimpressed and lets go of me. "What's yours?"

"Maybe I'll tell you later."

"I'll hold you to it." Tapping her knee, I do the naked strut to the bathroom connected to our room.

I have her for the rest of the day and a few hours tomorrow. That's it...until she wants to see me again. Bash can shove the work-chat up his ass. Nothing is going to ruin my time with her. Not a damn thing could compare to the way she makes me feel right now.

Chapter Ten | Affliction

Casey

Returning from the shower, I find Raine in the same place I left her, except she's rolled to her stomach with her phone in her hand, her curvy ass on display.

"What are you doing?"

"Texting Calle."

"Oh, didn't you check in with her yesterday?" I ask, concerned.

"I did, but she just texted me again. You know, making sure you're not a serial killer…or drug lord, or mafia prince. That kinda stuff," she says without even batting a lash.

"I wasn't lucky enough to have been born into the mafia," I groan. It may have been with sarcasm, but it's true. Cameron never laid a hand on Karson. I've taken the brunt of his abuse. I almost envy her. Then I remember, she's not special to him either. *Damn it.* Stop thinking about it.

"The shower is all yours," I say, changing the subject.

"Help me up," she commands, laying her phone on the pillow and rolling to her back.

"Give me your hand." I reach for her, pulling her to my chest. "You sure you don't want to skip the mountains today?" She pushes into my chest and walks to the other side of the bed to her suitcase. "Not going to answer me?"

"No." She roots around in her suitcase full of clothing. "If I say no, you'll just keep trying to convince me, and if I say yes, I won't be able to walk tomorrow, and I'll miss out on the mountain."

Dropping the towel from my hips, I step closer to her. "You would turn it down for snow? Now I see what you were talking about...I'm on your clock. That's new for me." A displeased wrinkle and more silence. "I can't convince you? I could make you cum over and over all day long." Her eyes flash over my body. "You would be lucky to survive, that part is true." I bend over, grabbing her chin, her eyes ablaze. "But you think I'm going to fall for you and you'll break my heart. Don't be naive, wildcat." Taking her lip with the brush of my thumb, she latches onto my wrist, playing into it. "You won't be the same after me either. Nobody will satisfy you. You break me, and I ruin you. We'll be even." Straightening, my erect cock is level with her gaze. Her gentle hands run up my legs, back and forth over my thighs. And oh...that smile. That sinister curve dragging up her face. Little brat. "You tease." I shake my head.

"What are you going to do about it?" Her warm breath and that mouth of hers. She's unshakeable.

"Fill your mouth, that way you can't talk any more shit," I reply, stony.

"Sounds like a challenge," she derides.

"If you want it, all you have to do is ask." I would love to read her mind right now. I can see she wants to say something. Growing harder with the thought of her, I stroke my cock. "You said I was a villain, so tell me, is it the bad boys that do it for you? Anything you want, I can be it."

"You look like a villain. You talk like a villain. But...you're not one, Casey." She runs her hands up and down my thighs, smoothing over my dark hair. "Bad guys don't cater to women."

"Maybe I'm not, but I've already given you a taste of how *good* a good guy can fuck." Tantalizing, she drags my thumb into her mouth. "It's only the beginning. Tell me what you want, Raine. Do you like to be tied up? Is that your weird thing? It's basic. It can't be that. Are you into sadism? Like it rough? Or is it something like urophilia? That might be too much for me."

"Right now? I want you to cum in my mouth."

Fuck. I run my tongue over my teeth and shake my head.

"Please?" She asks, teeth edging my thumb. Don't be sweet now.

I hide my thrill, starting to believe her warning. I want to trust that I'm the one with the upper hand, but I might just be miserable when she leaves. Not only because she's a wild woman and I want to explore every one of her kinks, but she's a woman who can do things to you in the sexiest manner and laugh with you at the same time. She's a Saint-Gaudens double eagle, not a dime.

I wave my fingers through her hair, brushing it back and grabbing it all in one hand. "Tell me again, once more, what do you want?"

"I want to draw circles on the head of your dick with my tongue." Every word she utters, so slow and soft, drives me wild. Her dilated pupils drift hungrily up my body. I unintentionally tug her hair, the thrill descending, heating my body even more.

"Since you're practically begging..." She's hungry and feral and everything more than I ever expected. Her eyes never falter from mine as she grips the base of my dick, moving her hand in long strokes, taking the tip between her lips. She pulls back to circle and traces it with her tongue. Every time she flicks across the center, I twitch in elation. "Ah, fuck," I groan. "You're never leaving this room again." Wrapping her lips around me, she takes more in, slowly inching down deeper. Feeling her tongue twisting around my girth, her lips widening, I drop my head back and moan. "That's my girl." She gags and draws my attention back to her face. I swear she sees right into my soul with those eyes. She is so determined that she tries again. "Keep going. Please, sweetheart." I exhale. "You feel so good." She gags again but doesn't stop, taking my cock in and out of her mouth. She draws up and down, her hand following from base to head. She gags at the same spot every time.

"Love love love, you're...good." Her tongue's tip glides along my shaft and circles again. I grasp her jaw with my free hand and pull her back down. She gags, and I let go before tugging her hair towards me. "What was that about good guys?" I adjust my hand that's holding her hair, bringing both hands to the back of her head as I thrust into her watering mouth slowly, deep into her throat till she gags harder and her gorgeous eyes begin to water. *She's going to murder me in my sleep.*

"You can do it. We're almost there. Come on, wild." I toy with her, thrusting a little faster, less deep. She squeezes onto my legs. With every pump, I feel the pressure build, the climb that comes from her touch, her feel, and the way she looks up at me. I release my hand from the back of her head and try to pull out, but she slaps my hand back, taking me deep once more. The heaviness radiates in my dick through my body as I coat the back of her throat. She twists her hand up and down, stroking my shaft. My cum runs across her tongue as she holds it out...waiting for my direction? Where did this woman come from? The one who listens, follows directions, and doesn't talk back. I'm never going to figure her out.

My eyes drag over her, and a crooked smile emanates. I wonder how long she can hold it like that. "Swallow me, wild." She runs her tongue across her lip, and I crouch down to her level, running my thumb along her chin, catching what's left before she sucks it clean. "You're amazing."

"Like extra fudge in the middle of a sundae. Sometimes I'll surprise you for shits and giggles. You eat a lot of pineapple?" Turning awkwardly, she almost falls over, reaching for her phone from her pillow. And she's back.

"You're a dirty girl."

"I know, and it's a quarter till eight. I need to shower," she says, dropping her hand to my knee. She sighs, using me as leverage to stand back up. The palm of her hand caresses my jaw. Our naked bodies brush against each other, and I steadily look at her.

"Kiss me."

Her lips softly press to mine, and then she's gone, dropping her hands from my body and turning back to her bag. I stop her, grabbing her wrist. Sliding my hands down her body, I hoist her up by the thighs. "I'm not done with you yet." I kick her suitcase out of the way, setting her on the nightstand. Liquid splashes onto her thighs. The fucking cup of coffee! "Shit. Are you okay?" I frantically look for my towel.

"That was your fault." Her unbothered response eases my racing heart. I would have felt terrible if I had burned her.

"I'm blaming you. Your ass hit it." I grab the cup and set it on the floor, out of sight.

"Did you just call my ass fat?"

I kneel in front of her. "It's juicy." Licking the dripping coffee from her thigh, a grin finds my lips. "I like it. Almost as much as your tight cunt." I push her legs apart, burying my face. Her hands brush through my hair, pulling me closer. She moans, and I nibble at her clit. Her legs wrap around my neck, squeezing, and I grab her ass, tilting her open.

"Casey," she moans, dropping her hands to the sides of the table.

I rest my thumb along her slit, applying pressure, pulling at her clit between my teeth. Her thighs choke me as she tightens more. She's cutting off my oxygen supply.

Her back arches, and her head hits the wall, moaning, riding my face. Her hips roll, dragging deeper. Her body shudders against me, pulling me in, heavy breaths and moans escaping her lips. It's such a fucking turn-on, getting her off.

Her legs fall to my shoulders. That happened quicker than I thought it would, but it lit my ego. I lick her once more, massaging my hands over her legs. Kissing the inside of her thigh before standing up, I admire her exhausted body.

"I can see why Nollan acts like an idiot when you're around."

"Can we not talk about Nollan while I'm naked?" She presses her head back against the wall.

"Why? Is he mad because he couldn't pin you down?" I grab her hands and pull her up to me, holding her taut.

"I'm mad," she snaps in an almost scolding tone. "He..."

"Hey...you can tell me." I brush my thumb across her cheek.

"He's a fucking liar." She bows her head.

"Bailey?"

"You knew?" Her face snaps back to mine, and her eyes level.

"The last few times I was in town, she was with him. I assumed they had something going on."

"Nollan is a long story. I don't want to talk about it standing here *naked*." She points down her body with both hands.

"Sit. Let's talk. No funny business, I promise."

"Shh," she holds her finger to my lips. I bite at it before she drops her hand. "I don't think I can ever talk to him again. I...hate him."

"Wait till he finds out I fucked his little obsession." She gives me her signature sour look. "I'm joking. Personal matters remain personal, no matter how many times you want to call me arrogant. Zipped, locked, and threw out the key." I throw the invisible key over my shoulder.

"What you saw of him was nothing. I've seen worse. You may be kidding when you say I'm his little obsession, but it's the truth, and it's my fault."

"How is it your fault? Did you make all his decisions for him?"

"It's not like that," she says, sitting down on the bed and pulling her legs into a pretzel. She drags her pillow to her lap.

"What's it like then?" I ask, picking up my towel and wrapping it around my waist. I grab a blanket and sit next to her, draping it over both of us and pulling her closer.

"Nollan and I have a lot of history." She looks at the floor with her face wrinkled. "He wanted to marry me. I told him it would never happen, but he went out and bought a ring and planned this big proposal. I can't believe I'm even telling you all of this." Her eyes fall to the floor, but she continues. "I was so angry. He didn't listen, or he didn't understand, and I got put on the spot in front of our families...friends...at this beautiful rooftop restaurant. It's like a nightmare I replay in my head. I see the rope lights in the distance, the stars, how bright they look, and the photographer. Oh, the photographer, it had to be the most traumatic proposal she ever shot."

I brush the hair from her forehead behind her ear. "You can't blame yourself for his choices."

She stares at me with dewy eyes. "I broke his heart that day in front of everyone. I loved him and cared about him, and it hurt. It hurt like hell. It hurt to put an end to everything we had—everything we had been through together. I've known him since I was six years old. I wasn't expecting him to do that, up and propose to me," she says, talking with her hands. "I broke both of our hearts that day. I could never give him the life he wanted."

"What life?"

"The American dream, I guess. A wife, a house with a picket fence, two point three kids."

"None of it?"

"That's not my dream. I want to be free to do what I want. Being a parent is such a selfless decision to take on that responsibility. I don't care if that makes me selfish."

"That doesn't make you selfish, Raine. It makes you human. You have desires in life. They're *your* desires. They don't have to be the same as everyone else."

She looks at me, sedate. "Do you want a wife and kids?"

"Maybe, someday. I'm not in a rush to make a decision."

"Don't your parents nag you about settling down?" She asks.

"Parents?" I shrug. "I lost those long ago."

"I'm sorry." She pulls the blanket over her shoulder, moving closer to me.

"Don't be. My sperm contributor is only dead in my mind. I wasn't joking yesterday about them. My grandfather, on the other hand, is a man worth mentioning. He taught me to work hard, and I'll get what I want in life. Up until now, the only thing I've wanted was financial freedom, to prove I could be successful without my father."

"That's horrible. I mean, I can't imagine not having my parents. They're good people. My mom is incredibly overbearing, but she means well. I lost it with her on Friday. *Raine, you're twenty-nine. You're running out of time.*" She rolls her eyes, making that face I can't get over.

"So I just fucked a cougar," I suck on my lip, and her jaw drops.

"*A what?* How old are you, Casey?" She asks, raising her voice by an octave.

"Twenty-six," I admit.

"God, you made it sound like you're twenty or something." She exhales in relief.

"What if I were? Would you fly home and never speak to me again?"

"I might sleep with you a few times first."

"I'd think a twenty-year-old would be perfect for you. That guy is not looking for marriage. He's not looking for kids. He's looking for a wildcat, *my wildcat.*" I move the blanket and adjust myself on the bed, resting on my arm. "My Grandpa had this weekend house in the mountains. Every time we went there, I would spot one of these beautiful Bobcats at night. The cabin must have been close to home. You had to see them because you would never hear them coming. They're solitary, except during mating season."

"Cool. I'm a loner who just comes around when I want to fuck."

I laugh under my breath. "I'm wrong, you are not a wild-cat. You are—what was that goddess? Pay-Pay?"

"Pele!" She tilts her chin to the ceiling, letting out a giggle.

"Throwing fireballs at me constantly!" I dodge and duck as if she were throwing something. She laughs and falls back against the mattress. I trace her palm, lacing my fingers into hers. "Now I'm going to hold your hand, don't get any ideas to set me on fire. Okay?"

"I don't know, you make me a little nervous. I might accidentally get *hot*."

"You're already hot."

"*Noo*, no. That was so corny. You're so cringe," she says, grabbing onto my forearm with her other hand. Her face scrunches up, sassy. She straightens, and I catch her eyes. I lunge forward and kiss her lips passionately.

"Stop doing this to me," I whisper against her skin.

"I tell you I'm fucked up and never want a life past companionship, and you get turned on? You need more help than I do."

"I could have a life of only companionship if it's with you." She stares at me for a moment. Her green eyes search for my face. I drop her hand and wrap both of mine around her jaw, pulling her lips to mine again.

Her words are soft-spoken. "What would your grandpa think of you having a companionship-only life?"

"My life, my choice."

"Sounds like a smart man."

I look down, twirling a strand of her hair between my fingers. "He was. He passed away two weeks ago."

"Casey...I'm so sorry."

"It's life. We can't live forever."

She smiles softly. "We can live now. Come on," she says, tapping me in the arm and rolling off the bed. She grabs what she wants from her bag and runs across the room, bare ass, into the bathroom.

"What do you want to drink if you don't like coffee?" I yell.

"Orange juice...or water is fine," she replies before sliding the shower door shut.

I get up, adjust my towel, and walk into the main room, heading towards the kitchen. Sebastian and Estella are still on the couch watching TV.

"Well, holy fuck, I thought you were going to be in there all day," Bash says, loudly.

"We'll be out of here by nine," I reply, grabbing two bottles of water out of the fridge.

"I'm guessing the coffee was a good idea," Estella says with an eager grin.

"She hates coffee. Me, on the other hand, she likes."

"You sure it's you and not your horse cock?" Bash clowns.

"Both, haven't you heard?"

Estella palms her face as Bash naturally pings another insult at me. "Yeah, and my attempt to cock block didn't work. Your disgruntled moose noises reigned on."

Hah, fucker. "You know I don't mind an audience."

"You two are ridiculous," Estella interrupts without moving from Bash's side.

"You should know by now who you married."

"And still the best decision I ever made," she flirts.

"Aw, babe." Bash kisses her head. "When are you finally going to let a girl tie you down, Case?"

"Never." I shrug.

"Since when are you against marriage?" He asks.

"Believe it or not, since Raine." Yeah, that sounds bad. Pussy whipped in three days. I said I wasn't going to fall for her. Fuck, why do I do this?

"She brainwashed you in there, didn't she?" He rests his arm along the back of the couch.

"She doesn't want to get married," I reply, casually throwing my hands up. "She's something else, man. If she wants to be with me forever and never get married, I'm sold. Fucking crazy, right? I hardly know her, but I don't want her to leave."

"I told you. When you meet her, you know, even after a day, and you used to call me crazy." He glances at Estella. "I knew right away I was going to marry that one. Now look at this bitchin' rock on her hand," he says, grabbing her fingers and pulling them in the air. His craziness is rubbing off on me.

Shaking my head, I walk back into the bedroom. She's sitting on the floor, tying her shoes. I wonder how much of that she heard. I probably sound like the last guy who wanted to keep her forever, like a fucking psycho, and it's the truth. I like her. I don't want her to go. What am I thinking? Don't date another rich girl; instead, take the first woman I meet who's not a plastic gold-digging bore and immediately claim her as my soulmate.

"Here's a bottle of water," I say, setting it on the bedside table next to the cold cup of coffee that she must have cleaned up from the floor.

"Thanks," she replies. Her hair is pulled back messily, with a few loose strands framing her face. She has a little bit of makeup on, dark leggings, and a slouchy green knit sweater.

"You clean up nice."

"I know. What's the temperature today?" She asks.

"Forty-nine degrees. I'll get you more clothes."

"You might be a little cold like that," she says, trying to hide her grin.

"If someone hadn't gotten me naked, I would be dressed and warm by now." She cracks the cap off the water and takes a drink, her eyes shifting to the side as if she's not accepting the credit nor denying it.

"Bash made eggs around six. There are leftovers in the fridge. There's fruit and oatmeal on the counter. Take whatever you want. I'll be out in a few minutes."

"Okay," she says, walking toward the door. I grab her hand and abruptly pull her to me.

"You're not going anywhere till you kiss me."

"If I let you kiss me, neither of us will be going anywhere, period." I softly kiss her and step back.

"I have more willpower than you."

"Says the guy who tried to guilt me about his blue balls." She replies, walking out the door. The view of her ass never leaves my sight till the door latches behind her.

I am drawn to every aspect of her like a moth to a flame, and she is a ticking time bomb in my possession.

Chapter Eleven | Alliance

MONDAY, AM

Holy Judas Priest. I lean against the door outside the bedroom, knocking my head against it. Scanning the spacious living room, I slide my socks across the hardwood flooring and leave my thoughts of Casey at the door. Catty corner couches surround a rectangular wooden coffee table. An unlit fireplace with a large flat-screen hanging above it plays music at a volume so low that I can't hear it. Large windows frame both sides of the brick fireplace and extend across the front. All the blinds are fully drawn, allowing sunlight to fill the cabin. Beautiful, crisp snow borders the driveway where Casey's SUV is parked. I don't remember it looking this pretty last evening. I was also pretty zombied out.

"Good morning," a voice greets me.

"Hi." I find a beautiful, petite woman with a knife in her hand. "I'm Raine. Sorry about that..." I thumb towards the bedroom door. "Um, noise." Please don't be stabby.

Her smile is soft and comforting. "Hunny, I can't blame you. We've all seen it at least once...not by choice." She stands behind the small island in the kitchen, preparing something.

I suck my lips inward, easing my way over. Ugh, I'm sore. "Mm... He's not really a businessman. He's an exotic dancer, isn't he? Upscale, of course, players' clubs where you have to dress to impress to walk through the doors."

Her pigeon laugh is reassuring. I sit on a stool across from her as she chops greens.

From the staircase, a deep voice emerges. "Casey is Casey. He doesn't give a fuck around us. Confident bugger," he says. "But I'm his lawyer, so I should know the line of business he's in. It's not shaking his joystick for money as far as I know." *His what?* He's the lawyer? The man is big, burly, bearded, and used the phrase *joystick* to describe a penis. He reaches out, gently shaking my hand. "I'm Sebastian. Bash, please, and I see you met my beautiful wife, Estella." He walks around the island to join her, wrapping his arms around her waist and nuzzling against her neck. She looks even tinier in his large arms. I don't know if I'm going to be able to borrow her clothes. I'm not much taller than her, but how my hips don't lie.

"I didn't get a chance to introduce myself yet. Thanks, babe," she replies, setting her knife down and tossing the greens into a blender. "Would you like a smoothie bowl, Raine?"

"I don't want to impose." *I'm starving.*

"There is plenty to go around. Is almond milk okay?" She asks.

"Yes. Thank you."

Bash reaches around her and slides a single, very spotty banana next to the knife. "Put that banana in there, too."

"It's brown and mush."

"It's the last one. I don't want to throw it out," he insists. "It won't taste bad."

"I'm not eating that." She doesn't budge.

"You going to throw me away when I'm this aged?"

She glares deadpan at him. "I'm not putting that in the blender."

"That's insulting. He's a wholesome friend...or fruit."

"Does everything that's dick-shaped need to be a he?" I stretch my fingers across its length. "He's about the same size as Casey, though, so I can see why you're making friends with him. Surround yourself with big banana energy."

"Ahh." He clowns. "Joke's on you because a long tongue is where it's at." He points at me with his spotty banana, then unpeels it and takes a bite. "Long tongue energy," he says with a full mouth.

Estella ignores him, continuing to scoop acai or something with a measuring cup from a container. "Have you been to Bender before?" She asks.

"No. Never. I couldn't pass it up when Casey invited me. I live fifteen minutes from Holiday Resort in New York. I got into snowboarding four and a half years ago, so I've only traveled to a few other mountains."

"Oh, you live in New York near Casey? That area is gorgeous."

"No. Several hours away, actually, but good to know he doesn't live in a dump."

"Babe, they just met Friday," Bash says, finishing his spotted dick banana.

"I'm out of the loop, I guess." She blinks. "Where did you meet?"

"The sexiest place to meet...the hotel gym. And then again, when my ex-boyfriend introduced Casey as his friend after we ran into each other in the lobby." Nollan can eat a bag of dicks.

"Wait. This fucker didn't tell me he stole you from another guy!" Bash says, exhaling excitement.

"I didn't steal her." Casey's voice pulls my attention.

A long-sleeve, heather gray shirt covers his chest, meeting dark jogger sweats. He drapes his arms around me, with his body against my back. I run my fingertips down his forearms. A goofy smile creases my face, and I try to shut it down. Everything with him comes naturally, like the sun rising in the morning and setting each night. Yet I repeatedly fight it. Okay, I like him. He's more than arrogant. Plus, he has a huge fucking dick, too. "I was at the right place at the right time, and she gave me a shot." He walked into my mental breakdown with temptation.

Shortly before he returned to bed, I climbed back under the covers. My ability to sike him out like a dead fish worked. It paid off—running to the bathroom and rinsing my morning breath away with peppermint. I didn't knock him out when I kissed him...as if he'd care. Casey wouldn't judge me or lie. I don't think...Maybe he would...Or maybe he'd tell me in a subtle, snarky way to pop a mint and get back in bed.

If I never see him after this week, I won't regret it. I couldn't forget it either, and by it, I mean *it*. Bigger isn't always better, but Calle got *all* the eggplant emojis I could type in three seconds. She doesn't need to know the part where I held a cold water bottle between my legs while he was in the shower. Neither does his ego. Casey Pierce's body was not just chiseled by Gods, so was his slightly curved to the right cock. She filled half my screen with double the amount of star-struck smiley faces. Oh, wait till I catch Ivy up on what I did during my time off from work. She's going to scold me badly for this one and then envy me.

My thoughts drown out the kitchen banter. My insides clench with the thought of him. His thick, tattoo-covered fingers sliding inside of me. I follow his fingers with mine, knowing where they had been.

"Come on, man." Bash laughs, drawing my attention back to the three of them. Estella raises her eyebrows, waiting to hear his reply before she presses the start button on the blender.

"Tell him, Raine." Casey winks. As he pulls the stool beside me closer and settles in, his hand drops to my waist. His dark stare analyzes me. Which one of us is the bad guy? Me—for almost hooking up with my ex and last-minute switching to the friend? Or him—the man who suddenly appears when I'm having a breakdown *over his friend* and casually sweeps in?

"I have commitment issues." I shake it off, scratching my brow.

"You found your match then. What was your longest relationship, Case? Three months? Might as well call them extended hook-ups."

"Don't listen to him. He's exaggerating."

"Yeah. Casey and the puppy love. It's all fun till the magic fades."

"More like till I realize I'm being used."

Estella presses the blender button, replacing their voices with the machine's loud grinding.

Estella is one of the most genuine humans I have ever met. It's either that or she has a soft spot for Casey. When he called her at the last minute for extra pants and a jacket for a chick she had never met, she didn't protest. I can't say I'd be as willing, especially knowing I'd have to take it on a flight. Add-on luggage fees? No thanks. Oh, right. Her husband is a lawyer.

The bibs are a little snug. Fit better than I expected. And they're pink. Not my favorite color. It's one less thing he'll have to pay for, though. Maybe it's me, learning to survive on a single paycheck. Mentally adding up the cost of everything is as natural as sarcasm.

On top of the snowboarding bags, I toss the light pink bibs and the two-tone jacket into the trunk. Then Casey pulls the hatch down till it latches closed.

With his keys in his palm, he holds out his hand. "You want to drive?"

"Don't ask me twice." I grab the black keyfob, pinching the blue plastic tag between my fingers. Playfully running to the driver's side, I open the door and hop in, adjusting everything I can adjust.

Casey sinks into the passenger seat and closes his door. "There is a small board shop about ten minutes down the road. Turn right down here." Clicking his seatbelt into place, he tilts his head at my Chucks. "We need to get you some boots. Those won't cut it." Looking over his shoulder, he calls to the angel of a woman in the backseat. "Stell, thanks for bringing extra gear. I owe you."

I pull the car down the gravel driveway to the road, looking in both directions before pulling out onto the pavement.

"I know how you can repay me," she replies.

"How?" Casey looks back and forth between the two in the backseat. "What is it?"

"How does being a Godfather sound?" She asks.

"Like I should brush up on my Italian." His eyes shift, and he smiles at me before returning to them.

Bash's boisterous laugh fills my ears. "No, a Godfather to our son."

"What!" His yell is like a whisper. Casey's forehead is full of lines, and his jaw hangs. "You're pregnant?" His voice grows in pitch.

"Not yet. He's *hoping* for a son. A daughter would be great, too."

"We're trying! It's pretty fun." I catch a glimpse of him winking before the echo of skin-to-skin contact. Estella gave him a whack for that comment.

"I'm honored." He sinks back into his seat, lasting seconds. Twisting back, the utter surprise illuminates his voice. "You trust me to take care of your kid, Stell?"

"You're our brother. We know he *or she* would be in capable hands," she says. Out of the corner of my eye, I catch him staring at me, his eyes cascading over my face. "Plus, you couldn't teach them anything worse than Bash can."

"Where am I going?" To avoid someone asking me about kids, I interrupt, changing the subject.

"Take the next exit."

A silver hatchback curves into my lane. "Come on, asshole!" My hand shoots up as I slam on the brakes.

"Yeah, asshole!" Casey yells.

I point and slap my hands against the leather. "The asshole cut me off."

"Fucking asshole," Casey replies.

"Motherfucking asshole," Bash yells.

"Total asshole," Estella adds.

I try not to laugh, letting out a giggle when I see Casey's huge, dimpled grin.

"Hey, Casey," I call.

"Yes?"

"I like your friends."

"Hey, Raine!" Bash leans his face to the side of my headrest and whispers. "We like you too. Just don't get us killed."

I let my forearm fall to the center console, sharply glancing back at him. As I straighten, the console lid flings open.

"What is this?" I nab the blue rectangular device from the compartment. "You could cut bra straps with this!" Before denying my impulsive, intrusive thought, I damn near hook it to the collar of my top.

Casey takes it from my flattened palm. "A lot of these rentals have emergency seat belt cutters in them, surprisingly."

"That's a good idea. They won't know it's missing." Bash holds out his hand. "Give it to me." His wife smacks his hand away, surely giving him another displeased glare. Casey shakes his head and puts it back in the compartment, latching the lid.

"Fucking lawyers. Think they're above the law," Casey sneers.

"Bitch, I am the law."

"I thought that was cops," I point out.

"No, Judge Dredd is the law," Bash argues.

"Bro, that's the same thing," I push back. "He's a dystopian officer."

"How do you know that?" His jaw hangs. "Casey, wife her up or lock her up. She's a keeper. A comic bookkeeper." He nudges Casey on the shoulder.

"Oh no. You started him up now." Her tone settles into tartness. "He's not going to stop talking about comics."

"You like to dress up in tights and a leotard, then pretend to fly? Actually, strike that. I don't want to know your kinks. We shouldn't talk about anything comic-related in case you get a hard-on. I've heard that's embarrassing in public...for some people."

His face stones over. "Damn, cutthroat. What do you do for a living?"

"Stare at computer screens in hopes they do all the work for me, and I can continue to eat popcorn in my pajamas at six AM."

"If you ever want to branch out, my office could use someone like you."

"If I'm going to change careers, it will be something far more exciting."

Bash and Casey exchange looks. Then he points. "Right up here, love."

Shit, I clipped in too early. Penguin walking, I catch up to Calvin—Casey's friend, who routinely does guided tours for special groups—AKA *his connection*. Overcast skies and fresh snow. It's gorgeous...and bizarre. This is what it's like to be him? Getting into places before the masses. I've never seen a mountain this empty.

Front knee bent, back knee straight. Press and rotate.

"What was that?" Casey yells. I twist to see him, blacked out in gear, from his helmet to his boots.

"Butter 180."

"No, it wasn't! It was a challenge," he calls. "It's a challenge, Bash! She's getting cocky over here. Eat some POW!"

Bash hoots, taking a side hit, a small jump, on the run, and grabs his board in the air. "I'll snort it too!" He yells back.

Casey hits a backside 180, catching air and flashing me with a big, arrogant smile like he won. It's only a low-rotation trick. I'll just let him think that for now.

"You snort stuff." I nod. "Explains a lot."

"Yeah, it explains why I'm friends with Casey, but what's your excuse?"

"Entertainment purposes." I instantly eat my words, catching the toe side of my board. Bending my elbows, I'm unable to avoid the fall and drop to my forearms.

Bash laughs. He's too far away for me to catch what he's saying.

Go snort snow.

Casey cuts below me, stopping. "Is this that coordination I heard so much about?" I wish he could see my face right now, behind the mask and goggles. He holds his gloved hand out, and I reach for him. The second his fingers close around my palm, I yank, pulling him to the snow. I like his mouth better when he's on his knees.

"Bash is so smooth with his comebacks, I felt weak." The back of my hand meets my helmet. "I almost died. For my survival, I only see one option. He has to keep his big mouth shut the remainder of the day."

"You'd better feed him then. Only time he's quiet." He knocks his helmet against mine. "Then feed me. You know how well I eat." He makes my stomach knot just in time to stand up, leaving me swooning. "Pull me down later." He holds out his hand for a second time, with faith I won't drop him to his knees again. Without his assistance, I pop back up.

"I got this." Like the Pillsbury Doughboy, I poke him near his belly button and curve down the slope. Hell yeah.

We spent most of the day riding like it was home away from home. A moment replays in my head: *Bash penguins his board, somehow managing to faceplant. Heavily laughing, Casey tries to avoid colliding with Estella.* It gives me this stupid, warm feeling in my stomach. Butterflies.

Bash again made reservations for dinner at The Lodge Restaurant after two of us missed out last night. The food was so good. Casey didn't even dress up in his overachiever suit and tie. I preferred his charcoal-rolled long-sleeve button-down and fitted jeans anyway. It was a relief that we didn't go to an upscale, black-tie-only venue.

I make my way from the massive, wrapped-around dining deck to a covered bridge below, overlapping a creek. Massive rocks line the water's border, and a woman closes her notepad, giving me a polite nod on her way past me up the rocks. I take her spot on the broad, flat surface, wrapping my arms around my bent knees. It's cold and damp, but cleared of the scattered patches of snow. My phone pings; this is the second text I received from Ivy today. I should reply.

I need a vacation. How's yours going?

I have sooo much to tell you.

You didn't hook up with your ex, did you?

> Better. One of his friends.

Girl, what the hell?

> Get on Insta and look him up. Casey Raiden Pierce.

Hold on.

This is a fake account. That man was created with Photoshop or AI. You're pulling one over on me.

> I almost wish I was. He's real. Very real. Maybe 'roids. Didn't affect his dong. I'll tell you about it when I get back.

Are you still with him?

> Yep. I swear I'll tell you everything asap. Gotta run. Love, love, love.

Stay safe. Love you.

"There you are." I tuck my phone away as Casey approaches. He sits next to me, his shoulder brushing against mine. I smile at him, then look back at the creek.

"Do you ever wonder what it would be like to live underwater?" My attention doesn't leave the rapids.

"All the time." He replies impassively.

I glance over, creasing my nose. "Stop fucking with me."

"I'm not going to do that, love."

I stare deadpan at him. "Think about it. Could you imagine communicating without actual words and being able to fully comprehend one another, respect one another? Well...if you don't give respect, you're eaten."

"Raine, you're making this too easy for me."

"Gutter brain, you have an *ocean beast* permanently printed on your skin. Have you never thought about what it would be like?"

"Like Atlantis?" He picks up a pebble, tossing it into the water.

"Atlantis is fiction, but yeah, if it were real, would you dive to the depths to see it? Live in a parallel world?"

"With my dying breath," he admits. "That would be on my bucket list."

"Mine too." I have a mental list that's so long that I doubt I'll ever finish it in this lifetime.

"You're weird. Don't get me wrong, I like it. It's entertaining."

"Normal is overrated...like decorative pillows on the bed. They look pretty, but you just throw them on the floor, never actually having use for them."

"That's a *colorful* analogy." He taps my knee. "What else is on your bucket list?"

"Chase a tornado," I reply, straight-faced.

A deep chuckle rolls from his throat.

"It's not that funny."

"Sorry. It was an unexpected answer." He exhales another short laugh, nudging my knee with his knuckle. "I guess I don't know what I expected. Uh, what else?"

"Dance on the beach in a foreign country."

He lets his lower lip protrude. "Specific, but doable." With his nod, I continue.

"Get on stage at a rock show, swim in every ocean, take a trip in a hot air balloon." I could have done that last one multiple times. Somehow, my trust issues interfere with my sense of adventure when it comes to festival workers and heights. Unless it's a major theme park, count me out. I'm not riding the big wheel you put together three hours ago, bud.

"Even the Arctic?" After a three-second dip, my titties may have cut ice. I could use them to carve myself out if I ever get trapped under ice.

"I'll try anything once." I quickly catch myself. "Almost anything." Before he hits me with another innuendo, I lift my shoulders, sighing. "What's on yours?"

"Go to Oktoberfest."

"I thought you said you *hardly* drink?" I side-eye.

"It still sounds like an experience, you know, like Mardi Gras in Louisiana." I picture him being flashed by hundreds of women, all desperate for his attention, and a massive amount of bead necklaces hanging from his neck. That *doesn't* make me jealous.

"Right." I shift on my rock seat. "What's one thing you already checked off your list?"

He rubs his finger over his chin, looking up to the clouds. "Mardi Gras." He smirks. Please do not go into details. I do not want to hear about how Sally Big Boobs and six of her friends went back to your suite for a private party. *I don't care who you were with before or after me.* It was something along those lines, he said.

"Totally because of your religion."

"I'll give another. I watched twenty-eighties movies after that trend on, shit, what's that app?" He tilts his chin up, searching for the answer. "Whatever it was, cult classics or something."

I laugh, pushing my hair behind my ear. Nice save. He's probably talking about Knack. "There are like...two communities. Creators who make short movies and those who discuss them?"

"Yeah. Are you on it?"

"Knack. Yeah, mostly for the book trailers."

"What kind of books do you like?"

"Dictionaries, remember?"

"Non-fiction aside, I like the occasional dystopian."

"I like romance."

"I didn't take you for a hopeless romantic. You give more of a horror feel."

"I'd expect that from a guy who learned his dance moves from Dirty Dancing."

"I think you can attest, those were sensual moves." His hand brushes my knee. "I liked those movies, the 80's hits. I find it...funny, how in teen movies the parents are never around. It's familiar." Our eyes meet, and his smile reappears.

I revert to talking about myself, unsure of what to say to him. "My Mom was always hovering, but she liked Nollan, so I got away with stuff that I swear wouldn't have floated with anyone else." Feels like a lifetime ago. I clear my throat and continue. "Were you the hot, popular guy or the smart, dorky nerd?"

"Believe it or not." He leans closer to whisper. "I wasn't the popular guy."

"You were a nerd!" I suck in air, squealing.

"Take it easy with that word. I wasn't like a loner or anything. I would have rather played video games—poorly—than party. You'd kick my ass if we played." He smirks. "Bash was the only reason I went to the parties."

"You're such a people person. It's hard to believe."

"You think I'm lying?" His shoulders slump, and he presses his elbows against his knees.

"No, no. Whatever line you want to give me, I'll take it with a grain of salt."

"Where did you fall in the high school hierarchy?" He lifts his chin.

"Um..." I giggle. "The skater-stoner kids."

"You hung out with the deadbeats?"

"Skaters, bro." Nollan & I weren't allowed to be degenerates. "Have you met Declan?" I lean back, dropping my chin toward my chest. "His dad's one-car garage was our hang-out. He worked the graveyard shift, so in a sense, we had *no parents around, an eighties movie thing* going for us. My mom was a quick call away, always checking up on me."

He laughs deeply. "Declan, I believe. Nollan? He could skateboard?" He skips another rock across the water.

"He broke his arm once. Told his mom that a cow ran over him while walking home from school."

"A cow?"

"He stuck with that story. Really committed to it."

"He is a great salesman," Casey admits. "What did you check off your list?"

"Kissing a stranger," I say, looking down as something draws my attention. Reaching between two rocks below me, I pick up a black permanent marker. The woman who was drawing must have dropped it. I twirl it through my fingers, catching Casey running his hand over the back of his neck. "I'm suddenly feeling like a teenage dirtbag." I nod at his black Converse shoes, crawling to the rock below us. "Don't move." Pushing my knees against the rough edge to balance my uncomfortable, obscure hunching squat, I pull the cap off and fix it to the top. Pressing the felt tip to the white rubber of his shoe, I write in thick black lines.

"The guys at the gym are going to pest the shit out of me for this, you know."

"Yep. It could've been a dick." Popping the cap back on, I nudge him. "If you don't like it, buy a new pair."

"What if I do like it?" He asks.

I hold back a smile. "Then you're in luck. You now have a custom pair of Raine Chucks."

"*I heart Raine*," he reads. "It's not a lie."

My eyes dance over him, bracing myself against his strong legs. I climb back to my rock, and the damp cold returns to my butt and legs.

"Do you have a passport?" He asks.

"Um, well yeah," I pause, taken aback. "I went to Blue Mountain last season." My first trip to Canada. The resort home we rented for a week was great. I'd go back any day. "Why?" He's going to ask me to go riding somewhere else. No. I can't do that. Well...I could. In another month or two, I'll catch another weekend getaway with him.

"My friend, Alistair, is getting married next weekend. It'll be intimate, but I'm granted a plus one."

"You want to take me?" Red flag. Red flag alert. Stage four clinger. Back the fuck up and pack the fuck up. "I've never met these people, and I've known you for a total of what? Fucking...four days?"

"It'll be seven days by the wedding. It's Saturday."

"Oh, a whole week." I bat my lashes. "You do realize that only someone with a death wish does this kind of stuff, right?"

"Goes to a wedding?"

I deadpan. "Running around the country with a stranger. It's equivalent to hitchhiking and thinking it's going to be smooth sailing after the trucker picks you up. Meanwhile, your friend who's getting married is wondering who the rotting carcass is that you brought with."

"He's going to be mind-blown that I even have a date. Rotting or fresh fleshed. Every single person I consider my friend knows I do what I want, and that means taking you to Italy, enjoying a wedding, and then fucking you to oblivion on the hotel balcony like you deserve, love."

"Hmm?" My eyes widen, blinking rapidly. What. In. The. Forking Fuck? "Did you just say Italy?" I lean towards him, holding my hand on my forehead.

"Lake Como, Italy," he replies, unbothered. "So, outside the country, too. You'll be running outside of the country with the...serial killer? Is that me? Look, I don't like blood."

My jaw drops, gawking. "Italy?"

He laughs. "Italy, Raine. Come with me. Run away with me again?" He asks, taking my hand. "Colorado today, Italy next weekend, maybe Thailand after that. I've heard they have great food."

"Bangkok, huh? Um...I wasn't expecting anything past this weekend." Swallowing, I stare at the water for a moment. "I would have to check with work. See if I can rearrange any assignments." *This is not real.* I'm dreaming. It's an all-expenses-paid trip to beautiful Italy with unlimited access to Eros, the God of love and sex. This is a steaming pile of horse shit, and I don't believe it. He'll cancel the day before. Guaranteed.

"It's a weekend, Raine. Don't you have off?" He demands answers. "What's it that you do for a living again?"

"I just took a week off."

"You do something with computers? You were telling Bash."

"I work for a company called Eleanor." I shouldn't have told him that. "I'm a copy editor," I softly scramble to hide my slip-up.

"And what does a copy editor do?" As he questions me, I look at him. His tongue rolls across his front teeth while his eyes intently fixate on me.

"I'm basically a human spell check. I read documents and check for errors and consistency, among other things."

"So you work from a computer, I'm guessing remotely, and you wouldn't have any meetings on the weekend?" He nods.

"Yeah. It's a pretty flexible..." I push my tongue to my cheek. "Shut up, I'm in." I'll double up on assignments and not sleep for two days.

"You'll be my plus one?"

"Is that whole balcony thing a promise?"

"Pinky swear." He extends his smallest finger toward me, and I wrap mine around his.

"One more condition." I tuck my chin and smirk. "You have to go dress shopping with me."

"Watch you try on a bunch of sexy dresses? No problem."

I loop my little finger around his. We're going to Queens & Cuties. Hands down. He wants me. He's got me.

It's been too long since I've visited Amie. I'll introduce him to Ivy and Elias. All of my friends will know if something happens to me; this is the guy responsible, and he has a shark of a lawyer.

"Hey, Estella." I collapse on the couch, catty-corner from her.

"I told you, call me Stell," she insists.

"*Stell*," I sass. "Are you and Bash friends with Alistair?" The fireplace lights the dim cabin, and a song I'm unfamiliar with is playing in the kitchen from a square wireless speaker.

"Yes, and his fiancé, Ginevra. Why? Did Casey invite you to the wedding?" She sits up straight, clasping her hands in her lap.

"He did. It's kinda last-minute. Less than a week away." I tuck my blanket underneath my legs.

"He must really like you." Her smile broadens before she picks up her brown marbled mug from the coffee table and brings it to her lips.

"Why's that?"

"This wedding has been planned for nearly two years. He hasn't asked anyone else to go. Plus, Casey isn't the type to make impulsive decisions." *And I am.*

"Lucky me." I clench my jaw.

"You don't want to go?" She holds her mug close.

"Italy, yes, a wedding...not so much."

"Oh, I love weddings, especially ceremonies." It's obvious, she's internally squealing over the idea of the romantic exchange. Someone else ask me why I read romance books and watch predictable rom-coms. "It's going to be beautiful. Why don't you like weddings?"

"I'm totally all about the romance," I snide.

"I saw Casey's shoe," she says, sucking her cheek in. "That's sweet, Raine. Romantic gestures come in all forms."

"Branding. Sweet." I nod, taking my lip in my mouth. "Okay, I'll make sure it's to skin next time."

"I know you only met Case a few days ago, but I'm sure he's already been whining and dining you. Even if romance is not your forte, he has it mapped out. Did Casey tell you I met him before I met Bash?" She asks.

"Nope."

"He was very much a gentleman. He introduced me to Bash at a winery event." She sips her tea. "I was a little nervous and had one too many samples. Embarrassing, right?" She shakes her head to the side, almost ashamed to admit it. "Casey had to attend to a business colleague before we could leave, and Bash ditched his date, picked me up, and carried me to the car. We talked for fifteen or twenty minutes before Casey finally joined us. I overheard Bash telling Casey he was going to marry me. Casey gave him the key to his car. Just like that. Sebastian was a total asshole for leaving his date, but he drove me to my apartment, helped me to the door, and asked if he could see me again. I gave him my number and the rest is history."

"He talked to you for fifteen minutes and knew he wanted to marry you?" If *what the fuck* was an expression, it would be on my face right now. I thought I was impulsive, but that is some stalker-grade impulsive shit. I hide my clenched teeth.

"He's a lot." Her lips press together, smiling softly. "Loud and blunt, and kind, caring, intelligent, witty, and passionate." Her eyes light up. They're full of love and joy, talking about him. Yet, I can't help...

"And you didn't have feelings for Casey?" It's a reasonable question.

"I knew him for a few weeks. I love Casey as family; he's a brother now. Back then, I thought he was a bit of an arrogant playboy. He was kind. It's his *tone.*" Her long lashes flutter.

"Satirical." I point out.

"Opposites attract. That's Bash and me." Her soft laugh makes me smile. "Now, I see the similarities between you and Casey. You two, you're twin flames. He needs someone like you."

Twin flames. I thought it was a dumb statement that celebrities had brought to light. Estella's saying it, however, makes it sound more meaningful. She's right. Casey mirrors me in many ways. Is he...he can't be that one in a million. The one in a million Calle only believed existed in elderly men with racks on racks—who don't know what that means.

I pull my lip into my mouth. *He needs someone like you.*

"Did you ever sleep with him?"

She smiles tightly. "That's a straightforward question."

"I'll take a straightforward answer. I don't need the details." I smile, unsure if she's uncomfortable with the question.

"No," Casey sternly answers.

"Just saw your dick," I respond, looking over my shoulder at him with a big cheesy grin on my face that I can't manage to hide.

"She's seen far more vagina than penis."

"That's out of context." Her eyes flash between us. "I'm a resident gynecologist." I rub my eyes, shaking my head.

"If you have any concerns, she's an open book." Behind me, he leans his arms along the back of the couch.

Stell palms her face, dropping her head. Here, I was afraid of making her uncomfortable, and he did it effortlessly in not even two full sentences.

"Casey, stop talking about your horse rod." Bash walks to the kitchen, grabs an apple, and takes a bite.

"I favor male doctors, though, sorry, Stell."

"Want to go play doctor?" He whispers in my ear, although everyone hears him. I swear he has a dress-up closet at his house. The man desperately wants to pretend to be a doctor.

"Can I watch?" Bash says, walking into the living room with his free hand in the air as if he's in a classroom, asking for a turn to speak. Casey chuckles, raising his eyebrows at me.

"All three of you are disturbed," Estella interrupts. "My job is far from sexual."

"Baby baby baby," Bash flops on the couch beside her. "You know, I only have eyes for you." He wraps his arm around her, and she takes his hand, weaving her fingers through his. "We weren't making fun of your job. You're a professional. We know."

I tilt my head back, looking up at Casey. I wonder what it would be like to fall in love with him. He lifts his hand from the couch and places it on my jaw, along my chin, extending my head back farther. Bending down, he presses a kiss on my lips, and his hand slides down my neck. I swallow hard against him, fading into his dark eyes.

"Let's go," he whispers along my ear, biting the cartilage, before releasing his hold and walking to the bedroom. As he reaches the door, I look back to Estella and Bash. His arm is wrapped around her waist. A wicked grin rises on his face as we make eye contact. He pulls Estella onto his lap, bringing her face to his. They lock lips, and I find Casey leaning against the door with his arms crossed over his chest, one ankle overlapping the other. He lifts one hand and curls two fingers, calling me over.

Walking into the dark room, I close the door behind me, quickly pinned between Casey's hands against the wood.

"Is it always like this?" I ask, flicking my thumb backward. His lips trail down my neck.

"Sexually open?" He kisses my jaw and steps back. His eyes float over my body as he sits on the edge of the bed. "It's not taboo, Raine. It's human nature. We're sexual beings. We're comfortable talking and joking about it, well, for the most part. Stell has heard all the pussy jokes and wants to kick our asses." His lips curve.

"Have you ever..." *I shouldn't ask.*

"Have I ever?" He leans back onto his burly forearms. "I'm an open book."

"Got it in while, like...in the same room?"

"No. I'm not into group play." He doesn't flip the pineapple upside down. "It's not for me." His words steady. "Is that one of those sex *things* you want to tell me about? Voyeurism?"

"It's kind of exciting. It seemed like you were into it earlier."

"I'm used to being interrupted. I mean, shit. With a previous partner, monogamous. Can't fuck in a hot tub without being walked in on when the guys are around."

I walk to the bed, standing between his legs. "Give me your hand." I'm about to do something I've only fantasized about, never imagining I'd have the opportunity or the right place and time, but nothing like the present. My mind is more experienced than I am, and that's okay because Casey's the right guy to experiment with. "Do you trust me?"

"Not at all."

"Casey," I squeeze his hand.

"Yes," he elongates in a grunt. "What is it?"

I pull at his hand, and he rises to meet me, his body mere inches from mine. To meet his glare, I look up. Rolling my hands down his chest over the soft cotton fabric, I pinch the hem, dragging it up his body to expose his firm abdomen and broad pecs. He fists the fabric outside of my hands and pulls his shirt over his head, dropping it. I turn away from his kiss and then return to his lips, letting my mouth hover over his, pulling away every time he tries to connect. Edging and teasing, my heart races heavier. Should I do this? Yes. Ask him.

"Are you open?" I whisper against his skin.

He chases my lips. "I'm listening."

I glance at the door. "Bash and Stell are hooking up out there. We would make out and touch and, um, feel...on the other couch. It would be tame. Nothing anyone hasn't seen on a big screen."

"I'm in," he agrees. His mouth meets my jaw. "It sounds hot." He kisses me once more. "Bash will speak up if he has a problem."

"Really?" I grab his hand before he can reply, leading him to the door. I open it, then walk back into the living room. Bash and Estella are at the same spot. Bash's shirt now hangs over the arm.

Casey looks at them and back at me. His dark eyes flicker. Where's that arrogant man of steel?

"Am I making you nervous?" I taunt in a whisper. His own words, used against him.

"What are your plans, wild? You're the mastermind behind this one."

"I'll show you." Returning to the couch we left, I steer Casey where I want him, gently pressing on his shoulders until he sits down. His friends both glance over at us. He shrugs them off with a smile in his eyes. The wireless speaker still plays, lips smack against one another, and my heart plays a rhythm that I can't seem to slow.

I kneel on the hard floor between Casey's legs, ignoring the discomfort. My hands run up the silken microfiber fabric along his legs as I look up at him. Did I run toward adventure and snow, or was it him? Was it him the whole time? Was it this moment right here? That view of the tattoo under his chin? The hills of his arms? His soft, gentle eyes that cater to me one minute and challenge me with encouragement the next?

I bring my hands to his jeans, cascading over the cotton threads, up to his belt. He stretches his arms back to put his hands behind his head as he watches me unfasten the silver hook. *God.* My lips part, then close again, unable to come to terms with how truly large he is. I trace the outline pressing against his pants. The curvature. The swoop of his cut head. I pull his belt twice until he lifts enough for the leather to slide free. Crawling up from the floor to straddle him, I waver above his thighs.

"Still trust me?" I whisper against his ear.

"I see through you, wildcat," he replies. "Kiss me."

I grind against his boxers, rolling my hips and devouring his taste. A flick of his tongue here and there beneath body-shuttering kisses, continuously deepening against my lips.

"I want more."

His eyes shift, unable to stop gripping my ass and sucking at my lips.

"Love, please...slow down."

"You turn me on."

"Where's the off?" I pull away and glare at him. "I'm kidding," he mouths. "Bash," he calls.

"Uh?"

"Cool if I get my dick out?"

"Do you?" He waves, holding his weight with the other hand.

Casey's thick fingers cup my chin, drawing me in for a gentle kiss. "You have my permission."

With Casey's belt in hand, I loop it through itself and lay it on his lap. I place my hands on his big arms, straightening them above his head. My chest is in his face as I lean into him, picking up the belt. I slip the belt cuffs over his hands, tightening them slightly at the wrist as I pull the end of the leather. I descend back down his body, causing his hands to relax behind his head.

"You're mine now, Casey Pierce," I whisper against his neck.

"Promise?"

The moment suddenly becomes intimate, as if we are alone. I have always had a distraction waiting, an interruption. When I wanted it, it was an easy way out. Is that what this fantasy is about?

I don't want that anymore.

The exit strategy isn't something I need with him. He is the exit. The escape. After the chaos, there was relaxation. I never want the scent of sandalwood and birch to fade, the dark look he gives me when I take control, and never do I want to go a day without hearing his acrimony, the sarcastic prick. I'm an idiot. Insta-love isn't real. Yet, here

I am, melting into a puddle of pussy juice and *pick me, princess.*

"Pinky promise." I tangle my fingers through his dark, soft hair. His eyes never leave me.

I kiss his jaw...his neck...his collarbone. My tongue runs circles over his nipple, feeling it harden, and I trail down to his navel, stopping before a light trail of dark hair. I drag my fingertips down the deep V that cuts above his unbuttoned jeans and reach along the waistband, tugging. He pushes to the floor, lifting his hips for me to shimmy them down. I stand, pushing his clothing to his ankles.

In my peripheral vision, I see Estella move. She stands, taking Bash's hand, and he rises. She doesn't even glance in our direction as she leads him to the stairs. Before disappearing, Bash tilts his head to the side and mouths yes, flicking his tongue and shaking his other fist in the air at Casey.

It escalated. All of this is insane. Who does this shit? I should stop. No, fuck it. Live for today, for bliss, for excitement, for sexual awakening, and for human desire. Regret nothing. When it's over, and I'm a bitter catless granny, I'll know I never ran away because I was scared. I ran towards me and my happiness.

I pull my top over my head and drop it. I slid my jeans down, letting them fall to the floor next. Ah fuck. This is going to hurt. Why does his dick have to be fucking eight or nine? I don't know, too much girth, too?

Kneeling over him, I smooth my hand down my warm skin, moving the gusset of my panties to the side. I circle my clit before sliding two fingers into my wet cunt. Pulling them out, I bring my fingers to his lips. He leans forward, lapping his tongue around me and sucking them into his mouth, his teeth running over my skin.

"Mm," he hums.

I brace myself over the smooth tip of his cock, gliding my fingertips over the vein that travels up the center of his length, slowly guiding him into me. Inching him in, my breath weakens, cutting out, and waiting for my lungs to refill. I should have known it would be too much too soon, sleeping with him again today after this morning. Motherfucker.

"I can't hold you down this time," he murmurs against me, as I lean into him. "I know you want to take it all. You want every inch inside of you, but take it easy, love." I don't answer, slipping deeper into him. He exhales a quiet moan. "You like to prove me wrong. I should use reverse psychology on you often."

"Shut up, Casey." I take the rest of him and the burn that comes with it. His thick, muscular thighs widen, pushing mine out further. I sink deep into him, using all that I have left to pull up. Those devious eyes run up and down my body.

"You wanted me, you wanted this," he whispers. "Come on, baby, keep going. Keep going for me. I want to see you cum." His demands invade my body. Every word is an assault, tackling the part of my brain that is telling me to take it easy, overriding the voice of reason with inflamed desire. "Just like that, come on."

In slow motion, I lift myself up and roll my hips back down. Then again, faster. I continue wrapping my hands around his enormous triceps. I lose focus on him. He keeps saying these words that set me over the edge, but they're fading under my breathless body, the pressure rising between my legs. It's building so fast—faster than it does when I'm home at night with my vibrator—and I don't know how I'm reaching the edge effortlessly faster than before.

Heavy breathing, moaning, and my arousal had traveled like sound waves. Now, all has vanished. Rhythmic contractions pulse through me. Grinding deeper against him, only intensifying every pulse, I fall to his chest, digging into his arms, moaning uncontrollably. His hips tilt, moving the pressure closer to my clit. They dip back down, only to return again. I tighten around his length. Just as I come off my orgasm, he drops his face into the curve of my neck, gently biting at the base. His intense breathing, behind his locked jaw, conceals his moans. The pain and pleasure fuse. Warmth and pressure return to my tensed pussy, setting another wave through my body. More fractious moans break out between my lips, my back arching passionately. And like that, I'm stripped of energy, plummeting to his shoulders as we both breathe against each other, mine more laborious. *Twice? Twice!* I'm playing the lottery when I get home.

"I thought you were going to make me do all the work this time?"

I smack one hand against his hard chest. "I guess I like the control a little too much."

"I don't mind it," he exhales.

"I can tell." I sit back, looking down at his glistening skin from the friction between our bodies. "I think you're going to need to sterilize this couch now."

He chuckles. "Think you need to untie me first."

"That wouldn't be any fun. Watching you try to escape would be more entertaining."

"I don't want to make you dripping wet for a third time today."

"Watching you clean would positively soak my panties like a waterfall." I raise my chin and stick my tongue out, rolling it.

"You have some cleaning of your own to do first with that pretty mouth." His dick shudders inside of me. "I'm not exaggerating either. Your lips are fucking beautiful."

"Don't beg."

I push from my thighs, gently lifting my body away from him. *Where's the ice?*

I kiss his smooth jaw, reaching to unstrap the belt from his wrists. He could have escaped them at any time if he wanted. The leather was never tight to his balmy skin. Despite this, he rubs his wrists as if they were constricted. His hands fold around my hovering thighs, rolling his fingers over the wet mixture on my inner thigh.

Two fingers from his free hand sail over my swollen cunt. I squirm and look down. Cum drips from his fingers. I slide to my knees and look up at him, grabbing his wrist and sucking his wet fingers into my mouth. The salty warmth settles on my taste buds. *Blegh.* I want to go mouthwash right now, but I'm not telling him that. It's a turn-on, sure. Unfortunately, it never tastes like whipped cream. Instead, I take them again, running my lips over one, pulling it back out, and taking the other in, my eyes never leaving his. *Vomit as fuck.*

"If you don't call me, I'm hunting you down," he mutters.

"What happened to never chasing me?"

My tongue circles his cut head, rolling over the wet bead in the center. I lick from the base to the tip slowly, my hand stroking back his dark, curled strands. A mixture of sweetness and salt, it's slightly better than the lone salty warmth.

"I'm never letting you leave," he says, weaving his hand through my hair.

"I'm yours," I reply, knowing that eventually, I'll have to go back to reality. I don't live in that world right now. This is fun…playing pretend. Now I see why kids are happier than adults. Here I thought it was the lack of jobs, bills, taxes, and corrupt small-dick energy that runs the world.

Steadying my hands on his knees, I stand, adjusting my panties. "Wanna join me in the shower?" I bend over and pick up both of our clothes and his belt, then extend my free hand. His fingers run across my palm, taking my hand.

I drop our clothes on the bedroom rug and proceed to the shower. Sliding open the glass door, he waves his hand. "Ladies first." The cold water hits my toes, and I sink back into him.

"Yes, I'm very lady-like." I glance up at him.

"Fine. Hoes first."

My jaw drops for a second, and then I pinch my lips together. Touché. "What happened to promiscuous?" I step into the water, having warmed.

Casey closes the glass door behind him. "You are far too dirty for *promiscuous*, wildcat." He grabs my chin, pulling my lips to his. He orbits around me, sticking his head under the showerhead.

Water cascades down his back, over every contour, down his spine, and over his firm ass. He turns back to me, blinded by water. It runs over his flattened hair. Streams of connecting droplets descend down his neck and chest, and I breathe in his aroma. I grab the bar of soap and a washcloth hanging on the door, lathering it over his bare body.

"My turn." He takes the cloth from my hand and moves it over my breasts. I hum, dropping my shoulders. It's pure calm and relaxation—a spa I didn't ask for. I reach for the knob, turning it to the left.

"Shit, woman. Are you trying to melt my skin off?" He shrieks.

I scrunch up my nose at him. "Oh, come on, sissy."

"What did you call me?" He wraps his arms around me, pulling me tight to his chest and tickling my sides. I struggle, trying to wiggle away from him as I laugh. He stops, holding me, and I look into his dark eyes. Struck.

How he's found a way under my skin and into my head…it was my drunken dramatics that told him my short story. I accidentally invited him in, and I purposely let him explore my brain now. Fairytales are bullshit…Why does it feel like I'm in one?

"Would you wash my seventy-year-old body like this?" Of all things to say in an intimate moment, that's what I felt was necessary? Well, I had to ruin it somehow.

His brows rise, a short, deep laugh following. "I'm hoping you stay twenty-nine forever." I close my eyes, turning my head away from the water. "As long as you're with me, I'm going to take care of you, beautiful. Fight me the whole way, I'm patient."

"I don't know why I asked you that." I try to laugh it off, evading his eyes. "Calle got inside my head the other day. We had this *great* conversation about sugar daddies."

"I knew you wanted me to be your daddy."

"I never said I wanted *you* to be my *sugar* daddy. I wanted a rich old dude who would just hang out and spend money on me. According to the requirements of being a sugar baby, I need to hang out in multiple ways, so I'm already thinking that I don't qualify. Then she *had to* ask me who would take care of me in sickness and some other bullshit." I press my finger to his lips. "Don't commit to that." Quickly, I shrug it off. "Nurse bitchy Brenda, who decided she wanted to change adult diapers for a living and therefore can't snap herself out of her monotone mood, will be dealing with my sour ass," I ramble. "Fuck, I hope I die before that."

He laughs. "Don't hate on Brenda. She chose the shit life so you don't have to."

My cheeks rise and tighten, holding me back from laughing at his dumb joke. "Fuck Brenda."

"I'd rather fuck your eighty-year-old ass than Brenda," he declares.

"Seventy," I correct.

"Pardon me, seventy. I bet you would still be smokin' at seventy."

"I'll be tying my titties up and throwing them over my shoulder so I don't trip over them."

"I'll be sucking on those saggy tits and trying to get my elongated balls in your mouth."

"Oh God, can you imagine? Brenda walks in on a deep throat competition. Matching saggy balls and tits. Doesn't quite hit the same as matching Converse chucks." Our laughter echoes in the shower.

"You'll make me laugh till the day I die."

"And you'll make me sore, you giant dong...gorilla."

"That's all I'm good for?" He nudges my chin. Soapy bubbles float in between us.

"And satire." I shrug.

"Plenty satire."

I press my finger to the fogged glass, drawing a heart. Casey looks at it and back to me before swiping his finger in front of the heart, creating an *I* and a curve behind the heart, making a *U*.

"You ever been in love, wild?"

"In love? Once. Love without being *in love*? More than enough. I've cared about people, and sometimes I left, and sometimes they did," I admit. "It goes for more than men I was getting dick from. Friends, people I called family…"

"They weren't as good as me." You know what…he's right…for right now. Everyone has the power to disappoint, and most of them do.

Stop the mush. Back to sex. "I can't relate to women who say they *had to fake it*. Never had. Never will. If they aren't doing it right, why would I tell them they are? Like…no. That's pathetic. Do better."

"If you tell me to do better, I might chop it off." His hands run over my hips, taking water with them.

"Good." I nod once, sheepishly tugging my lower lip into my mouth. *Good.*

Chapter Twelve | Legacy

Casey

TUESDAY, 1:30 PM

I reach for Raine's hand, pulling her back to my chest. "Where are you going, wildcat?" I ask.

It's worth being exhausted to have spent half the night talking and kissing this woman. I'll never forget her favorite color—black—or that she couldn't live without her friends, especially Ivy, and she's a pretty good poker player, which I learned firsthand. I had to be a miner. Swinging, swinging away to find what's inside her snarky shell, layer by layer.

I had to check in with Estella this morning. Bash gave me the green light. Not her. If she wasn't comfortable, I'd feel like an asshole. What she told me, I know, would be hard for Bash to admit. Trying to get pregnant was becoming a robotic chore, and last night brought new excitement to their tired routine. Nobody wants to confess their sex life is lacking, especially not to the guy who's having a great time.

"We said goodbye three times already. I gotta catch a cab." People bustle around in the airport terminal, few paying attention to our locking lips besides two young women who stare with envy. Are they recording? Hah, whatever.

"I'll see you in two days."

"Thursday at five. My apartment. You have the address." Her lips gently skate across mine.

235

"Call me when you get home," I insist, not wanting to let go of her.

"Are you getting a little attached, Mr. Pierce?" She's right. "Oh shit. My bad." I'm going to let that slide. "Casey. Casey, Casey, Casey."

"I only want to make sure you get home safe." I draw her chin up. "Don't break my heart." Her eyelids fall closed as she sighs.

"You know I will one of these days. We left the fantasy. Back to reality." The reminder is stale. I have clients to deal with on top of the estate and *Karson*.

"I know you're done with me yet." I run my fingers down the strands of hair framing her face, twisting them at the end.

"Yeah, that free trip to Italy is a good reason to keep you close."

"Liar." I slide my hands down to her ass, giving it a spank before letting her go. "Call me, Raine," I call out.

"What's your number again?" She yells over her shoulder. "I think I lost it." Her hair sways against her shoulders as she smiles one last time and walks off.

Home, sweet home. There is nothing like it after being out of town for a week.

"Molly! How's my girl?" I pick her up and rub my wiggling Dachshund's tan belly. "Did Erica give you a lot of treats?" I put her down, take off my shoes, hang up my coat, and drop my keys into the crystal dish on the mahogany entryway table. Peeling my socks off and tossing them into a short, dark wicker basket, I head across the crisp, authentic wood flooring. As I walk around the corner, a silhouette emerges from the kitchen near the window overlooking the front of my property. Who the fuck—I freeze in my steps. The statuesque man turns, bringing a glass of golden liquid to his mouth.

"Casey. It's been a while." A voice that could curdle milk. Why the fuck is he in my house?

"Try eight years. I see you found the Hennessy," I grumble, glancing around the open floor. "How did you get in here?"

"That little thing isn't much of a guard dog." Come at me and find out how well she protects, dick. "The woman, Veronica? She let me in when I told her I was your father."

"Erica, the pet sitter," I clarify. "How did you find me?"

"I'm Cameron Pierce. You have to try harder to hide from me." He sips his drink, and I walk slowly toward him.

"Took you eight fucking years. I don't want to catch up with you. What do you want?" Moving to the sink, I keep him in sight as I grab a glass from the cabinet and fill it with water.

"You know what I'm here for, Casey. I want you to take over the family business. You are next in line. It's what your grandfather would have wanted."

"You know nothing of what he wanted." I shake my head, unamused. "You're only here now because he's gone. I don't have his protection keeping you away. You can pretend all you want, but I'm not a child anymore. I see through your bullshit, Cameron."

"Karson's resilient. An iconic Pierce quality. She will get what she wants from your grandfather's estate." If this is his sad attempt at a scare tactic, he's losing his touch. I'd give her that place in a heartbeat along with any share he thinks I own in CP Banking. The legacy dies with our generation, either through me or her.

"Let her run CP. That's what she wants. You know as much as I do that's the only reason she's interested in..." I laugh in an exhale. "You don't know what she's after, do you? Keep fishing old man," I reply.

"I don't need to know. Generations of men have run CP Banks. Karson is not built for it. She's...too emotional. She's a woman." He turns back to the window, looking at the rocky cliff edging my property.

"Women are just as successful as men. If she can't handle it, it's because you didn't prepare her. It wouldn't surprise me. The only thing you ever taught me was to protect the dynasty at all costs. Fuck over anyone who gets in the way. Pay off all problems that arise." I stare out the window just behind him. All the ways he could disappear out here in the woods. Living in the mountains, hidden away, has its advantages. He taught me more than he realizes. The biggest one is how not to treat others.

"Sebastian Canter may be a fine young lawyer, but we both know the CP team could drag this out and make your life hell till you finally give in to Karson's demands," he says, changing the subject.

"How's Mom?" I counter. "Still covering up bruises with flower arrangements?"

"I never hurt your mother," he argues, finishing his glass off. "Your memory is mistaken if that's what you believe."

"Just me then?" I snatch the glass from his hands, taking it to the sink.

He slips his hands into his slacks, slightly trailing behind me. "I know we have a rough history, Casey, but people change. You have obviously changed…You have a lot more tattoos now." His eyes roll over me in disapproval.

"Not the clean face of CP you were hoping for? How unfortunate."

"Could have done without the neck and the hands." His forehead wrinkles, and he turns back to the window. "Not exactly resembling a CEO."

I exhale in a huff, half laughing. "You will never change. You're still the same asshole you've always been. Still trying to make me think I'll never be good enough for the Pierce name. Sorry to break the news, but I don't give a fuck about your opinion."

He turns back to me, his face in shock, as if this is the first time I've told him off. It's not. "Never seemed to complain about everything my money has paid for, all the trips and expensive toys. It's always how I disciplined your smart ass as if I beat you on a daily basis. You were an impossible child. You needed structure." He pulls his hands out of his pockets, throwing them in the air. My body tenses as I watch his every movement. I've worked through this, it's what I started therapy for. I can handle him without losing my temper, without becoming him.

"Verbal abuse is abuse," I reply, slowly and clearly. "If you changed you wouldn't blame your actions on me or anyone else."

"One day you will want this company. When Karson—"

"Karson is getting nothing." I exhale, smiling. "She's going to take CP from you. She's going to hit the board and force your hand since you won't willingly give it to her. She's doing everything to make herself desirable to them. And you have been foolishly chasing me for months, knowing she's working on a plan to overthrow you. It didn't even take me a week to figure it out. Do you think I'm going to suddenly change my mind? I don't want CP. I don't need it."

"One of these days you're going to need me, Casey. I'll be waiting."

"You can get to that now." I nod to the side. "Right there's the door."

He stands outside for a few minutes on his phone. Finally, a limousine pulls up the hill, and he leaves. I feel nothing for him. He's dead.

I'm being haunted by shadows from my past. It's almost humorous that I joked with Raine about her past Friday night because hers is nothing like mine. Valid and not mine. Years of being told I'm an idiot, I'm worthless, I'm nothing but a troublemaker who's bringing shame to the Pierce name. That was more taxing than the times he threw furniture at me and slapped me across the face. I was a fucking child. He can't take me back to that dark place. Years of therapy...I buried you six feet below. Stay in the fucking ground.

"Yes," I grumble, holding my cell phone to my ear. "He was in the house when I got here."

"You can put a restraining order against him...and maybe get a new dog sitter? Otherwise, you can't touch him. You know he's a fucking ghost." *You have no idea.* Actually, he does. If I had a dollar for every time Bash had to sneak me into his house at night after I took off from my parents' home, I'd invest it and watch my pain turn into paper. Bash knows what money can get you into or out of. He grew up with plenty of privilege.

I placed my phone down, massaged my temples, folded my hands behind my head, and exhaled deeply. "Thanks, Bash." Brushing my hair from my face, I glance down at the granite kitchen counter. "Has Karson furthered her demands?" I pace, listening to him talk.

"Case...She wants your grandpa's foundation."

My lips curl in realization. "That's her first step in taking over his legacy. I don't get it, man. She could use his name, and I'd never know, making her way into CP with the board. She's that manipulative, could easily convince them that his dying wish was for her to join the board or some shit."

My phone beeps, and I tap the screen to reveal the incoming call. The name that pops up puts a smile on my face. "Raine's calling. Set something up for next week, Tuesday?"

"Bow chicka wow," he hoots. "I got it."

"Yeah, yeah. Appreciate it." I switch the call, answering my girl. "Hey, wildcat."

"Finally sat down." Her voice instantly creates a calm over me. I collapse to the couch, kicking my feet up.

"I guess you made it home in one piece then?"

"Almost got kidnapped by the Uber driver, but I told him I was a cannibal on a men-only diet. After I told him his knife wasn't sharp enough for filleting, he threw me out. Amateur."

I dip forward, picking Molly up, before leaning my head back against the leather. "Thanks for the dark humor. I could use the distraction."

"What are you procrastinating?" Her sassy tone evades my ears, filling every crack in my soul.

"Avoiding..." A sigh escapes my throat. "The unfortunate battle over my grandpa's estate."

"I'm sure it's a hassle."

"Raine," I hesitate. "There are a few things I haven't told you. I..."

"Okay, *villain.*" She's in a better mood than I am.

"*Love*, I need you to close your mouth, respectfully."

"Respectfully? Well, you have my attention, *Mr. Pierce.*"

"You'll understand...I need you to understand this part of my life. It's...messy. It's why I don't care to be called Mr. Pierce outside of business." I breathe out any reluctant feelings I have, revealing something deeply personal to someone vastly new to my life. I have to tell her. It's for her own safety. "My grandpa was a very wealthy man. If I'm Macaulay rich, he's Lauder." She hums in realization. "Multi-billionaire," I slowly add.

"That's...wow." Her words fail.

"Exactly. This isn't something I wanted to tell you on the phone or, honestly, tell you at all, at least not any-time soon. If it wasn't affecting my life right now, or if I didn't have some concerns about your safety during this mess, I wouldn't have told you. It's easy to tell people that I'm estranged from my family, but I don't share who they are...ever." I run my fingers through my hair, and the line stays silent for a brief moment. "Generations of my family have owned CP Banks. I was born into a dynasty of very wealthy, privileged men. My dad, who currently holds the position of CEO, is planning to retire and pass it on to his next-of-kin, me. I haven't spoken to the man in nearly a decade." I rub the tips of my fingers over my brows. "Here is where it gets...complicated. My sister, I have a sister. ..*Karson*, she's always wanted to take over. Cameron, our father, refuses to let her have it because she's a woman. He's a fucking sexist pig, among other things, not to mention that traditionally, CP has been passed down to the eldest son. My grandfather left nearly everything he had to me, besides CP." Is she still there? "Sorry." I clear my throat. "It's fucked. I know, and it gets better. Karson is trying to legally fight me for… bear with me, his *legacy*." I wipe my hand across my face, realizing how ridiculous that sounds.

"Um, yeah. I was expecting something like…" Her breath plays against the speaker. "Not his *legacy*? How does one take another to court for *legacy rights*?" She lets out a short laugh. "*Knuckles* with the ring grabs, meanwhile, *Sonic* is already nearing the finish line. It makes no sense." Her wit is amusing, and her analogies always come in strong.

"Right? It wasn't till her lawyers demanded she take controlling ownership over his charity foundation that I made the connection. Taking over means that his reputation becomes hers. She's the *caring grandchild* of the outstanding Charles Pierce. I have no idea what she's been doing the last four years since she graduated high school, besides working in marketing at CP. It can't be just that, though. She's a vindictive little bitch. She's up to something. And honestly, I don't care as long as it doesn't affect me. If she seeks vengeance on Cameron, it's between them." I look up at the ceiling, propping my head on my folded arms and holding my phone to my ear with my brachium. "Cameron paid me a visit today, too."

"What?" She whispers.

"I walked into my house to find him drinking Cognac in my kitchen."

"How did he get in?" She asks.

"The dog sitter." I don't blame Erica. She had no idea, but now we need to have a conversation.

"Why don't you want CP? It's not just Cameron's. It's generations of Pierce families, right? You would be filthy rich.

"Filthy...yeah. Money is a fucking plague. I've seen first-hand how wealth only buys greed. It's not for me," I insist. "I wanted comfort. I got a little more. Nobody needs billions."

"Casey?" Raine calls my name.

"Yes, *wild*?" I kick my feet up and wait for her voice to soothe me.

"Thanks."

"Thanks for what, darling?"

"For telling me all of...that."

"I come with baggage, Raine. And Cameron is capable of doing...I wouldn't put it past him to try recruiting my friends. I'm not trying to be forward or scare you off. You know I don't want that." I'm not telling her everything.

"I think we've passed being forward." That's it. Stay positive. Keep me in the same place as you.

Raine listens to me vent and offers up her highly illegal solutions. She talks about work. Snooze worthy, but I listen and ask one or two questions. The way she explained her friend Ivy's reaction to our *little escapade*, I think she called it, was brilliantly Raine. Her descriptions are...imaginative. She mentioned getting a stomp pad for her snowboard, and I'm half tempted to order a few styles and ship them to her. I would have indulged in her conversation longer, but she had plans with friends.

I check client accounts and send emails for the night before going for a hike with Molly till she's tired with the cold. Some days, I wonder why I didn't get a Malamute. Simple. That's a lot of dog to care for.

As soon as we walk into the house, my phone buzzes.

Heard you had a visitor. You doing alright?

Bash and his big mouth. He had to tell Alistair.

I'm good. You ready for the big day?

I hang up Molly's leash and my coat, kicking my shoes off and walking to the kitchen looking between my phone and the empty room.

Yeah, if we make it on the plane without eighty bags I'd be even better.

I refill Molly's water bowl and pour myself a glass of water before typing my reply.

Gin taking a year's worth of stuff?

She has an entire suitcase filled with swimsuits! What the fuck does one woman need that many swimsuits for?

I laugh out loud, walking to the living room couch. "Come on, Moll," I call, smacking my hand on my thigh.

BASH:

Tell her the beaches are nudies.

There's the big mouth now.

The beaches are NOT nudist Ky. I know you're in this chat. Don't even think about it.

ALISTAIR:

> It's going to happen now. Ky's going to be running down the beach with his wang out and Bash is going to be chasing him shouting obscenities and all five of us are going to be in foreign jail.

BENJI:

> I opened this to read Ky's going to be running with his wang out and I'm already in. I don't know what it is, but I'm in.

KY:

> What the hell? Why is it always me who gets accused of being the naked guy?

"Because it is always you!" I yell out loud before typing the words and hitting send. Granted, I may walk around a cabin half-naked or go skinny dipping at the lake at night with these guys; everyone knows Ky is the dumbass willing to do anything he thinks will get a riot going. I'm a nudist for convenience, and he's doing it for the attention.

ALISTAIR:

> It's always you. My sister's wedding two years ago…

BASH:

> High school graduation.

KY:

> That doesn't count, it was a dare and I was wasted at Kinley's wedding.

Kyle running across the stage with his cap over his family jewels was the most memorable thing that day. He's lucky his mommy was on the board of education with deep pockets. She kept his ass out of jail for indecent exposure. Too back she cut him off after that stunt, besides paying for his college expenses so he wouldn't drop out. I lost touch with him for a while. I'm glad we reconnected when he made it to Alistair's sister's wedding. Between him and Bash, it's never dull.

ALISTAIR:

> You keep your shit in check this weekend. Gin will kill us both if anything gets messed up.

> No she won't.

ALISTAIR:

> Yeah, she'll cry and that's worse.

BENJI:

> Word is Casey has a woman finally.

Bash with the mouth again. I already told Alistair about my plus one first. I run my hand through my hair, typing with the other.

> I do.

BASH:

> She could give Ky a run for his money.

> Easy. Raine doesn't need a hype man.

ALISTAIR:

> Guess we'll see Saturday.

THURSDAY, 5:30 PM

I look up at the building, and a red open sign is lit by the door. "Where in the hell are we, Raine?" This can't be the first place she chooses to take me when I step into her everyday life.

"A dress store." The look on her face is ten times worse than any wrinkled nose glance. She's up to something, and I don't like it. I stare at the neon sign in the window next to the door, trimmed in red paint. Shaggy beaded strands hang against the glass, and a deep blue dress covered in white shiny stones hangs on a headless manikin.

"*Queens & Cuties*?" It sounds like a mother-daughter shop. "Are you sure this is the right place?" She pulls the door open, and I follow her. *You have got to be kidding me.*

I was wrong. Dead wrong.

"Hey, babe, how are you? I have dresses hanging in room four for you." She's greeted by a tall blonde with blue and white powder or liner—whatever it is—across her eyes, sculpted cheeks, and cherry red lipstick. "Is this the lucky man escorting you all the way to Italy?" Her hair is perfectly curled with matching bangs and a long, black, form-fitted skirt with a matching blouse tucked in.

I look back and forth between Raine and the floor, gathering my thoughts. "Casey," I extend my hand. This is...W hat in the hell is she up to?

"Welcome to Queens & Cuties. You are definitely in our cuties category. Nice job, Raine." She winks. "I can see you're a fish out of water. Don't worry, this is a judgment-free zone. Inclusive sizes for every individual would loves a sexy dress."

"Raine could wear a trash bag and be stunning."

"Oh, suave." Her eyes run over me. "We love those compliments around here. Now repeat to me, you deserve a dress as beautiful as you." She wafts her hands. "Come on."

My teeth press to my lower lip as I smile and glance at Raine. "You deserve a dress as beautiful as you, love."

"Oh, I like the little personal touch. *Love.*"

"This is Amie," Raine introduces. "She's better than any personal stylist in this city, and I'm lucky enough to be friends with her."

"You're too sweet, but you don't even know any stylists in this city, girl." We all know that's the truth. "Come on, let's try these dresses on. I don't have all night." She wraps her arm around Raine's shoulder, hurrying her to the dressing area. I trail behind, looking around at the alien shop. An entire wall is covered in wigs, aisles of makeup and shoes, dresses, corsets, and embellished jumpsuits. It's like any other women's store that I avoid. I sit down on the white leather couch, waiting for Raine to return.

"Perfect," I whisper under my breath, taking her in her curves as she walks to a circular podium. A taupe dress layered with black lace hugs her hips, illuminating her waist. The deep neckline plunges along the front, and a slit carries along the side of the mid-length gown. It's elegant and sexy, and...yeah, I can see her on the balcony now.

"Ring it up." I circle my finger in the air. "Bill, please. Ring it up."

"This is the first one. Don't you want to see the rest?"

"No, you're getting that," I insist. It dawns on me that this is the first time I've seen her in a dress besides that photo.

I can't wait to watch her dance in this number. Hold her in my arms, against my chest. My fingers smooth over the fabric along the lower back. Would she agree to do this, get dressed up, and dance with me on a semi-regular basis? I'm jumping the gun. *This is Raine.*

"Well, if you're paying, maybe she needs three." Amie grabs two more dresses, holding them up.

"Anything you want, you can have it, as long as that is one of them." It doesn't really matter what she wears. Whatever it is, I'm taking it off of her and tossing it off the balcony if I must to keep her bare ass.

"How about this?" She holds up a dress that is clearly too large for her frame.

"Looks a little big, but I like the color."

"Oh, it's not for me." She pushes out her glossy lips, looking like the most gorgeous duck, before walking over to me and grabbing my hand.

"Raine..." What in the fuck is this crazy woman thinking? I don't like to call women crazy, but she's out of her mind thinking I'm putting that on.

"I know a really cute guy that would fill this baby out in all the right places." I'm not putting it on.

"My best feature would be downplayed in that." I suck my cheek in.

"You just said anything I want, I can have it," she argues.

"You really want me to wear a dress?" I whisper-shout, widening my eyes.

"Live a little, you might like the breeze."

Ah, wild. You button-pushing woman.

"I'm not playing dress up." I stare at her deadpan.

"If you can't handle a little shopping montage, I'm not forcing you." She turns around, allowing her tone to do the work. Fuck...She's going to win.

"Shopping montages are usually of women in the movies. I have plenty of the hit chick-flicks I can reference."

"My story isn't a classic. Besides, haven't you seen White Chicks?" She twirls with the dress pressed against her body.

"I'm not an undercover cop." That big smile of hers turns me into putty in her hand. "You don't think I'll do it, do you? Give it to me," I sigh, pulling the hanger from her and walking into the dressing room. Finally, I get the damn thing on and walk out of the stall onto the pedestal. The long cream dress has this weird overlapping skirt with a tie around the waist, long sleeves that are stretched around my arms, and a low-cut neckline.

"Meow." Her giggles engulf me. The things I'd do for this inexorable woman.

"You're dirty. How did you talk me into this?"

She walks over to me and circles the podium, her hand cascading over the fabric. I wrap my arm around her waist, pulling her frame to my chest. Her warm smile greets me.

"You have an amazing rack," she whispers.

"The power of protein," I whisper back.

Amie walks around the corner, cupping her hands over her mouth. "Yes! We need accessories!"

"And cue the upbeat playlist." Raine steps down from the pedestal, dancing to the music in her head.

"I kind of like it. Very freeing." I shift my hips from side to side. "Think I should wear this to the wedding?"

With liveliness in her eyes, she pinches her lips together.

"Yeah, this color washes me out. Do we have anything in black?"

"I like this one." Amie gestures her hand towards me. "The man, not the dress. He's right, that is not his color."

Raine wraps her arms around me. "Yeah, I might keep him."

Keep me, love.

I glance at the diamond-shaped clock hanging on Raine's wall. Ten past eight. The cracking of thunder levitates in the distance. Raine's one-bedroom apartment is filled with dim light, white frames with photos of everyone she loves covering her intimate living room, and the smell of fresh popcorn rests in the air. I scanned the place while she showered. A tall black bookcase shelves rows of books, followed by a row of vinyl albums. On the center shelf, a pair of snowboarding goggles is propped up in front of the books with a sticker across the right side reading, " If *my mouth doesn't say it, my face will*. Fitting.

She sits down next to me with a large bowl of popcorn, eating a piece.

"Did I pass the test?"

She laughs. "I just wanted to mess with you a little."

"You bitch," I laugh, pulling her legs on top of mine as I recline on her loveseat sofa, throwing a blanket over both of us.

"I prefer this new pet name—*wildcat*—opposed to bitch."

"Better than, what's that one Nollan called you...*rainbow*?" I chuckle.

She closes her eyes, throwing her head back against the sofa. "Don't remind me. It's awful. Like, yeah, I get it. Everyone gets it. It's also a nickname for a kid or...someone that's bright and wildly imaginative."

"And you're not?"

"I'm average."

"You're exquisite," I say, raising my hands.

"Sure. Okay." She sarcastically agrees. "I'm not the smart girl or the pretty girl. I'm the girl who...gives the worst first impression. The one who knows a little about a lot. The girl who weaponizes words in my head, but I wouldn't dare speak my peace when it matters the most. I'll bottle it up and shake it, ready to explode at any given moment."

"You can count on me to listen when you think you're about to explode." Her eyes drift away, and she holds back her thought. "So what are we watching?"

She hits the play button on the remote, lighting up the sleeping screen. "I figured it would be time for you to start working on a nineties movie list, so don't get any Netflix and chill ideas. The movie only counts if you actually watch it."

"I would never," I reply, unreadable. She sees through my false line.

"We have an early flight tomorrow. Movie and sleep."

"But Raine...we don't need sleep," I say convincingly. I pull the blanket from her, dropping it to the floor. Moving her legs back to the couch, I kneel on the floor beside her and push her arms above her head, letting my lips skate across her neck, kissing her collarbone.

She shakes her head, pulling her lips tightly together. "Casey."

"Wildcat." I slide my hands down her arms, running my fingertips along the sides of her covered breasts, to her waist, where I start unbuttoning her flannel shirt at the bottom, till only two buttons at the top exist. I kiss her navel, her ribs below her breast, and then again at the last button. "Tell me, what can I do for you?"

"Casey," she drags my name out, staring at the ceiling. I could compare it to her moans, but it had more frustration and denial attached to it. "I want you, I do." Her words hang. I withdraw my hands, leaning back with a sigh.

I look back at her beautiful face, and her hair is every-where. We had a great time together in Bender, and now she's pulling away. I thought she was mine. "What's the problem?" I calmly ask.

"I like you," she blurts out, abruptly.

"You like me," I repeat her words, looking up at her. "Elaborate, please."

She sits up, pulling the blanket from the floor. "Look, I haven't felt...connected, really, since..." Her eyes wander away from me, and sorrow overwhelms her. I join her on the couch, grabbing a corner of the blanket to pull over my legs.

"Since Nollan and you're afraid it's going to end the same way? I'm not Nollan. Don't compare me to him ever again," I reply, frustrated. I reel myself back, catching the tenseness in my jaw. "Please. You need to understand that if you want to be with me, I'm not playing games. You have to be open and communicate. Yes, I've spent time with women who liked the cars, the vacations, my body, more than who I am as a person. I'm tired of it. Look at me, please." I touch her chin. "Whatever sorcery you have over me, I don't want it to end. So if you want to backtrack, then fine. I'll keep the snake in the cage tonight." Her lips curve. I'd say anything stupid for her smile. "Please, just stop comparing me to Nollan." I take her hand. "Transparency. Let's talk it out.

Right now. I've known you for a week, Raine. Not months or years. You were upfront with me, and I'm willing to give you what you want in a partner. Do you want to try this, or is this the last time we take a trip together?"

"Insta-love isn't real, Casey. I can't—"

"You won't."

"We're arguing."

"No. This is open communication. A little tense because I'm frustrated, because I want to be with you. I want to talk to you. I want to fucking touch you. And you're shutting down because it's scary."

"You don't know me enough to make that accusation."

"Then let me get to know you. What do I need to know about the men you've dated? Why did the last guy fail?"

"Okay." Her voice softens. "Leo," she whispers. "I tried to save him. I thought I was the hero this time. I was wrong." She won't look at me. The vulnerability in her words is as if she's spoken them very few times.

I brush her hair behind her ear, watching the pain invade her face as she continues, stumbling over her words. "It's okay."

"No, it's not," she cries out.

"I'm listening."

"I don't talk about what happened with him. It was over a year ago." She tugs on the blanket, wanting to hide.

"I'm listening," I reassure her. "Talk to me."

"He was an alcoholic." She sucks her lip into her mouth, and I slip my fingers down hers, weaving them into the back of her hands. "He was doing so well, going to his meetings, staying clean. We had this petty fight over something so stupid, I can't even remember what it was." She shakes her head. "The next morning, I called him. It just went to his voicemail." Her lower lip shakes, and she chews at it. I thought Nollan had a hold on her, but she's edging on a breakdown now. She's been pained by more than one relationship. It's all starting to make sense to me—why she's suddenly keeping me at arm's length. "Later that day," she musters the words together. "I heard about this car accident...that happened just after two AM," she says, breathy. *Oh fuck.* I close my eyes, leaning my head back, knowing what she's about to reveal. "Involving a...drunk driver and...a telephone pole." She struggles to get the words out, her eyes welling with tears. I pull her face to my chest, wrapping my arms around her. She pulls back, looking up at me with dopey eyes. "Casey, this is what you're getting into with me. Darkness follows me, consumes me; no matter how far I run and how deep I hide, it finds me. Everyone around me suffers from this...storm."

I bring her face back to mine, holding her beauty in both of my hands. "You can't control the weather, love."

"I don't want to hurt you." A drop of liquid runs down her cheek, and I wipe it away with my thumb.

"I'm unbreakable, baby."

"You're just a man, remember?" She sneers.

"I'm a man who's been through more than you know. You can't put skeletons back in the closet without knowing they exist." She stares at me, bewildered. "When I said my parents are dead to me, there is a deeper reason than my dad being a greedy pig. He was abusive."

"Casey," she says in that tone, squeezing my wrist.

"Don't do that. Don't feel sorry for me. I grew up in one of the wealthiest families, went to the top schools, had everything I could desire."

"No, you didn't. What every child, every human, desires is love, care, and respect. They failed you on the one thing that they should never have failed at," Raine replies, pensive.

"Then be angry with them, but don't feel pity for me. If you must, release this dark bullshit on them. I used every strike and every deplorable word to my advantage. I got out of there. I felt the love of family. I built my own empire. And now I've found you. You gave the wrong men your attention; bad things happened, and you moved forward. That's life. We fuck up, we deal with pain, and we move forward."

In pouring her deepest, pained secret into my lap, I ended up telling her mine. She's quiet for a moment before whispering. "What am I to you?"

"You're calm on the surface and crazy underneath. And you're my person, wildcat. I'm yours. Bitch about unrealistic expectations, your anti-fairytales, and how fucked you think insta-love is...because you know an inch of truth exists in all of those things. It adds up, and people like you and I spontaneously meet."

Thunder cracks, shaking the house and lighting every window up. She jumps, wrapping her blanket tighter to her body.

"Come here." I pull her to my chest and stroke her arm. "For someone who describes themselves as a storm, I'd expected you would enjoy this weather."

"I don't."

Chapter Thirteen | Sempiternal

Raine

The sun beats off the lake as I lean against the white, intricate stone wall, overlooking the breathtaking view. It's like nothing I've seen before. Every architectural design, every aspect of this place, is detailed and magnificent. Even the vines that wrap around the stone artwork and the arched walkways are perfectly placed. I pull my single-button blazer tight around my body before Casey's warm hands seize my hips.

"Beautiful." His mouth sweeps across my neck.

"It's like a postcard."

"It doesn't compare to you."

I turn to meet his lips. His tongue twists around mine, and his soft lips instantly warm my chilly body. I'll take the compliment and assume he's being a sweetheart. There's no way I hold more beauty than this country. Man, this is what I've been dreaming of since I was a kid. Not getting dicked down by Money Bags McGee. *Adventure.* The world.

It's not fair that I'm only here because of him. I should have been smarter. Invested. Grew an online business. Figured out how the influences do it. Something. Anything.

Maybe the whole time I've been making fun of people who have sugar daddies, I should have been thinking about how I could take advantage of an opportunity like that. In my head, I hum a spoof of Wannabe by the Spice Girls. *If you wanna be my daddy. La la la la la.*

"You know that list you have, your bucket list? You should write it all down. Put it in a notebook."

"Why?"

"That way you can keep track of everything we cross off."

"We? I can—"

"You can do it without me, I know, and I'm hoping you let me do it with you. It only seems fair since I'm going to need someone to tag along on my adventures, and I'm hoping it'll be you."

The rowdy group of groomsmen near us. "Hurry up, Alistair, the exhibitionists are about to turn your show into theirs," Bash yells as he walks around the curve of the sidewalk. Alistair, Benjamin, and Kyle follow behind. All four men are dressed in suits tailored to perfection, looking like Wall Street gods. None of them looks as good as Casey. His charcoal suit, white button-up shirt, and tie look good on him. He traded his marker-covered Chucks for something expensive in leather.

"Hey man, don't get us kicked out," Alistair jokes, smiling.

"You ready to do this thing?" Benji grabs Casey's shoulder, squeezing.

"He's ready to do something," Bash interrupts. All the men laugh. I smile tightly, unsure if I want to admit it to them. He's right. We're both patiently waiting to rip each other's clothes off. What stupid idea did I have Thursday night? *Oh, let's just talk.* It was an eye-opening conversation, though. I guess we're all a little fucked up, some more than others.

"Alright, men. Time to drag this fool to the altar." Benji nearly puts Alistair into a headlock, pulling him up the path. Bash & Kyle follow.

Casey pulls my hands behind his neck. "Like Benji said, let's go watch these fools get married." His lips meet mine once more before he takes my hand and leads me to the ceremony.

These people mean a great deal to Casey. The corner of his lips arch upward as he listens to Alistair's vows. This isn't as bad as I thought it was going to be. It's intriguing and...it's a scene from a romance book. Casey said we get some kind of gift at the end of the evening, like a favor, but more symbolic. He called it a Bomboniere.

The shattering glass makes me flinch, looking back at the bride and groom. Casey wraps his arm around me, holding onto my waist. "You okay?" He whispers.

I nod. "What are they doing?"

"The shards of glass symbolize each year they will be happily married." He looks at me with one of those soft, dimpled smiles before looking back at the altar. Those are not bedroom eyes. They're dreamy...and I was right. He is an Eros. While I'm a Ludus.

Shut the hell up. I'm doing this. We're doing this. Commitment. Monogamous, mutual fun, and freedom, and...God, I'm hungry. When are we eating?

"May your life be like good wine," Bash says, raising his glass in the air.

"Congratulations," I tell Ginevra for the third time. These women hate me. "You look amazing." *Oh, look, here comes weird bitch Raine. Let's try to be nice for Casey's sake.* "Beautiful gown." Her Mikado ball gown flares out from her waist, a slim belt highlights her frame, and an off-shoulder Chantilly lace bodice with long matching sleeves covers her torso. I did my research. It wasn't in my plans to be the only chick at this fancy venue who was confused by terms like *Chantilly lace bodice* and *ball gown versus A-line*. Her dark hair is in an up-do, tightly tucked away from her face.

"Thank you. I'm so glad Casey invited you." It's cool. She's being polite. I'm being polite.

We dance across from each other on the balcony of the massive hotel suite. If that's what you want to call it. I'm shuffling. *Shufflllling.* Eight o'clock has the bride and groom's family calling it a night, and the ten of us hanging out in the newlywed's golden suite. It's insane. The shower. *The shower!* It has two bathrooms. One has a massive Jacuzzi tub. Golden drapes surround every window, and a huge gray microfiber couch with matching massive chairs fills the living space in a "C" shape.

"You don't have to lie. Your posh, Stell, is collected, and I'm here with a guy I met a week ago."

"I'm going to stand on a limb and say you've had experiences with mean girls." Before I can answer, she continues. "They're sad bitches. Nobody here is sad."

"Marie might be. Sad bitch vibes," I deadpan. "Kyle must suck in bed."

"Decent in bed, not the best at keeping women."

"Sounds like you know from experience."

"We've all been friends for a while. Some of us had to switch teams mid-play. To be clear, it was a mutual departure, and I didn't get with Alistair till a year later. I won't be the one to judge you." She grabs a bottle of champagne from one of the outdoor tables, refilling our glasses. I knock it back like a shot and find myself dancing again. This time with less shuffle and more sway.

"Estella!" I yell as she joins us. The fourth glass of champagne snuck up on me. "I need some water," I say, pointing to the open doors.

The men are scattered around the living space. Benji's date, Hannah, is leaning over the island in the kitchen, waiting for a mixed drink. Scanning the room, I notice Kyle's date, Marie, is not with Kyle. *Sad bitch vibes* is sitting so close to Casey that they are touching.

Alistair looks up from the end of the couch, spotting me. "She was talking shit to Hannah."

"Huh?"

"Ky's date." He up nods. "I'd put her in her place if I were you."

"I'm not confrontational enough for hair-pulling and titty punches."

He laughs and tips his glass back. "Yeah, I heard you were funny." He glances around the room.

"Hey, Ky," I call out. "I heard you're notorious for picking up chicks from Trader Joe's?" I ask, loudly. "No offense, Gin," I call over my shoulder.

"Bob's Discount, actually." His tone is apathetic, but a half smile creeps from the corner of his mouth. I don't blame him for being annoyed. He brought her to freaking Italy. To a wedding. As his date. And she's flirting with *my* date. There's a fine line between fucking with someone and bullying them. And sometimes, the only way to get through to people is to be a bit of an asshole. Shit, am I Bailey? No.

It's not the same. It can't be. Stop overthinking. Save your man.

"I prefer Ashley's," Bash joins in, raising two fingers. I try not to laugh, knowing I started something viciously hilarious. Shit, what did I start? If the girls liked me before, they're going to change their minds now. God, weird Raine.

Estella walks in behind me, nodding. "I can live with that. Affordable style."

"No man, Ikea. IKEA has the best. Those tables have legs for days," Alistair chips in, raising his brows up and down as he holds his glass of mystery booze in his hand. The lovely bride passes Estellla, brushing her hand against my shoulder as she smiles, and makes her way to sit beside him. Either everyone is buzzed out, or they all have a great sense of humor.

Benji hands Hannah her fruity mixture. "Hooker Furniture." As he walks out of the room again, his voice carries.

"Excuse me." She glares at him, disgruntled.

"Sorry, babe," he mutters.

I cross my arms and lean into one hip. "Casey, what's your go-to store?"

He shakes the ice around in his nearly empty glass. "RH. Only the finest design is suitable."

"I could call my mom and double-check, but I'm pretty sure I was manufactured there," I answer flatly before smiling divertingly. "It sounds like her taste, and I'm sure I'm adopted. Do you, do you want me to give her a call?" I flick my thumb back, pointing over my shoulder. "Hey Benji, can you grab me a water? Pretty please with cherries and sugar tits," I shout to the kitchen.

"In a glass on rocks?" He yells back.

"Only the finest." Casey scans my body. Our eyes lock, and he smiles. I roll my eyes and walk off, meeting Benji as he enters the room. I take the glass and thank him.

"Steer clear of Hannah till that juice kicks in. Fucking PMS. She's out there grumbling about *sugar tits.*" I push out my lip.

"Whip cream makes everyone feel better." His brows jump, finding an idea. I walk off before I get roped into it.

"Love," Casey says in his usual calm manner. "It sounds like you're fitting in." Is that dry humor?

Everybody in a bar are friends. The same goes for this situation. Except—I look over at *Marie* and sit on Casey's lap—*her.* What more do I have to say to get her to move? *Why did I drink?* I'm going straight edge for the rest of my life. *I'm leeeeaving.* Shit, now I'm going to hum Jessie McCartney's Leavin' all night. Is that the one they remixed for Pop Goes Punk? No, no, no. It was Beautiful Soul. Man, I'm making an ass of myself. Windows down, hair in the wind, and drunk on moments instead of using alcohol to cope with disappointment and anxious feelings—that's where I should be.

Marie finally gets the hint and slides down the couch, farther away from us.

"Are you alright?" Casey asks.

No. I dazed out. I got lost in my head with a cracked-out glaze plastered to my face.

"Mhm. How's it going over here?" I drank, and I drank till I landed in a spiral of embarrassment. I'm fine. I'm fine, I'm fine, I'm fine.

"Just watching you shake that ass," he returns.

"You could have joined."

"I'd rather do other things with you," he whispers.

"Like what? Charades? Pin the tail on the donkey? Scrapple?" I could look around the room and see if anyone is paying attention. Other than Kyle, everyone is amused by something else. I lean my head back against him, closing my eyes and biting my smile.

"I heard Twister is fun." He presses his lips to my neck. "I have plans for you. They have some requirements," he whispers.

"What are these requirements? If it involves long-distance running, I'm out," I answer, opening my eyes and looking over to find Marie sporting a scowl on her face and her crossed arms. Musical chairs?

"For starters, sober up, darling."

"I can't make promises." I tug pins and bands out of my hair, dropping them between my feet.

"Yes, you can." He runs his finger under the strap of my dress. "You're lucky I don't pull this dress off now," he says before pressing his lips to my neck.

"That's not luck. It's torture."

"Kyle, come get your rocket pocket before Raine bites." I glance up at the broad man, yelling—wait, what did he call her? Bash shouldn't drink either. I'm starting a sober club with him ASAP. He's ten times more crude. It's to vomit point. Her mouth drops open, and she storms out of the room. "Look what you did." His hand shoots out in front of his chest.

"Yeah, I'm the one who just used the phrase *rocket pocket.*" Casey quietly laughs behind me. "If you could unlearn that one, no woman needs to hear it, including us innocent bystanders."

Bash walks up to me, extending his hand. "Stop being a bystander then. Let's go dance." My eyes fall upon Casey.

"Have fun." I tug the last band out of my hair and take Bash's hand.

"Stell, I need a dance partner. Your husband is stealing mine," Casey calls.

I take Bash's hand, immediately being pulled from Casey's lap and spun in circles. He rests his palm loosely on my waist, and the other holds my hand, leading me to the balcony. Casey and Estella follow behind, mimicking our moves a few feet away.

"Your meeting with Casey was fate," he says, authentically. "He's got a lot going on, and you're one of the good things."

"Yeah. I see that. He's a good guy."

"He really is." His tone becomes less playful. "He usually comes to my house for Thanksgiving and then visits his grandpa. This year might be a little rough for him. I know he's told you something about his past, but I lived it with him. That man was his saving grace. He refuses to let any of us see how much he's been hurting."

"I get it. I've lost people, and I've…" I sigh, unable to swallow my words. "I've hidden pain."

"Do you have anything going on for Thanksgiving? It's only a few weeks away."

"Uh, yeah," I hesitate. "I'll be in Florida for the weekend."

"I'm going to overstep and ask, are you going to invite Casey?" He glances back at Casey, having a conversation with Stell. I follow, watching the handsome, sweet man whom I judged as everything he's not. He's only ten percent, bad boy. He's not arrogant and self-absorbed. He's kind and loves hard. He's been through a lot but never shows it. His smile brightens every dark shadow that lingers in my mind.

"I haven't really thought that far," I admit. This is happening too fast. My eyes jump back and forth, unable to catch a clear glimpse of anything. What am I doing here?

"You should." I look into his blue eyes and nod, smiling tightly. In my panic, I turn silent. The uncertainty cripples me. I want to leave and sit in the dark with my earbuds in and my music cranking up. I want to go home.

"Can I cut in?" Casey asks. Whatever Bash says to him doesn't register in my head. He slides across the floor to his wife, pulling her close and dipping her side to side.

"What was that smile about?" He asks, sliding his hands around my waist.

"Nothing." Am I smiling?

We drift side to side, and I let my hands fidget along the back of his neck. Can we be alone? Can you sit in the hallway with me? Can I hold your hand and simply exist? *Talk, Raine. Communicate. Tell me everything.* Everything will make you hate me. If I leave first...you'll be okay. You will find your person. You will be so happy together. You'll see the world with her, splash in all the oceans, dance over miles of sand, slide down mountains, and laugh through snowball fights. I'll be content in my apartment...with my friends...Calle...my local mountains and occasional vacations. We'll both be happy when this is over.

"Seriously, what's that look? That soft smile and dreamy stare. Am I *piquant?*"

"Not as piquant as you were a week ago. Have to say, I liked you more when I thought you were going to chop me up into pieces and put me in your dehydrator."

He tips his head back, loudly sighing. He swiftly drops his hands to the back of my thighs, pulling me to his body. I wrap my arms around his neck, giggling as he carries me to one of the two black cushioned chaises. He sets me down on the end and straddles the top, leaning back.

"Come here, gorgeous." I scoot back, allowing my back to press against his chest. He brushes my hair from my neck, kissing me. "What would it take to get you to leave with me?"

"Hmm, I don't know," I hum. "A new pair of boots, a trip to the bookstore, that Porsche you dangled in front of me, a new—" His hand quiets me, covering my mouth.

"Shh," he hushes. "Close your eyes." His fingers run down my neck and between my breasts, smoothing across the fabric of my lacey dress until his palm rests on my navel. "I can't wait to get you alone. I'm going to have to carry you tomorrow through the airport because there is no way in Lord's creation that I'll be able to stop myself from fucking you over and over till your lungs are deprived of oxygen."

"Don't think I'm above crying. I will and make you feel bad."

"I wouldn't hurt you."

"Not with ill intent." My brows draw close as I tilt my chin up to see him. "I read the average sexual penetration lasts three to five minutes, not thirty to forty."

"I could give you multiple orgasms without penetration for hours and then use my three to five minutes."

"Hours? I'd die."

"Hence lungs deprived of oxygen."

I clench my legs together unintentionally. His hand drifts lower. Here? My eyes snap open, and I look around to see if anyone notices, but the balcony is empty. His fingers slide between my legs, pushing against the fabric of my dress. I softly moan, my eyelids closing again with his touch.

"You're everything," he whispers, pressing into my soft flesh, wetness coating my dress. "You're not doing any of the work tonight. Let me show you what you deserve."

I'm going to walk out of here with a huge wet spot on my dress if he doesn't stop. "Casey, slow down."

"Okay, love."

Ky's tall figure approaches the balcony doorway, walking backward while talking to someone inside. As the breeze picks up, his short blonde hair blows.

"Casey, my dress." I adjust the fabric.

"We're setting up for poker. You want in?" When he finally turns to look at us. "And Raine, thanks for the entertainment."

"The what?" I sit up, putting my feet back on the ground and smoothing my dress over my legs.

"With Marie. I sent her ass packing. Well, back to the room since I couldn't throw her onto the street. How the hell do you meet a fine woman a week before the wedding, and she's cooler than the date that I've had for six months?"

"Luck," he answers with signature Casey confidence.

"Then get in the game, you lucky fuck. We have the lawyer, the pilot, and the investor here tonight. The honey pot is going to be deep."

"What about the nightclub owner? I know he has enough to gamble."

"Yeah, yeah. I'm in too," he replies, walking back into the suite.

"What do you say, wildcat? Go home or show 'em your poker face?"

"Front me, and I'll double your money."

Without moving a muscle, he looks back at the door. "Deal."

"He's bluffing!" Bash points, then holds his hand in a fist up to his mouth. "Attention passengers, this is your captain. I'm straight full of shit." He stands at attention with his arms straight in front of him, waving two fingers on each hand up and down.

"He's not a flight attendant," Benji laughs, smacking Bash in the chest with the back of his hand. "You have a pair, two pairs at most."

"Two pairs?" Someone mutters.

"You both folded. Go plug your mouth with another bottle." Alistair flicks them off.

"Already in intoxication nation," Benji replies, holding his lager bottle up. Bash laughs, and the two play punch each other. Estella and Hannah walk in from the kitchen, laughing. Hannah has her hands full of shot glasses, while Estella has a bottle of Campari in one hand and vodka in the other.

"What's it going to be, Raine?" Ginevra asks. She's pretty good. It's nearing two hours into the game, and it's between the newlyweds and me. Mostly because everyone else is drunk or distracted by the drunks. I've sobered up somewhat.

I grab the first shot glass that Estella fills and slam it back. "Raise."

"Oh! Oh!" Benji and Bash hoot and yell. Casey's face says it all, a tight-lipped smile he can't hold back. The shot was for dramatic effect. I'll do what I have to if it gets inside their heads. I'm not losing.

"I'm awake!" Ky shoots up from the floor, like the living dead from the grave. Estella hands him a bottle of water that she grabbed twenty minutes ago before he passed out.

"Hey, wildcat. You sure you're going to double my money?"

"Watch and learn," I reassure him.

"Oh, she sounds confident. Will the Mr. and Mrs. call or fold?" Bash hypes. The commentator brothers are actually doing me a solid by running their mouths.

"I told you she doesn't need a hype man." Casey winks.

I look away from the table when I catch something from the corner of my eye. *What in the hell is that man doing?*

"I'm on top of the world!" Kyle yells, drawing the room's attention. He stacked a dining chair on top of the table and is standing on top of it in his boxers and a tie around his forehead. How he stripped that quickly, well, I'm kinda blown away. That's a new kind of talent, maybe even a sport. Velocity disrobing?

"For fucks sake," Alistair mutters.

"At least he's not naked," Bash laughs, looking back as he walks toward Kyle.

"Yeah, he might poke an eye out at that level." Benji follows him, standing on the opposite side of the table.

"Come on, time for bed."

"Bash, it's amazing up here. You can see the whole world!"

"The whole world is in a hotel room?" Estella asks.

"Alright, I fold. I'm evicting half of you."

"Be my guest, but I'm not folding. Ky can run across this table bare-ass, and I'm still in. What's it going to be? Gin?" I look down at my cards and return to her.

"Babe, get him down. I don't want to spend the rest of the night in an Italian ER with the drunken Three Stooges."

"He can walk off a concussion." Benji smiles, but changes his tone quickly when both Stell and his sober date look at each other. "Let's go, Ky. Easy does it."

I laugh under my breath, feeling Casey's eyes on me.

"Look, I have all night, but you still won't beat this hand. What's it going to be?"

Ginevra stares at me, pursing her lips. It's hard not to look away from the chaos to the right, but I don't move. Finally, she looks down at her hand and drops the cards on the table. The room's attention is back on the game as I lay down my cards.

"She's a fucking shark!" Bash yells and points. Gin could have easily beaten a straight. If anything, this game was an ego trip for any of them. The money never mattered.

Kyle's jaw nearly hits the floor, as if his drunk ass knows exactly what just happened and he's mind-blown. Benji jumps up and smacks Casey in the back a few times, excited.

"Damn baby, she got you," Alistair wraps his arm around his bride. I gather the money on the table, stacking the bills tightly on top of one another. I can't even fathom the amount of money I'm holding from a *friendly game*.

"I'll give you a personal dance for a few ones from that stack," Ky bargains.

"Nobody wants you to dance," Estella says, grabbing his arm. She leads him to Bash, who grabs his other arm and starts skipping towards the door. "We'll see you all in the morning," she says as she waves.

"You're quiet." I elbow Casey in the side.

He smiles, standing from his chair and bending below the table to retrieve my heels. His touch along my calf, gliding over my freshly shaved skin, pulls me closer, his lips meeting the inside of my ankle. He slides one on and fits the strap around, securing it.

"What are you doing?" I softly ask.

"Admiring you." His dark eyes hold a gleam of happiness. Strong and yet...incredibly delicate. "Come on," he says, taking my hand in his. "Time to take your winnings and split."

"You never take my warnings seriously."

"Oh, I never had any doubts. I knew you'd win."

We say our goodbyes for the night and walk out the door to find our home away from home. He intertwines his fingers in mine, his charming smile twisting my heart in every way I didn't think he could.

I close the door behind me, not getting a moment to think when my back is pushed up against it. The room is nearly pitch black and silent, aside from Casey's lips diving into mine like he's waited years to taste my kiss. I part my lips, letting him in deeper. His gentle hold on my heart turns into the drilling of a tattoo machine on my inner lip, desirable pain biting into me. I guess he wasn't kidding about that *can't breathe* thing.

He murmurs into the hollow of my neck. "Here, kitty, kitty." His hands tighten around my wrists, and his body presses against mine. "You're mine, wildcat," he hums, his sultry breath heating my ear. I inhale, bringing my lips to his neck.

"You." His lips press to mine. "Are." His lips find my shoulder. "Mine."

He kisses my shoulder again and releases with suction to the base of my neck. He grabs my arm, turns me around, and holds my wrist to the door. His other hand tugs the zipper on the back of my dress, slowly guiding it to the end, where it stops just above my ass. Heat overwhelms my body; my heartbeat hastens; butterflies leave my stomach and reappear between my legs.

"Here I thought maybe you had a daddy kink, but you're secretly possessive, aren't you?"

"Your mouth is uncontrollable." His fingers gently massage my shoulders one by one as he slides the straps over them, causing my dress to fall to the floor. "I thought we were back in fantasyland?" His subdued words make me smile.

"What's tonight's fantasy then?"

"I just want to shut you the fuck up for an hour, respectfully."

"An hour?" I snort, giggling.

He slams my hands against the door above me; his warm palms apply pressure. His chest presses against my back, the weight of his massive muscles sinking me deeper into the wall.

"Take your sardonic ass in the bathroom, love. I'll be right there."

I could argue. I almost want to. Another part of me doesn't. This time, it wants to lose control. Slipping out of my dreadful heels, I walk to the bathroom in my matching strapless bra and panties. As he said, special occasions make us...I don't know; I do special things. I'm glued to the sight of him from the doorway. He loosens his tie further and kicks his shoes off. His fingers trace his belt, adjusting it before joining me. His chest brushes against my back, leaning around me to turn the water on, filling the jetted tub.

His lips remain still, a sexy calm laced with dominance under his gentle touch and sensual words. "Turn around, please." I cautiously spin, licking my lower lip. "Close your eyes, love." The smooth silk fabric blinds me. Before tying my hair tight, he adjusts it. His touch sails down my spine, unhooking my bra. As it falls to the floor, his hands cover my hips, turning me to face him. Lips deepen against my thigh, a simplistic kiss nonetheless erotic and consuming. He slips my panties to my ankles, carefully lifting my feet one by one to get them off. I weave my fingers through his thick hair, trying to maintain balance. The man should know better by now that this is a mildly dangerous situation. In the midst of blindfolding me and peeling off my clothes, Casey is a gentleman.

"How did you get like this? This kind and generous?"

"I'll tell you about it later." His comforting hand caresses my jaw, his thumb running over my chin. "I'm going to pick you up, darling."

I open my mouth to answer, only allowing a whisper comes out. "Okay."

He pulls my naked body to his, hooking an arm under my legs and the other behind my back. Against his chest, I feel like the most petite five-foot-eight woman on the planet. Delulu much. His skin's scent is as inviting as his touch. I nuzzle my face close until the warm water catches my skin as he lowers me into the bath. The water splashes over my chest, covering most of my body. Within the warmth, my body stiffens, nipples turn into peaks, and I sit in silence, waiting for him. The sound of soft music fills my ears, and I turn my head in an attempt to look around. *You can't fucking see, Raine. Blindfolded, duh.*

"Casey?" I timidly call out. "Casey," I repeat, scoldingly.

"You're safe, beautiful."

Relieved to hear his voice, it's good to know he didn't take me to a foreign country, blindfold me in the bathtub, and then walk away. "Do you like what you see?" I tease and shimmy.

"Oh, sorry, I wasn't paying attention. I'm on my phone."

"You're such a liar." I scoop water in my palm, splashing in hopes I'd make contact.

"Easy, you wouldn't want to drown." *I knew it.*

"I'm an excellent swimmer," I argue. "You don't have to save me."

"Villains don't save people, love."

"Baby, you're not a villain. You're the prince who somehow fell in love with the evil witch."

"Evil goddess." The water splashes around me, and his legs brush mine. His touch smooths over my smooth skin as he sits opposite me.

In the dark, a sensual base and rhythm play. "I like this song." I roll my hips in the limited space, causing ripples each time I bounce a thigh off his legs.

Pulling me abruptly towards him, I sink back. My head and hips sit slightly above water while the rest of my body is engulfed. I wrap my hands around the tub's sides, my heart pounding. "I got you, wild. I got you. Okay? Do you still trust me?" He tightens his hold, squeezing my ass in his hands.

I exhale slowly. "Yes, I trust you."

"Good."

"Casey, I'm sorry."

"For what?"

"Drinking," I admit.

"It's a wedding, love. Special events make us get carried away."

"I hate it. It's like…I'm ready for people to hate me. I know they won't get me, and if I do this, it'll take the edge off."

"None of them hate you. I promise." His fingers stroke over my arms, his lips meeting my temple.

"Most people do. I get it. I'm odd and look like a bitch. Mildly, I am a bitch. And how many times have I heard that sarcasm is the lowest form of humor? And dark humor is for the fucked up. I know for a fact the girl who has it all shit her pants in second-period PE junior year, and that homie hopper who was trying to ride your lap peaked in high school, so she's looking for the best free ride now. I don't know that second one for a fact. I am sour about it, though."

"Love, I'm glad you're comfortable and want to vent to me. I really am." He inhales. "And we can talk all night. Right now, I need you to relax. Give me your stress and hold on. Will you do that for me?"

"Don't ask me twice. You could ex—"

"Remind me to make a killer kit the next time I'm at the hardware store. Extra tape." He shifts in the tub, changing positions. "Why are you nervous?"

"Asks the murderer."

"Raine Violet Cree, I'm trying to eat you the fuck out. Are you going to settle your ass down and enjoy this?"

Pinching my lips closed, I shake my head up and down. His shadow of facial hair nuzzles my inner thighs as he holds my legs against his arms. His tongue glides effortlessly into my flesh, causing my body to melt and shudder. Strokes of his tongue and gentle suction automatically push my body into a frenzy. I can't avoid arching my back as I draw my hips up into him. Heat rushes to my face; that ever-loved pressure builds so quickly, I swear this is the only three-minute wonder a woman could be perfectly accepting of.

Holy shit, we're doing this blindfold thing all the time. I tighten my thighs, pressing them against him. He stops and gently lets go of me. "Not so fast, love. Come here." He grabs my waist, lifting me forward onto his lap. I'm certain the water spills to the floor as it splashes. He slides his hands over my wet thighs, lifting my ass. His fingers dig in, pulling me closer and pushing me down onto his dick. I drop my head back, undoubtedly losing control of my facial expressions as my jaw drops in a moan. Balancing my hands against his chest, I rock, splashing water over both our bodies. Casey pulls my nipple into his mouth, tugging it in between his teeth, and I grind faster, moaning, arching in pleasurable pain, chasing the pressure. His hip bones drive me, lifting up and deepening.

"Not yet, love. I'm not done with you." Ugh. No.

He rises, stepping out of the tub, lifting me up. He grabs my hand before hoisting me over his shoulder. My feet don't even hit the floor. I feel like a doll draped over his hard body. A naked, soaking wet doll.

"Where are you taking me?"

"I said I was fucking you on the balcony." He slaps my ass, and I flinch, squealing.

"What if someone sees?"

"Suddenly shy?" Excuse me. This is a high-scale hotel in Italy! "By the time they complain, we'll be fucking somewhere else."

A rush of adrenaline labors my breathing further. The moment he walks outside, cool air stiffens my already hard nipples.

"It's fucking freezing!" He sets my feet to the ground, and I wrap my hands across my body.

"Hands here." He places my hand on the railing, guiding my legs open with his feet. I'm blindfolded, and I'm naked on a balcony in Italy. *What the fuck is happening?*

The warm air he exhales hits my back, his hand wrapping around my hip, the other cupping my breast, squeezing my nipple between two fingers.

"Still cold?"

"And wet...really wet," I yell, far louder than I anticipated. I can't help it. He got me exactly where he wanted to, pulsing, reaching for the friction between us as if I could pull him into me with nothing besides thought. "Fuck me."

"Fuck," His voice sounds an octave deeper than usual. "Tell me again, baby."

Wanting to please him in all the ways he desires turns me on. He keeps doing that thing with his finger and thumb. Does he even know how feral that makes me? "I need you. I want *you*."

I gasp. My wet body steadying under my barring hands, Casey pushes into me. With each thrust, I sink my ass into him. I squeeze around him, pressing my toe tips. My heaving body shakes, and I hold onto the railing tighter. The cold nightly temperature disappears, and heat pours over me.

I moan. "Casey."

He knocks the air out of me, and I inhale short, deep breaths, trying to recover. "Casey, I..." He brings his hand to my neck, his fingers applying pressure just below my jaw, wrapping the other farther around my waist.

"Tell me, love." I'm losing control as his thrusts continue without interruption. I've never felt this aware of my surroundings while being unable to slow the tension rising, the waves crashing into me. Look where the fuck I am! How...how. The edge of euphoria steals my breath, and every thought my mind once processed. The pressure is built so high that if he keeps hitting that spot, I'm not going to be able to stop it. I don't want to stop it.

"Casey," I pant.

He pulls out, spinning me. I arch my back over the railing, holding the metal railing as tight as I possibly can, pressing my forearms to the cold iron. My body pulses, gripping the emptiness, reaching. He wraps my legs around him, clutching my waist, and pushes back in.

"Don't let go of the rail," he says. "We have to be careful." I tighten my hold, taking thrust after thrust, and his moan finally sets me off. I shake underneath him, moaning through heavy exhales, holding onto the railing so tight my hands are probably turning purple. His moans grow, meeting mine with deep, slow pumps. I squeeze around him, unable to stop. He runs his hands up my back, pulling me against his body as he slips out of me. My limp frame falls to his chest, fully dependent on him. I'm a doll again, weak to his will.

He carries me to the bed, laying me down gently, slowly kissing my lips before he removes his tie from my eyes. My chest rises and falls, staring into his dark gaze. *God, he's fucking gorgeous.*

"I'll be right back," he whispers against my ear, pressing his lips to my hairline.

I could want this forever. I could watch him walk away bare-ass over and over again, too.

Casey returns with a washcloth, declining it down my leg. "Am I worthy?" He smiles.

"If you ever leave, I'm going to go full-on stalker."

He laughs. "You said you would break my heart. Who's breaking who now?"

"You literally almost broke my back, so…" I shrug.

"That means I fucked you right."

"Arrogant."

"Keep talking like that, and I'll have to shut you up…again."

"Intermission first?"

"Go," he gestures to the bathroom with a flick of his head.

I let the water out of the bathtub and pull my hair up into a ponytail. Washing my face and immediately going pee, I grab a robe from the closet and wrap it around my body. Casey relaxes in his gray sweatpants and glasses, lying in bed with *my book* in his hands. What is he doing, and why does he look so cute doing it?

"I like the parts you have highlighted in pink." His grin widens.

"Are you going through my things?" I climb into bed, sliding close to him and pulling the quilt over my legs.

"I was going to get you something to wear, and this was on top." He holds up the book with a shirtless man on the cover.

I shrug. "I read it for the plot." I reach over the top of him, awkwardly struggling, but manage to grab my oversized tee.

He shakes his head and tosses the book back on top of my suitcase. "Come here, please," he says, pulling me to his chest.

"I'm so tired."

He holds my hand in the air, threading his fingers through mine. "Me too, but I don't want to close my eyes."

"Why not? Mine are closed."

"If I close my eyes, the night ends. Tomorrow we go our separate ways. I don't know when I'll see you again." He strokes my messy hair, swiping it off my face.

"Thanksgiving," I murmur.

"What about Thanksgiving?"

I open my eyes and look up at him. "Come with me to Florida?"

"You know that's a questionable choice, right?"

"Not really. Yeah, my mom is going to have a field day, and we could run into Nollan. Well, we probably will run into Nollan if he finds out I came into town with you, which he will find out, but fuck it," I ramble off.

"Fuck it? That's your answer? Fuck if there is a bunch of drama over the holiday weekend, I'm taking my fuck buddy to the family dinner."

"You said fuck three times."

"Love." His glare cuts into me. Rolling his eyes would be less harsh.

I roll on top of him, looping my arms under his and hugging him with my face pressed to his chest. He exhales and takes me in his arms.

I look up at him. Even from this angle, the slight double chin that appears when he looks down is still sexy. "Casey, be my boyfriend?"

"Say that again." His brows crease, drawing together. *Oh shit*, are we not on the same page? I slip away from him, sitting up and crossing my legs.

"I'm...I don't know if I'm saying the right thing or taking the right path...I don't want this to end."

He meets me, reeling my lips back to him. "I've wanted to get to know you since that first night."

"You've got to know parts of me." My eyes stretch wide. He places another gentle kiss on my lips. "I'm yours."

Chapter Fourteen | Landslide

Raine

NOVEMBER 23RD - WEDNESDAY, 1:00 PM

I don't know how I got in so deep, so quickly. Elias scolds me for not paying attention to the ski lift and looking at my phone again. I almost take him out, managing to miss him and not fall myself.

I forgot this feeling. This new, exciting, low-key obsession comes from the fact that I truly like being around him. I'm checking my phone too often, hoping I missed a message.

"Get your shit together, Raine." He reaches down to readjust his binding.

"But did I hit you?" I yell, sarcastically.

"You're seeing him tomorrow, right?"

"Yeah, why?" I look back, waiting for him to catch up as I watch a little girl cruising from the top.

"I need to know what time to stop by so I can tell him you're losing phone privileges when we hit snow."

"I can multitask."

"Multitask right into a tree and you'd end up taking me with you."

"Exaggerations," I shout, adjusting my mask and heading down the mountain.

Casey has had a lot going on between work and his family's legal drama since we got back from Italy. So don't mind if I do. I can't wait to see him tonight. I actually miss his arrogant ass. We fly out in the morning to visit my parents. I've been more consumed with the thought of seeing him again that I haven't had the time to overthink going back to Florida. The man has some kind of voodoo over me, stripping me of my fuck you attitude and anti-fairy tale attitude.

Elias tugs his helmet off, and his bushy, jet-black hair is flat.

"Helmet head glory," I cheer. He drops his chin to his chest, shaking his mane around. "E, Calle's calling. I'll catch up with you next week. Have a nice Thanksgiving." I begin walking to the lodge door when he yells back. It's slowly starting to pick up here, particularly after the snowfall we were blessed with Sunday night.

"You'd better come back next week without the phone."

"Got it," I answer, not bothering to look back at him, and swing the door open.

"Hey Calle," I answer the phone before it goes to voice-mail.

"How come you didn't tell Mom you're bringing your new boyfriend tomorrow?" She immediately asks. Making my way to the lockers, I rest my board against the silver units and pull mine open. It only takes me a few seconds to grab my stuff and let the door hang as I juggle between my keys, drawstring bag, snowboard, and phone.

"I did, kinda. I told her I'll have a plus one." I quickly thank the patron holding the door and shuffle through the keys on my ring. Then, I almost dropped my board, but I managed to take the save before slipping on the smallest patch of black ice. I desperately reach for the sidewalk railing, trying to find something to prevent my fall. A squeaky yip makes its way out of my mouth as I slam to my butt on the cold, wet asphalt.

"That's not telling her you are bringing your six-foot, heavily tattooed boyfriend to Thanksgiving dinner, Raine. But I'm not mad. This is going to be a great distraction when I tell her we're moving." I lay on the ground for a minute, holding my keys in one hand and my phone in the other.

I groan, trying to sit up. "He's only five foot eleven. Ugh...ouch."

"Did you just fall?" I can hear the light laughter behind her question.

"Yep," I announce and regather my items. "Did you say you're telling her this weekend?" My eyes widen. We are going to be in the center of a hurricane. "You're going to put her in the grave."

She laughs. "You're going to first."

"Yeah, she'll die, Dad will resuscitate her, and then you'll go in for the double tap." I steady my legs and try to make it the rest of the way through the parking lot without joining the Cree family resting plot.

"Moving day is December twenty-ninth." I pack my bag and board into my car, open the driver's side door, and put the key into the ignition. Putting Calle on speaker, I tuck my phone into the holder and fasten my seatbelt.

Pulling out of the parking lot towards my apartment, I get back to Calle. "Dude, you could have told her any other time. Why would you wait till I'm coming home and a holiday weekend?"

"Because I don't want to tell her! Try being the golden child."

I narrowed my eyes as if she could see my expression. "Thanks, Calle," I reply dryly.

"That's not what I meant! She just has these expectations of me."

"Cal, she has the same expectations of me. I've already disappointed her. Paved the path for you. Don't worry, she gets over it."

She huffs, likely rolling her eyes, then returns to her energetic self. "I'm so excited to see you." She puts an end to the topic. "Do you need me to pick you up tomorrow?"

"Yes, please."

"Okay, I have to go. Text me your flight details. Love you. See ya tomorrow."

Nearly a month ago, I went through an earth-shattering disconnect. I told people off, I hurt feelings, and I felt that same pain back. Now I'm flying back in, and it's going to be worse than ever. I shouldn't have invited Casey. It's too much, too soon. If we run into Nollan, what will I say? *Oh, hi, glad you're doing well. I'm fucking Casey now. He's a better lover than you. Thanks for introducing us. Have a nice Thanksgiving and a nice life. Bye.*

That text I sent Bailey last week was left on read. I don't know when she's going to talk to me again. I'm afraid to tell Declan. He wouldn't be able to keep it from Nollan. God, this is a mess. I should get a quick workout in when I get home, finish packing, and reset my alarm for the flight. It's going to be fine.

Standing outside of the house I grew up in, I squeeze Casey's hand. My palms are sweaty, and I don't know why he hasn't asked me to let go of him yet.

"Hey, love." He squeezes my hand. "It's going to be fine." I reluctantly smile. "This is your family. They want you to be happy."

"I know. I'm fine," I snap, refusing to admit how anxious I am.

"Your hand is disgustingly sweaty."

"Hush it," I whisper, walking into my parents' house.

"Raine," Dad stands from his recliner, greeting me with a hug.

"Hey, Dad." I hug him back. "Um, this is Casey. My boyfriend." Casey extends his hand, and Dad shakes it firmly.

"It's nice to meet you, Mr. Cree. You have a beautiful home."

"Thank you. Call me Josh." Dad looks back at me as if he wants to state the obvious. "Mom said you had a friend coming, but *boyfriend*? This is relatively new?"

"Yeah, I purposely left that part out." I nod.

"I don't blame you," he says with a smirk. "Well, come on in. Take a seat." He chauffeurs us with a hand. Casey sits on the end of the brown microfiber sofa, closest to Dad's recliner, and I sit next to him.

"Mom's working on dessert now. Dinner should be ready shortly. Are you hungry?"

"Famished," Casey replies. "The airport was so busy, we didn't bother attempting to get food. Raine said you like to fish. Do you catch and release or keep?"

Way to get him talking. He's not going to shut up about fishing or his boat now. I rub Casey's leg, smoothing my hand over his dark-washed jeans. Before I rise to head to the kitchen, I stop and smile at him.

"Raine! Just in time. Can you open the fridge?"

"Sure." I round the counter, opening the refrigerator.

On the center shelf, she places a tray of mini assorted pies, topped with a swirl of whipped cream. "How was your flight?"

"Awful." I lean my forearms against the kitchen peninsula countertop.

She shuts the door and begins rinsing a bowl from one side of the double basin sinks. "I told you not to travel on Thanksgiving Day."

"I know, but Casey couldn't leave any earlier. Work stuff."

"Where is this *Casey*? Did you meet her through work or snowboarding? No family to spend the holiday with?" In typical Mom fashion, she rambles off questions before I can answer the previous one. She's also assuming Casey is a woman.

"Um, *his* family is estranged. His only close family was his grandfather, and he passed away a few months ago."

She finishes drying the bowl, opens the cabinet to her right, and stores it. "Oh, *he*?"

I stand up straight, watching her pull serving utensils out. "Yes. We're dating."

She smacks a wooden spoon on the counter, setting it down dramatically. "Since when have you had a boyfriend, Raine?" She stares at me, dumbfounded. "You could have told me." I can't tell if she's in shock or if she's pissed I didn't tell her. "Did you invite him as a friend, and he asked to grow your relationship at the airport?" She winks.

"You hang out with Calle too much. It's new, only a few weeks old. He doesn't have any family to spend the holiday with...ours is welcoming, *right Mom*?" I ask with a guttural tone.

"It is the season for giving. I'm glad you decided to bring him here this early on. Can weed him out if he's a dud sooner rather than later." She pulls her mitts on and opens the oven. "I'm glad we get to meet at least one of your New York boyfriends. You are thinking long-term, right?" And there is the spurn. A few simple words that make the difference between ratifying and rejecting clear every time.

"Oh, it's this one, Mom," Calle coos, walking into the room and sneaking a crescent roll from the basket on the counter. "He's keeper material." She flashes me a look, her eyes widening, and her forehead creases. She moves around the peninsula, where she props herself against the counter in the farthest corner and takes a bite.

"What's he do for a living?" Mom glances from Calle to me, wanting more information.

"I enjoy being with Casey," I shrug, pressing my elbows back into the countertop. I suddenly seem to float away, trying to piece together my thoughts. How do I express the connection we have? I— "We went to Italy a few weeks ago for his friend's wedding. It was...incredible." I blink. Italy! She's going to freak.

"What! Raine Violet Cree, you left the country and didn't even think to inform your mother! How long did you know this man when you fled to Italy with him?"

"A week," I shrug. Be glad I didn't tell you I left early from my last visit so I could go to Colorado and fuck him.

"A week, Raine!" Her hands swing up and tensely back to her sides, tilting her chin up, and rolling her eyes. "Did you at least do a background check?" She asks, placing her hands on her hips.

"Well, I'm still alive. Think we're okay." Both of her hands spring to her temple.

"This is not funny. You could have been murdered."

"I only murder brunettes," I hear his voice in the background, and I rise from my hunching position. He kisses my cheek and stands behind me. "Nash is here. Your dad went out to look at his new car."

Mom is frozen with her mouth hanging open. Calle's looking at the floor with her lips pinched, holding in her laughter.

"I'm kidding, Mrs. Cree. I'm not a homicidal maniac. Casey Pierce of Pierce Investments, feel free to internet stalk me." I smile at him. "I'm going to head outside." He looks at me, then back at Mom. "Nice meeting you, Mrs. Cree. Dinner smells amazing." His gaze drops to me for a fifth of a second, quickly sending a flutter of butterflies into the pit of my gut. "Calle," he raises a hand, giving her a subtle wave and nod.

"Have at it." I watch him walk away, turning back to Mom.

"Are you serious, Raine? That man is covered, *covered* in tattoos," she whisper-yells, walking closer to me. "And how old is he?"

"Twenty-six. Sexy, right?"

"Not even the slightest. They're all the way down his hands and his neck, *his neck too*. Good Lord. Where did you meet him?" She sighs.

"Why does it matter? He treats me well." I spin around, lowering my elbows to the granite. "Calle," I exclaim. "Finish the freaking roll already and vouch for me." I twist back and glare at her.

"Mom, he's cool," she says with a mouth full. "Nash knows him, he's friends with Nollan, and he's like, filthy rich."

Flipping Calle and her big mouth! That's not what I meant by vouching.

"He's Nollan's friend?" She raises her brows with her arms crossed over her chest.

"Yeah, he was one of his clients. Comes to town every few months," Calle adds.

"Wait, what did he say? Pierce Investments? What is that? What does he do for a living?"

"Filthy rich," Calle repeats, digging a deeper hole while I stand here with my palm over my face, trying to figure out how to fix it. "He did just take her to Italy and Colorado before that."

"Calle!" I yell, not knowing how else to shut her blabbering mouth up.

"Are you sure you actually like this guy and not just his over-the-top lifestyle?"

"He could live in a freaking cardboard box, and I would like him. Can we stop discussing this?" I reposition myself. "He's a good man. It's not up for discussion."

"Excuse me..."

Nash, Dad, and Casey walk into the dining room behind me, crowding the small space.

Mom's daggered look cuts me bloody before she smiles to greet Nash. "Hi, Nash. How's the family?"

"Good. My mom mentioned stopping by tonight after they leave my Grams."

"The Broack's are welcome anytime!" She waves her hand in the air, swooping it inwards. *Petty.* I hope they wait till we leave to show up. I smile at Nash when he glances in my direction. Casey grasps my hand, lacing his fingers between mine. Nash's loyalty is to his brother. He's foolishly going to find a free moment and text him. I'm sure of it. I hope he doesn't. It won't bring anything good.

"Shall we eat?" Dad asks, pulling out a chair.

While most of the house is in a food coma and crashed in front of the football game, I excused myself to the restroom. I walk back into the dim hallway, lost in thought, before heading to the living room to rejoin everyone. Jolted back into reality, Casey's fingers wrap around my shoulders.

"Coincidence meeting you here, beautiful," he proclaims, shuffling around me till my back is against the wall.

"Real coincidence. This is an elite establishment. How did you get in?"

"Fucked the owner's daughter." My smile appears like lightning during a storm, abruptly occurring and fading as fast.

"Lucky woman."

"No, I'm the lucky one." His lips press into mine, and his tongue slips into my mouth.

"We should be getting back." I look toward the hallway entrance.

"Nobody knows we're missing," he replies.

"Somehow I find it hard to believe that not a single person missed the exotic cuisine sitting in the middle of a family-sized box of McNuggets, getting up and leaving the room."

"Someone subbed the ordinary soft drink for a thick-ass strawberry shake."

"A strawberry shake goes amazingly with Bastila," I reply. I've never even tried Bastila. I only saw it on one of those cooking shows one night when I was bored, flicking through channels, but if he were a dish, this famously sweet and savory food would be a little more accurate.

"It does. I'll prove it to you." He takes my hand, spinning me till I'm facing the wall, and slides his hands along the waistband of my jeans till he reaches the button, undoing it and dragging the zipper down.

"What are you doing?" I whisper. "What if someone comes over here?"

"The greater the risk, the greater the reward," he says in that lower tone, the one that challenges me to listen instead of argue. "I give financial advice for a living. Don't question me." He slides his hand down the front of my open jeans, his finger slipping between my thighs, his palm covering my pelvis.

"Speaking of finance, did Bash get your paperwork drafted?"

"I don't want to talk about it. And you...you're already soaking." He draws his hand back, and I look over my shoulder at him, pulling his dick from his jeans.

Holy shit. "Casey, this is fucking insane," I stage whisper. "I'm not doing this."

"You started it."

"I did not, and this is my parents' house. My dad walks around the corner and catches us—the opposite of hot. It's mortifying."

He inhales deeply and breathes out. My eyes wander down to the hard dick in his hand. Someone would have to walk into the dining room before finding the short corridor to the bathroom. Ugh, no. This is a bad idea. He wraps his hand around my hip, settling it over my pelvis and pulling my back against him. He lines up using his other hand, and I instinctively push my ass back. "Two minutes? Please, darling. I missed you." He pleads. His lips meet my neck, and I feel the pressure of his head ready to slip into me.

"You said I make you do stupid things..." I'm the biggest dumbass in the world right now. "This is the one that's sending us both to hell."

He chuckles, a sign of amusement and pleasure. "Yes?"

"Yes."

Pants around my thighs, he doesn't waste another second. Skin to skin, heat to heat—the tip of his cock slides in my arousal. He pulls my hips back with each micro thrust until I'm stretched around him and he can slide easily. The initial discomfort lessened, and I let my head fall to his shoulder, digging my nails into his forearms. This is wrong. This is stupid. This feels...so fucking good. A moan eludes my lips, and I push my ass into him, trying to apply more pressure to my clit.

"Shh," Casey hushes, covering my mouth with his hand. "Tell me your dad isn't a gun owner."

I pull his hand down, holding onto it. "This is Florida, the Gunshine state, baby."

"Then you'd better shut your pretty little mouth. I want to survive the night." He drives into me, and I lean back against him, wide-mouthed and muted.

"Casey, let's go into the bathroom. We need the full five minutes."

Between laughs and panting, we make it inside, locking the door. He rails me against the sink, and it's hot. His balls tap against me, and his breath on my neck, but it's not getting me there. "Can you sit down? There are towels in the closet."

"Right here?"

"Yeah."

I straddle him on the covered toilet, grinding deeply when a knock rattles the door. *Fuck you! I was so close.* "Yes?" I ask.

"Raine, you'll never guess who just showed up."

"Wait," I whisper as quietly as possible, pushing my hand against Casey's chest to stop him from kissing my neck. "Who is it, Calle?"

"The Broacks' and Nollan."

I look at Casey, unable to speak. A flush of lightheadedness overwhelms me.

"Where's Casey?" She asks.

"Calle," I practically grunt, climbing off Casey's lap.

"Ew. I shouldn't have asked."

He stands up, cleaning himself the best he can given the circumstances, and tucks himself back in his boxers, zipping up his jeans.

I sit on the toilet, and Casey smirks at me, shaking his head. "I have to pee. Look the other way," I scold. "What are we going to do?" I whisper.

"Smile and say Happy Thanksgiving."

"Right." Quickly washing my hands, I open the door. Calle is still standing in the hallway, her arms crossed over her chest, and she has a condescending glare.

"Don't give me that look." I walk past her.

"I wasn't the one doing the dirty in the bathroom. I hope you washed whatever surfaces you touched."

"It started in the hallway, so you've always been contaminated," I scoff, continuing down the hall with Calle behind me and Casey trailing in the rear. I don't look back, imagining the look of pure disgust on her face.

"There she is. Raine, Linda, and Mark wanted to say hello," Mom says when I walk into the living room.

I force a smile and give Linda a quick hug. "How are you?" I ask. Nollan steps out from behind them. His blue eyes catch mine for a moment.

"Wonderful, but how are you, dear? It's been too long." She rubs my arm with a concerned, almost pitying smile.

Before I get the chance to reply, Mom answers for me. "She's doing so well in New York. Thriving at work, nicest group of friends. We love it when she comes home to visit us." She smiles proudly. What in the *my toy is shinier than yours,* is this?

"And she brought her boyfriend to meet the family," Dad adds. She turns to look over at him sitting in the recliner. Her head spun so quickly that she made the devil shit his pants.

"Right. I guess you know him already, Nollan," she chirps. Nollan looks past his parents toward the kitchen entryway, where Casey stands. His blue eyes couldn't be colder, and his jaw clenched tightly.

"Casey," Nollan acknowledges.

"Come sit," Mom tells them. "Are you stuffed, or could you take some sugar? I made assorted mini pies. Raine, could you bring the tray and a few plates in here?" I nod, walking past Casey into the kitchen.

I open the fridge and look up, only to find Nollan standing next to the man I was screwing in the bathroom five minutes ago. "What the fuck is this, Raine?"

I glance at the doorway, seeing if anyone followed the two of them. "I didn't plan it." The tray clings against the counter, and I kick the fridge door closed with my foot.

Nollan turns to Casey, pointing a finger. "And you, I told you to stay away from her."

"You have no say in who I date," I disagree. "I'm trying to live my life and let you live yours. I had no idea you would be at *my* parents' house. Why are you here?"

"My parents wanted to stop in. I rode with them to my grandparents' house. I had no choice. It would have been odd if I sat in the car."

"Look, we obviously can't avoid each other all the time. Our families are friends, and my sister is dating your brother. You respect me. I'll respect you. Keep everything civil."

"Civil." He nods. "You want me to be civil, while you're fucking someone I thought was my friend. Of any man you could have chosen, you had to pick him? You did this on purpose."

"Yeah, Nollan. My life's goal is to make you as miserable as possible. That's the only thing on this planet that makes me happy."

"I'm sure it has nothing to do with his money either. Was it money, Raine? Did he offer you money?" He turns to Casey. "I knew you wanted her."

"Are you suggesting I'd exchange money for sex?" This bastard.

"Well, you are pretty easy."

I clench my fists together, ready to knock him out.

"Nobody needs to act like a child," Casey finally cuts in.

"Fuck off, Casey. Did she tell you all our history? Did she tell you how I was her first?"

"Yes. Everyone has a past."

"I bet she didn't tell you everything." Nollan looks at me, rage and envy in his voice.

"She doesn't have to. It's her choice what she wants me to know."

"Don't expect her to marry you or stick around when things get rough. Raine always runs." His intense stare is terrifying. He knows parts of my life that I haven't shared with anyone else, not a soul. My chest pounds, sinking into the pit of my stomach.

"It's between us." Casey keeps his composure.

"So this is just a fling?"

"Nollan! My relationship is none of your business," I snap. Casey's hand warms the curve of my back, reminding me I don't want to make a scene. Everyone is still content in the living room, and I don't want to draw them in here, especially since Nollan holds secrets I don't want him sharing with the classroom. He'd do anything he knew would hurt me right now.

"It's only my business when you come crawling back, right? Or no? You're not going to do that again." He sucks his lips in and nods, brushing his hand over his stubbled jaw. "I think he should know everything. We're friends. I'll do the friendly thing and tell you what kind of person Raine is."

"Nollan, please." I clench my teeth together. "I'm sorry," I plead. "Be the good man I know you are and let this go."

"How do you know who I am anymore, Raine? I haven't been the same person since I lost you and the baby in the same month."

I can't breathe.

My lungs are hollow. Hastily vacillating up and down, my chest reaches for oxygen.

He...he said...and Casey.

I look back and forth between the men before grabbing the tray from the counter and walking between them to the living room. I'm heavily panting, on the verge of a full-on anxiety attack. Calle looks at me and stands up from the sofa, rushing over. No one else notices the color has faded from my face and my puffy eyes, my happiness being stripped.

"Go," she whispers, taking the tray.

I walk back into the kitchen and out the back door, settling into a rocking chair and pulling my legs to my chest. I bury my face into my thighs and try to slow my breathing down. Why did he do that? He thinks he's the only one to suffer. I've buried that horrible night so deeply that I couldn't find it if I wanted to, and he unearthed it with ease. I didn't want any of this.

The presence of someone standing in front of me almost makes me want to lift my head. It's Casey. Nobody smells as amazing as him. His warm hands caress my back, rubbing my shoulders gently. "Love," he sighs. "You know I'm not a stranger to loss or trauma. If you want to talk about it, I'm here. If not, I'm still here."

"I hate him."

"You don't." He breathes out. "It's okay. He was an asshole. He purposely hurt you because you've hurt him. It's fucked up, I know. Nobody wins." He bends to my level, wrapping his arms behind my bent legs.

"Casey, I've never told...*anyone*. I've never spoken those words. I don't know if I can say them out loud to you, to Ivy, to Calle. I'd rather die." I swallow the saliva in my mouth and wipe my undereye with my thumb. "The story behind my tattoo...it's this. I want to tell you. I'm scared." My lip quivers, and streams of water coat my cheeks.

"I'm not going anywhere."

"You should. I warned you. Horrible things always happen around me."

"I'm not leaving." He presses his lips to my knee.

"I…I found out when my period was a week late, and I was terrified. I didn't want to keep it. I had to wait two weeks to get into the doctor's office to discuss my options. They were the longest two weeks of my life. I told Nollan right away, and…he was happy. We were twenty-two years old. I was about to graduate from college. I couldn't understand how he was so excited."

"Because he loved you and he wanted a family with you."

"He knew I didn't want that. It was so unfair. And then…" A hard lump sits in my throat. I work up whatever saliva I can manage in my dry mouth and swallow. Casey takes my chin between his fingers, pulling my lips to his. My eyes fall on his, weaving back and forth.

"When I finally saw the doctor, they couldn't find a heartbeat." My words are nearly silent. Casey's expression tightens, sorrow filling his eyes. He combs pieces of hair from my face, tucking them back. "They told me that miscarriage is common in early pregnancy, and I couldn't have prevented it. I thought I would feel relieved, as horrible as that sounds, but I didn't. I was as heartbroken as Nollan…and I shut down. I buried it. It's been seven years, and nobody has ever known. Nollan never heard a word from me about it. Now you know, and not by my choice, but because that greedy bastard will say anything, no matter how painful, to make sure I don't get to move forward if he can't."

"You don't have to be strong all the time. You can tell me or don't tell me; tell a professional. Whatever you want to do, I'm not afraid of life. He thought that was going to chase me away? Something out of your control that doesn't tell me shit about your character other than how you've coped?" He chuckles. "Fuck, I ran from my past for years before I faced it." He taps my knee. "I'll give you the name of my therapist."

"You go to therapy?"

"Twice a month." He leans in, kissing my forehead. I don't want to go back inside. I don't want to face Nollan, my parents, or his parents. "Look at me, please." I find his dark eyes. "I want you to scream." Huh? "Just scream." He tilts his head back.

"You want me to scream?" I shift my gaze. "Right here?"

"Yes. Give me the loudest, over-the-top scream of your life."

"This isn't going to help," I protest. People are going to think I'm being attacked by a rabid raccoon and call the police.

"Yes, it will. I pinky promise." He takes my hand in his. "Do it. Scream for me, baby. You'll feel better when you just let it out." I stare at the ground, contemplating the scream of my life. He takes my jaw into his hand and regains my attention. "I'll do it with you. Okay? You ready? *Peer pressure*," he exaggerates his words, squeezing my shoulders. "One. Two...Three," he calls. He belts out a scream, and I can't contain my laughter. Covering my mouth won't even mute it. "Don't you laugh! Let's go."

"No." I shake my head.

"You want to know something I'm starting to hate? This villain bullshit. You're getting, I don't know," he shakes his head and tilts his chin upward. "You're getting spanked, that's it! If you try to tell me you're a villain again, it's a physical red ass for you. I want to hear you yell *I'm the fucking savior.*"

"A savior of what? I can't save myself, let alone anyone else."

"You save me. Every day, you save me."

"Hey, is everything okay out here?" I look up to see Nash stepping to the deck from the doorway, and I nod. "My parents and Nollan left. Are you sure you're okay?"

"I'll be fine." I softly smile.

"Okay, we'll no rush, but uh, let Calle know when you're ready, and she can drop you off at the hotel."

I nod again. It is after six, and it's been a long day. "Hey, Nash...thanks." Wrapping my arms around Casey, I take in his warmth.

"Yeah, no problem." I look back and see him standing in the doorway. "And if it means anything, I didn't tell Nollan about Casey." He pats the door frame, turning back inside.

"Are you ready?" Casey asks.

"Yes. Rom-com night?"

"As long as it's from this decade."

"Movie roulette. Let it up to the luck of the draw," I suggest.

"Can we take some of those little pie things?"

My laugh returns. "Mom's mini pies. Absolutely."

His mouth softens, and he sits on the rocking chair beside me, weaving his fingers through mine and stroking the length of my thumb with his. "Raine, what are the odds of you getting pregnant again?"

"Why?" A feeling of uneasiness washes over me, and my heart begins to pound more quickly. I thought this conversation was over. It was out in the air, blowing away.

"You said you had it covered. Permanently covered?"

"Um...I have an IUD."

"That means there is a small percentage that it could occur." He looks me up and down.

"It's like a one percent chance. I don't understand. What are you trying to ask me?" I talk faster, frustrated or afraid...both?

"I don't want you to be put in a position where you have to make a complicated decision if that decision is made for you by nature or not. I won't be that man."

"I know you won't," I reply softly. "I'm confident in what has been working for my body for years, but if anything changes, you'll know. Want some educational pamphlets in the meantime?" Ah, the dimples. He stands and grabs my hand, pulling me from the rocking chair into a bear hug. "You could work on your pull-out game, too."

"Oh!" He throws his head back. "You're breaking my heart now."

Chapter Fifteen | Opacity

Casey

When I close my eyes, I see Raine covered in flour, her face speckled with a huge smile, and her laughter carrying throughout the kitchen. I never imagined I'd be making cookies all day with her, her sister, and her mom. Now, I would give any amount of money to be there instead of in another office, sitting at a long, blank table in a tailored suit, waiting for Karson.

The clicking of her red-bottom heels draws me from the papers I've been reading. Her noisy pumps are covered by light purple flared pants. A strong-shouldered jacket cinches at her waist with a far too low neckline, revealing her ample cleavage. Exactly what I wanted to see this morning. I refrain from letting the disgust show on my face.

"Good morning," she greets the room. "Did everyone have a nice holiday weekend?" Others reply, but I ignore her. "Not having a good morning, Casey?"

"Well, you made me come here, Karson."

"All you have to do is agree, and we can both go our separate ways. In and out, done." She brushes her hands together. "You can go back to that plain life of yours, and I can go on to becoming the new CEO of CP Banking and, respectively, CP Reach."

"What's your plan?" I lean onto my elbows. "Genuinely, I'd like to know. Does Reach somehow tip the scale on qualifications to take over CP?"

She presses her palms to the table across from me, narrowing her greedy chocolate eyes. "If you didn't walk away, you would know exactly what I'm after."

"I knew you were after something. Glad you can admit it."

She purses her red lips and straightens. "I'm willing to give you partial ownership of CP Reach."

I laugh. "You want to give me partial ownership of something I already have control over?"

"The man had two grandchildren. He would want us to have an equal share of his beloved foundation. If I were on board, it would free up your time. Fundraisers, events? Press and grant presentations? All public appearances? Work is my life."

"Right. This is all for my benefit."

"I'm your sister, of course I care." She pushes her rouge lip out as if pouting will make her appear innocent.

"That's funny since I haven't heard from you in years."

"It's hard to keep track of you, hiding from daddy and all." Right. That's what I've been doing, Karson.

"Are you trying to tell me the queen of social media couldn't find me anywhere? You must be off your game. I do my research as well."

"Fighting for my birthright from a chauvinistic ass that refuses to invest in me tends to be distracting. You would know if you didn't desert me." Here it is. This all comes back on me because *I was rescued* from him when I was a teenager.

"You could have left, like I did," I reply, as professionally as possible. "You had the choice."

"You could have stayed for me."

Don't put that guilt on me. "Cut to the chase, Karson. Why the foundation? If you want to be partners, tell me why I should trust you."

Her cheeks hollow, twisting her lips. After a pause of silence, she answers. "The office. I've been trying to get office space near Hudson Yards for months. I can split it, putting CP Banking and CP Reach together."

"The location, that's it?"

"From a business standpoint, it's perfect. Gramps was smart, but not smart enough to utilize one building for two purposes. The board will be impressed, I'll have the credentials, and the old man won't have anything negative to protest. He can't run the company forever, and with nobody else to replace him, I look pretty damn good placing a market space in Hudson."

"Sebastian," I call. He walks to our end of the table, and I step away, discussing the details of our conversation.

"Sure. Take your time." She flings her arms up, grabbing the top of a chair and pulling it out.

"It's up to you, Casey. As your friend, I don't trust her. As your lawyer, we can get a clean contract with all the details hammered out to protect you from anything shady, if this is the direction you want to take."

I pull out my chair and sit down across from her. "I haven't been to the office in at least a year. I'm open to discussing terms, but before I sign anything, I want to walk the building with you and go over all details of this...combination."

Her brash smile drags from her lips as she stands to leave the room. "As you wish, brother. This is going to be a good partnership, just you wait and see."

"Are you sure about this?" Bash asks in wary.

"No. This allows me access, though. I want to see that she gets all of CP. It's the only way to shut Cameron up and end all of this."

3:00 PM

On the countertop, my phone buzzes in a circle. I hope it's Raine.

How did it go today?

I close the text message and open her contact, hitting the call button and switching to speaker.

"Good or bad?" She answers, cutting right to the chase.

"Hello to you, too, love." I put my phone on the counter and adjust the pan on the stove. "I've missed you."

"It's been one day," she scoffs. "You're delaying."

"No, I'm not. Business is second on my list of things to do. You're number one."

"Well, do me while doing business. That would be hot. Instead of a desk walking pad treadmill thing, a desk hump and grind." Picturing her under my desk in such a position, I couldn't agree more.

"You're right, they would be hot. Add it to our list."

"We have a list?"

"We started checking boxes off your bucket list, right? Now I'm thinking we make a second list, a *fuck-it list*, for all the rated R things we'd like to do." I scrape my knife against the cutting board till it's emptied into the pan. Her silence worries me. Did I lose her? "Raine?"

"When are you coming to see me?" She abruptly asks.

"My schedule, uh, I've come to an agreement with Karson. It might make my schedule a little tighter for a few weeks...or months," I admit.

"Months?"

"Yeah, I know. We'll figure it out." She doesn't say much. "It's temporary."

"I was hoping you'd make it to the mountain with me."

"I'll make it happen."

"So, did you give her the foundation?"

"*Partially.* I have a few things to check into, and Bash has legal jargon to go through." I reach for a wooden spoon from the utensil rack and stir the chopped zucchini mixture sautéeing in my skillet. "What are you up to tonight?"

Snowboarding with the girls. Audrey and Rosalin just walked through the door." Their chatter grows in the background, with one of them yelling, "Hi."

"Alright, I'll let you go then. Behave, please."

"I never behave," she sasses.

"Yeah, well, I don't want to earn the emergency contact call quite yet." I grab my spices and return to my skillet.

"I'll be safe, Dad."

"That's Daddy to you."

"Oh, I also wanted to tell you really quick...hold on." The laughter and chatter quiets. "I wanted to let you know that Nollan texted me this morning."

"Okay, what do you want me to know about it?" Women drive men to do some crazy things. Act like an asshole and try to ruin any relationship she has that's not with him? The worst he could do at this point is stalk her on social media and text her every day.

"He was apologizing, telling me he wants to be friends again, that he can't live without me. He'd rather have me as a friend than a stranger. Total bullshit."

"It's your decision." Since the day I met Raine, I knew she wasn't going to listen to a damn thing I said. She's smart. She'll cut ties with him on her own terms.

"I don't know how to feel. I'm angry, shocked, hurt, and I'm sympathetic. He felt betrayed and lashed out."

"Raine, he gave away your deepest secret. Tried to use it as a bargaining chip. I—" It's not my place. "You still owe yourself that scream."

"I'm fine," she says lightly. "I just wanted to let you know."

"I'm glad you told me. I might have found out the next time I go through your phone, and that wouldn't have ended well. Would put some holes in the wall or something. Who knows what kind of violence I would evoke? Nobody talks to my woman." My satire is well-received, earning her bold laugh.

"Your possessive boyfriend role needs a little work. Like, you have to at least threaten to cut the man's tongue out for even *thinking* about *saying* my name."

I laugh at her, turning off the burner along the back of the range. "Possessive boyfriend training starts at 0800 hours. Send me an audiobook."

"I got you."

"Go have fun. I'll talk to you later." I drop my voice an octave to deliver a worthy warning. "Behave, wildcat, *don't make me come find you.*"

"Instant improvement. It's all about that confidence."

"Bye, love."

"Bye."

December 1st - Thursday, 8:45 AM

The open white walls and wood flooring, along with the scattered tan rugs under sets of cushioned chairs and small tables, remain unchanged from the last time I was here. I round the corner, reaching for the door handle to Grandpa's office. He won't be sitting at his desk when I turn the knob and pull it open. Regret is the worst part of losing someone you love. Sadness and guilt twist into the rope I want to hang myself with. It's not that I want to join him. I want to feel anything other than this. I'll take pain. It's the easiest to concoct. While living in the state of the present, I can't change the past, and I can't hold what is already gone. I thought it wouldn't be this difficult to turn a knob.

I twist the bronze grip, only to find an empty disaster in his place. There are papers scattered on his desk. I'm sure the staff have been struggling to assess them. A floor-to-ceiling bookshelf, filled with hundreds of books, including the entire encyclopedia, covers the back wall. Without a doubt, he regularly referenced them. Technology wasn't his strong suit. I run my fingers across the spines, meandering down the wall of literature till I reach his desk, front and center. Leather turns my fingertips cold as I trace the stitches. Pulling out his chair, I sit and roll closer to the desk.

I lean back, staring at the ceiling. "What do you want me to do here? Should I go through with this? Should I let Karson take this place and turn it into something new? Potentially something better. She's right, you know. And don't be stubborn." Separate entities owned by the same man. It's not wrong to house them together. "A sign or...something would be useful." I let out an audible breath, my eyes falling to the center drawer.

I glide it open, and lying along the left side of a desktop calendar is a photo of him and me. I pinch it between my fingers and hold it up. My last race. I lost. I was disappointed in myself for the stupid mistakes I made. He wasn't. He was so proud to call me his grandson. He took me around under his arm, introducing me to all his rich, big-shot friends and talking me up like I was the next Andretti.

Laughing out loud, I run my hand over my chin. *I miss him.* I pull out my wallet and slide the photo inside. Closing the drawer, I open up the two on the right, going through them. I check the opposite side, finding nothing of inter-est. Everything looks in order. I glance around the room, spinning in Grandpa's chair. The bookshelf has cabinets on both ends. What does he have in there?

I rise, finding myself opening every door. All empty.

"Find anything good?" Karson calls.

As she drops a large binder on the desktop, I turn around. "Yes, the encyclopedia."

"That sounds great and all, but this has more pictures. You seem like a picture book guy." She turns around, walk-ing away.

I sit back down and open the binder. It's very profession-al—a complete redesign with all the original branding. "You had this done in three days?"

"I'm a Pierce. You should know, so are you," she replies, walking back to the desk.

"Don't remind me," I mutter.

"Seems to have done you good. Your business is successful, is it not?" She walks around the room to the bookshelf, rolling her finger across the surface and brushing it off as if the room hadn't been cleaned since his death. Every building has a cleaning service that arrives each evening.

I don't answer her, continuing to read through the pages.

"I'm not here to ruin you. I'm here to take everything from the fucking devil." She grinds her teeth, flipping her wavy brown hair over her shoulder as she walks to the cabinets at the end of the bookshelf.

"I already checked them. They're empty." She opens them anyway, then begins pulling books and paging through them. "Looking for something?"

"I'm just curious what this old man spent his time doing."

"You could have found out. Now you'll never know."

She shoves the book back in place, staring at me. "You and I may have grown up in the same house, but you have no idea what it's like to be me. You say I could have left, then what? I would get *nothing*," she enunciates. "The fucking devil set me up from the moment I was born. Everyone for generations has had a name starting with C. He gives me a name that clearly should fit with the rest, but changes it to a K. A fucking K! What a sick fucking joke. He would fight till his dying day to keep me, *a simple woman*, out of CP. Do you really think that if I left, I would have any way back in? If I moved with you to Grandpa's, I would be right here, with half of his foundation and none of CP. I've worked my ass off, interning, earning my position, and still not being good enough. He would hand you the key after not seeing you in years."

"We agree on one thing." I look up from the binder. "He's the fucking devil."

"What do you think?" She asks.

"It's well thought out."

She walks back to the desk and flips the page, pointing. "I added a second front desk here, that way CP and the foundation remain separate entities, respectfully, and account holders will see it every time they enter the office. The marketing rule of seven."

"I'm impressed." With my hands behind my head, I lean back.

"Nobody wants to make a trip to the bank if they can access their needs from the palm of their hand. Having this location will make it convenient to come in, and with all of the shops, seeing that bold sign enough times, you'll be curious enough to ask questions. Rule of seven. Trust me now?"

"No." I cross my arms over my chest. She knows what she's doing. She's smart and on top of it, and very *Karson*. A god of her own rules. Sometimes cutting away from the rest of the sheep isn't good for those surrounding the one who's telling the normies to fuck themselves.

"What do you want me to do to prove that I'm a trustworthy partner?"

"We haven't talked in years. I'd compare it to working with a new colleague, except that's not possible. You're not a stranger. You have a proven track record of greed and selfishness. You want my trust? I don't want to run the foundation. From a business standpoint, it's logical to bring someone capable in to oversee it."

"Let's get this straight, you are not my boss. We are partners. If you want to be the silent partner, then be the silent partner. You can relax. I'm not going to bury it. I need this foundation."

"That's what I mean, Karson. *You need it.* That's why you're here. It's to your benefit. It has nothing to do with carrying on our grandfather's legacy or whatever bullshit you want to tell me next."

"Transparency, Casey? We both know my image is better than *yours...*" Her eyes roll up and down. "For the face of Reach."

"You're such a cunt."

"Aw, big brother is jealous." She pouts, quickly pulling a compact from her clutch to check her lipstick.

"You got me. I'm green with envy for your life, Karson."

"I have a meeting to get to. Finish your inspection, and have your lawyer contact mine. In fact, tell Sebastian I said hi while you're at it...and if he's snappy about it, I'll invite him to my next foam party. I'd like to have this finished as soon as possible."

"Of course you would." I exhale as she disappears. I pull the photo back out of my wallet, stuck under history. "So would I, so would I," I murmur to myself.

December 14 - Wednesday, 4:15 PM

After circling twice, I finally found a place to park. I look up at the brick building, double-checking the address again on my phone. This is the fitness studio Raine said she takes classes at every Wednesday. I pictured something more...obvious, a large gym? It's hidden on a quiet back road with on-street parking. The only signage is the large decal on the lobby window.

"Hello, how are you?" A young woman greets me.

"I'm well, thank you. I'm hoping you can help me. I'm trying to surprise my girlfriend."

She lowers her chin, smiling with reddening cheeks. "Which class is she in?" She looks between her computer monitor and me.

Shit. I don't know. "Honestly, I'm not sure. I know it started about fifteen minutes ago."

"Mm," she hums. "This is only my second week on the job. What's her name?"

"Raine Cree."

"I think…" Her lip protrudes. "Can you describe her? We have two classes that have just started. Let me see if I can get you to the right room on the first try."

"Her face tends to be stuck in a look that could kill, but when she smiles, church bells ring."

"Aw, my goodness. That's adorably poetic, but I need a little more descriptive words like *hair color* and *height*. Those would be more helpful in this situation."

"Of course. She's a few inches shorter than me, strawberry blonde hair, green eyes."

"I'm pretty sure I know who you're looking for. She's in pole, Studio B." *What* did she just say?

"What is *pole*, exactly?"

"You're about to find out." She grabs a desk plate from the corner and flips it, setting it in the center of the L-shaped counter. *Back soon.* "This way." She walks around the desk. Following her through a small gym with various machines, she makes small talk as we walk.

"If you don't mind me asking, what's the surprise?"

"I live out of town. She's not expecting me."

"Oh, you're the surprise. How cute."

She holds the door open, smiling as I walk past her into the studio. Dim lighting and seductive music fill the room. Six women, with their backs to me, spiral around poles. Fucking stripper poles. I shouldn't be surprised. This is exactly the unexpected stuff she does. It's definitely not jazzercise.

The young brunette walks in behind me, leaning into my arm. "Do you see her?" Amongst the reflections in the mirrored wall, one in black sweatpants and a gray cropped tank top calls my soul.

"Abso-fucking-lutley," I say under my breath. Clearing my throat, I look at her. "Sorry. Yes, she's here."

"Take a seat. The class is an hour long." She points to a few metal chairs along the wall and walks away, whispering something to a tall woman with a long braid down her back, presumably the instructor. They both look at me and back at each other with wide smiles before she leaves, waving.

Raine follows the direction of the braid woman while quietly observing. At least two of the other women have noticed me, occasionally glancing in my direction. To avoid making anyone uncomfortable, I try to ignore them.

"Ladies, before we run through the full dance with music, we have a guest today." She presents me with a twist of her hand, all eyes following. Raine's eyes find me, and her smile grows. She speedwalks over to me and wraps her arms around my neck. "Raine, do you want to introduce your patron?"

"Um, yeah," she hesitates. "This is my boyfriend, Casey."

"Hello, ladies," I reply with the flick of my hand.

Her instructor unfolds a chair at the front of the room. "If you could come to the front of the room, you'll be in for a treat."

"What?" Raine groans. *She's going to kill me for this.*

I take her hand, joining the instructor as requested. "We finished a new dance routine today. Raine, I'll have you switch poles with me if that's fine," she says, walking to the row behind her. "Have fun with it."

"What are you doing here?" Raine whispers, side-eyeing me.

"I came to surprise you, but now you're surprising me instead." I raise my shoulders, grinning.

"Are we ready?" The instructor loudly asks, looking around at the women surrounding her.

"I'll kill you if you laugh," Raine threatens. "Don't you dare," she mouths.

Wrapping her hands around the pole, she twirls, spinning till her butt is against it with an arch to her back. The slow motion of a simple forward bend is incredibly sexy. She reaches back, taking hold, and with the drag of her toes against the ground, she lifts her body against the pole. I sit up straight, surprised by the amount of strength she has.

She grabs a hold, swinging around and dropping to the ground. Her knees drag across the wood flooring, and she crawls to me. *Geez, woman, it would be a nightmare if you didn't have knee pads on.* Her palms push against my thighs, and our fixated eyes lock as she mouths the dirty lyrics.

"Yes! Hit, hit, hit that move. Turn it up." The instructor coaches the class, hyping them.

It's been over two weeks since I last saw her, since I kissed her, or touched her. She dips her ass to my lap, letting her back rest against my chest. Her hips circle, grinding away. *Stop it.* I grab her jaw in warning, pulling her eyes to mine as she tilts her head back. She drags my hand down her body and slides off. I hold the excitement off, watching her swing around the pole with each seductive move.

I get it. This is for her, not for me. I admire it more than she could realize.

She exhales, walking back to me as the song comes to an end. "What do you think?"

"I think I'm installing one of these in my house."

"The house I haven't seen yet?" She sasses.

"You're coming home with me. Till Monday, then I'll fly you back, okay?"

She fans her sweat-glistening body. "A four-day surprise getaway? Hmm...should I agree or should I make you work for it?" She looks back at the pole.

"No. Wild, fuck. No." I point. It's the dress shop all over again.

"It only seems fair. I dance. You dance."

"Damn it."

Chapter Sixteen | Teleport

Nollan

She's doing this on purpose. Liver-deep in misery, I swipe through the photos of Raine and the traitor I used to call a friend. She went to a wedding with him. The dress that hugs her frame doesn't feel like her. It's too tight, too revealing, it's a fucking dress. I can count on one hand how many times I've seen her put on something like that. What has he done to her? The suited little bitch manipulated her into a carbon copy of every other woman he's dated. He has her so tightly wrapped around his cock, she won't reply to my text. I sent it twice. She saw it. It says *read.*

I type three letters and delete them. Casey is dead. He's fucking dead to me. His money isn't good enough to blind me from this.

"Nollan, baby," Bailey's groggy voice calls in the dark. "What are you doing down here?" She stops at the end of the kitchen, where the lamp lights the space between us. She no longer blinks away her sleep. She sees me sitting on the couch, half-naked, phone in one hand and a half-empty glass of liquor in the other. "Not again." She wraps her ivory robe around her petite frame and ties it closed. "Not again, Nollan."

I stare into my glass at the solid ice cubes. I can't bear to see another disappointed glare from her sad, round eyes. "You don't know what it's like."

"How am I supposed to understand when this is how you handle everything?" She hugs her body, walking into the dimness of the living room, on the other side of the glass coffee table. I hesitate, cautiously finding the look I've been avoiding.

"I'm fine. I can handle it," I insist.

"No, you can't. This isn't healthy." I wish she were angry. If she were to yell, it might justify my actions.

"What is, Bai?" I snap at her. "Going to fucking yoga and meditating?"

Her doe eyes soften. "You didn't have to say that."

"Oh, I did. I can't go for a jog or pottery class to find peace and thank the Lord for what I have. He's not going to help me."

"I hate it when you drink."

"I know." I hold the glass to my lips, tipping it back and drinking what's left in one shot. What does she want me to say? I'm pissed she's not Raine? I'm fucked because one of my friends is hooking up with the first woman I've loved? It's not fair that I can't forget her, and she can have everything she wants without me. I bet it would go over well. She might yell.

"Don't you think it's a problem?" As her tone becomes strained, I test her patience.

"What if I don't?" I lean back, resting my arms along the couch's length. "Are you going to leave me?"

"I don't want to leave you." Lies. I'm not fun anymore. When the fun ends, so does the relationship.

"I think you do. You're searching for any excuse."

She stands in silence long enough that I sit forward, pop the top off the single malt whiskey taunting me, and fill my glass halfway.

"Nollan, what do you do when you come down here at night and drink?"

"Nothing. Why?"

"You have your phone. I thought—"

"Now you want to know who I'm talking to? I'm not fucking cheating."

Her eyes widen, and she swallows back. "No." She shifts in her place. "I thought you might be gambling again, and losing money is making you upset. Therefore, you drink because that's what you do when you're upset. I didn't think...I didn't want to think that there could be someone else keeping you up."

Fuck. I don't want to do this to her. "Babe." I rub my face down, tossing back the blond strands that hide my eyes. "I'm sorry. There's nobody else."

"I've excused your behavior before. I don't know how much longer I'm going to be able to do it."

"I...I just need time. Okay? Can you give me some time?" I plead with her.

"If you pour that down the drain, we can talk."

"Here." I hold the glass out. Her baby pink nails meet my skin. She wraps both hands around mine and takes the glass. She sets it on the table and tucks her knees between my legs, sitting on the black and white geometrical rug in front of me. Her hands wrap around mine, and her saddened eyes hold my face in pity. "I don't deserve you."

"You have accomplished so much in life, Nollan. You had a dream, and you put your mind to it and accomplished it. Running a successful business can be a lot." My business isn't what's driven me to this state of mind.

"There's more I want to do."

"Exactly, and drinking yourself into an early grave won't get you there."

"Yeah." She's right. I'm not the guy who sits around and waits for things to happen. I take control, and I make them a reality.

"I have that flower bouquet workshop with Kat and my mom tomorrow, but after that, I was thinking we could take one of the cars and go for a nice drive and just talk…like we used to." The red Corvette Z06 is her favorite. She's a domestic girl, and Raine likes the imports.

"Whatever you want." Red 'Vette.

"Then, dinner at your parents'?"

"Uh, yeah. We can do that." Her slowly spilling cleavage reels my attention.

"Great. I'll call your mom in the morning. I want to try that recipe I found for Brussels sprouts, the maple bacon one."

I brush her silky, dark hair from her shoulders. "Sounds good." Following the line of her robe, I trace the collar, peeling it back.

"Hey." She snatches it shut. "You've been drinking."

"Don't worry so much." I reach for her hand.

"Baby," she whispers.

"You want one?" I kiss her jaw, inhaling her fruity-sweet scent.

"After I get married."

"You know I like to roleplay."

"The doctor doesn't impregnate the patient. His bedside manner isn't this handsy either."

"Sometimes they do. You're thinking about it." The telltale smile proves my accusation. "You want my cum dripping out of you."

"Stop." Her eyes flash wide.

"It would drip down your pussy, and I'd push it back in." Her cheeks flush pink, and she rubs her lips together. "Look what you did to me." I grip the length of my cock, testing the durability of my boxer briefs.

"You charged yourself up without much of my help."

"Because you're so sexy." I slide my black briefs to my thighs, my cock jutting out in front of her.

"Nollan, right here?" She pulls away. "Our guests sit on this couch."

"We're not gonna make a mess." I reel her pretty painted fingers back to me, gliding her hand up and down my stiff shaft. "Feel how hard that is. All for you, baby."

Her brown eyes travel between mine and my mouth, then meet our hands. I let go of hers, wrapping my fingers around her neck. I pull her to my mouth, laying into her soft lips.

"Not so aggressive," she gasps. I let go of her, falling back until my grimace meets the ceiling. "Nollan."

"Sorry." I noisily exhale. "I'm sorry. Let's...Let's go to bed."

"I can get on top."

"Yeah, let's go upstairs."

DECEMBER 22ND – 5:10 PM

"This is delicious. You should have saved it for Christmas dinner," Mom compliments Bailey's cooking.

"I saw it on Pinterest a few days ago and had to try it, but I already planned on making strawberry shortcake and my favorite roasted garlic cauliflower dish for Christmas. I'll keep this in rotation."

The four of us sit at Mom's new kitchen table. I didn't think the light oak would suit the room, but it does. All the gray blues and sandy tones fit. I could do without the portrait of me at two years old with a bowl of pasta on my head. At least Nash has a matching frame next to mine, with a slightly different meal.

"You're going to put me to shame when you take over the menu."

"I will not. If I stray from what the boys are expecting, I'll catch hell." Bailey has been a copycat version of Mom for a few weeks now. From her cooking style to her straight, shoulder-length bob, the imitator comes over here more than I do.

"How's business?" Dad asks.

"Good. Steady growth. Nothing I can't handle, nothing underwhelming." I fork more food into my mouth.

"Would you consider taking some time off then?"

I rinse my palette clear with ice water and answer. "For what?"

"A cruise. We're looking at The Bahamas," he replies. He quickly brushes the side of his full silver mane back in place with his fingers, then combs out his matching beard. He hasn't grown it out in...ever, wanting to stay clean-shaven for the courtroom. He must be trying it out for his upcoming retirement.

"I could probably work something out."

"Good. I think you could use to some away."

I narrow my eyes, closing my mouth before I can shovel the next forkful in. "Why's that?"

"You've been tense lately," he continues.

"You've been a raging dick." Nash opens the fridge, snatching the glass jar of orange juice.

"Nash," Mom scolds him. He leaves the door hanging while he reaches for a cup.

"If I was a dick to you, it was deserved."

He nods, chugging six ounces of juice. "You're a dick to Bailey, too."

"What?" My face becomes a muddled contortion. "I am not."

"You're in denial," he insists. "I gotta go. Calle said Merry Christmas in case she misses our call." He rinses his cup and sets it in the sink.

"What time is your flight?" Mom asks.

"Early."

What is he talking about—I'm a dick to Bailey?

"Hope the surprise goes well." Bailey smiles at him.

"It will. She has no idea it's coming." He joins the table, patting Dad on the back and hugging Mom.

"Have a safe flight. Call one of us when you get there. I love you."

"Love you," he replies and walks off.

"Am I a dick to you?" I hold her beneath my gaze.

"I don't think you're doing it on purpose."

"I have no idea what you're talking about. What did I do or say?"

"You're always in a bad mood. You don't want to do any-thing besides work and drink."

"My job is stressful too, son, and sometimes we lose ourselves in that. It's nothing to be ashamed of as long as you accept the responsibility and redirect your actions. We know what happened the last time you got stressed with life. I don't want to get a call like that again." If I had known this was an intervention, I would have never come.

"That's not going to happen."

"I'd hope not," he agrees.

"I'll go on the cruise if that's what everyone wants." Anything to get them off my back.

"Great!" Mom cheers. It seems she has as much interest in discussing my current state of mind as I do. "I'm so excited. We could make it a family affair. Bailey said Tiffany and Grant would like to go." Her parents, too? "We might be able to get Nash and Calle on board since it's the week after Christmas. I'd imagine he would have accumulated vacation by then. Kim and Josh, too." The Crees? Come on. Fuck. Whatever.

"Yeah. Let me know when you need the money." I push my chair out and stand. "I'm going to excuse myself to the restroom."

"Ahh fuuuck," I groan, staring into the bathroom mirror. I push the air, wishing I could slam my fist into the mirror. It would make everything worse. And if they want me to be okay, I'll show them I am.

The door rumbles twice with a knock. "It's Bailey. You've been in there for a while. Are you feeling alright?"

"Fine."

"It wasn't my food?"

"No."

"Are you sure?"

I open the door with a growing smile. "You know it wasn't, Bai."

"Okay. Good. I'm ready to head home when you are."

"Do you mind if I go for a drive after I drop you off?"

"I could go with."

"I need some time to myself...To think." I take her cheek in my palm, letting my thumb rest below her lips. "Equivalent to your bubble bath regimen."

"Okay. Come back in one piece."

I place a tender kiss on her mouth. "I intend to."

DECEMBER 23RD

"Nollan, where are you? I've been trying to reach you. Why didn't you come home?"

"My mind is clear, Bailey." The pavement only has one end, and I'm counting the hours between paddle shifting and missed phone calls.

"What do you mean? Are you okay?"

"I started driving, and I stopped a few times."

"Where are you now?"

"I love you, I do. You're amazing, sweet, and do so much for me."

"Nollan." She reaches out in agony.

"Sometimes that's not enough...The girl that's perfect on paper."

"I don't claim to be perfect." Desperation.

"You're not. I know that. You jump to conclusions often, and at times, you're naive when you're truly a very intelligent woman. You don't always get my jokes, and I can't tell you about the dark thoughts that take control of me at night."

"You can tell me," she insists.

"I could, and your answer would be to trust in your faith."

"Faith is hope. It keeps you strong in hard times. I never said it erases the bad."

"It couldn't mend my heart. I've been asking for that for seven years," I admit. "It's time to take matters into my own hands."

"Seven years? Nollan, where are you?" I'm upsetting her.

"One day you'll forgive me." I need to merge.

"Forgive you for what? Nollan, where are you?"

"It's going to be okay."

"What is? Nollan!"

"A man will give you the world. He'll drive miles for you and jump barricades. He'll be everything you want him to be that I'm not."

"I'm going to call the police if you don't tell me where you are." They won't do anything.

"Be with your family today. Don't think about me. Eat and be joyous."

"Nollan!"

"Goodbye, Bailey."

"Noll—"

I hang up, turning the volume up, and sing along to the lyrics of a random song on my playlist.

Chapter Seventeen | Ammunition

Raine

"Hey, beautiful," Casey rolls over, looking up at me. "You're dressed already?"

I sit at the end of my bed, putting my socks on. "My family will be here in a few hours. I want to make sure everything is ready." I turn from the mirror, wrinkling up my face. "And you're not off the hook yet."

"Off the hook for what?"

"Molly." I point to the *donut of a dog* curled up in my bedroom.

"Slipped my mind." He shrugs.

"It won't ever slip mine after nearly stepping on a giant hot dog the moment I walked into your house. She looked fucking dead. She looks dead eighty percent of the time."

Casey's arms scoop me up and pull me into his chest. "I'm sorry. Everything is set. The food prep is done, the tree looks like it came straight out of a Hallmark movie, and it couldn't be any cleaner in here. It's perfect, you're perfect, and one day you'll come to realize how perfect my giant hotdog is." He kisses me. His morning breath is awful, but I kiss him back anyway.

"You need to brush your teeth," I whisper. "Molly's breath smells better."

"Molly girl, she's making fun of you again." She looks up from her bed and wags her tail.

"She likes it. She doesn't care if she's getting positive or negative attention, as long as someone is talking about her."

"Sure. But speaking of attention whores—" He veers to the subject of Karson. I've been waiting for an update. His family drama makes me forget about mine. It also makes me realize how many people say and do petty things, not just in small towns.

"Did she sign?"

"Yesterday, finally." He leans back against the headboard, tucking his burly arms behind his head. Every time he does that, I get the urge to jump on top of him and touch the ridges that stretch across them. *Put a shirt on, man, I can't focus.*

"It's about time. I thought she was going to argue with you over every detail."

"The only reason she gave in on some of my terms is that she wants to start the remodel next week to make her timeline," he says, unamused.

"At least it's done, and Brent will be in contact with you if she causes any problems." He stretches his arms behind his head. It's like I know these people from everything he's told me, but I couldn't identify one of them in a lineup. Brent is the office manager who excels at organization and communication.

"That's if he doesn't fall into her manipulation. It will be harder than showing her tits since he's not exactly someone who desires the female body. This isn't an end by any means, and I'm stuck with Karson back in my affairs as long as I stay on as her partner." He sighs.

"Then don't stay on forever. If she succeeds, give it to her. You didn't want the responsibility of it anyway."

"Okay, brainiac," he replies, rolling his eyes upward.

"And you can share my sister. She's fun...eh, wait." The bunny lines take over my face. "Only in like a sisterly way. I thought I'd be cool with sister wife-ing it once. I evolved. Two months can have wild effects on the brain. Ten out of ten revolutionary."

"You sicko." He wraps his arms around my waist, pulling me from the edge. "That mind of yours."

"But I'm perfect, Casey, so perfect," I sneer, shaking my head and dramatically throwing my arms up, nearly smacking him in the face. He dodges without letting go of me, like a skilled professional.

"I like your disturbing humor and anything else that you think is a flaw. Your imperfections make you perfect."

"That doesn't even make sense. I like you because you're rich and have muscles *for days*," I exaggerate. "It makes complete sense."

"Quit acting. You know what I have *for days* that really keeps your attention." He brushes my hair back and whispers against my ear. "My arrogant personality."

I shove into his shoulders, knocking him back, and climb on his lap. "Let's run away. Fuck this dinner party."

"Let's go, love."

"I've been working on that bucket list."

"Which one?" He laces his fingers between mine, drawing one hand to his lips and kissing it.

"Both. Mostly mine."

"What did you add?" He asks.

"Hike to Fanes Waterfall in Dolomites, Italy, feel the adrenaline bungee jumping in Switzerland, see the beauty of Nymphenburg Palace in Munich, Germany, take a hot air balloon ride in Turkey, go wine tasting in Portugal—"

"Wine?" His face turns blank. "You will be the death of me."

"That's not remotely funny."

"Yes, it is."

I lunge forward, covering his mouth and nose with my palms. "This is death, Casey. You said it's funny." He easily pulls my wrists down, flipping me to my side. His large arm wraps my lower back, holding me close and tight.

"Where to first? I'll book a flight."

"When am I supposed to work?" Running around the world on adventure doesn't leave much time to pay for it. At least I'm not picturing it that way. If you prioritize and set aside a time frame every day to nail out projects, I guess it could be possible.

"Take vacation." He gently traces my jaw.

"I've taken all of it."

"Fine. Quit."

"I can't quit my job, Casey."

"I'll pay your bills."

"That's not happening. I'm not going to be dependent on you."

"I knew you'd say that." His handsome smile appears. "Get the calendar out sometime this weekend and look at your schedule. We'll plan trips throughout the year."

"One at a time."

"Where are we going first? Switzerland?" His morning breath would be my cause of death if I weren't burrowing my face into his shoulder.

"Um...Barcelona." I connect with his upturned eyes.

"What's calling you to Spain, darling?"

"Skateboarding...At MACBA. It's a contemporary art museum. I've wanted to go there since I was a teenager." I hear myself and can't shut up. Let me tell you all about my teenage dreams, Casey. Next, it'll be a story about the boy band I never got to see, and which of the five members was my crush. New flash, it was Lance. You can see how that fantasy would've turned out for me.

"Travel all that way so you can bust your ass? I wouldn't miss it."

"Classy, clumsy is my wheelhouse. You'll learn."

"You'll like the Gothic Quarter," he tells me.

"You've been?" On some days, it's as if I've known Casey my whole life, and on others, I'm reminded that he had an entire twenty-six years of living before we met, and that was a mere two months ago.

"I've traveled a good bit, love. How about you start the coffee for me, and I'll get dressed, then while you pace the apartment, I'll tell you about some of my adventures besides the mountains."

"Yeah, I'm already jealous of those. Please don't tell me again."

"We have all the time in the world to get to them."

"Raaaine!" Calle sings.

I run out of the kitchen to find Casey had let her in. She throws her bags to the floor, wrapping her arms around my neck. Nash walks in behind her with more bags than he can carry, struggling to get around the furniture.

"What's with all the bags?" She looks like she's moving in. I love her, but no.

"We can't check into our hotel yet. We should have flown in last night like Mom and Dad. Where are they?" She adjusts her top at the neckline.

"Not here yet." It's a relief that Calle is here first.

"Great, then I can show you first." She holds out her hand, giving me ten seconds to see she has a band on her ring finger before she begins to wave and spew the entire story. "He proposed last night at Gerald's. It wasn't a snowy ski lift, but oh my gosh," she squeals. "We had the patio to ourselves, champagne on ice, and it was sweet and intimate. He kneeled down, and I started bawling." Nash nods with a smirk on his face, and we both know that she's not exaggerating about the *bawling*. Is that the restaurant where they had their first date? Looks like I'll have a Broack as a brother-in-law. "Nash thought of everything. He booked a photographer for an engagement session, too. So I still get my snow-covered photos."

"Well, are you going to keep talking about it or show me the rock?" I grab her hand, impressed by the large rectangular diamond. "Holy shit, that's beautiful. Did you rob the jewelry store? Why is it so big? I mean, congrats." I point to Nash. "You'd better be a good husband to this one."

"I will," he answers.

"Don't make me dig deep for my inner crazy."

"You don't have to dig that deep," Calle returns.

They're cute together, matching their outfits. Outside of their red-and-tan ensemble, their energy matches in a unique way. I love how happy he makes her.

Casey picks up Molly and leans over my shoulder to see the sparkling jewelry. "Congratulations. Very nice."

"You got a dog, Raine!" Her hands drop to her knees as she dips forward, bending to Molly's level and making a kissy face.

"She's Casey's, calm down." Is the dog as exciting as the sparkles on your hand?

"Can I hold her? She's so cute." She reaches for Molly while looking back at Nash. "Babe, I think we should get a wiener dog when we move."

"Can we focus on one thing at a time?" Nash replies, moving luggage to the corner.

"Where are you moving?" Casey asks.

"Oh, I forgot to tell you, they're going to be about an hour outside of Albany for a year."

"I'm about two hours away," Casey calls to Nash. "If you need help moving or anything, feel free to let me know. I'll give you my number."

"Did you tell Mom yet?" She avoids eye contact and puckers her lips. That tells me everything I need to know. "Calle, are you kidding me?"

"My family knows, but the procrastinator keeps avoiding telling Kim," Nash says.

"I'm going to tell them today."

"Oh, you're going to do the good news and the bad news thing. I don't see it helping you at this point. You should've told her weeks ago."

"Hello. Anyone home?" As he opens the door, Dad calls from outside, with Mom following behind. They had to hear us carrying on.

"Wow, Raine. The tree looks beautiful. Who did it for you?" Mom immediately asks.

I sigh. "Nobody. I managed myself." Seriously, who would pay for their tree to be decorated? Not me in my one-bedroom apartment.

Molly barks, wagging her tail. "Whose dog is that?" She asks, detached.

"Casey's," Calle answers.

"Oh, thank the heavens. I thought you picked up a stray," Mom adds. That was undeniably more insulting than my remark about her breath. I'd take pity on her, but the dog has more gifts than anyone else under the tree. I slide my hand along her belly, taking her from Calle and handing her back to Casey.

"Can you please take her upstairs for now?" I raise my eyebrows, waiting for my family's craziness to implode.

"Sure." He kisses my head and looks around the room before leaving.

Everyone manages to squeeze into the living room, finding a place to sit. Calle welcomed this. If there's anyone to put the blame on, it's her. If it weren't for the dividing wall, it might actually feel more spacious. Nash sits on the recliner, and Calle parks her tush on his lap.

"So, Calle, did you say you had some news?" It's now or never. Break the ice, lady.

She holds out her hand. "We're engaged!" She yells. The good news first to lighten the blow?

"Oh my gosh!" Mom cheers, jumping up from the sofa. She fans her hand out in front of her, searching for the shiny band on Calle's finger. "Let me see the ring." She holds Calle's hand, examining it. Finally, she glances up to smile at Nash. "Well done. It's absolutely beautiful. Do you have any idea of dates yet? Spring, summer? Or maybe a nice autumn ceremony?"

"We're thinking...next spring." She pulls her hand back, sits down, and moves her mouth so fast it's as if she doesn't want anyone to understand. "Plus, we'll be in New York for a year, so it would work out well with getting settled back in Florida." Mom's eyes enlarge, and her chin tucks as she processes the lightning-speed statement that is the bane of her existence.

"Come again? New York for a year?" Yes. Here we go. She's going to explode.

"Nash got a job. It's contract." Calle runs her hands over her knees. I feel like I'm looking at a reflection of myself. Why do we always want to please her? "It's one year, and the pay is so good, we couldn't pass up the opportunity."

"When are you moving? When did you decide this?" She fires off questions, crossing her arms over her chest.

"We're moving next week, outside of Albany."

"Next week! Calle, how long have you been planning this move?" I look away, hiding my smile on my shoulder. This isn't funny. *I'm not a child, stop.*

I look back at Calle. Her upper lip curls to the side, and she shrugs her shoulders. "Since October."

"Calle June Cree. You wait a week before you plan on moving, leaving for a year, to tell me about it!" She scolds.

"I didn't want you to be upset. I'm sorry. It's only a year, and we'll still fly in for the holidays like Raine does."

"I'm disappointed...but I'm happy for you. You're getting married and going to have many new strides in life." What did she just say? Just like that? "And Raine..." What? Not me. This isn't on me. "I owe you an apology." Come again? "I talked to a good friend. Do you remember Rodney Martin? He ran the cafe on Whitley. Such a nice man. He always gave you girls free cookies. Anyway, his nephew is a desk officer at a police station. It turns out your...boyfriend is a well-respected businessman. I was surprised to hear who he was related to." Oh. That was...nice, I guess.

"Um, thanks?" I'll choose my battles wisely today.

"Now, where are your board games?" She waves her hands in front of her, again pushing me to show her in the right direction. "It's not Christmas Eve without Monopoly."

December 25th - Sunday, 3:00 PM

"Mm, something smells amazing," Casey says, wrapping his arms around my waist and nuzzling his mouth against my neck.

"I nearly burnt it, but the pie survived." I lick my finger, then turn around to kiss him.

"Oh, I wonder why?" He taunts.

"If you would stay out of my pants for one day, I wouldn't have to light the apartment on fire just to get you to leave."

"Are you saying you would rather burn the apartment complex to the ground on Christmas day than get in a secret quickie with me? Because if that's the case, I could leave. The exit is this way." He points to the door and slowly walks towards it.

"Not happening. My Mom likes you now," I taunt with a cocky head tilt. "You're stuck here, and I guess I'll just have to suffer the consequences." I run my fingers over the collar of his shirt, unable to look away from his lips.

"I see, now I'm just a pawn in your mommy-pleasing plan."

"You're suffering so much, aren't you?"

"You can burn it down if you want," he whispers. "I'll still find a way to roll in the ashes with you all night."

"So I have to shower for a week straight to get ashes out of my ass crack?" I slap my hands to my sides, and his deep laugh fills my ears.

"Honey, I'm home!" Calle yells. "And so is everyone else, FYI!" She walks into the kitchen, uncovering her eyes. "Just making sure you were clothed."

"We're not rabbits," I reply flatly.

"Could have fooled me. I witnessed that Thanksgiving fiasco, remember." She shivers. The pictures that must have popped into her head make me chuckle and roll my eyes.

"Help me take these dishes to the table." I look between them and offer each a bowl.

"Your outfit is cute, Raine."

I glance down at my distressed black sweater. "Thanks, Cal."

"How's the food?" I ask, looking around the table as everyone shoves forkfuls in their mouths. It's kinda the best part about the holidays. Well, family and food. Everyone is getting along, smiling, sharing memories, and it's...okay. It's all going okay.

I see a lot of nods. "It's bussin'," Calle answers, covering her full mouth with her hand, nodding.

"Very good," Mom adds. "I approve. You can help with dinner next year at our house." *Great.* This was a setup.

A knock at the door catches me off guard. Maybe Elias decided to stop by, but I thought he had a dinner to attend. Who else would it be? I slide my chair back, standing, and Casey rests his hand on my thigh.

"I'll get it," Casey offers. He brushes my shoulder and walks around the divide to the living room.

"Thank you," I shout as he walks off.

Who is that? Sounds like a man. Elias? Tuning everyone out at the table, I try to figure out who he's talking to. It sounds like...no fucking way. Is that Nollan? For fucks sake, who invited him?

I excuse myself, connecting with Calle as I push my chair into the corner of the table. My sister knows me too well, instantly picking up on my tense glare before I walk into the living room.

"Nollan, what are you doing here?" I whisper yell. "Did my mom invite you?" Why would she do that after she decided she's okay with Casey? Was it a load of bullshit?

What the hell is Casey doing? His hands—Casey's hands are up, and he steps backward slowly. Past him, Nollan stands in the doorway. My heart races, blood pumping through my body so fast I swear it drowns my lungs. All the oxygen is suffocated. A twisted knot of adrenaline and the worst anxiety attack I've ever encountered. In chills, I sweat while the hair stands straight up on my arms.

I heard your brain shuts parts off when in dire situations in self-preservation. Speaking calmly and softly while my insides shake, I choke back the terror and muster up any words I can find. *It's a gun.* "Nollan, why do you have that?"

"Raine, I can't live without you." He walks into the room, leaving the door hanging open. My gaze is unsettling, switching back and forth between his trembling hand and glossy eyes. "You won't leave my head." He taps the muzzle against his temple. "Stop with the games. I know you're only dating him to mess with me. You win. You. Win." He is surrounded by the odor of alcohol.

"Nollan, I'm not playing games." I look down at his hand. "That is not a game." My sharp exhales hang on to each syllable. "That is a life sentence."

"You would choose him." He flicks the gun up toward Casey as if the mechanism were a laser pointer, and I sink back. *I'm going to puke.* I am going to vomit everywhere. Involuntarily, I shake my head from side to side. "You have known me since the first grade, but you would choose a man you met what? Fucking two months ago? Over me? Over me." The tone of his voice rises, and he swings the gun in the air, his hands meeting his head. He paces to the side before looking at me again. "I'd give up everything for you! I drove all the way here for you. That's a long fucking drive, Raine." His unsettling chuckle vibrates. "I'm here, babe. Tell me you're ready to be with me. I'll do whatever you want. I swear. He won't stop us. It can be you and me again."

"Okay. I want to talk. Let's go talk." Stay calm. Don't upset him. "I need you to do one thing for me first."

"Anything, babe."

"I need you to put the gun down, okay? Can you put it down, Nollan?" I step closer to him, hoping that if I touch him, he'll trust me. "Please. Hand it to me, and we can sit down together."

"Oh, my God!" Calle yells behind me.

"Calle. Quiet." My eyes stay locked on him. "Nollan, look at me. It's me. I know you don't want to hurt anyone. You're a good man. Please...hug me. Put the gun down and hold me in your arms," I plead. I take another step toward him, holding out my hand.

"You're lying. You're fucking lying!" He yells, looking between Casey and me.

No, no, no, no, no. This isn't right. How was I to predict this?

My heart beats in my ears, and I shake my head, not wanting to fall into the fetal position, hugging my knees as I spiral into a massive panic attack. I can't. I can't let anyone get hurt because of me. Because I fucked with his head. I did this to him. I should've stayed away. I should've found another man who wasn't one of his friends.

"Nollan, I need you. It's only you." I close my eyes. "It's always going to be you."

Everyone at the table is likely behind me. How could they not be at this point? They must freeze upon seeing him. Dark circles below his eyes, his usually styled hair in a mess, and...his fingers are laced around a pistol.

"Nollan, what are you fucking thinking!" Nash yells. "Put that shit down!"

"You know what I'm thinking, little brother," he chuckles again. "The same thing you feel. You would die for little Calle Cree." He exhales. "I'm prepared to die for you, Raine. Is he?" He points the gun at Casey, tilting his head sideways. His eyes are fixated on Casey, and he aims for his chest. Gasps and groans start to drown out my calm.

"What the fuck is wrong with you? Put it down, now!" Nash screams.

"He's leaving right now!" Nollan yells. "Out the door," he waves the gun. "Get out!"

"Go," I mouth.

Casey steps to the side, his hands remaining in the air as he moves towards the open door. I'm utterly frozen, breathless, standing in what feels like the deepest silence and longest second in time. What, what do I do? My eyes well with tears. None of them escapes. Frozen. Fucked. There's no way to rewind.

What is he —

Casey!

"No!" The screaming surrounds me. It consumes me. It is me. I'm the one screaming. My ears ring as I fall to the floor. I told Casey I'm not the type to be rescued. He tried anyway. The noise gets worse. The pounding in my eardrums meets the echo of a loud bang. Once. Twice. Three times. The screaming becomes distant. It's not me anymore. It's the voices all around me. I'm underwater, and they're fizzed out. I get to live underwater. It's not like I imagined. It's hard to communicate. It's more about the...touch than the faces. Atlantis would be beautiful if it weren't a myth. This isn't real either.

"No, no, no. Raine, love, come on. Open your eyes." Casey. Are you underwater too? His hands...they feel warm. Warmer than usual. Or am I just cold? "Wake up!"

"Raine, I'm sorry. I'm so sorry. Please, please, open your eyes." Nollan. You feel fuzzy. This is my water world. I like it here. The waves are calm.

"Nollan!" *Casey.* Don't stop talking. "He's losing too much blood. Nash, put pressure here." I'm cold, but Casey's here. I knew he'd swim like a fish with me. "Come on, wildcat," he whispers. "You're too strong, open your eyes. Stay with me. Please."

"I love you," I breathe out.

"Fuck. Beautiful, I love you."

I open my eyes enough to see his face. His dimples are out of sight, and his gentle, dark eyes are filled with tears that run to his lips. "This is exactly where I'd want to be as I die...With you in our own Atlantis."

He chokes out a breath. "You're not going to die. Pinky promise." His warm fingers thread through my hair. "I pinky promise.

Chapter Eighteen | Valiancy

Raine

January 1st - Sunday, **6:00 AM**

Casey never broke a pinky promise. I didn't die. I almost wish I did. I never thought love was the root of all evil. How could it be? It's supposed to conquer all. It is though—evil. Lust entraps you with its beautiful disguise. It reels you in and convinces you with its thrill. You choose to stay and let love grow. You choose to give all of your emotions, all of your time, and all that is delicately you to another. Then it doesn't work, and you feel pain you never imagined—pain worse than a bullet piercing your flesh. Heartbreak.

It fucks you over. It warps your logic and turns good people into savages. The lengths one would go to for love. I've heard mothers would kill to protect their offspring...And some men would kill to keep the love of their lives.

I hate hospitals. They're cold giant petri dishes made into a white-walled cube.

"Miss Cree, how are you feeling today? Are we ready to get out of here?" Dr. Saeben asks.

I pull myself upright, leaning against the back of the stiff hospital bed. "I'm thinking about staying long-term. The food isn't amazing, but I'm rich here. Butlers and maids by the dozen."

"Raine!" Mom scolds from a recliner along the window. It's her shift to babysit me. I'm such an infant. That shit was pretty traumatic for her, too, so I won't protest. It's weird how well she's been getting along with Casey. Yeah, she gave me that acceptance speech, and then I almost died. I don't know what I missed when I blacked out. Or the first day after being admitted to the hospital. They've been chill buddy-buddy ever since.

I'm lucky my injuries weren't life-threatening, and it was the mass trauma that sent me into the Atlantis world. What a clean shot. Great aim, Nollan. Missed all major organs. I wonder what's going to happen with him. Are the police going to push for charges, or is he going to be placed in a mental health facility? What's going to happen to his business? His dad is going to give him that dry look accompanied by silence. Will it hurt, or is there something seriously wrong in his brain? Does he understand what he did? Does he grasp how wrong it was?

"The sarcasm is a good sign, although I think we experienced plenty of your personality this week." He chuckles. "You will be remembered."

He looks over at Mom, and she looks away, her face becoming flushed. I'm the center of attention, and it's for something I can't remember.

"What did I say?" I ask, rolling my eyes. They got me hopped on painkillers and watched me unravel. Do I even want to know? Yes. One hundo percent. I want to know.

"Your mind is brilliantly colorful, but there are things I wish I had never heard." Mom shakes her head, rolling her eyes right back. Dr. Saeben continues looking at his chart, pretending I can't see the smirk on his face.

"The ocean is a little less mysterious now," he says, not bothering to look up from his tablet.

Oh no.

"Well, you look great. Everything is healing well. You will probably need to continue with assistance when walking for another week, and feel free to eliminate the pain medication as you can tolerate it, but I don't see any need for physical therapy in the future. Just take it easy. Don't overdo it. Your body went through trauma. I also suggest that when you follow up with your primary, you discuss mental health. If you need resources, there are many available. You as well, Mom." He sympathetically smiles.

"Can you give me an update on Nollan Broack?" I unapologetically blurt out. I'm sure he thinks I'm missing some bolts now, asking about my shooter's well-being.

"I can only disclose that he is doing well. If you'd like to speak with him, he's open to visitors. An officer will be present outside of the room at all times while the case is under investigation."

Mom shakes her head, either in disagreement or disapproval. It doesn't matter which one it is, I won't leave here till I see him. "Mom, I need to do this."

"We appreciate your time, Dr. Saeben. You have been so wonderful." Calm down, lady. You're both married. I hope my parents aren't the people pushing a shopping cart around Publix with an upside-down pineapple in the kiddie seat. The thought alone gives me the shivers. *Vomit.*

"I'll be fine." Does she think he's going to strangle me with his IV? "I can manage to limp a foot into the room," I remind Mom. Outside of Nollan's hospital suite stands an officer, as expected. I'm sure he'll love having her blab his ear off for the next five minutes.

"Okay, but I'll be right outside the door waiting."

"If I wipe out, I'll yell *help, I've fallen, and I can't get up.*" She stares at me, deadpan. "I'm joking. I'll be fine. Don't ask the cop a million questions, please." *I tried, buddy.* I turn away, walking into the room.

Colorful mylar get-well balloons float in the corner of Nolan's room, and I'm curious if they're from his parents or from Bailey. Does she know what happened? The real story. "Hey loser, how long are you in for?"

"The hospital or jail?" He replies, smiling.

"Glad you still have some humor, even if it's not nearly as tasteful as mine." I hobble to the window, sitting down on the closest chair.

"Surgery went well, and they think I'll be able to leave next week." He looks away. His face is stained with shame. His blue eyes are less confident, and his smile is nowhere to be found.

"Nollan, what were you thinking?"

"I've been asked that exact question about five times now." He pushes himself up against the back of the bed, adjusting as he winces in pain. "I had to talk to you. I had to see your face. You with him. I got a bottle of pumpkin spice vodka at Keller's Spirits before I made the trip. It's your favorite...or it was. When I saw you two, I..." He sighs. "I drank a lot of it. I couldn't tell you how much. I started spiraling, and I couldn't walk away without seeing you. He answered the door. It was Casey again, fucking my day up. Keeping you from me." He rubs his neck, and those familiar blue eyes search my face. "Raine, I wish I could take it all back. I swear, I didn't want to hurt you."

"I know. You need help, Nollan. It's terrifying how dependent your life is on mine...How easily my piss-poor actions gain your reaction."

"Raine, this is on me. I could have...I could have fucking killed you." His fists hit the mattress, and I watch the tears pour down his cheeks. "I could be doing life in prison for a murder, and I wouldn't have cared because it's what I would have deserved if I took you from this world. I'd deserve worse. You are a beautiful person, inside and out, and I can't forgive myself. For you, I'm going to get help, and I'm going to let you go."

"Don't do it for me. This can't be another route to winning me back. I'm serious. Do it for you because you are a good man, Nollan, and I want you to find happiness, love, build a family, and have everything you wanted. I will love you for the rest of my life. That is a fact. But I will never be yours again. That's a promise." Exhaling, I look at the shiny white floor. "You know, some bridges aren't meant to be rebuilt. With millions of people in this world, we're two who aren't meant to stay connected for a lifetime." I swallow the saliva pooling under my tongue. "If I never texted you after I left all those years ago, would you have moved on?"

"I don't know," he softly replies. I pull myself from the chair and slowly make my way to his bedside, grabbing his hand and holding it tight. "I love you, Raine. I'm fucking sorry. I'm so fucking sorry."

"I know."

"I have no idea what's going to happen. My dad's firm is working on it. I wa—I want to make sure you're okay and that you know—"

"I know, Nol."

A knock on the door startles me, and I pull my hand back to myself.

"Can I come in?" Casey asks. "Raine, can I have a minute with Nollan?"

"Um, yeah." I nod. This is it. I hate heartbreak. "Goodbye, Nollan. Take care of yourself." I smile softly, taking him in once more.

After all these years of hanging on to him while telling myself I was over him, this feels different. I've lost him forever. He might as well have died. That sweet six-year-old who made me smile, that punk I smoked weed with in Delcan's garage at fourteen, and the first man who loved me when I didn't know how to love back. He never gave up on me, and I deeply hope that he finds everything he needs in this life.

"Casey, help me to the door, please."

He rushes over to me, taking all my weight on his shoulder. "Are you okay?"

"I'm fine. Are you okay?" I ask, concerned.

"I need to take a minute to talk to my friend. It won't be long."

I nod in understanding, but it doesn't mean I'm not going to eavesdrop. I wait a moment, then crack the door. The officer gives me a look and lets it slide without saying a word.

"Casey, you can save it. I feel guilty enough."

I slide to the floor, letting my back meet the wall as I listen intently.

"Raine, get off the floor," Mom whispers, and I shush her.

"I'm not here to tell you off."

"Then what do you want?"

"To apologize to you. I didn't listen when you said *not her*. A broken heart...I know what it's like. It doesn't heal, it just...*mends* over time. You're never the same. You learn to move forward. I could have called you and told you I was into her, but it wouldn't have made a difference. I'm sorry that." Silence. "None of it excuses your actions. You need to move on. Find help, a mental evaluation...whatever you need. Do it."

"Easy for you to say, you have her. If she left you right now, would you *move forward*?"

"I don't give a fuck. You got shot. I got shot. Raine...Raine got shot. Your stupid obsession could have ended all of our lives. I've been in therapy for years. Own up to it and get the help you need. And Raine or not, you run a well-maintained business, and I would hate to lose that relationship at the least." He sighs. "If she left me right now...I'd move forward. It's what I'd have to do. That's life."

"Yeah, you've always been the bigger man, Casey," he huffs, unimpressed. "At this time, Broack's would like to decline your business and let me know when she leaves you if you still feel the same."

"Respectfully, I understand. Disrespectfully, I'll make sure the bullet hits something more vital if you bring harm to her again." I hear shoes tapping across the floor, and I shuffle over to Mom, disturbing her from reading her book.

"Raine, what are you doing?" She yelps.

"Mom, shh. Help me up. Hurry." I reach for her arm, putting my weight against her as I stand. "Hey. Everything okay?"

His eyes scale my body, and he meets my eyes with a smile. "No problems."

Mom paces my apartment for a while, then she finally gathers her purse. "I cleaned your flooring and spoke with your landlord. He's not happy about the incident by far, but I've charmed him over enough to not make any hasty decisions. I'll stop over in the morning. Take care of her, Casey." She fluffs the pillow under my legs. If the woman didn't insist I need to prop my feet up, I'd be walking around instead. How she cleaned the furniture is beyond me. The hardwood flooring has everything to do with me not losing my security deposit.

"Thanks, Mom."

"I'm here anytime you need me." She walks out the door, Casey closing it behind her. He sits on the sofa next to me, slowly rubbing my thigh. Looping my fingers through his, I extend till I feel his calloused palm.

"You need to moisturize. I have hand cream upstairs," I say, letting my head fall back.

"It wouldn't help. It's from lifting." Could help. "I'm so glad you're okay."

I nod silently.

"I heard I may have had some *brain-to-mouth explosions* when I was high on painkillers," I smoothly avert. "My wild came out?"

"Oh, love. You flipped the nurse off like ten times while repeating, " *Don't look at him. He took a bullet for me.*" His tongue slides across his lower lip, unable to contain his smile. "You liked the doctor, though. Told him all about your underwater theories. They were just a little crazier conspiracy than usual," he says, laughing.

"Oh, God." I palm my forehead.

"I do have a video I was thinking of posting all over the internet. Maybe I can title it Wild Gone Wild?"

"Shut your face." I look at him deadpan. "Where? Show it to me." I tap his pocket where his phone is tucked away. "Did I flash my titties too? No wonder Mom wanted me to shut up today."

"You're great at demonstrations. I mean, it only would seem right to share with the struggling public." He opens the gallery on his phone and clicks the video. Taking his phone, the image of my *under-the-influence* self doing the backstroke on the hospital bed, followed by my breath-holding skills, is mortifying. At least it's not a titty show.

"Delete that. Nobody ever needs to see that. You shouldn't have even witnessed that."

Casey laughs, slipping his phone back into his pocket. "I'd rather that be the image of you stuck in my head than the one of you on the floor...this floor." His focus falls. "Bleeding out in my arms." He laces his fingers back into mine.

"I'm sorry." This is my fault. I put everyone in danger, and now this will be the memory when they think back to the first and last Christmas that *Raine* hosted.

"So I had a talk, you could say, with your mom." Casey interrupts my spiraling thoughts. "Honestly, we got into it. I shut her the fuck down, and she didn't like it. By the end of the conversation, we came to an honest understanding."

"What did you say?"

"I told her she's the reason her kids don't want to open up to her," he answers confidently.

My jaw drops, accompanied by tightly furrowed brows. "Why would you say that to her?"

"Because it's the truth. She was looking for someone to be angry with, and if anyone, it should be herself. Look at Calle. She held off on telling your mom she was moving for weeks because she was afraid to disappoint her. And you do the same shit. You didn't tell her about me until you couldn't avoid it." He leans back, staring at me.

"That's not your place. It's between my mom and me. You shouldn't have said anything."

"I know. It's your choice to accept it or not. I wasn't trying to get involved, but she pissed me off."

"Like Nollan pissed you off. Are you going to threaten my mom next?"

"What?" He blinks. "I won't be made out as this horrible person who got her daughter shot. She can think anything she wants to about me. I will shut her down when she tries to say I don't care about you. I'm not going to threaten her."

"So tell her Nollan was holding the gun," I call out, my hands springing up almost involuntarily. "Don't tell her she's a bad mom. She's not. She's a wonderful person who, yes, can make mistakes and can be overbearing. Doesn't mean she's not...she's never been a bad mom." I push the hair out of my face, wishing I had a hair tie nearby.

"That's not what I said."

"We don't always see eye to eye. That's it. She never put a hand on me."

"That's coldhearted. You have good parents. You want to defend them. I get that. She's put these big expectations on your backs, both you and Calle, and you may act like you don't care, while I know you care. You care far more than you want to admit. That's why you become a nervous wreck every time you go back to that town. Keep telling yourself it's Nollan or every other excuse you use. Don't admit you need to work on your relationship with your mom. Live in that delusion and don't tell me *I don't know what I'm talking about* because I had an abusive father and an absent mother," he says defensively.

"I can't do this, Casey," I told him this day would come.

"Do what? Confront your mom? Work on your relationship with her?" His snide tone pisses me off more.

"No. This. Us. I can't be with you because *you're right*. My life is a mess, and as much as I say I'm okay, you figured me out. I'm not put together. I'm not as confident as I pretend. I fight with myself, secretly seeking acceptance. I say I'm okay being alone, and I've done it for so long, but I don't always like it. Wanting to be with you just to fill that void, it's what I do. I cover the holes in my life with something or someone else till I can't hide those holes anymore, and I end it. Are you happy? I admit it. You have enough going on. You don't need to be here. You don't need to rescue me."

"I'm not trying to rescue you." He throws his upward palm out before bringing it to his forehead. "I know that you can survive without me. I want you. I choose you. I don't care how much work it takes." He grabs my hand, and I try to pull it away. He refuses to let go. Why does he have to make this difficult? "I understand days will be rough and we won't always get to live in fantasyland. Still, I choose you. Choose me, too, Raine."

I pull his fingers from my hand, turning away. "I can't. I can't drag you down." Please don't make this harder than it has to be.

"Stop!" He slams his hands to the sofa cushion, catching me off guard, and I jump. "I'm sorry," he retracts. "You keep trying to play this villain, and you're not her. You're not. I told you, you're the fucking savior, you're the hero. The hero, Raine. You save all of us without knowing. You are always there for everyone around you. You care so hard," he enunciates the last word passionately, and I follow his heavy eyes. "You babysit for free for your friends, you literally agreed to host Christmas dinner because Calle wanted you to, you think you hurt Nollan, yet you made such an impact on him he can't move on, and you can't help him with that. You can't fix him. This exterior of a balanced wild spirit who couldn't care less...It's only part of you. I know because I'm the same. I always look like I have my shit together. I struggle too, and you...You fucking see it. Wild, you made me realize that there is a woman on this planet who is my soul's reflection. She's not plastic or a temporary thrill. She's someone whom I could talk to for hours about the stupidest shit and be completely satisfied. You can't let this go because you're afraid."

I stare at him with the same fiery passion heating my core until my heart finally slows and I softly reply. "I'm darkness. I'm not your hero."

"If you're darkness, if you are so set on being this darkness, then I'm despair. Drag me to hell because I don't want to survive in this world without you."

"Don't say that. Don't do that to me." I close my eyes, shaking my head in disbelief, feeling my teeth grind together. "Don't be."

"Do you remember what you said to me after you got hit with that bullet? You told me you loved me. *I fucking love you.*" He cradles my face in both hands. "Do you hear me? I love you." He lets go, sitting back in a huff when I refuse to answer. "If you need some time, I can give you time, but don't push me away because of fear. Don't run away from what we have when you know you love me too."

"I'm not running!" As I sit up, I yell, grabbing the pillow under my legs and throwing it to the floor. I hate that phrase! I cross my arms over my chest, staring at the black television. His silence makes me fidget, pinching at the skin along my elbow. Say something. I close my eyes and tip my head back against the couch.

His dulcet tone returns. "Living...is to experience heaven's grace and hell's hail. Where both places collide, they create something unspeakable...us. People who struggle every day but still give their all trying...because we want to be happy, no matter how hard we have to fight for those moments. Fight for us."

The calm washes back over me as I replay his words in my head. "You shouldn't struggle to be with me."

"I'm not. You are not my struggle. You're being difficult right now; it's what you do. You've never been easy, and I don't give a damn. I'm here for it."

"Casey, please. I..." I push a deep breath out of my nose. "I can't do this." No matter how convincing he sounds, I can't let him turn out like Nollan. "You need to book a hotel for the night. Fly home tomorrow. I appreciate you staying here, but you didn't have to...You knew this day would come." As he shakes his head to the sides, his jaw tense. His eyes narrow, shaking and shaking. "I'm sorry it had to end this dramatically, and I'm sorry you lost your business relationship and friendship with Nollan. I'm sorry. It's...We've reached our expiration."

"With the circumstances, I understand why you're being irrational right now. I don't think that's necessary. It feels childish. That could be me, angry with what you're doing...So, I'm going to be careful with how I use my words."

"Don't fight me on this. You won't win." I bow my head and rub my eyes. "Casey...you're too perfect for me. You deserve someone who can give you more."

"Perfect," he says in a huff. "You think I don't have flaws?"

"Nail biting is a minor offense. You're every woman's dream."

"A man who goes to therapy to keep his fucked up past from affecting his daily life. A man who gets bored easily in relationships yet falls deep every fucking time. A man described as arrogant, whose appearance demands attention wherever he goes. Should I be apologetic for every woman who hits on me while I'm in a commitment? Those are the things women dream of?" He raises his brows. "Being attractive and kind does not make me the perfect man. I'm flawed just like you and every other soul on this planet. Perfect is a state of mind."

"I'll save you the trouble of becoming bored and end it while it's still...exciting," I quickly respond before I can think it through and change my mind.

"Are you fucking kidding me?" He stands to his feet, bellowing. "I took time off from work to be with you after I got shot by *your* ex-boyfriend, if you forgot that part, because yes, Raine, I got shot too. *Oh, it was a graze!* Yes, I'm not crying about it. It happened, and I'd do it again for you, and you would call it quits all over." His tone switches quickly, sarky, yet far worse than his arrogant flirting. It's ridiculous. "Oh, shit's getting rocky, I'm out," he sneers.

"No!" I wag my finger. "You shouldn't have ever jumped him. I could have talked him down. You should have left the house. I would have calmed him down and gotten the gun. Nobody would have been hurt," I shout defensively. "I keep telling you to stop trying to rescue me, and you say you're not, but you are, Casey!"

"Fine. Fine." He flaps his arms. "Maybe I did try to save the day, maybe I wanted to be the hero for once, and maybe you were right the first time. I'm the bad guy, just like Cameron Pierce. Am I cut from the same cloth, Raine? Am I him?" He leans forward in the most contemptuous manner, which irritates the hell out of me, before he paces once, returning to me. "I told you, I'm not the guy who's going to chase you. I'm not going to come begging on your doorstep like Nollan. If I leave, I'm done."

"I know. I heard you."

"If you don't want to be with me, I'm not going to keep trying to convince you, and I can't keep trying to make you see how wrong you are. Right now, yes, you're breaking me. I've been hurt enough to know not to wallow in self-pity, to pick my ass up and find happiness somewhere else, though I want it to be with you."

"Don't forget the dog bowls in the kitchen," I reply, disconnected as I stare at the wall, avoiding his connection. I soak in my thoughts, not moving from the sofa as he walks around my apartment gathering his belongings. I don't want this. I don't want him to leave. Why am I so fucking stubborn and stupid? I should stop him. I should apologize. I can't. He's better off. I'm better alone. I'd be better with a beer. I quit drinking except for wine...wine tasting in Portugal.

"I'm leaving. Are you sure this is what you want?"

I stare at the floor, slowly finding his face. His beautiful face, that tattoo under his jaw, the shape of his lips, his missing dimples...everything that caught my eye the first day I met him, and it's the first words he said to me that hooked me, still subconsciously playing back in my head. *I didn't think you could dance to a Bring Me The Horizon song like that.* "I'm sorry."

"Goodbye, wildcat." Stop him. Stop him! "Take care of yourself."

Casey closes the door, and my eyes fill with tears. I don't want to feel anymore.

Chapter Nineteen | Fortitude

Casey

JANUARY 9TH - MONDAY, 9:00 AM

She cut my heart from my chest. I once joked about this zombie stuff. Those first two days, I felt like the walking dead. Nothing compares to getting your heart ripped out. I want to move on, move forward, and find happiness again, and there is an ache inside that creeps up on me every time I think I'm doing fine. It smacks me in the back of the head. It tells me to fight for her. Every night when I go to sleep alone. Every morning when I wake without a text message on my phone. After a long day of work, when I'm dying to vent, and she's not there. She should be the least of my worries.

My phone buzzes in the holder above my dash. I glance at the incoming call and keep my finger steadily wrapped around the steering wheel.

Brent again. Stop blowing up my phone. I'm two minutes down the street. *I'll handle it.*

Karson has gutted the entire office. I'm about to see what Brent considers gutted. I have meetings scheduled with clients on the West Coast next week and a weekend booked at Mammoth for snowboarding with Bash and the guys. I'm not canceling because Karson wants to play the drama queen.

He wasn't kidding. Walking into the building, it's a vacant warehouse. What in the hell is she doing? Where did she put everything?

"Karson, what the hell is this, and why is this place empty?" I rant, entering Grandpa's office.

"Didn't you know? Daddy likes to keep secrets." She spins in the leather chair, pushing it back from the desk and rising.

"What does that have to do with this place being empty?" I ask, picking up a book from the floor. Stacks upon stacks of books are scattered around the room. The area rug is rolled up in the corner, and she looks like she's trying to flip over the desk in her high yellow heels.

"Because my entire life is a disaster right now," she huffs, holding her breath. "And unless I find that fucking paper, I'm screwed!" She steps back, her arms dropping to her side as she gives up for the moment.

"What paper?" I ask sharply.

"Don't worry about it. Just let me look. I'll have the renovators in here as soon as I find it." She leans her weight into her hip, attempting to flip the desk again. That desk is easily a hundred and eighty pounds.

"Move over. You emptied the drawers, right?" I glare at her as she rolls her eyes before I push my palms against the top along the opening, lifting upward and through my legs. Grunting, I test my fingers, setting it down gently on its side. "I knew it." I inhale as Karson rushes over to the desk, wasting no time inspecting it. "I knew you were looking for something in here. Is that the whole reason you wanted the foundation?"

She looks up from the floor, her hair flinging back. She blows it off her face, then brushes the remaining strands with her pinky. "No. I need the foundation. It's working to my advantage as planned. It's father. I know he's up to something. That old bastard would do anything to keep me off the board, and I'm going to be ahead of him, cut him off before he gets the upper hand because I know more than he thinks I do."

"What are you going on about?" I ask, entertaining her for a little longer.

"Don't worry about it." She smacks her hand against the floor. "I told you, I'll have this place back together as soon as I find what I'm looking for, and then kiss-ass Brent can get back to doing his job."

"Brent is excellent at his job. You're pissed he's been tattling. Try to fire him, and we'll see who has the last laugh." I pick up a book from a two-foot-tall stack and flip through the pages. "I could help you. It would take less time with another set of eyes." What could be so important? She said a paper. A paper. A secret paper.

"No, I can handle it," she insists.

"Karson, what are you not telling me?"

"It's not your concern." It's entirely my concern.

"I'm half-owner of this building, and you're refusing to move forward with these *quick renovations* because you need to find a piece of paper." I set the book back down, walk to the bookshelf, and look around before I face her. "Is this any way to earn my trust?"

"Oh, don't give me that bullshit, Casey." She stands, flattening out the creases on her corduroy skirt. "I don't think you could handle this one, big brother. Didn't you just get your heart stomped on a week ago?"

"My personal life has nothing to do with business, nor do I want to know how you found out that information." I follow her, tucking my hands back in my pants pockets.

"This is your personal life, too." She looks at me with this devious, curved smile that lights through her eyes like she can't wait to ruin my day. Fuck it. She's telling me now.

"Tell me what the fuck is going on right now, Karson. Enough of the games and bullshit. What are you looking for?"

She looks back, walking from room to room before grabbing a hammer and heading back towards Grandpa's office. "Proof," she says, looking back at me briefly.

I could bang my head off the wall.

"Of what? Proof of what, Karson? Come on." I snap my fingers twice, stopping in the doorway.

She abruptly spins around, the hammer dangling between her fingers by the head. "That Cameron had an affair." She slowly walks over to me, swinging her hips as she takes the hammer by the handle and taps the head off her other hand. Give me a break with the dramatics. "And the bastard child he fathered was born less than one year *before* you." She boops me on the nose with her finger like I'm a cat. "You know what that means..." She turns around, walking back over to a stack of books. "He has the legal right to everything, Pierce. How's that firstborn rule sounding to you now?" She sticks out her lower lip in a fake pout.

"I, um." I shake my head, closing my eyes tightly for a second. "How does this give him rights to everything?"

"Now, big brother, I know you're not a lawyer, but you are a smart cookie," she taunts. "You know CP Banks has it all documented that the oldest male of the family gets first dibs at running the dynasty, and only if he refuses does the second-born and so forth have the opportunity. No, that doesn't affect you because you never wanted to run it anyway. It does, however, change the foundation because in Grandpa's will, he addressed everything to his eldest grandson. Which, of course, you took as being addressed to you, as did everyone else, but here's the biggest secret...Pops knew the whole time who his firstborn grandson really was. He had even been sending the woman money since the kid was born. Pops had the only documents that could announce *you are the father*," she cheers, shaking her fists above her head. She grabs the chair while I stand halfway to the middle of the room with my head floating, trying to collect my thoughts. "Take a seat," she says, pushing it over to me. "It's a lot to process." Who does she think she is? My therapist? "Let me know if you think you're going to pass out. I'll call someone to deal with it."

I pace the room, running my fingers through my hair. What in the horse shit? How long has she known about this? How did she find out? Why the fuck didn't Grandpa tell me? This is the type of crazy I thought I could avoid. I should have known that when Karson is around, something is always going to catch fire.

"Where's the truth in it, Karson?"

"It's all legit. I overheard Cameron and Charles arguing a few years back. This was sometime after you went to live with him, and Cameron didn't want you to stay there. Pops said something about how he had to take care of both *his* boys. I've done some digging over the years. It's never too early to gather some blackmail, you know. I know it's here...somewhere."

"How do you know it's *definitely* here? And what are you even going to do with it? Hold it over his head, force his hand?" I ridicule.

"I'm going to stop the old bastard from treating the little bastard to the luxury life." She bobs her head, grabs another book off the shelf, and begins to page through it. I guess she decided to hold off on whatever that hammer was for. "It only takes a taste, once he knows he could be filthy rich and the power that comes with it, getting over an absent father becomes a little easier."

"Not always," I disagree.

"I'm not waiting to find out. If Cameron finds out where the bastard spawn is and tells him he's the heir and he wants CP, there is nothing I can do. No amount of blood, sweat, and tears will overcome the first rule. I'll tell you one thing, though, as soon as I get in there, it's the first damn thing to go. Any kin that wants to take over will have to prove their worth, equal privilege, not just get a golden token because they were the first to pop out of their mom's coochie."

"Nice." I scratch my brow. "You do know you have to find a man who can tolerate you and is at least somewhat attracted to you, and then you have to birth those humans for that to be worth it?"

"Excuse me. I've got several eligible bachelors dying to take my hand. And ew, I'll pay a surrogate to do that birthing stuff."

"Will the nanny raise the kids for you, too?" Father likes daughter.

"I can run a successful empire and still raise beautiful, strong daughters. Don't get all brotherly love and act like you care. I know as soon as everything is straightened out, you're going to cut ties again. It's fine. I get it. This isn't the life for you, and well, I'm perfectly cutthroat." She smirks.

"You're not lying," I reply.

"Are you going to help or just stand there?" She complains.

I stiffly walk over to her. "What am I looking for exactly? A random loose piece of paper?"

"My guess is an envelope with a birth certificate copy or blood test results," she says, still flipping pages.

"Did you look through all these books?"

"A through Z and all of those over there. That last section needs to be paged through."

I walk to the last section of the bookcase and run my finger across the spines.

"So why did your woman leave you?" She interrupts.

"How do you even know about that?" I sigh. "It's complicated."

"People love to share their drama on the internet. The ex-boyfriend was airing his and, well, your dirty laundry out on Good Friday. He's cute." I half-roll my eyes and look down at the book in my hands.

"He's also borderline psychotic."

"I like a little crazy," she says, shimmying her shoulders.

"He shot me, he shot her, he shot himself. Still like crazy? It was a shitshow, and then she broke up with me. That's the story. Can we leave it at that?" Two books down, a hundred more to go. Hopefully, Karson will shut the fuck up for the rest of that time.

"You got shot?" She walks over and lifts the back of my shirt. "Where?"

"It was a graze. Right here." I show her my right lumbar region. I'm lucky he didn't hit two inches over and take out my kidney.

"That's nothing. I dated this guy, Danny. He had some scars," she says, excitedly.

"God, our parents really did some work on us." I tuck my shirt back in, grabbing the next book.

"Speak for yourself. I'm doing just fine," she insists.

"Karson, you just got excited about a scar and proceeded to tell me how you dated a mutilated man that I can only assume you were attracted to."

"Fair enough. What about you, though? This woman dumped you because of her own drama? Sounds like she did you a favor."

"Probably."

She drops the book and looks me dead in the face. "You want to get a drink tonight?"

"I don't drink, and why would I go out with you? We don't speak in years and only rekindle over your greed."

"I'm having a rough day, and well, you are having a rough week, sibling bonding for one night for old times' sake?" A snake can't grow legs.

"What do you want?" I add a book to the stack.

She puckers her lips before finally admitting her intentions. "I'm going to Heart, the new club that's opening tonight. Press is going to be everywhere. It's an elite event. Imagine Casey and Karson Pierce together on every tabloid in the city. That would get under Cameron's skin." Her rapacious grin reappears.

"And going to a club would be really good for your image?" I let out an airy laugh.

"It's about balance. I don't get trashed. I don't get involved with drama. I go for a max of two hours and stick to the VIP booth. No negative press." There is always a catch.

"So you want to use me again? Cutthroat Karson has a ring to it."

"Want me to lie to you again? I miss hanging out with you so much," she squeals. I didn't think her voice could be any more annoying.

"Enough. I'll go." It's better than going home to be left with my thoughts.

"It's because of her, isn't it?" Always have to stick your nose in everyone's business.

"What petty shit do you think I'm doing because I haven't even thought it up?"

"Post a picture or two with some top-tier women hanging on your arms on Insta and watch her come crawling back. Or is she the jealous, raging type?" I relax my furrowed brows, rubbing my hand across my face, and set another book on the stack.

"She's not you, Karson, and I'm not trying to hurt her. Here." I hand her a book. "Find the paper."

"Hey! Smile." Karson looks at her phone, her fingers speeding across the screen after she catches a picture of me that I didn't smile for.

"Do not tag me in that," I order. "The selfie with you was enough. I don't need any pictures showing up with all your friends hanging off of me."

Stretching my arms along the back of the booth, Karson's friends crowd around me. I undoubtedly look like a pimp with his hoes. All these women in tight dresses and tits spilling out of their tops make me think of Raine. God, that's awful. *California hoes.* New York hoes. I'd be the kettle calling the pot black if I were judging them solely by their appearance. It's their attitudes, the way they can't keep their hands to themselves, general observation. Reading people is my strong suit.

The lights strobe across the dance floor. It's packed full of people. Crowded, sweaty bodies. The overwhelming lack of personal space. I'd only venture out there for one woman.

"If the media wants to find you, they will." Karson retrieves a flute from the table and sips her wine.

"You know it's not them that I'm worried about." I rest my head back, wanting to close my eyes, and resisting.

"She's the crazy type, isn't she?" She smirks, tipping her glass toward me.

"Who's crazy?" The burgundy-dress blonde sitting next to me asks.

"Casey's ex." Karson tips her glass for the second time.

"And you just took a picture of Everly and me on his arms?" She scooches over a foot. Karson's friends are dripping in daddy's money and still afraid to ruin their lash extensions.

"Don't post pictures of me on social media, and you won't have to find out." If Raine showed, flicking them off and telling them to stay away from me the same way she told her nurses, I'd need to be resuscitated. I laugh under my breath and pull my phone out of my pocket. Opening the gallery, the first video is the one I never deleted. I shouldn't, but I click on it, playing it back from the backstroke demonstration. I swipe to find another picture of her. One I took while she was sleeping. No makeup, no filters. Unapologetically wildcat.

"What's she like then?"

Huh?

Oh, this woman again.

"I don't really want to talk about it." I slide my phone back into my pocket. "How about a round of shots?"

I need to call my therapist.

"Say hi to the camera!" Who the hell is this? I don't even remember this woman being here five minutes ago. I'd remember that dress. It's like a disco ball.

"Hey! Stop recording," Karson scolds.

"It's just a harmless video." Sparkles shrugs.

"I'm fine. Nothing's going to happen," I respond.

Karson stands beside me, talking in my ear. "You don't know these bitches."

"I thought they were your friends?"

"They'll double-cross me when the opportunity arises." She looks around with a fake smile. "Mica, the car!" She calls to her driver. "It's only ten, I'm going back to the office. If you want to get rid of me, then help me find what I want."

"We checked every single one of those books."

"We missed something. I know it."

Karson's work ethic is the only thing about her that I relate to. She can't quit till she finishes the task, can she? Now, I get to follow her around like a lost dog.

"Meh meh meh," I mumble. I can't think of a better come-back, resorting to fighting with my sister in the same manner as I did when I was twelve.

"Watch what you're doing. I'm wearing four-inch heels," she snaps.

"Wouldn't it be a shame if you tripped right now?"

"I swear if I break a heel or an ankle..."

"You'll what? Sue me? With what legal team, Karson? Cameron is about to cut you off. He just needs the prodigal son to return." I walk around the room, unsure of where to look at this point. "Does he even need this paper? What if he finds him, this son, and contacts him? All they need to do is get another blood test?"

"I'll find him first. As soon as I get his information," she grunts, moving a stack of books for I don't know what reason.

"What makes you think he isn't already in contact with him?"

"Because I've had access to the same resources for years, trying to find out who this kid is and where he lives. If I couldn't figure it out, neither can anyone else. Someone buried this deep enough that it would stay hidden." She growls, her hands balled into fists, as she kicks the cabinet several times.

"So much for not breaking a heel." I laugh, watching her lose her mind. "Wait...I have a thought. Have you looked behind these?"

"Behind the cabinet? I'd have to destroy them. They're built in."

"Not the entire cabinet, just this." I point to the bottom. "These toe kicks." I look around the room, spotting the hammer. "Hand me the hammer. It's the heavy thing you've been swinging around for half the day and not making real use of." I wedge the claw along the top of the quarter-inch plywood, pulling it off. Karson hovers over me while I lie on the floor, blindly reaching around. I run my fingertips across the top and feel it. Is this it? I pull out the envelope, and Karson snatches it before I can sit up, tearing the seal open.

I stand up and look at the letter in her hands. *Holy shit.*

My Dearest Grandson Casey, I knew you and Karson would eventually find this. I don't know the circumstances or where this may take you, but I need you to know I kept this hidden for your best interest for many years, but you deserved to know. I failed my son, and we both failed you. Do with this information what you will. I know you'll make the right choice, no matter what it may be. Till we meet again, Grandpa.

Karson turns the page, revealing exactly what she predicted.

"It's a copy of his birth certificate." She lifts the page, revealing a third sheet. "And DNA test results."

"We have a brother." This is real. There's the proof.

"Half-brother. Christian. Of course, he got a C." She sharply exhales. "I'm burning these."

"And that's the end?" Rubbing the back of my neck, I look around the room. Books are everywhere, and the desk is still on its side.

She follows me as I circle the office, catching my wrist in her hand. "You know any other route would end badly."

"I agree." I lock my tense jaw, watching her pull her hand back to herself.

"Sorry, Christian," she mutters, flipping through the papers once more.

"Wait. What's on the back?"

She stops and flips the bottom sheet. "It looks like an address. 113 Parson Street, Jay, Vermont."

"Is there a date anywhere?" Is this a recent address, or is that where he grew up? Vermont.

"Nothing. Why?" Don't give me that look. I'm not going to look for him.

"Nevermind. Do you have a lighter?"

"Look in the break room. I think they left one in a drawer."

I can't not be a little curious, but he's better off not knowing who his father is. Look at that. She was actually right. There's the lighter.

I walk back into the office to find Karson still holding the letter, reading it over again. Maybe I'm not the only one with doubts. This is the right move.

"You want to do this?" I ask. She puts all three papers back in the envelope and holds it toward me.

"Light it." Holding down on the spark wheel, I roll my thumb, catching the paper in the flame. She watches it burn in her hand until over half is ignited, then she drops it into the empty metal waste can.

"You'll have this place put back together by Friday, right?" I ask.

"My assistant has been on standby, awaiting my call to get to work. It'll be done in three days, and in three weeks, CP will be mine," she says, not batting an eyelash as she walks to the door.

I kick the can as I follow her to the front of the building. "Good luck. You know how to reach me if we have any problems, which we won't, correct?"

"Karson Pierce, hello," she retorts, opening the door. Before she leaves, she looks back. "And Casey." She pauses.

"I know you wouldn't listen to my business advice—as if I would share it freely—but listen to my woman advice. Call her."

"I've been drinking," I call out.

"Perfect time to beg like a bitch," she yells back, halfway down the hall.

Karson stabbing me in the back wouldn't be a surprise. Her telling me to call Raine—that's shocking. What's her agenda? Should I care? Raine is more important to me than anything Karson has to gain.

I'm calling her.

I need to at least know that she's doing okay.

Falling to my bedsheets, I hit the call button.

"It's midnight," she answers. "Can we not do the *dial your ex when you're drunk and want to talk dirty* thing? Doesn't end well."

I missed her voice. Since I left her, this is the first time my heart has beat this fast, adrenaline coursing through me. Snowboarding couldn't give me this high anymore.

"Why would you think I'm drunk, wildcat?" She's quiet. I don't like it. "Wildcat?" I call. "You still there?"

"Yeah. I saw the club photos Karson tagged you in. She's pretty for someone you said you hated. Cute dress."

"Still hate. It probably cost a small fortune. And that was Karson's idea to promote the Pierce siblings *teaming up*, but turns out we aren't Cameron's only children."

"No way." She shuffles around. "I guess be glad you didn't inherit his hoe gene." I hate how good it feels to smile at her commentary.

I laugh breathily. "You said no dirty talk."

"It's not really dirty when it's about someone else. I mean, unless you get turned on by their sex life, and in this case, that would definitely be a red flag," she replies. "For me, anyway. Incest isn't my thing."

"Karson, who told me to call you?"

"Why would she do that?"

"She's a social media stalker." I chuckle. "And she can see that I care about you. I don't know why she gives a damn about my feelings. It was solid advice, though."

"Perhaps she's not as terrible as you think. Take it from me. I've judged plenty of books by their covers. You, for one. Can we blame our parents for everything?"

"That works for a while. At some point, the responsibility lies on us to change."

She yawns. Her voice has that slightly rough tone that she always gets when she should be sleeping. I bet she's in bed, wearing a tank top and shorts with her eyes closed, wondering why she answered my call.

"What do you think of me now, wild?"

"I think you should stop calling me that," she says without hesitation.

"Why?" I adjust my pillow with one hand, turning to my side.

"Because it makes me miss..." She stops herself. "Just call me Raine."

"I miss you." Why won't she just admit it? She misses me, too.

"Casey, it's late. If you need someone to talk to about the family stuff, call me tomorrow."

No. I don't want you to hang up.

"Okay. I'll let you go, but first, tell me you're doing okay. You've been to your follow-up?"

"I'm fine," she says, vaguely.

"Are you back to work yet?" I ask, wanting to keep her on the line a little longer.

"I have this week off. Ivy picked up my work. I'm starting to feel like shit about her having to cover my ass. I'm thinking about...Ah, never mind."

"Tell me. Please?"

"If I want to travel, I need to find a way to increase my wealth. You know? I'm not going to get promoted within Eleanor. They were supposed to be my *experience company* to get my foot in the door. I know it, Ivy knows it, and it's time I give a damn."

"What do you want to do?"

"Sell my pussy."

"I got a few dollars."

"Yeah, well, I'm going to spend the week at Calle's. See what happens after that. Anyway, like I said, if you need someone to talk to...I have some time to listen. Don't bug me all day."

A friendship. It's what she wants. It's what she needs.

"Friends?" I ask.

If it's my only choice, it's better than living without this woman. I hate the way she ended things. It hurts, and it sucks, but what am I going to do? I can either accept it and be her friend, or I can accept it and lose her completely. I can't do the second one right now.

"Pinky promise." I can hear it in her voice—how it made her happy to say that.
"Goodnight, Raine."
"Goodnight, Casey."

Chapter Twenty | Manifest

Raine

FRIDAY, 8:00 AM

A princess carries the weight of the world on her shoulders while kicking ass, fighting dragons, and letting everyone believe that the charming prince is the one doing the saving. He's offering something she deserves. Friendship, unconditional love, respect, no judgment, and time. He's not her identity...her sole reason to exist.

I'm a fucking princess, aren't I?

Vomit, bitch. *Vomit.*

It's challenging to move forward when I have to dredge up my past after I buried every psychological injury a million times over. I foresee therapy being a long road. I don't want to go. I also don't want to get shot again.

It's back home tomorrow. I'm going to miss these ugly light pink walls. This comforter, too. Will Calle notice if I shove it into my suitcase? I'll miss Calle's burnt toast and her *never-failing* loaded oatmeal. How she can bake and ice a beautiful cake yet never get the toast quite right will always be baffling.

It's crazy how one brief moment of time can change the way your brain is wired. Mine has always been tangled as fuck...Now, those cords are woven tighter. I'm afraid to start over for the first time.

But I can do this.

I shouldn't be lying here on top of the blankets, staring at the ceiling, staring at this fucking phone. I made a mammoth-sized mistake breaking up with Casey. It's been days since he's called me. It's not going to light up with his name. He's moving on with his life like I wanted him to.

"Hey, you ready?" Calle walks into the guest room. A cozy purple sweater wraps her arms, and a pair of flared gray joggers finishes off the comfortable outfit she models. She was filming again, judging by her hair and makeup. She doesn't want me to know that she's been making content. I can't wait till she's ready to tell me about it. I hope she connects with the people she wants to be surrounded by. She deserves it.

"Ready for what?" I answer her without leaving the comfort of bed.

"You know damn well for what. What happened to that live-for-moment momentum?" Her hands cover her hips, optimistic that she's going to get me to listen. "Go get that cute ass man! He doesn't want to let you go, and Raine, I've never seen you as I saw you with Casey."

"I don't..."

"Shh shh shush." She leans over me, cutting me off, her ponytail dangling above my head as she holds her finger to my lips. "Give it another shot."

Sitting on the side of the bed, she flips her hair as I push her finger away. "Oh Cal, no...Your wording has horrible timing."

"Yes, and now the entire family is in therapy. It happened, I'm still shook, but everyone is alive, and you are not going to blame yourself and miss out on happiness." She's loud and peppy, and I'm not ready for full-on Calle spirit yet today.

"He doesn't have to be my only source of happiness," I protest.

"Well, duh, you have me," she sings. "Really, though, you and Casey are great together. Go talk to him. Look, you don't even have to do it for yourself, do it for me." Her wide smile takes over, and she lowers her chin onto her flattened hands with a pose.

"For you?" I laugh deep from the gut.

Nash steps into the doorway. "Please, go see him so Calle stops talking my ear off about it."

"Let's go. Get up, get up," she grunts, pulling my hands while she stands at the side of the bed trying to get me moving.

"Fine. Okay. I'll go, with one condition," I bargain, sitting up.

"Anything." I don't think her smile could take up more of her face.

"No matter how honest you are in group therapy, you never tell Mom about Thanksgiving in the bathroom."

"Deal," she agrees.

"What happened in the bathroom?" Nash asks cluelessly.

We smile at each other, simultaneously speaking. "Nothing."

The view from Casey's deck is gorgeous. Snow-covered trees for miles, and the most captivating horizon. Sitting out here every night in a rocking chair wrapped in a blanket with a mug of hot cocoa after a day of promising work...I want that.

"I'm supposed to do these daily positive affirmation things. I get to look in a mirror and tell myself I'm a weird bitch and I fucking rock."

Casey walks beside me, strolling from his deck, down his driveway toward Nash's SUV. The burn against my cheeks should make me want to move faster. It's blustery as hell out here.

"Calle downloaded this app on my phone that gives me a new one every day since she got tired of hearing me yell *I'm a weird bitch, and I like it* every morning."

"I like that one. What did your affirmation app give you today?" He asks, pinching the rim of his hat and securing it.

"I am worthy of love," I admit, stopping in my tracks.

"I can't wait till you believe it wholeheartedly...because you are." He holds my gaze.

"Thanks, Casey. Really, thank you."

"You don't need to thank me."

"I do. You saw me carrying this chip on my shoulders, and you embraced it. I wanted to keep believing I was the bad guy, and I didn't need anyone to help me. I was strong and badass, and I would be happy all on my own."

"You are badass."

"I know that, and I don't want to be alone or on my own all the time."

"I will always be here, you know, if you want someone to scream with." He smiles, pulling his supple pink skin between his teeth. A breathy laugh escapes me as I turn to walk down the driveway.

"Raine. Stop." Casey's warmth takes my palm, holding me. "Can you look at me and tell me your life hasn't felt like total shit without us? I don't chase the past, but here I am, chasing you. Please, stay."

I swallow the lump in my throat that's been holding me back. "I messed up, like really messed up. I was horrible to you after everything."

He weaves his fingers into mine. "I trust you with my life," he says. "You make me stupid. What can I say?"

"Forsaken, stupid inducer."

"Wild, you are so utterly impossible to top. I'll be your hero when you want me to and sidekick every other day."

"Why do you always say the right thing? There's a book with dreamy lines in it that you secretly read every night in hopes of seducing women with." The amount of attitude I let slip with that question still proves I can't change overnight, and drawing hearts on dirty shoes is as romantic as I get.

"Only one woman. She's hard to impress." The pressure of his finger against my jaw draws me back to his eyes. "It's you."

"Bullshit."

"Behave."

"Do you love me?"

"Is that even a question?" He sneers. "I'll love you till we have matching sagging body parts," he says, making me instantly laugh.

"Only until then, right? Then we go our separate ways?"

"Yeah."

"But we can still be best friends, right?"

"Yeah."

"Pinky swear?"

"Pinky swear, I won't complain when you play your ear-piercing metal music early in the morning."

"Good because you know it's going to happen," I point out.

I wouldn't survive without my morning music sesh. It's my morning coffee.

"Oh, I know, your Spotify is still connected to my phone. I've been listening to the same song every morning for a week."

Yet he didn't turn it off or switch it. Must've been feeling the morbid lyrics. It's growing on him, I know it.

"Sorry, I've been feeling vampy lately." I shrug, pulling my sweater tighter to my body.

"Did you know they're touring?" He asks.

"Yep."

"But I bet you didn't know four hours ago, when Calle called me, telling me she was bringing me a surprise, I decided to do some surprising of my own." He takes his phone from his pocket. "One second." I grab the phone as soon as he holds it in front of me, reading the email.

"You bought tickets?" *What!*

"Just checking a second box off your bucket list. They're backstage passes. You're going on stage at a rock show."

"No." *He did not.*

"Yes." *He did.*

"But you hate this stuff."

"I couldn't hate anything that I'm doing with you." His smile tugs up his face. "Well, are you excited?"

"Ahh!" I tiptoe dance. "Yes. I can't wait." With the tightest hug, I wrap my arms around his neck, pressing my body against his. He lifts me from the ground, spinning me in his arms.

"Scream for me, baby." I scream and scream, and his entangle with mine. We're surrounded by clouds of steam and slapped red with wind. And it doesn't matter. It's our fantasyland.

"So uh, are we leaving without you?" Calle yells out the car window.

"It's going to get freaky soon! Run for the sake of your eyes."

"I got her," Casey yells.

"Keep her!" She yells back, waving. "Love you!"

"I love you!" I scream, watching them pull down the driveway. "I love you," I whisper.

"I love parts of you."

"You're a terrible liar. Every part of me is lovable." His doe eyes drift to my lips, where his fingers run. "That's three. You checked three of my bucket list boxes. Dance on the beach in a foreign country, go on stage at a rock show, and kiss a stranger. The best fucking kiss of my life."

"I'm not a stranger anymore. Any things I can check off that list as your boyfriend?"

"Um, take me inside because it's freaking cold out here." I scrunch my nose up.

"Make that face one more time, and I'm tying you to the bed. Boyfriend or not, you're never leaving me again."

"I think you said that once before, and well, I defied the odds."

"I also said I'd never chase you, and I think I just broke that promise. Aren't we both full of surprises?"

"Casey."

"Talk to me, wild," he says, brushing hair from my face.

"If you needed to put that circle on my hand, I'd never take it off."

"Did you bump your head, love?" *Stop laughing.*

"I'm not saying I want to get married. It's...I want to accept a symbol of commitment. If that's the symbol you...I don't know. Is that a symbol you need?" I ask, realizing I don't know what he wants.

"I got a better idea. You'll see." He picks me up again, tossing me over his shoulder like a rag doll, and carries me toward the house.

"I missed you," I say, letting my hands drift underneath the front of his shirt.

"And I missed every pain-in-the-ass part of you."

When someone sees you when you can't see yourself anymore, they're worth keeping around. It's what Calle meant when she gave me her better or worse speech. Having that person who holds you accountable for your bullshit while endlessly caring, supporting, appreciating, and laughing with you. God, I sound like the worst rom-com of all time. Let's, hehe, haha, all the way to sweet smoochies-ville. I'd rather be tied to this bed.

The weight of Casey's arm over my waist is my comfort blanket. His labored breaths against my neck, his chest rising and falling against my back—his...dick, yes. His dick twitching against my ass.

"Are you awake?" I whisper. He doesn't answer, and laughter takes my heaving chest.

"Mm," he hums. "What?"

"Nothing."

"You're laughing. Why?" He pulls me tight, wrapping his hand around my waist.

"Nothing. I can just tell you're happy this morning," I reply.

"Do you want to find out how happy?" The warmth from his whispers caresses my neck.

"Maybe after you brush your teeth."

"Don't you want to smell my morning breath every day when you wake up?"

"Just ask me the question, Casey."

"I have no idea what you're talking about."

"Fine." I pull away from him, trying to stand up, but he tightens his hold, and I fall back to the bed.

"Where do you think you're going?" His fingers dig into my sides and along my rib cage, causing me to squirm from his tickling.

"Casey!"

"Will you move in, wild?"

"Eh...I guess."

"Enthusiastic."

"You show me happy, I'll show you enthusiastic."

"Behave."

"You know I don't know how to do such things."

"I could devour you right now, but you should take it easy for a little while."

I roll my eyes. "Thanks, daddy," I sneer. The smile that curves from his lips and those sexy dimples—I can imagine the wheels turning in his head.

"I told you—"

"No. I do not," I cut him off. *I do not have a daddy kink.*

"Maybe someday you'll admit it, but one day at a time."

"Arr-o-gant," I emphasize. "Stop being a know-it-all."

"Get in the shower, wild. I'm taking you somewhere special today."

My hands explore, smoothing over his silky shorts. "Are you sure your *better idea* is still a better idea?"

"Love," he growls. "It'll be worth the wait."

I roll off the king mattress, losing the warmth of his body and comforter. A wiggling weiner dog greets my bare feet. "I'm mad, Molly. I got kicked out of bed."

"You did not."

I walk toward the kitchen, looking for Molly's bowl. "Did so," I call back.

"Am I supposed to join you?"

"Yes."

"It's going to take longer to get on the road than."

"I have all day." I run the water and refill Molly's bowl.

"Start the coffee. Please."

After extending my shower time, we eventually make it out of the house and to a gray building with tinted windows and bold letters along the top reading TOTEM. Casey takes my hand as I step out of his shiny car onto the sidewalk. Salt and dirty snow coat the streets, yet his car remains immaculate. I swear he washes the thing daily. Below the flashing light on the door are stickers that match the letters. *Totem Tattoo.*

"Why are we at a tattoo shop?" Casey closes the car door behind me and rests his hand on the small of my back. "Remember when you talked about that finger circle, and I said I had a better idea?"

"Uh, yeah." I swear, if he wants a ring tattoo, I'm out. I'm highjacking his car and yeeting it so hard. "How is this a *better idea?*" I mock.

"I recall you saying how you said our nautical tattoos didn't really match, since *everyone* has one, and well, I had to do something about that."

"You want matching tattoos *over* marital status? I fucking love you."

"I fucking love you more."

"Wait, not like ring bands or names, right?"

"Too tacky for me, love. Doesn't go with my aesthetic."

Casey opens the door, and I walk into the shop. It looked bigger from the outside. In a small open lobby, three dark brown leather-wrapped chairs sit around a circular table with artist booklets placed on top. A water cooler sits along the opposite wall, next to a small rectangular table where steam rolls from a freshly brewed pot of coffee. Casey walks past me, meeting a man with slicked-back jet hair and a curled mustache.

"Casey, good to see you." They shake hands.

"Thanks for making time for me. I know it was last-minute."

"I couldn't have you hiring someone else," he jokes.

"Raine, this is Tyler Rendley." He glances back at Tyler. "This is my girlfriend, Raine." I smile and coyly say hi.

"Awesome. Great to meet you."

"All of my art is by Tyler."

He gives a thumbs up. "So are we doing matching or yin and yang style? What's your idea?"

"An air tank," Casey replies.

My neck nearly snaps, turning to look at him. "A what?" I ask, tucking my chin.

"Like a diving tank, scuba diving."

The smile rips at my lips, and I shake my head. "So we can breathe underwater together?"

"Yeah, I'm thinking a Leopard Eel wrapped around mine," he adds.

"With spots like a wildcat? I thought you didn't do symbolic tattoos?"

"I didn't say that. I said they don't mean shit. I just like them. This one is a little deeper."

"No pun intended. Oh shit, you're not going to try to fuck me while I'm getting a tattoo, are you?" January has been a dark romance week. My bad.

"Well, I wasn't, but now…"

"Not sanitary," Tyler interrupts, shaking his head.

"I want a Manta Ray. They look rough and edgy, but they're harmless, gentle."

Casey wraps an arm around my waist, pulling me to his chest. "Perfect."

"Okay, where do you want these?" Tyler asks unfazed.

"Ribs," we both say simultaneously.

"Ouch. Suit yourselves," he replies, walking back to a black desk. "Give me a couple of minutes to sketch these."

Casey takes my hand and leads me back to the cushy leather chairs, sitting down and pulling me to his lap.

"I can sit in my own chair." I thumb to the seat next to him.

"I'm feeling needy. The ribs are not fucking enjoyable."

"So how much does it hurt?"

"Not as bad as a bullet." His scowl replies before his mouth.

"Pussies could never." His smile returns, and his fingers brush my skin as he tucks loose hair behind my ear. "What do you have planned after this?"

"Taking a short drive to Bash's office." He scales my body.

"Why do we need to stop there? It's Saturday."

"Because it's the only parking garage I have access to," he whispers.

"In the car, on the roof of the parking garage." I wet my lips. "Checking a box of the fuck-it list."

"In the car, on the car, against the car. You think you can handle it?"

"Seems manageable." His eyes roll up, and he shakes his head. "But I want to know, could you identify my..." I lean closer and whisper. "Pussy in a lineup?"

His eyes narrow. "A pussy lineup? Mugshots?"

"Yeah." I shrug. "You're thinking too hard about it."

"Wait a minute. I need to know how many mugshots there are. Like six? Yeah, I can nail you. Six-hundred? That's a lot."

"Cool. Also, could you help me with a business idea?" I casually ask. "I'm tired of what I'm doing. I want to quit my job, and I spent all week researching. I think I have something."

He gives me the lightning look. A shiver travels along my spine, and the hair on my arms stands tall. His lips curve up, and dimples mark the ends of his smile. "I'm your sidekick."

"Partners."

Stay Connected

The easiest way to find updates and future releases is to sign up for my mailing list at **www.krbrendlinger.com**

Find me on social media at @kr.brendlinger.

If you want to make my day, be sure to send me a message if you enjoyed this book or join one of my online groups. I'd love to hear from you!

More Books From K.R.
Yield – contemporary, second chance, motocross.
When Everything Ends – dark, sci-fi, mysterious.

About the Author

A quirky free spirit, K.R. resides with her family on the East Coast of the United States. Her favorite form of caffeine is chocolate, she's unapologetically awkward, and multi-tasking is her way of life. When not writing or reading an alternative reality, K.R. can be found seeking out laughter, music, or something with a motor. You may also catch snaps of her adventures on socials.

Her undeniable Pisces energy emotionally steers her when the pen hits the paper, writing stories with realistic characters you can relate to and plots that submerge you.

www.ingramcontent.com/pod-product-compliance
Lightning Source LLC
Chambersburg PA
CBHW020330010826
48973CB00005B/1196